LIFE IS LIKE A FLOWER GARDEN

A Novel

Pamela Frances Basch

LIFE IS LIKE A FLOWER GARDEN © 2014 Pamela Frances Basch
All rights reserved.

ISBN: 1503106977
ISBN 13: 9781503106970
Library of Congress Control Number: 2014919883
CreateSpace Independent Publishing Platform
North Charleston, South Carolina

This book is dedicated to

Gary

For his love, loyalty and friendship
throughout the years and for
never dimming the light
of my creativity

Also by Pamela Frances Basch

EACH TIME WE SAY GOODBYE

A SCARY KIND OF HONESTY

ACKNOWLEDGEMENTS

Again, I am deeply grateful to the dedicated team of folk who have taken the time to read my manuscripts. Your thoughtful feedback, editing and innovative ideas are immeasurable, besides which the process wouldn't have been half as much fun without you: Amy Sager, at bebetterstudios. com for designing the beautiful cover; Vivian Foster, at www.bookscribe. co.uk; Vanessa Talbott; June Donnelly; Gary Basch; Roger Manternach for his knowledge on fire fighting, and last but not least, my very special anonymous friend.

Also, it is impossible to express how much I appreciate those of you who have taken the time to give me such great reviews and feedback for my two previous novels. Thank you.

Thank you also to all the staff at CreateSpace. It's comforting to know I can always rely on getting prompt and professional assistance just by sending an email or picking up the phone.

CHAPTER ONE

THEA—MASSACHUSETTS
NOVEMBER 2005

It all started with an out-of-the-blue phone call, a Thanksgiving invitation from Thea Chamberlin's friend Ellie, and a job offer. Thea procrastinated, sat on the fence, gathered the children around her and asked their opinion. Peter, arms-crossed belligerent, took some persuading, saying, "We always have Thanksgiving with Aunt Margaret and Uncle Bill," making his point, resisting change. Izzie and Jessica, the seeds of adventure sown, pulled their brother along with them, said it would be an adventure. Thea, nervous about the five hour drive from Maine to Massachusetts, hiding her white-knuckle fear of passing trucks on the highway and having too much time to think, allowed her mind to roam around the land of what-ifs. The pluses and minuses of taking up a job she had left twelve years earlier; of coming back to Massachusetts; of leaving Maine behind—her mind doing a loop-the-loop until she was dizzy with confusion.

Now in bed in Ellie's beautiful house, mulling over the puzzling turn of events, unable to sleep, her thoughts fixated on her sick friend just across the hallway, she was still in shock from Ellie's surprising revelation earlier that evening of an inoperable brain tumor. Thea wanted to go home. She lay on her back staring at the ceiling, uncomfortable and too warm in her sweats, afraid to get undressed in case she was needed in a hurry. The silence pressed down on her, made her ears sing. Conflicted with emotions, one minute mad at Ellie for not being honest and dragging her and the children to Massachusetts under false pretenses, and then incredibly sad. She had raised Thea's hopes, opened the door to opportunity to return to Aladdin's Cave, the arts and crafts emporium she so passionately loved, only to have it slammed shut in her face by Ellie's illness. Not once mentioned since her arrival by Theodore Blunt, the owner of the store, she wondered whether Ellie's offered partnership a figment of her imagination, the tumor pressing on her brain creating wild ideas.

Frightened by her predicament, guilt-ridden because she was healthy and Ellie was not, she got out of bed, padded over to the window seat, tucked herself into a corner, pulled her knees up to her chin, covered herself in a blanket, hugged one of Ellie's bright yellow pillows for comfort and counted her blessings. For one thing, she wasn't alone: Mr. Blunt was downstairs in his apartment; Robert, Ellie's younger brother, was asleep in his basement room, and then there were the children. On the other hand, Mr. Blunt was elderly and Robert an emotional, exhausted wreck, and if she didn't get some sleep, she'd be in the same boat. Her parents lived twenty minutes from Ellie's house, but lacking in empathy for shoulder crying, she discounted them, although things had changed between them for the better. Ellie, thoughtfully inviting them for the Thanksgiving meal, forced Enid and Henry into the company of their grandchildren with surprising results. For her mother and Peter, her ten-year-old son, an instant love affair; for her dad, jolted out of his self-absorption, rowdy card and board games; for Thea, her mother's revelation of her orphanage upbringing, an "aha" moment. Now she understood Enid's timidity, her lack of self-worth, but she still had a million questions. Over the past two days, with the gift of acceptance, she had finally, at the age of thirty-three, forgiven her parents their shortcomings and appreciated them for her childhood stability.

Thea wondered whether the children were as eager as she to go home to Melford Point, back to the familiar routine, to the people they loved: Bill and Margaret Gilson, their substitute grandparents at the Country Store, hub of the small town; their daughter Nan, recently engaged to Stanley; MaryAnn and her two boys—Johnny, friends with Jessica, and, Ian, friends with Peter. Their adaptability this weekend filled her with pride—the one warm sunshiny spot in her otherwise bleak landscape. Visiting her parents' house, showing them where she had grown up, taking the kids out to breakfast out of necessity so as not to disturb Ellie, helping out at Aladdin's Cave—they had taken it all in their stride. Unfortunately, the children would never know the true fun-loving Ellie, but Mr. Blunt won their hearts, captivated them with his story telling. Older now, the same kind, bumbling, elderly man—a little more stooped, stomach noticeably rounder, tufts of gray hair thinner, his blue eyes paler, framed by the ubiquitous wire-framed spectacles—still loved an audience.

The room was chilly, only warmed slightly by the occasional thrust of the vented hot air, and she was forced to go back to bed where she finally slept fitfully only to be awoken a couple of hours later by what could only be described as a primeval cry of anguish. She sat bolt upright, heart pounding, stomach contracting out of sheer panic; chilled to the bone, it took her a moment to spring into action. Flinging the quilt aside, consumed by concern for her children, fumbling towards the door in the dimly lit room on shaky legs, gasping in pain when she caught her toe on the bedpost, she hobbled out into the hallway. With her uncanny knack for allowing the ghost of misfortune to darken her door, she wondered what on earth had gone wrong now. But, much to her relief, the children all fast asleep had not been the ones to cry out—no tear-stained cheeks, no damp brows, no whimpering for her in their unfamiliar surroundings.

Deathly afraid of what she might find, her pre-sleep premonition of disaster possibly coming true, playing for time by walking slowly, she arrived at Ellie's room. Greeted by the leaden weight of sobbing and the eerie whining of Ellie's dog, Honey, she nearly turned and ran. Gingerly pushing the door open, she found Robert kneeling on the floor, holding onto the lifeline of Ellie's hand. She ignored him, stared at Ellie, constricted her throat against the unpleasant odor, and stroked her tiny fingers down the coldness of Ellie's face, closing her sightless eyes. Moving in a half-conscious state towards Robert, she rested her hand on his dark cap of neatly cropped hair. Detached and nauseated, her breathing shallow, she swallowed the rising bile and said, "Hush now, Robert."

Robert turned and put his arms around Thea's waist—a small comfortless child, his tears soaking her sweatshirt—and she stood still as a statue waiting for him to compose himself. Shrinking from Robert's crying and Honey's soul-destroying whimpering, horribly aware she and the children were now in this strange house with a dead person, her mind created a safety valve by dissociating Ellie's soulless body from that of Ellie her friend. How on earth was she going to handle this and spare the children from even more trauma? Somebody would have to tell Mr. Blunt. He was an old man. Would the shock of losing Ellie kill him too?

She attempted to pry Robert's hands from her waist, remembering how they had held each other in comfort a few hours before. "Robert, listen to me. You have to try and pull yourself together." She put her fingers under his chin and lifted his bearded face. "Please look at me. I don't know what to do." He drew in a deep shuddering breath, let go of Ellie's hand, pushed himself to his feet, wiped his sleeve under his nose, and eventually found his voice. "I'm sorry, but this is all my fault."

"How can it be your fault?"

"Because I left the medication where Ellie could reach it. That's why she asked you to get her a glass of water before you left her last night. Don't you see?"

Realization dawning, Thea said, "Oh . . . Now I feel terrible. Then it's just as much my fault, but I didn't know what she had in mind any more than you did; it was her choice and not really anything to do with us."

"That's easy for you to say, but I never got to say goodbye."

"Neither did I. Come, Robert. Let's leave Ellie to rest in peace. We need to decide what to do." She held out her hand, but he didn't respond. Honey continued to whine, and much as she sympathized with the dog's distress, it was beginning to get on her nerves. Taking hold of Robert's arm, she pulled him gently towards her, waking him from his stupor, and he walked away. "Here, Honey," she said, hoping the dog would follow. Thea breathed a huge sigh of relief once they were all out in the hallway, the door to Ellie's bedroom firmly closed. She turned to face Robert. "When did you say Dorothy was coming back?" Thea had never met Dorothy, but judging by what Theodore had said about how helpful she was with the after-school program at Aladdin's Cave, she sounded caring and dependable, someone they both desperately needed.

"Monday, I think," he said, his voice barely a whisper.

"Do you have a number for her?"

"There's a list of numbers on the fridge."

"What about Ellie's doctor? He or she will know what to do." Terrified of the situation, of having to handle it all by herself, Thea wanted to keep Robert talking.

"It's a she—Penelope Randall."

"Technically, we should probably call 911, but I'm sure if we call her first, she will help us. Have you any idea what time it is?"

Robert glanced at his watch. "It's just after four."

"We need to move away from Ellie's door. It's not fair to Honey; we need to distract her. Let's go call Dr. Randall and I'll make some tea. How does that sound?"

Robert nodded, shuffled his way to the kitchen, sullen and brooding, his shoulders slumped. "I wish I could just disappear. I'd rather be anywhere but here," he said. Thea echoed his feelings, but someone had to be practical and her motherly instinct kicked in. Now was not the time to fall apart, and even though Robert, a visiting nurse by profession, had probably dealt with death before, she realized she was better equipped emotionally to deal with the current situation, dreadful though it was.

She seemed to spend her life making tea. She had shared a cup with Robert late last night and here she was back in Ellie's kitchen, setting the teakettle on the burner and putting out mugs. "This is déjà vu," she said, pushing him towards one of the stools at the breakfast bar, the mutual attraction of the night before out the window, a fleeting thing. Beginning to suspect he might be rather a weak man, she inwardly chastised herself for judging him under the current circumstances. She remembered Ellie mentioning Robert not handling her illness well and it saddened Thea to think her brother had added to Ellie's burden rather than detracting from it. Had Ellie known his true character, been aware of his limitations, when she had summoned his help a year ago? The age difference was quite considerable—Ellie, the oldest child, now forty-six, and Robert, the youngest, only thirty-two, part of a large French-Canadian family living in Northern Maine. Leaving home in 1987 to seek her fame and fortune in Boston, rapidly disillusioned by the city life, Ellie eventually found her niche in 1989 working for Theodore Blunt at Pens & Paper, changing the name to Aladdin's Cave shortly thereafter. Thea, startled out of her reminiscing by the teakettle's piercing whistle, removed it from the burner.

Thea set a mug of tea down in front of Robert. "Drink that. You'll feel better," she said, maternal in her concern, determined to keep busy, no time to dwell. "Now where's this list of phone numbers?"

"Should be there on the side of the fridge."

Thea found the list nestled in amongst many photographs of Ellie, all smiles, taken with different groups of kids, some of them in the craft room at Aladdin's Cave, the room Ellie had created and which Izzie and Jessica had made full use of when she and Peter were helping Mr. Blunt yesterday. Thea dragged her eyes away from the pictures. Running her finger down the list of numbers, she eventually found Dr. Randall's. She turned, glanced at Robert, a picture of misery, his head bent, hands curled tightly around the mug of tea, oblivious to its heat, and asked, "Should I try and get in touch with the doctor now? She may not be the one who is on call, but at least it's a start. I know this is different, but what do you usually do when a patient dies?"

Robert ignored her tactless question, continued his monotonous monologue. "Why wasn't I able to help her? I'm a nurse for heaven's sake. I should've been able to ease her suffering." Thea, stopping her impulse to run away, planted her feet firmly. She glanced at Honey curled up in her basket consumed with her own wretchedness, looking at Robert, eyebrows twitching. Robert continued, his voice low and subdued, "How am I going to tell Maman? She will be devastated when she finds out Ellie took her own life. She firmly believes in the Catholic doctrine that we are stewards, not owners of the life God has entrusted to us and that it is not ours to dispose of."

"Robert, I'm sorry this is all so difficult," deciding now was not the time to tell him she didn't believe in all that mumbo jumbo. "But we can't do this on our own. We have to have some help, so what do you want me to do?" She was getting desperate now, her voice rising, fearful one of the children might appear. Becoming increasingly agitated, absolutely petrified of doing the wrong thing, feeling sick to her stomach and close to tears of hopelessness, she wished for lovingly dependable Margaret.

Robert looked at her as if he were seeing her for the first time, his eyes cold. "Do you understand the finality of death?"

"Up until now, no."

"Then you have no idea what I'm going through. Go back to your children. Leave me alone. I don't want you here." His hand shot sideways and the hot tea she had so carefully prepared fell to the floor—the hot sticky liquid spattering everywhere, the mug shattering in a million pieces. Thea stared at Robert in disbelief.

Scared of his anger, she said, "I'm going to talk to Mr. Blunt."

She heard him mutter, "Go to hell."

She checked on the children, breathed a sigh of relief to discover them all still sleeping soundly. Flipping the light switch, she padded down the stairs into the basement, walking to the far end through the rec room, past the Ping-Pong table and Robert's bedroom. She ran her damp palms down her sweatpants and rapped sharply on Mr. Blunt's door, a prickle of nervous perspiration in her armpits. Shivering with the cold, she looked down at her feet encased in nothing but a thin pair of socks. She continued to stand there, put her ear against the door—nothing but silence. Unable to stand the inactivity any longer—needing to get this unwanted conversation over with—she turned the handle and pushed the door open. Familiar with the layout of the apartment, having only been there a few short hours before, she walked past the ornate hallstand with its antique mirror and hooks for coats towards the light coming from the sitting room. She found him dozing in his old and comfy reclining chair. She hated to disturb him, but she didn't want to waste any time; worried about the children, she needed to get back upstairs just in case one of them woke up.

Kneeling down by the side of the chair, she took one of his hands. "Mr. Blunt, it's Thea," and as soon as she spoke his name, the tears started to roll down her face. It took him a moment to realize she was there and all he said was, "She's left us, hasn't she?" And all she could do was nod her head and take the large white handkerchief from his shaky hand.

CHAPTER TWO

❧❧❧

MaryAnn—Maine

On the Friday after Thanksgiving, MaryAnn Wilkinson, her two boys—ten-year-old Ian and five-year-old Johnny—and Jim Hudson were in Thea's house looking after Smokey, the Chamberlins' cat. Her sons, eager to tell her all about their day with Jim, quieted her earlier misgivings about leaving her children with a man she had only met a week ago. She could see by their bright faces that her fears had been unfounded, the day an obvious success. MaryAnn's attempt to reach the pantry to retrieve a can of cat food with Smokey underfoot threatening to trip her up was a hazardous exercise that made Jim and the boys laugh out loud. "You could rescue me, you know." Jim took pity on her and scooped up the cat. "So, tell me all about your day," she said, wielding the can opener, wrinkling her nose at the fishy smell.

"We're going to build a tree house," Johnny said.

Ian jumped in. "Mr. Hudson turned on his computer and showed us this website with all these neat designs and we're going to send for a book to show us how to do it. The tree house will have a trapdoor, a real tiled roof and windows. And best of all, we'll be able to build most of it on the ground so we can start before spring."

"That sounds like so much fun," she said, catching Jim's eye and smiling. Pleased to see Ian so animated and enthusiastic, a child of few words who seemed to carry the weight of the world on his shoulders, he appeared lighter somehow. How quickly life changed. Forever grateful for the hand of good fortune that had tapped her on the shoulder, nudging her to accept Thea's invitation to dinner the Sunday before, she had tentatively joined the lively gathering. Even though the other guests were virtual strangers, she and Thea still getting to know each other, she had felt at home. Margaret and Bill Gilson had been warm and friendly; their daughter Nan flushed and happy in her love for the hilarious Stanley, and this was how she had met Jim. A brief encounter that set the wheels in motion, wheels which rapidly gained momentum. The instant attraction that penetrated her grief, destroying her widow's resolve to be loyal to Sam, had happened fast, leading her to this situation. Jim Hudson, a pillar of the community, an easy man to love, had taken her by surprise.

"So what else did you do today?" she asked, bending down, putting Smokey's dish on the floor and picking up her water bowl.

"Did Will miss us?" Johnny asked, always her sensitive little man.

"Of course, but he wasn't too sad because he knew you'd have fun with Mr. Hudson."

"That's all right then."

MaryAnn, run off her feet at Will's Diner, missing the boys, but secretly pleased they didn't have to spend the day cooped up in Will's office at the back of the restaurant, hummed while she worked. Will had been kind to her after her husband Sam's death three years ago and welcomed Ian and Johnny knowing she was unable to afford daycare. It wasn't an ideal situation but waitressing gave her an income, albeit small, forced her out of the house in her time of grief and gave her contact with people. "I was a little late, so I got hissed at by Evelyn."

"That must have been scary," Johnny said, giving her a wicked grin.

"She's harmless enough," MaryAnn said, thinking about the sour-faced elderly waitress Will kept on out of the kindness of his heart because she was a fixture and part of the diner's charm.

Jim, sitting on one of Thea's kitchen chairs, listened to the interaction. Wise enough to know there were kinks to be worked out with the relationship because MaryAnn was fiercely independent and proud, he lived in hope she'd eventually come to trust him enough to accept his help. His day with Ian and Johnny exceeded his expectations and he was as excited as the boys about building a tree house. And this time he would make sure he included the Chamberlin children. Still mad at himself for forgetting to ask them when he had invited MaryAnn and the boys over for supper on Monday, he deeply regretted hurting Peter's feelings—a fatherless boy, like Ian and Johnny, needing extra care. Jim, in love with Thea for years, once dreamed of being her husband, but not any more—MaryAnn had broken the spell.

Smokey stopped eating, calmly and methodically washed, rubbing first one and then the other of her bright white paws over her ears and down the side of her face. Johnny sat down beside her, reached out to touch her tabby fur, only to be rewarded by a lick from a very rough and fishy-smelling tongue. "Ugh," he said, but undeterred she continued with her grooming and he just sat next to her watching in fascination.

Comfortable with each other, despite the oddity of being in someone else's house, Jim still thought he could detect Thea's lingering scent of roses, but it may have been his imagination. He listened to Ian tell his mom all about the library his grandfather had created, gratified by the boy's enthusiasm. "I've never seen so many books in someone's house, rows and rows of them. Some of them are very old and smell like far-away places. The shelves go from the floor all the way to the ceiling," Ian said. "There's even a ladder. It runs along a metal rail and it has wheels at the bottom. Mr. Hudson let us climb so we could reach the books right at the top."

"Is that right?"

"Yes, it's fixed to the shelves so you can just slide it along. We pushed Johnny, and he loved the ride."

"I did, I did," piped up Johnny in a muffled voice, coughing and spitting out cat hair.

"We also learned something called Cockney rhyming slang. Mr. Hudson's grandfather was from London, England, and he showed us a list of all the funny things he used to say," Ian said.

"Give me an example," MaryAnn said, pulling out one of the kitchen chairs and sitting down opposite Jim.

"*Apples and pears* are *stairs* and *Uncle Ned* is *bed*. *Bacon and eggs* are *legs* and . . ."

Johnny jumped to his feet, his dark hair flying, interrupting Ian and saying, "*April showers* are *flowers!*"

Ian, totally unfazed by his brother's rudeness, continued, "'Course there were lots of words we didn't understand, but Mr. Hudson explained them to us. It was so much fun. I'll be able to call Peter my *dinner plate* as he's my *mate* and instead of answering the *phone*, we will be answering the *dog and bone!*"

"And did you know me and Ian are *dustbin lids?*" Johnny said. "*Dustbin lids, kids*. Get it?"

"Because if you didn't you'll have to use your *down the drains, brains!*" and Ian started to laugh and soon they were all laughing. MaryAnn looked at Jim with tears of joy threatening to brim over and mouthed a silent, "Thank you." She hoped he realized how much pleasure he had given

18

these children of hers in the past few days, enriching their lives beyond measure.

"You've really started something haven't you? You know the kids are going to drive us nuts with this. They are the kings of redundancy!" She looked into Jim's kind brown eyes, felt the connection, a rekindling of the flame they had been forced to extinguish earlier that day. He was giving her a glimpse of the man who resided beneath his calm exterior and it excited her, left her wanting more. Not only a talented carver of the little animals he had given her boys and the Chamberlin children, and a lover of all kinds of books, she was also delighted to discover there was so much more hidden beneath the surface of this humble man.

Jim's cell phone rang. He pulled it from his pocket, flipped it open. MaryAnn listened to him say, "I'll be right there."

"Is there something wrong?" she asked.

He stood up and pushed the chair away from the table. "I'm sorry to break this up, but I'm on call and there's a house fire on the other side of Melford Point. I guess I forgot to mention I'm a volunteer fireman," he said, winking at her, making light of his revelation, thrusting his arms into his coat and pulling his hat down over his ears.

Hiding her surprise, she said, "Go. We need to get home anyway. Please call me as soon as you can." She walked around the table and gave him a kiss on the cheek, a natural reaction—an old married couple ritual. "Stay safe."

"Goodbye boys. Be good and thank you for spending the day with me." He touched MaryAnn briefly on her face. "I'll talk to you later," he said, opening the kitchen door, letting in a blast of cold air. She stood at the window, the boys at her side, watching as he backed out of Thea's driveway, blue emergency light whirling on the top of his truck. There was no end to the mystery of Jim Hudson, but he had left her with a sinking sensation in her stomach, and an out-of-proportion concern for his safety.

CHAPTER THREE

JIM

Jim made a left turn out of the Chamberlins' driveway. Driving swiftly but carefully, he listened to the details of the house fire on his two-way radio, cursing the static, the blue light on the truck roof casting eerie shadows across the hood. Through the years, he always found fighting fires and going to accident scenes an amazingly stimulating and emotional experience, a heady rush, but no one had prepared him for the intensity and the abhorrence, the resulting haunting nightmares.

Melford Point Fire Department at Main Street and Pine, although well equipped, wasn't a busy station. The trucks didn't normally roll out more than once a day, the mundane more common than the dramatic—a house fire such as this one, unusual. They were much more likely to be called out by folks trying to figure out what to do, unable to afford a repair person at two o'clock in the morning. Jim enjoyed those calls, a Mr. Fix It at heart, co-owner of Hudson's Hardware and Lumber with his brother, Ben, he had the skills, the tools and the materials to fix a hole in a roof; to temporarily stop a leak, and calm down an elderly resident living alone. He liked going into the local schools and talking about fire prevention; loved it when the kids came for a visit to the fire station—one of the reasons why he had held on for so long. It was the ravaged faces and the tragedy that haunted him: the man he had talked to patiently for hours who still jumped off the bridge; the dog that died from smoke inhalation; the twitching deer on the side of the road, the impacted vehicle twisted against a tree. Some of the guys were able to develop a sick kind of humor, but he never could. His problem was his inability to talk about it; all the terrible stories buried deep inside.

Jim wrenched his mind back to the present, the horror much too close to home, the wailing of the station siren getting louder and louder. He turned into the driveway and parked over to the side, well out of the way behind Tom Nealson's truck. The station, brightly lit, was a hive of activity. One of the pumpers, Engine 16, already fully manned, was pulling out, lights flashing and siren blaring. Jim didn't waste any time. He removed his uniform from the container in the bed of his truck, ran into the station, grabbed helmet number 10—the one he signed out for everything—hung up his own jacket in one of the metal lockers, tugged up his bunker pants, hauling the straps over his shoulders, thrusting his feet into his boots. Tom called out to him to hurry. Impervious to the cold, he tucked his jacket under his arm, snatched up his helmet, ran to Engine 8, hauled himself in, and sat down in the jump seat area. One man short, they couldn't afford to wait any longer. Chuck Jones, the driver—one of the old-timers like himself—pulled out of the bay and onto the road, the ambulance following close behind.

Jim leaned forward and shrugged into the heavy jacket; no easy task in such a confined space. He put on his headset and listened for any instructions from Andy Maynard, the captain, sitting in the cab up front next to Chuck. Other than the preliminary greetings, the seven men were silent. Fire fighting, always a serious business, every ounce of energy conserved, Jim had learned early on firefighters had little tolerance for idle chatter. Riding with Tom, Roger Chartwell, Tony Billings and Vernon Addison he couldn't have wished for a better team of men; they were family. Roger, although only in his early twenties, had the makings of a fine firefighter— Jim hoped with all his heart he would be spared the nightmares. The other men wore their experience in the set of their jaws—brave and competent to a fault.

Jim hated fighting fires at night, dreaded the gathering dark, making it so much more difficult to see when entering a building looking for people and domestic animals. He wondered what had ignited this particular fire and he hoped to God the first response team had been able to get a good start on the blaze. It was possible they could be there for hours.

The pumper sped through town; Chuck's driving skillful, watching for other vehicles pulling over to get out of the way. At least at this time of the day there weren't any school buses—a blessing. Buses always caused a delay out of their control; no matter how urgent, they weren't allowed to pass without coming to a complete stop first and only when signaled by the school bus operator were they able to proceed. Chuck took the turning for Route 1 and Jim realized with dismay they were heading towards the area where both he and his brother lived. As with any fire, his thoughts always turned to anyone he might know. However, in this instance his fears were unfounded and he breathed a huge sigh of relief when Chuck pulled off the highway a couple of exits prior to his own. They could smell the fire before they saw the thick plume of dirty yellow-black smoke through the leafless trees—the odor a combination of wood, roofing tiles, tar, siding and plastic.

When they got there, two firefighters from the first truck were inside the house, two others on top of the ladder making a hole in the roof. Chuck drew to a halt. The firemen clambered out of the truck, awkward in their heavy gear, and Andy ran over to the first crew to find out how much water they had left in their tank. Larry Swayne, manning the levers and switches on top of Engine 16, gave him a thumbs down. Andy ran back to his men to tell them they needed to make their pumper ready. "Sixteen is running low," he shouted.

Jim and Tom, breathing apparatus on, waited for orders. Engine 16 had already used its deluge gun causing the pumper to run low. Despite the quick response, the blaze was fierce and still in danger of getting out of control. The windows on the ground floor were already out, flames devouring the front of the old farmhouse, licking their way into the second floor, and there was thick smoke throughout the whole of the upstairs. Carl, 16's captain, shouted, "We've got to get this sucker under control. We don't want sparks igniting the horse barn!" Roger and Vernon wrestled a hose around the back of the house and tackled the blaze that way.

"Anyone inside the house?" Andy shouted.

"Just two of ours, Brian and Shane. They're in there right now breaching walls and hosing everything down." Jim felt a shudder of relief, pulled his mind away from scenes gone bad. He shouldered a hose from their own truck, leaning into the weight, dropping the flat yellow loops onto the frozen ground. He gave Vernon the green light to start pumping, and he and Tom watched the hose fill, the water ironing out the kinks. Grabbing the end, they tugged it past the exhaust fan placed in the doorway and into the house. He heard a horse whinny and it sent shivers up his spine.

The smoke enveloped them, their familiar world disappearing as they crossed the threshold. They dropped to their knees and crawled, dragging the hose with them, and it fought them every inch of the way, the brass couplings catching on corners. Jim created the same repetitive diagram in his head: always follow the right-hand wall, count the turns, figure out the maze. He crawled into a walk-in closet, backed out, bumped into a piece of furniture, eventually finding Brian and Shane in what he assumed was once the living room. Shane was making holes in the ceiling, directing the water upwards, and Brian was using a sheetrock puller; the two of them rapidly running out of air, indicated to Jim to take over. He grabbed the pike pole from Shane, put his mask next to the side of Shane's head and yelled, "Get out!" Shane nodded and he and Brian crawled away.

Salvage covers placed over the furniture, barely discernible humps, protected the men from noxious fumes. Jim created a sizeable hole in the ceiling and Tom directed the hose up into the opening. Though the roaring of the flames appeared to be lessening, he didn't trust the unpredictable beast, and even with the bright flashlights on their helmets, it was difficult to see. Despite Brian and Shane's aggressive attack, they still needed to be wary. Holes had already been punched in the kitchen ceiling; the area well doused. He came back into the hallway and gestured to Tom they needed to get out. A mixture of water and foam poured from overhead, aimed through the hole in the roof made by the men on the ladder. The building creaked and shuddered; the ceiling and the floor above the living room fell, leaving a gaping hole. They needed to get out before they were buried.

The low-pressure alarm on Jim's breathing apparatus went off, a vibration he could feel right through his coat, a fluttering in his armpit. He had to get out before the bell stopped ringing. "Don't panic, follow the hose, remember the pattern," he talked himself down. He could hear what sounded like beams collapsing, sodden sheetrock falling. He crawled faster, Tom on his heels. The bell stopped ringing just as Jim reached the front door. The front of the mask smacked hard against his face like a plastic bag and he couldn't breath; nothing left for his lungs to pull. He panicked, foolishly ripped the mask off his face instead of reaching behind his back and checking the override and the main valve. He took a great gulping breath of the cold, smoke-filled air, remained on his knees coughing convulsively—his throat thoroughly irritated, his jacket steaming with residual heat. He pushed himself to his feet and in a raspy whisper told Tom he was okay. "You're sure, man?"

Jim nodded. "I'll go see the medics. Just need water," he said, his voice hoarse. He was worried about toxins, but not letting on. He wandered over to the ambulance, helmet and mask in hand, no longer sure Helmet number 10 his good luck charm. Pete, daydreaming behind the wheel of the cab, engine running to keep warm, jumped when Jim knocked on the window. He took one look at Jim's soot-covered face, wound down the window and told him to go around the back and get into the ambulance. Jim knew better than to argue. "What happened?" Pete asked, producing a bottle of water, removing the cap and holding it out. Jim pulled off his gloves, drank gratefully, the cool liquid soothing his smoke irritated throat.

"Air pack gave out sooner than it should have, but I was outside so it was okay. Just breathed in a little smoke."

Pete, reluctant to let Jim go, said, "You know the drill, man."

"Yeah, I do."

"At least let me do a pulmonary function test. We can do a tox screen later, if necessary."

Pete hooked up the machine, gave Jim the mouthpiece, told him to breathe in and out for at least five minutes. Tom's dirty face appeared around the side of the ambulance. Jim gave him a thumb's up. Tom smiled, his teeth glaringly white against his sooty skin. Firefighters dreaded a man down, made the danger too personal. Pete gave Jim a temporary all-clear, told him to come back at any sign of increased shortness of breath, fast heartbeat and chest pain, weakness, pale and clammy skin . . .

Jim cut him off. "Aye, I will, and thanks."

He clambered out of the ambulance, stood for a moment, his legs a little shaky. There was a full moon and it was cold, the stars white and shining against the navy-blue sky; the roof still sending up wisps of smoke, but no more flames, no more sparks, and once the structure cooled down, it would become an ice sculpture—macabre and grotesque. Water was still being directed down into the hole in the roof and would be for some time to make sure the fire was well and truly out. He wondered who lived here and went over to ask Carl. "A young woman was hanging around outside when we arrived. The house belongs to her grandparents and thanks be to God they'd gone to visit her sister in Portland for Thanksgiving and were staying there for a couple o' nights."

"Where is she now?"

"Over in the barn with the horses."

"I'll go talk to her."

Jim turned away from the house, walking slowly in his heavy gear. In all his years as a volunteer firefighter, he had come across very few house fires and he was very thankful for that. He couldn't imagine what it would be like to lose a home and he thought of his own, so steeped in history, and he suspected this old farmhouse was the same. He had no trouble seeing where he was going—the lights still flashing on both engines, the moon shining bright.

The barn, a single story low-slung building containing six stalls with double doors securely closed against the frigid temperatures, faced onto a fenced-in paddock. He headed towards a side door, attracted by the lights within. Turning the knob, he found himself in a well-lit hallway; the odor of warm horses, hay and sweet feed a welcome relief from the acrid smoke. Each horse or pony, well protected from its neighbor, looked out over their half doors onto the aisle—six in total in varying sizes and colors—the first a beautiful dapple-gray mare. He held out the flat of his hand, but she blew through her nostrils in alarm and stepped backwards. He immediately felt bad for bringing her the unwelcome gift of the odor of his smoke impregnated gear. "Hello, Moondancer," he said, reading the name on her door, moving away. "I'm very glad we didn't have to rescue you tonight." Fearful now, she remained in the back of her stall.

Even though he stayed well away from the remaining horses they still retreated, ears alert, showing the whites of their eyes, a sign of alarm. He shouldn't have come. He passed utility rooms on his right: a place to store feed, an office, a big wash area and finally a tack room where he found a young girl sitting on a trunk, her head in her hands, a big hairy lump of a dog sitting at her feet, its huge head resting on her knee. She jumped when she heard him and looked up; her face tear-stained. "I'm sorry. I didn't mean to startle you and I'm sorry I spooked the horses. I wasn't thinking," he said, and coughed, covering his mouth with his hand.

"It's okay. I'm in a bit of a daze I'm afraid. Is there anything left of the house?" She stood up and offered her hand; made no comment on his sooty face. "I'm Jemma Moorehouse and this is Rufus. As you can tell, he's not much of a guard dog."

"Jim Hudson. I just came to see if you were all right."

"Physically, I'm fine. I just don't know how I'm going to tell my grand-parents," and she looked at Jim as if to say, "Please make this all go away." A tall and slender girl, wearing a dark blue vest over a gray sweatshirt, a bright red woolly hat pulled down over her ears, her long legs encased in tight jeans, over which she wore sturdy knee-length leather boots, she stood in a state of melancholy rubbing the back of her neck. Her brows dark, her lips full, her nose a little upturned, her eyes a light hazel, she was an extremely attractive young woman, young enough to be his daughter

and he thought how wonderful it would be to have a child of his own.
"Can I get you anything? I could make you a cup of coffee," she said.

"I'm sorry, I have to get back to the crew and help pack up, but let
me give you my phone number and I'd be happy to help you in any way I
can. You're rather isolated here aren't you and do you have somewhere to
sleep?"

"Yes, I have a bedroom here. In fact I live in the barn. I prefer the company of four-legged critters to humans. They don't let you down."

"Have you any idea how the fire started?"

"No. In fact I haven't been in the house much since my grandparents
left. I haven't done any cooking, or lit any fires."

"It could be electrical then, or possibly the furnace. I'm sure the insurance company will be able to figure it out."

"All the insurance money in the world won't bring back the photo
albums, my grandmother's hand-sewn quilts, my grandfather's paintings,
but more than that, the house was their sanctuary. You didn't see a huge
marmalade cat by any chance?"

Jim shook his head.

"I have to believe he escaped through the cat door."

"I'm sure he did."

"I've been calling him. I hate to think of him out there frightened and
alone. He's a house cat and doesn't usually come anywhere near the barn.
My grandmother will blame me if he doesn't come home."

"Jemma, I'm sorry. Have you got a piece of paper and I'll give you my
number."

"I'll just put it in my cell phone," she said, pulling a phone from a back
pocket in her jeans and flipping it open with shaky hands. "Jim Hudson,
you said, right?"

"Yes," and he gave her his number, shook her hand, walked out of the
tack room—the smell of leather and saddle soap lingering in his nostrils—
back down the aisle, pausing outside Moondancer's stall, but staying well
away. Jemma, on his heels, said, "She is beautiful, isn't she? It's a shame she
won't keep her dapples, but she's young so she'll have them for a while."

He opened the door and stepped outside. He turned and faced her.
"A skeleton crew will remain to make sure there aren't any flare-ups. We
covered up what we could, but I'm not sure how much you will be able
to salvage. I'm sorry. Please don't hesitate to call me if you can think of
anything and then you can tell me all about the horses."

"I'd like that," she said, giving a little wave before closing the door against the cold of the night.

Jim walked back towards the house and went over to talk to the crew who were busy reeling hoses. He was tired. He went over to help Tom hold the hose to make sure it stayed straight, the automatic winder pulling it back in, whining under its load. "Is the girl all right?" he asked.

"Seems to be. She's worried about telling her grandparents, but thankful they weren't home. Things could've been a lot worse."

"Does she know how it started?" Tom asked, picking up the second hose and guiding it as the truck did its job.

"Says she has no idea and I believe her. She actually lives in the barn and prepares all her meals there too. It's an old house—could be electrical. I gave her my phone number just in case she needs anything."

"Always the Good Samaritan, eh?"

Jim shrugged. "If it hadn't been me, it would have been another member of the crew. You know that."

"I do. Just giving you a hard time."

Jim removed his air pack and placed the empty canister and harness with Tom's in the special rack. The canisters would be refilled and ready and waiting at the station for the next time, but this one would have to be carefully examined, find out the cause for the malfunction. All hoses stashed, Andy said it was okay for them to leave. Engine 16 would stay behind. Jim, saddened because of not being able to relieve Jemma's burden, imagined how difficult her conversation with her grandparents was going to be. He didn't envy her the task. He remembered another fire: a child's bicycle on the front porch, scattered belongings on the lawn, scorched curtains blowing through the broken windows. Jim believed Jemma's grandparents' house unsalvageable. Smoke had a way of infiltrating everything, sneaking into every single cupboard, leaving sooty rings around and under objects, turning every single thing yellow with heavy, sticky goop. The men hauled themselves into the truck one by one—somber, dirty, and weary. Wedged between Vernon and Roger, Tom and Tony on the jump seats opposite, Jim put his hand on Roger's knee. "Okay, son?" he asked.

"I'm good," he said. Jim couldn't see his face because it was dark now that the lights on the truck were no longer flashing, but the young man seemed to have weathered his first house fire well. Sometimes it was easier to be a rookie, although Jim remembered only too well the menial tasks back at the fire station—cleaning toilets and grocery shopping, preparing simple meals.

"This was a tough one," he said. "Fortunately, there aren't many like this. We get the occasional chimney fire that we're able to douse quite easily, but folks don't usually lose their homes. For some reason, this took hold fast and no one was home to report it. By the time Jemma saw the smoke it was already burning out of control." Jim realized he was talking too much, so he stopped. There was a great deal of bantering back and forth when they were all in the communal room in the firehouse waiting for a call, but after a fire such as this they were all exhausted and no one was in the mood for talking. Eventually, they would discuss this fire—how well they had responded and whether they could have done better—always looking for ways to improve procedures.

Jim leaned back, closed his eyes and thought of MaryAnn; the vision of her that morning when she had innocently walked out of his bathroom, just wrapped in a towel, with her silvery blonde hair pulled up onto the top of her head; this image of her his secret, a little golden nugget of good fortune. Thinking about her, remembering her initial reaction to his revelation, he decided it was time to retire, take the worry away. Time for the young firefighters like the Rogers of the world to replace a veteran like him, but the decision was not made lightly and there was still no escaping the dreams and the nightmares when he would wake up sweating with imaginary smoke in his nostrils, unable to breathe.

CHAPTER FOUR

THEA

Mr. Blunt rested his hand on the top of Thea's head. "Let me get dressed," he said, "then we'll figure out what we're going to do." She sat back on her haunches, pushed herself away from the chair, moving to one side. They didn't hear Robert come in, his footsteps muffled by the carpet, startling Thea when he appeared in the living room doorway with three envelopes in his hand. He offered no apology to Thea for his earlier behavior, and she eyed him warily. "Ellie wrote notes to all of us. I found them in the drawer of her bedside table. Here," he said, holding one envelope out to Thea and the other to Theodore. They remained frozen to the spot, afraid to touch the letters, unwelcome intruders into their grief, poignant reminders of Ellie's death. "For goodness sake take them," he said, losing patience, thrusting them at Thea. "I can't even bring myself to read mine."

Taking the long ivory-colored envelopes from Robert's hand, she placed the one addressed to Theodore on the coffee table by his chair. The old man, standing as if transfixed, seemed bewildered and perplexed so Thea suggested he go get dressed, and he seemed happy to have someone tell him what to do. He shuffled off to his bedroom and they heard him opening and shutting drawers, an encouraging sign.

Left alone with Robert, she tried to gauge his mood, wondered whether he was likely to explode again. He lingered, his face a picture of abject misery. Summoning up her courage, Thea went to him, slid Ellie's letter out of his hand, immediately stepping backwards. "Would you like me to read it to you?"

"You never give up do you? The letter is written in French. Ellie and I always revert to our native language when we're miserable." She noticed his use of the present tense, his tone rude and abrupt, she the unhappy scapegoat.

Trapped and nervous, foolhardy in her response, she said, "Oh, well that makes sense. It would probably be a good idea to read it though, because knowing Ellie, I'm sure her words will make you feel better."

"How can anything make me feel better? She took her own life. She shut me out." He muttered something in French, which she was unable to understand.

Thea swallowed, remained silent. She could have cut Robert's anger with a knife, and running the risk of further chastisement, she said, "Where's Honey?"

Robert sat down heavily on the couch and looked up at her. "Lying outside Ellie's door. She wouldn't budge when I tried to make her come with me. I'll wait for Theodore. Why don't you take your letter and go be with your children. I don't need you hanging around."

Longing to give Robert a piece of her mind, she held her tongue. Gone were the days when she allowed people to treat her badly, but if it helped Robert to be nasty to her then so be it. Clutching the envelope, she made her way back upstairs, wondering what arrangements Robert had made with Dr. Randall, if any. She went to her bedroom, stopping to talk to Honey on the way, but the dog refused to move. Sitting down on the bed, she plumped the pillows, pulled the quilt over her legs, and turned on the bedside lamp. Taking a moment to catch her breath, being on her own a welcome respite from Robert's glowering presence, she looked around the pretty bedroom, brightly decorated in corn-flower blue and yellow, white blinds softening the early morning light. Bringing her wandering attention back to the envelope, she ran her finger across her name, boldly written, feeling the slight indentation, holding the lavender-scented paper to her nose. Turning the envelope over she lifted the unsealed flap, gently removed the letter and started to read:

My Dearest Thea

When you hold this letter in your hand, I will hopefully be at peace. It has been a long struggle, and despite my belief in God, I just didn't see any point in going on and I hope both He and you will find it in your hearts to forgive me.

I wish now that I had made more of an effort to spend time with you over the years, and I know you will blame yourself for not staying in touch. Please don't. Let me explain.

The two years that you and I had together were the best of my life. Even though you were only eighteen and I was thirty, the age difference was irrelevant because we had a common bond—Aladdin's Cave. Your love for the store was as great as mine, as was your love for hard physical exercise. Even though I didn't share your enthusiasm for running (!) there were plenty of other sports we enjoyed doing together. You used to say, all the time, how much you learned from me, but I learned from you too. As you know, cooking wasn't my favorite thing to do, but you loved to create tasty meals and you were never afraid to try new recipes, even though sometimes they didn't quite work out. Remember the raspberry tart with the crunchy crust that was too hard to eat? We threw it out to the birds and forever looked for birds with bent beaks! We had so much fun, but we worked hard, too, and I did go on to create an after-school program, the one we'd planned together. Did you find the craft room when you went to the store? I spent so many happy hours there teaching kids how to be creative, telling them stories, listening to music, and keeping them off the streets, but there was always someone missing.

Thea stopped reading, the writing swimming through her tears, leaning back against the pillows, she closed her eyes and wiped her hand across her face. Sensing Thea's distress and seeking solace, Honey padded silently into the room, rested her head on the bed, and looked at Thea with sorrowful eyes. Thea, deciding Ellie's *off the furniture rule* no longer applied, patted the bedcover and said, "Up, Honey." The dog, not needing to be told twice, backed up, made a running leap, landing next to Thea's legs. "It's all right, girl. It's going to be okay." She gathered the big dog to her, put her arms around her neck, took comfort in her warmth; Honey gently licked her face. "We're a bit of a mess, aren't we? Why don't you lie down?" She did as she was told, sinking down with a sigh. Thea continued reading:

I never wanted to get married. I had seen what it had done to my mother. Don't get me wrong, Papa was a good man, but Maman bore too many children. I have always thought the Pope should be a woman and then the stance on contraception would be very different, I'm sure. I was cooking and caring for siblings at the age of nine and it never occurred to me to complain. I wasn't angry or resentful, just realized at a very early age that I wanted something different. I didn't want to be responsible for the health and happiness of either a husband or a cluster of children. I never regretted it. Of course in my naiveté, it never occurred to me that you might not feel the same way and I wonder what unhappy twist of fate would have happened to rock my world if you hadn't met Michael when you did. I knew I'd lost you the minute the two of you set eyes on each other and I'm sorry things went so wrong. I could sense disaster in the making, but even had it

31

been my place to say something, you wouldn't have listened anyway! I let you go, and wallowed in my own self-pity for quite a while. It was unfair of me to stay out of touch, but you hardly had time for me. You were twenty years old and blinded by a handsome and worldly man who didn't deserve you. Anyway, all that is water under the bridge now.

I hoped I might be able to lure you back this way once you and Michael divorced, but then you took up with Kenny and I thought, won't she ever learn? But I believe you finally have.

"Oh, my gosh, Ellie. You're really doing a number on me. I'm not sure I want to read any more. If you're saying what I think you're saying, then I had no idea." I have to put it down to the ramblings of a sick woman and put it behind me otherwise I will be haunted for the rest of my life.

Words cannot express how very sorry I am that you find yourself in this current mess. Yes, it was selfish of me, but I wanted to see you one more time and I honestly didn't know the end was so near. You would have smelled a rat if I had invited you without the children, and in any case, you wouldn't have left them behind, especially Jessica, who you say is still so vulnerable after the abduction.

I am writing this in the hope I will meet your children soon because I know they are wonderful. I couldn't run the risk of waiting to write to you in case my demise came fast. No one knows what causes brain tumors, and unfortunately, mine was malignant and aggressively invaded surrounding tissue. I was lucky to feel as well as I did for as long as I did. Of course I chose to ignore the symptoms—in my case headaches, tingling in my arms and legs, problems with memory and an inability to concentrate—until the seizure I had in the kitchen. Fortunately for me, Theodore was there, but it frightened him to death and it was shortly after that he begged Robert to come. He is the youngest member of the Tetreault family and sixteen years my junior. He was only four when I left home!

So Robert came and we soldiered on with the radio- and the chemotherapy in pill form and a range of drugs including steroids (which gave me super human energy!) to reduce the swelling in the brain, and anticonvulsants. I experienced some hair loss, but I was lucky, I followed instructions to the letter and had few side effects. Lately, we added anti-nausea pills to the regimen. It was hard to keep going when there was no hope of getting better. Of course I prayed for a miracle, ate all the right foods and laughed at a lot of funny movies. After all, laughter is supposed to be the best medicine, isn't it? You would think that after all the laughing we did during those two charmed years enough of a reserve would have been created to keep either of us from getting sick for ever, but it wasn't to be. Cancer is frightening and lonely, and even though I had hands to hold and give me strength, it was my journey and mine alone. I was fortunate in that I had a fantastic doctor—Penelope Randall—and if you ever meet her you will know. She truly listened and that is a gift. Anyway, now I'm getting melancholy, but I didn't want to leave you hanging with unanswered questions and I suspect we had little time to talk. If there is no footnote to this letter, then you will know I was too weak to write anymore.

I have a request, and before you cast the idea aside, my request has already been discussed with Robert and he is in full agreement. I would like you to take Honey home with you. Oh, she's fond of Robert and Theodore, but her heart has always been with me.

"So, Honey, our friend Ellie has just dropped another bombshell. At this point, I'm finding it hard to be sympathetic, but of course we will give you a home. She has the uncanny knack of either reducing me to tears or making me very cross. And now I'm talking to you. I think I must be losing my mind." She shook her head and went back to the letter:

I'm sorry about Aladdin's Cave and the partnership. I know it would be a lot to ask you now to stay on, especially as you would be on your own without my support. I could have helped your children with the transition and I know we could have made a good life for all of us here, but again, I was being unrealistic. Aladdin's Cave always did belong to Theodore and we never discussed what he would do when I wasn't around.

Well, my lovely Thea, this truly is goodbye. I'm sorry I dragged you all this way to no avail, but you will take a little bit of me back to Maine with you in Honey's heart. She is a great dog and will bring you much happiness and especially Peter, I suspect, because I remember you telling me he always wanted a dog. Hopefully, she will make up for the loss of Lady just a little bit. God bless.

Love Ellie

Exhausted by Ellie's outpourings, not quite sure what to make of it all, frustrated because she was now unable to talk to her friend, she folded the letter and tucked it back into the envelope and sealed the words inside. She doubted she would ever read it again. Honey sniffed the envelope, whined when she recognized Ellie's scent, doubling Thea's despondency. Sleep, the best escape, Thea leaned her head against the pillows and closed her eyes.

Robert, finally plucking up enough courage to read his sister's letter, sat in his dimly lit room. He wasn't quite sure what he expected, but he was disappointed—it was nothing more than a thank you note. A beautifully written one, yes, but devoid of emotion, done on purpose perhaps to help him miss her less. Well, it wasn't working. He felt sorry for himself and he was still angry. Too angry to call Maman and Papa, or Dorothy, besides which he saw no point in waking them up when there wasn't anything they could do.

He stomped upstairs to wait for Dr. Randall, closing Thea's door on the way. No reason for her to wake up. Why was he so mad at her? He couldn't figure out why she got under his skin. He had certainly burned his bridges as far as a relationship was concerned. He shrugged, wondered how she had reacted to Ellie's request to take the dog home with her.

Robert saw headlights turning into the driveway, a welcome distraction. He opened the door, stepped out onto Ellie's brightly decorated porch with the scarecrows and Indian corn, the mums beginning to look a little tired and sad. Dr. Randall got out of her car, leaned over and retrieved her bag from the passenger seat. He walked towards her and said, "Thank you for coming."

"Come, let's go inside. You must be freezing."

He was cold, both inside and out, ridiculous to be standing outside in these frigid temperatures with no coat. Dr. Randall, silvery gray hair tucked inside a frivolous pale pink fluffy hat, matching scarf fashionably knotted, looked at him intently, her smile sympathetic. She exuded a timeless quality, wore her age well, and seemed to have an endless wealth of knowledge she imparted with kindness in a language her patients could understand. Meeting with her many times during the course of Ellie's illness, he had always come away comforted, even during Ellie's darkest times.

She shrugged out of her coat, handed it to Robert, waited while he hung it in the closet, and walked with him to Ellie's bedroom. "If this is too painful, you can stay outside," she said, resting one of her delicate hands on his arm, the nails neatly trimmed, fingers unadorned except for a simple gold wedding band.

"It's okay. I'd like to be with you." She nodded and slowly opened the door.

"Despite the cold, I think it would be a good idea to crack a window in here."

Robert couldn't agree more, wished he'd thought of it earlier, cut himself some slack. Dr. Randall placed her fingers on Ellie's wrist, a purely mechanical gesture; she found no signs of life. She shook her head and pulled the sheet up over Ellie's face. He saw her glance at the empty pill bottle lying on its side on the bedside table. He had made no attempt to hide it. Neither of them said anything. After a few moments, Dr. Randall turned to him. "Does anyone else know about this?"

"Yes. Theodore Blunt."

"Yes, yes. I know who he is. Anyone else?"

"Thea Chamberlin. She's visiting from Maine for the weekend."

Robert picked up on Dr. Randall's nervousness. "Why didn't you tell me this before? You know you should have called 911. This puts me in an exceedingly awkward position. I would be struck off if it ever came to light, but I'm a middle-aged woman and close to the end of my career so I am going to suggest you throw the bottle away and remove the glass Ellie drank from. I know this goes against all that you believe in. You didn't hear this from me, so we'll say no more on the matter. I will call the funeral home for you." She paused, mulling over her decision, deciding it was the right one. Robert would talk to Thea and it would be conveniently swept under the rug. Sometimes medical and religious ethics just got in the way and she didn't see any point in causing any more stress, especially for Robert's deeply religious Catholic family. In this case, she was happy to turn a blind eye, especially as she had absolutely no sympathy for the archaic and rigid dogma and the human suffering it quite often caused.

Robert broke into her thoughts. "Ellie left a letter for me in which she named a funeral home, one that will transport her body to Maine, honoring her request to go home and be buried with family."

Dr. Randall held up her hand. "I will sign the death certificate. The remainder of the form will be completed by the mortuary and filed with the state registrar. You will need a certified copy of the death certificate every time you need proof of death. Did she make it easy on you and leave a will?"

"Yes, she did. It was something she tried to discuss with me, but I wasn't very co-operative. I'm afraid I didn't handle her illness well. She was much braver . . ."

"Don't sell yourself short, Robert. It's always much harder for the caretaker. Believe me, I've been in your shoes."

"Thank you for understanding."

"How's Mr. Blunt holding up? Would you like me to talk to him while I'm here?"

"I'm sure he would appreciate it, and so would I."

They both left Ellie's room, the lingering smell of death on their clothes and in their nostrils. There was no sound from Thea or her children and he tiptoed past their rooms, putting his finger to his lips. They found Theodore sitting in his kitchen, clutching a mug of tea, a partially finished crossword on the table, his face lighting up at the sight of Dr. Randall. "Well, this is a nice surprise," he said. "The water in the teakettle is still hot if you would like a drink."

"You know, I would, but Robert can make it," and she winked at him, walked around to where Theodore was sitting and felt his pulse, pleased to feel its steady beat—not too fast, not too slow. Despite his sorrowful demeanor, he seemed remarkably healthy. "How old are you now?" she asked.

"Now that's no question to ask a gentleman," he said, a little of his natural humor returning. "I'm seventy-seven years young." She looked into his faded blue eyes, amazed at the whiteness of the sclera, a reliable indicator of good health. "How are you holding up?"

"Oh, I'm a bit creaky in the joints," he said, "but other than that, I feel fine. Sad of course, but Ellie wouldn't want us to be gloomy. She always continued to attack life even when she was sick and that's what I shall continue to do in her memory."

"That's the spirit and Ellie was quite remarkable in that respect. That's why I was sure we would beat the disease in the long run, but it wasn't to be." She took the steaming mug of tea from Robert, declining both milk and sugar. "Do either of you have any questions for me?"

"None that I can think of. How about you, Theodore?"

The old man shook his head and said, "But I do want to thank you for coming so quickly. It's very comforting to have you here. There aren't many doctors who make house calls these days, but sometimes the old-fashioned ways are the best."

"I still visit my patients at home when I can. It's not an orthodox approach and my fellow specialists have no wish to follow in my footsteps, but I have never been a slave to convention. It works well for me and I feel more connected. I'm sorry Ellie went downhill so fast because I would have liked to have seen her, but I'm glad I have been able to bring at least a modicum of comfort to you both. If you're sure there's nothing more I can do, I really should get going," and she stood up, pushing her chair back and taking her mug over to the sink. "Thank you for the tea." She held out her hand to Theodore; he clasped it firmly. "The medical profession would be a lot better off with more doctors like you."

"Thank you," she said with a smile. "I hope you go for regular physicals."

"I do. I have an excellent primary care physician, Dr. Robertson. He gives me a thorough once-over every year."

"Cameron Robertson; I know him well. He's a bit of a crusty-old curmudgeon at times, but you're in good hands. Well, I really must be going. Goodnight, Mr. Blunt. Robert, will you see me out?"

Robert waited while Dr. Randall buttoned her coat and pulled the ridiculous pink hat down over her ears. She turned to Robert and said, "Don't try to do this all by yourself. I can write you a prescription for anti-anxiety or sleeping pills if that would help."

"I'll be all right, but thank you," he said, holding the door open for her. "Just knowing you cared enough to come has made a huge difference already."

"I'm glad," she said, stepping out onto the porch into the frigid air. "And as I said before, don't hesitate to call if I can help in any way. Good luck with all the arrangements and I'm sorry you're going back to Maine. The VNA here will miss you. You are an excellent nurse. Please take care." Robert watched until she was safely in her car with the engine running and then stepped back and closed the door.

He stood outside Ellie's room. He didn't want to go in there, but knew he must, one last time. Stepping inside, he pulled the door shut behind him. The room was cold as a tomb. Pretending the sheet-shrouded figure was somebody other than his sister, hands shaking he picked up the yellow container now empty of morphine tablets, together with the lid, and the glass from which Ellie had taken her last drink of water. He felt like a criminal, but Dr. Randall had been right, and admiring her courage, he ran a steamroller over his little voice of guilt. This was one confession he was not going to make. He wasn't going to ask his priest to forgive him; he was going to go straight to God. After all, God was love, and having his own conscience get in the way would serve absolutely no purpose whatsoever except to make a great many people unhappy.

He took one last look at Ellie's room taking in all the bright colors she had loved so much. The quilt over the bed mimicked the sign painted above the window of Aladdin's Cave with its moon and stars in vivid purples, yellows and blues—the lamp itself delicately rendered in gold cloth in the bottom right hand corner. Duplicating the colors from the quilt she had used them for the furnishings, the total effect rich and luxurious and slightly exotic, tempered only by the flimsy white draperies. Pictures of the children she cared for in her after-school program hung on one wall in old and interesting frames gathered from tag sales and flea markets. The result was a display of pictures of all different shapes and sizes, grouped together in a way that showed them off to their best advantage. An uncanny knack with a camera, Ellie had captured the kids' faces, their various expressions reflecting their love of clowning in front of a lens. Robert eventually pulled himself away, wondering what he would do with all her belongings, especially a rather large and whimsical giraffe sitting in one of the corners. "*Au revoir*, Ellie," he said. "*Je t'aime. Être en paix*, be at peace," and he closed the door.

Placing the glass in the dishwasher and thrusting the pill bottle down the bottom of the garbage pail, he made sure it was well buried. He washed his hands, staring at them as if they had committed a murder, still blaming himself, even though Ellie in her weakened state could just as easily have died from natural causes. He knew it was ridiculous and totally irrational to feel this burden of guilt, but he did and he would have to live with it. He glanced at the digital clock on the stove, surprised to see it was six o'clock. He needed to go see Thea before her children woke up and all hell broke loose. He knocked gently, opened Thea's door, stepped into the room, and touched her gently on the shoulder. "Hi, Thea. I'm sorry to wake you, but we need to talk."

Dozing fitfully, instantly awake at the sound of Robert's voice, eyes wide with alarm, she resisted the urge to flee. Honey thumped her tail on the quilt but made no attempt to move. "I see you've found a friend," Robert said, leaning down and running his hand along the dog's sleek fur, noticing Ellie's letter in Thea's lap. "You read Ellie's request, then?"

She nodded to this new friendly Robert, relieved his counterpart had disappeared, but not convinced Mr. Hyde wouldn't return. "I'd be happy to take her, but are you sure she wouldn't be a good companion for Mr. Blunt?"

"He loves her, but she's young and needs a lot of exercise. He's already agreed she would be too much for him."

"What about you?"

"Why do you have to ask so many questions?"

She didn't answer. He continued, "She should have a family and lots of people around her. She wouldn't have much of a life with a single guy like me."

"Well, if you're sure . . ."

"How can I be sure of anything anymore, but that's what Ellie wanted so end of story."

Thea wanted to tell him how thrilled Peter would be, but decided he wouldn't be interested. "You can rest assured we will take good care of her." But he wasn't listening.

"There's one other thing." He shuffled from one foot to the other, swaying slightly from side to side, his kneecaps shivering; a nervous little boy trait. "I called Ellie's doctor and she was kind enough to make a house call. She left about twenty minutes ago. She's going to complete a death certificate for me with *natural causes* as the reason. She turned a blind eye to the empty pill bottle, and is prepared to sweep the whole thing under the rug unless you have any objections."

"Robert, I saw nothing, so there's no need to say anything more."

"Thank you." His whole body slumped in relief. "Dr. Randall is going to call the mortician Ellie named in her letter. She left instructions to be buried in the family plot in Maine, and as soon as that is all arranged, I will be going home. I know that leaves Theodore on his own, but I know he has a friend in Dorothy. She will help him out and be much more useful than I could ever be."

"I think it would be best if the kids and I just packed up and left. Perhaps you could put all Honey's stuff together in one place with any special instructions. Does she have a vet record with her shots? We definitely need that so we don't repeat anything she's already had. I want to make sure she stays healthy."

"*Oui*, for the dog's sake, I can do that."

She had to get away. She'd had enough of Robert's rudeness. "I'm going to go down and talk to Mr. Blunt," she said, thrusting the quilt aside. Honey jumped off the bed and Robert stood back as Thea brushed past him, the dog following close behind.

Thea, somewhat reassured by how quickly Honey had decided to adopt her, hoped it would help to ease the dog's transition to her new home. Knocking on Mr. Blunt's open door, she walked into the apartment. On the phone in the hallway, he held up a finger. She waited for him, pacing the floor in the sitting room, fingering the old-fashioned photographs in their ornate silver frames on top of the piano—a young Jenny and Theodore in their wedding finery. She heard him say, "Dorothy, it's Theodore. I'm so sorry to call you this early and I hope I didn't wake you." Thea imagined the woman's reaction, the sharp intake of breath, hearing the bad news. So much had happened in such a short period of time, the Thanksgiving visit bearing little resemblance to her anticipation. She sat down on the sofa, Honey's head in her lap, absent-mindedly fondled the dog's ears, hated eavesdropping. The conversation continued. "Are you sure you don't mind?" he said, followed by a prolonged silence. Finally saying, "Thank you, Dorothy. I'll see you later today. Bye, bye," and he hung up.

Thea heard his soft shuffling steps as he walked towards her. "Mr. Blunt, I've come to say goodbye. As soon as the children are awake we are going to pack up and head home. I'm going to stop in and see my parents on the way. Here, I've written my address and phone number so we can stay in touch and if you would like to come for a visit, we would love to have you. I hate to think of you being all by yourself. I know a place where you could stay, where you would be welcomed with open arms."

Theodore sat down next to Thea on the sofa and took her tiny hand within his chubby one and squeezed. "Thank you. I will definitely think about it."

"Maybe you would like to come for Christmas, and I know someone who could give you a ride," she said, turning to look at him, her face bright with anticipation. "The children would love it and you would have time to tell them some more of your stories. You'd also be able to see Izzie as Clara in *The Nutcracker*. Even though it's only a local production, it's very well done, besides which my daughter would be thrilled to have another grandfather, as would Peter and Jessica!"

Theodore tugged his large white handkerchief from his pocket, removed his glasses and polished the lenses madly, his usual diversionary tactic to hide his emotions. "You have a big heart, Thea, and you've certainly given me something to look forward to. Rest assured I will give serious consideration to your invitation, and thank you."

"It's the least I can do. You were always so kind to me when we worked together." She wanted to ask him what would happen to Aladdin's Cave now that Ellie was gone, but figured now wasn't the time, let it go, put an arm around his shoulders and hugged him tight.

"I see Honey has found a friend."

"Yes, she seems to have latched on to me. I'm assuming you are aware of Ellie's request."

"I am. She, Robert and I discussed it at length. We assumed Robert would go back to Maine and I'm too old for a young and energetic dog like Honey. She'd be lost and lonely and much better off with you and the children. I'm glad you've agreed to take her."

"It wasn't a difficult decision and I can't wait to see Peter's face when I tell him. He has wanted a dog for the longest time. He used to help look after Lady, our friends' the Gilsons' black Labrador, but she's no longer with us. We all miss her and Honey will help to fill the hole. Well," she said, standing up, "if there's nothing I can do for you, I really should get back upstairs."

"I'm all right. Dorothy will be here later and then we will work out what needs to be done."

"That makes me feel better. Give me a hug." She and Theodore stood up, putting their arms around each other in a proper heartfelt hug, rocking back and forth. "I'll call you when I get home, and promise me you'll think about coming for Christmas."

"I will," he said, and Thea walked away with Honey sticking like glue to her side.

CHAPTER FIVE

CHRIS

Christopher Morrison couldn't get the images of the young woman who had helped him with his Black Friday purchases at Aladdin's Cave out of his head, and he was determined to find a way of getting in touch with her.

Getting up early Saturday morning, deciding to go for a run before breakfast, locking the door to his loft apartment on the third floor in the old mill building on the outskirts of Great Barrington, he pocketed the key. Lithe and fit, he jogged down the three flights of stairs and out onto the sidewalk, the cement blocks gritty beneath the soles of his sneakers, playing the childhood game of *minding the cracks, break your grandmother's back*. The hazy blue sky and cotton candy clouds, the sun just rising, the air brisk and cold, hinted at the promise of a decent November day. Crossing the deserted street to the park opposite the mill, he stopped at one of the wooden benches, lifting his foot onto the seat, stretching his hamstrings. He loved this time of the day when there was no one around with the exception of a squirrel, cheekily sitting on a stone wall, lured from its nest by the pale wintry sunshine, darting away from his approaching footsteps. The path looped around the edge of the park for about a couple of miles and at one point joined the bike trail's eighteen-mile stretch. He ran for about an hour, passing through the neglected cemetery, the gravestones like soldiers, some at ease bending this way and that, protruding from the coarse texture of the frost-tinged grass. He glanced at their moss covered faces, names eroded with the passage of time, and shivered at the eerie shadows cast by the light filtering through the stark winter branches. He jogged on the path between them. Tiny American flags, tattered and discolored, fluttered in the breeze to commemorate those who had served their country in all of the dreadful wars. It didn't matter which one; Chris, a peacemaker at heart, believed they were all terrible.

Chris removed his sweatshirt, tying it around his waist, warmed up now. At the peak of fitness, he loved the exertion of hard physical exercise and the resulting euphoria. Meggie, his ex, unable to understand his obsession with staying fit, had pouted and sulked when he spent time away from her. With so little in common, her fluctuation of mood exhausted him, but blinded by her beauty, he chose to ignore all the irritating little things that secretly drove him crazy. After a year of mourning for the lost relationship, he finally believed the old cliché that beauty really is only skin-deep. If only he had realized it earlier. Meggie, now happily married to a rather dull and unambitious man—equally as handsome as she was beautiful—they suited each other perfectly. Now expecting a baby and living a life of domestic bliss, she had fulfilled her dream. At first Chris had been resentful and angry, but now he was hugely relieved that she had at least had enough courage to break up with him. His wounded pride and his broken heart had healed and now he was ready to start over. He had learned his lesson well and vowed never to get himself into such a situation ever again.

Chris stopped at the same bench to do some more stretching after his run and then walked back to his apartment. The street no longer empty, he dodged the traffic; the cars growled up the incline, trapped in their deep-pitched lower gears. He passed a young man and a woman—she bright in a turquoise jacket, he drab in grays and blacks—the heated voices of their argument hanging in the air. Before opening the door to his building, he glanced at the young woman's face to see if she needed any help, but she didn't appear to be frightened. Conscience clear and with a bounce in his step, reveling in his good health, he bounded up the three flights of stairs, hardly out of breath.

Invigorated from his shower and hungry after his run, he poured granola into a bowl, added walnuts, blueberries and skim milk, took a mouthful, and added hazelnut coffee to his French press while waiting for the teakettle to boil. He decided to go back to Aladdin's Cave just on the off chance the woman with the soft sandy-colored hair and the scent which reminded him of his mother's rose garden might be there. To kill time, he checked emails. There was one from the East Coast Greenway giving all the updates on the bike trails. As a subscriber, he participated in the advertised group rides when they were local enough. The next one was from the ski club inviting him to a pre-ski get-together; he made a note of the date on his calendar. They were a fun group and he was looking forward to seeing them. He clicked on the one from his kid sister, Madeline, who lived in New York City with her husband, Colin. Never one to waste words, it was just a brief sentence asking when he would be coming for a visit. He hoped the mystery woman lived close by, fantasized taking her with him, knowing his sister would be thrilled to know he had finally moved on.

He sat at the breakfast bar with his mug of coffee, looked around him at the starkly modern space, the angular lines of the big open room, the ceiling beams and the duct work exposed—the huge silver pipes adding their own charm. One wall was brick-faced, another partially taken up by a compact and functional galley kitchen with pale wooden cabinets and stainless steel hardware, countertops a luxurious granite in various shades of brown; the flooring throughout a pale maple, the light from the skylight reflected in its gleaming surface. A metal staircase wound its way up the third wall to a bedroom above. Chris, on a trip to Ikea, picked up a simple bed with drawers underneath, complementing the one wall of built-in closets, adding a chair in bright green, and a geometrically designed scarlet and black rug. To the left of the door, bookshelves lined the wall on which sat a Bose radio and CD player, listening to music while lying in bed a favorite pastime. Downstairs, a chocolate brown sectional sofa ran along the brick wall, turning the corner, resting beneath the windows, brightened with throw pillows in reds and greens, a multicolored rug in front on which to rest his feet. Meggie had helped him decorate and he begrudgingly admitted he was pleased with the results; despite being colorful, the decor was suitably masculine, and a great hangout for his friends. He had tucked a TV into the right hand corner opposite the brick wall and a desk to the left of that for his laptop and printer. Floor to ceiling bookshelves on the remaining wall, again in light blonde wood, were crammed with books and magazines. He had to walk through the kitchen to reach the bathroom and washer and dryer, an awkward drawback at first, but he was used to it now.

His taste in modern architecture came to a dead stop when it came to his car—an elderly white Jeep, now rust-pocked and dented. Meggie had hated it—a huge bone of contention between the two of them. She didn't want to be seen dead in it, convinced it would ruin her credibility with her, what he considered, shallow friends. To him it was an old chum, and to date had never let him down. He carried out his own maintenance, and when stumped, he called a skilled mechanic at a shop just down the road. Jasmine the Jeep had safely transported him for many years, and despite her age and her one hundred and fifty plus thousand miles on the clock, she still ran like a dream. Meggie had told him many times that he had taken better care of Jasmine and paid more attention to the car than he had to her. She'd probably been right, but he didn't understand her jealousy over a motorcar. He loved Jasmine because she was convenient for all kinds of things such as hauling furniture and being big enough to house his bicycle when he felt like riding further afield. He rarely raised the back seats so he was ready for anything and Meggie had never complained when it was convenient for her to have him pick up items too large and cumbersome to fit into her compact car. Anyway, it was all past history and she was no longer his concern.

Chris unhooked his jacket from the hooks beside the front door, pulled a hat down over his ears, picked up his gloves and headed out. Part of the mill building had been converted into a covered parking area and extra storage. The storage was pretty useless, too humid for cardboard boxes and the like, but an okay place for his bike and skis. The covered parking was a great luxury; Jasmine appreciated a roof over her head, besides which on-street parking was a problem—the street narrow, necessitating her removal every time it snowed. He looked at her all shiny with a new coat of wax, but oh so homely, not that he would tell her that. He patted the hood, unlocked the door, slid into the driver's seat, and turned the key in the ignition—his reward a rumble of life. "Ready for an outing, old girl?" She gave an answering growl when he pressed his foot on the accelerator.

When he reached Stockton and pulled up outside Aladdin's Cave, he was disappointed to find the store still in darkness. He left the car running, glanced at his watch, went over to read the store hours and found a notice on the door saying the store was closed until further notice due to unforeseen circumstances. Although this was a serious setback, Chris wasn't about to give up. He got back into the car, pulled the door shut and fastened the seatbelt. "Well, Jasmine, I have some detective work to do," deciding his mother would be a good place to start.

Jasmine purred along, eating up the miles to Lenox and Chris was parking in his parents' driveway in no time in front of their big white, green-shuttered, colonial house. The mums on either side of the front door in their concrete urns looked faded and brown-tinged but the wreath of silk leaves and bittersweet made a colorful splash against the deep green of the front door, its brass knocker bright and shiny. The stone driveway crunched beneath his winter hiking boots and wiping his feet on the welcome mat, he opened the door to the right of the garage into the breezeway. He looked through the panes of glass at the top of the kitchen door, pleased to see Audrey, his mother, standing at the sink. He knocked and she looked up, a bright smile of welcome lighting up her delicate oval-shaped freckled face, her vivid green eyes crinkling at the corners; her thick luxurious auburn hair, now tinged with gray, pulled away from her face and held back with a fancy silver comb. She dried her hands and held out her arms to hug him. "Well, this is a nice surprise."

"I've come to pick your brains, but first, let me go say hi to Dad."

"I'm intrigued. Your dad's in his office, of course."

Sure enough, Derek Morrison was sitting behind the large mahogany desk that had been such a feature of Chris's childhood. He understood Meggie's jealousy of Jasmine just a little bit when he remembered his resentment of this piece of furniture and the hours and hours his father seemed to spend behind it. Of course it was work-related, and as his dad always used to say when he complained, "Money doesn't grow on trees, son." Chris would shrug his bony little-boy shoulders and try and coerce Maddy into boyish pursuits like tree climbing and kicking a soccer ball around. She adored her brother and tried, but she was a poor substitute. It wasn't too bad for nine months of the year, but when tax season started, his father was lost to all of them. That was when they all wished his office were someplace else where he could work with other accountants who would lighten his load, but it wasn't to be. Instead they had to put up with the constant stream of clients who traipsed through the house forever invading their privacy. It was November, a fairly quiet time, but his dad was still working, and according to his mom, the hours spent behind his desk had increased after he and Maddy left home. Feeling sorry for his mom with her bright outlook on life having to live with this work-riddled man with his overdeveloped sense of responsibility, Chris vowed long ago that if he were ever lucky enough to have a family, it would come first.

"Hi, Dad. Busy as ever, I see."

Physically, Derek bore little resemblance to Chris, except for his once-splendid physique, now gone to seed. Maddy was more like her dad with her light brown hair and brown eyes, but she'd inherited her mom's oval face and shapely brows. Mentally, neither of the children was burdened with his serious demeanor; they were sunny by nature, taking after their mom with her ability to look at life with the glass half full. She had a busy social life, and although Chris knew she loved his dad and enjoyed the quiet evenings they spent together, she needed more than that. He never complained about her not being home so she was content to let him bring home the bacon, a trade-off for her freedom. Her life as a teacher came to a halt with Christopher's birth, closely followed by Maggie, and she raised her children, contented for the most part, but now they were grown she was teaching once again. She would have liked more children, but Derek persuaded her otherwise by saying two was enough. She just shrugged her shoulders, knew there was no budging him once he'd made up his mind, compromised by filling the house with Chris and Maddy's friends and ignored Derek's complaining. That was one thing on which she would never budge, and in all fairness, she kept them well out of the way of his office and the constant stream of clients.

His father looked up from his papers. "What are you up to these days, son?" It was the same question he always asked and Chris always gave the same answer.

"Not much."

"How's work?"

"Keeps me busy."

Derek didn't understand anything about computers so trying to explain to him exactly what it entailed to be a programmer was a waste of time. He hadn't kept up with the times and Chris wondered what he would do when one of his clients asked him to file his taxes electronically! He'd offered to help set his dad up with a PC, but the offer had been declined, dismissed offhandedly. Not so his mom who was always eager to learn and excited when he gave her a laptop and printer. An insatiable thirst for knowledge of any kind whisked her off to evening classes where she learned Microsoft Office. Her love for PowerPoint satisfied her creativity, never declining a request to design posters and artwork for the community.

"I'll stop in again before I leave. Do you want me to bring you a coffee?"

"No thanks, I'm all set," and he went back to shuffling through the piles of paper on his desk, eventually, Chris knew, to be filed neatly in alphabetic order in the big antique oak filing cabinets in the back of the room. As children, they had been admonished, "Not to touch." Many times in a fit of pique, he had wanted nothing more than to pull open all the drawers and throw all the files on the floor. He wouldn't have destroyed them, but he dreamed of creating a giant pile of papers that would take his father hours to sort out. He and Maddy steered clear even though they made up secret games to try and get his attention, all to no avail. Chris wandered back to the kitchen. He had resigned himself long ago to his father's short-comings; his childhood could certainly have been a good deal worse.

His mom, sitting at the kitchen table, a mug of coffee steaming before her, was working on the daily crossword. "What's the English word for a car's hood?"

"I think it's a *bonnet*. Does that fit?"

"Yes it does. Why the people who create these puzzles have to include all these foreign words, I'll never know. Anyway, never mind. What did you want to ask me?"

He poured himself a mug of coffee, sat down opposite his mom. "How many years have you been going to Aladdin's Cave?"

"Many years. I remember it when Jenny and Theodore Blunt were running it together when it was called something else—Pens & Paper, I think. Why do you ask?"

"Do you remember a young girl with sandy-colored hair?"

"Yes, I do, now you come to mention it. She wasn't there for very long, just a couple of years. She and Ellie Tetreault really put the store on the map."

"What was her name? Do you recall?"

"Let me think. It was unusual."

Chris took a sip of his coffee, appreciating the nutty flavor of the hazelnut—another example of his mother's quest to always try some-thing new. Now there were all sorts of flavors, and he knew his dad didn't approve, but he went along with it. Audrey sat twirling an escaped piece of hair between her fingers. "Thea, Thea Marchant, that was it, but I believe she married so I've no idea what her last name is now. Do tell me more."

"She was in the store when I went in there yesterday to buy Maddy's birthday present. She helped me choose a birthday card and wrapped the pendant for me—the one Maddy had admired when she was here last. I know she has a son, but she wasn't wearing a wedding ring, so I would really like to try and find her."

"I know this is probably a stupid question, but did you go back to the store?"

"I did, but it wasn't open and there was a notice on the door saying the store would be closed for a while due to unforeseen circumstances."

"Oh boy, that's going to throw the quilting ladies into a panic. I wonder what happened. Are you sure it's wise to try and trace Thea?"

"Probably not, but it's something I think I need to do. I can't get her out of my mind and I'll go nuts if I don't at least try."

"I think her parents still live in the neighborhood. Why don't you start with them? Marchant isn't a very common name around here so let's look in the phone directory. The directories are out in the hallway by the telephone just where they've always been."

Chris came back with two or three phone books, started running his fingers down the M's and found a Henry Marchant listed in the Stockton directory. "I'm going to try this one," he said, taking his cell phone out of his pocket and adding the name and number to his contact list. "Thanks, Mom. I'll call first and then go round there with a letter they can send to her. That way I won't be invading her privacy if she wants nothing to do with me."

"Sounds like a plan, Stan. Let me know what happens and I hope you won't be disappointed in your quest, but on the other hand, I'm pleased you're moving on from Meggie. I know I'm biased because you're my son, but you're worth two of her."

"Thanks, Mom," and he gave her a huge grin. "Well, Madame, my carriage awaits. I'll just go say goodbye to the chief and I'll be off."

Chris headed home in an optimistic frame of mind; he was getting closer, he could feel it in his bones.

CHAPTER SIX

MaryAnn—Friday

MaryAnn, uncomfortable staying at the Chamberlin house any longer, braced herself for the boys' disappointment when she suggested they go home. Staying over at Jim's had given them all a taste of luxury and even Thea's modest home was so much more comfortable than her own dismal rental. The decision about what they were going to do for the evening had been taken out of her hands by Jim being on call. Even though she had been sorry to see him go—frantic for his safety—his leaving had solved her dilemma. She didn't want him to see where she and the boys lived, convinced, rightly or wrongly, he would be horrified. The last thing she needed was Jim's charity and with this thought came the resolve to do something about her current living situation. She had been foolish to squirrel away the money Sam's parents had sent. They needed it now. She had to swallow her fear of not having a "rainy day" fund, make their lives comfortable, and find a home where she could invite Jim and be proud. She refused to allow him anywhere near their current residence.

Drained of all energy and motivation by Sam's death, she was mad at herself now for allowing herself to live in such dreadful poverty. She had dragged the boys down with her, but no more; time to climb out of the hole, find the bright light of day. And she would start by looking in the local paper for somewhere decent to live within the same school district. They'd be better off in a two-bedroom apartment than the spacious and drafty run-down house she could ill-afford to heat. She told Ian and Johnny they needed to go home, ignored their anticipated groaning, and used to not making a fuss they accepted the inevitable. "Come here," she said, holding out her arms. "I know this is difficult and I would much rather stay here too, but it doesn't feel right taking advantage of somebody else's home." The boys stood there looking at her with bubble-burst solemn faces, deepening her resolve even further to improve their lives. "Things are going to change for the better, I promise you, so I need you to be brave for just a little while longer. I'm going to get us out of that miserable house, find somewhere warm and cozy for us to live and you can help me by looking through the ads in the newspaper."

Johnny stepped back from MaryAnn's embrace and looked up into his mother's face. "Couldn't we just go and live with Mr. Hudson? He really likes us and we like him too and he has lots of space."

MaryAnn sat down on one of Thea's kitchen chairs and held out her hands, taking hold of Johnny's thin shoulders. He leaned forward and pressed his small body against her knees. How on earth was she going to make Johnny understand they couldn't just move in with a virtual stranger? Ian saved the day. "We can't do that until we know we're sure we really like him."

Johnny's lip began to quiver. "I'm sure. I want to live with Mr. Hudson cuz he's kind and he looks after us. I'm sad my daddy's in heaven, but Mr. Hudson makes the sad go away."

"I know," and she hugged her little boy, letting him cry it out. She looked at Ian over the top of Johnny's head, gave him a watery smile. "Okay, champ?" He nodded, but she could tell he was struggling to control his own emotions. Jim had opened a window onto a new world, a world hard to resist; the boys had stepped all the way through, but she was still perched on the sill. Yes, she was undeniably sexually attracted to him, but there had to be more than that. Her marriage to Sam had been rock solid, resting on a foundation built over the years and she wanted to do that with Jim. It had to be right for her and she didn't want to rush into a situation she would live to regret. Better the boys suffer for a little while now rather than sometime down the road if the relationship didn't work out. She pushed Johnny away from her, and taking a napkin from the basket on Thea's kitchen table, she gently wiped his face. "I'm certainly not going to stop you seeing Mr. Hudson all you want because I know you have lots of plans, but we just can't move into his house. Okay?"

He nodded. "Sorry, Mommy."

"Oh, baby, it's all right. And, guess what? Tomorrow we are going to go out and buy ourselves some new winter coats—big, thick, fluffy ones that will keep us really warm. Are you both up for that?"

Their eyes lit up—expressions hopeful at the thought of having new clothes rather than hand-me-downs—going shopping a novelty, giving them all something to look forward to. "Come on," she said. "Let's say goodbye to Smokey and be on our way."

MaryAnn's feet, encased in the grease-spattered sneakers she wore in the diner, were freezing by the time she got home. The boys bundled in blankets in the back seat chattered about their outing with Mr. Hudson to his hardware store and lumberyard; how he had proudly introduced them to all the friendly people who worked for him and how they had shaken their hands, feeling very grown up and important. He took them out back where all the wood was stored to show them what kind they would use to build the tree house. Breathing in the smell of all the different kinds, scuffing their feet in the sawdust on the floor, they stood back looking up at the stacks of wood piled high above them until their necks ached. He had answered all their questions, lifted Johnny onto his shoulders so he could see all the things on the top shelves in the hardware section. Cans of paint and a whole display of those little sample cards in every color of the rainbow filled one wall. They discussed whether they should paint the tree house or stain it and Jim showed them the difference between the paints and the stains. Their fingers itched to get hold of a big fat brush and get started and he told them that in all probability they would be able to select the wood and paint the pieces over the winter months so they'd be all ready to put it together once the winter was over. They thought that was a great idea, their excitement and enthusiasm contagious, and both the boys sensed Mr. Hudson couldn't wait to get started too. What a day it had been—quite beyond their wild imaginings.

MaryAnn noticed they had come down to earth with a bump, their busy chatter lapsing into silence on pulling into the driveway. The night was pitch black, cloudy and overcast without even the slightest reflection from the moon; the house isolated with no welcoming lights from neighboring houses. She opened the glove compartment, pulled out a flashlight, turning it on after she doused the car's headlights to dispel the gloom. A sad and dispirited trio, they walked towards the front door and MaryAnn almost hated herself at that moment for being the cause of her children's unhappiness. She also had no idea what they were going to eat for supper, and kicked herself for not asking Will for some eggs. God she hated this existence because that's all it was. It wasn't a life; it was survival and barely that at times. She was so tired of being cold.

They trooped into the kitchen still wearing their coats. Even flipping the light switch did little to cheer up the room—a stark contrast to Jim's kitchen with its bright white cupboards and sunny yellow walls. Relieved to finally be out of her grief-born lethargy, she was no longer blind to her surroundings: the truly dreadful drab green counter tops and the worn wooden cabinets. The permanently stained beige linoleum tiles, and the ugly maple table with its equally ugly matching chairs, rendered the room even more uninviting; the warm temperature its only saving grace. The house had come miserably furnished and she had cleaned out the cabinets of all their dreary and not very clean contents, alarmed at all the little mouse droppings. Packing up the dented aluminum pans and greasy skillets, the sticky plastic containers and a variety of well-worn and dirty kitchen gadgets, she had vacuumed and scrubbed, but to this day, there was still a problem with mice. Will had given her a *Havahart* trap because there was no way she could kill the soft brown field mice with their creamy white chests. Setting the trap with peanut butter, she lured her prey, picked up the trap filled with the tiny mice, stopped at a field on her way to work and coaxed them out of the little metal box, ignoring the boys who pleaded with her to keep them, desperate for a pet of any kind.

"Let's rustle up something for supper. Why don't you go wash your hands?" MaryAnn said. The boys, in good spirits, jostled each other at the sink; Ian lifted Johnny so he could reach. She opened the freezer, hoping to find something she could thaw out fast, but she was disappointed. Absolutely nothing looked appetizing; the unlabeled foil-wrapped mystery clumps the result of her lack of organization. She shut the freezer and decided a couple of cans of chicken noodle soup would have to do. At least it was the hearty kind and with some cheesy toast, it would make a passable meal. Setting the boys to work, the kitchen was soon full of the aroma of simmering soup and toasting cheese bubbling away under the broiler.

A large wicker basket sat in a corner of the kitchen filled with newspapers taken from the diner at the end of the day. Sometimes the food-spattered papers had pieces missing, but still afforded her a way to catch up with the news for free. She stopped stirring the soup and turned to Ian, asking him to pull out the most recent paper and find the housing section. He didn't need to be told twice. Taking off his jacket and hanging it over the back of one of the chairs, he went down on his knees and started rummaging and found Wednesday's. Johnny also struggled out of his jacket now that the warmth of the kitchen had thawed him out, dropping it in the corner by the door. MaryAnn didn't say anything. Normally a tidy little boy, unlike Ian who had to be persuaded to put his things away, she was surprised Ian hadn't been the one to fling his jacket on the floor. She piled the cheesy toast onto a plate, ladled the soup into bowls, poured a couple of glasses of milk for the boys and a glass of water for herself and carried everything to the table. Ian moved the newspaper over to one side, took a spoonful of his soup, absentmindedly blowing on it while he ran his finger down the listings of apartments for rent. "What are we looking for, Mom?"

"Is there anything around five hundred dollars a month?"

Ian continued searching, his soup completely forgotten. "There's one over a store in the center of Melford Point for four hundred and fifty, heat and hot water included, but there're only two bedrooms."

"Why don't you read what it says?"

"Two-bedroom apartment, eleven hundred square feet, heat and hot water included, newly finished hardwood floors and renovated kitchen and bathroom, washer and dryer. Garage available for an extra $50 a month."

"I wonder which store it's over. How would you boys feel about sharing a bedroom?"

"We wouldn't mind, would we?"

Ian shrugged. "I suppose."

MaryAnn liked the idea of being in the center of town, but it would be hard on the boys without anywhere outside to play. As far as being cramped inside, they were used to being restricted to a couple of rooms during the winter months—all she could afford to heat. "I'd like to go look at it. What about you?"

"Yes," Johnny said through a mouthful of toast, and for once, MaryAnn didn't tell him not to talk with his mouthful. A little of his brother's enthusiasm rubbed off on Ian and he said, "Why don't you call?" He read out the number while she dialed and after several rings she heard a cheery female voice say, "Hello."

"Hi. I'm calling about the apartment you have for rent. Is it still available?"

"It sure is. I could show it to you tomorrow. Would that work for you?"

MaryAnn, free from waitressing at Will's Diner on Saturdays, asked if ten o'clock would be a good time. The woman introduced herself as Georgie Simpson, told MaryAnn she would meet her outside the store and gave her the address. "Georgie, I have one question. Do you have any objections to children? I have two sons, a five-year-old and an eleven-year-old."

"No, that's not a problem at all, but I do have a no pet policy. The rooms are quite spacious and currently the store is vacant so there won't be anyone to complain about any noise coming from above. Are you familiar with the area, because if you are, I'm sure you're aware there's a lovely park within walking distance where your boys could go run off some steam. I look forward to meeting you."

"See you tomorrow. Bye," and MaryAnn hung up.

"Well, that's all settled, and I'd quite forgotten about the park. We went there and fed the ducks. Ian, do you remember?"

"Yes, I do. It's a great park."

"Well, let's hope the apartment is as nice as it sounds."

CHAPTER SEVEN

❧❧❧

JIM—FRIDAY

Back at the firehouse, Jim removed his heavy gear, folding it neatly and placing it on the floor. He put on his winter jacket, hat and gloves. After checking to make sure his wallet and keys were in his pocket, he said good-night to his fellow firefighters, stowed his bunker suit, helmet and boots in the container in the back of his truck and headed out. No longer starved for company because of MaryAnn, he had no desire to sit around the table in the common room rehashing the night's events, sharing cups of not very good coffee. It would be impossible to tally up the number of hours he had spent with these men, putting off the inevitable of going home to a house empty of people. Carrie always gave him her usual welcome, and much as he loved her, canine companionship was nothing compared with his three favorite human beings. Now he couldn't wait to get home, take a shower and call MaryAnn and the boys. He hummed along with the radio, his truck eating up the miles, overcome with emotion when he heard Kenny Rogers singing *Lady*. The lyrics mirrored his thoughts of wanting to wake and see MaryAnn every morning. Boy he'd got it bad, but he couldn't ever remember being this happy, even though he chastised himself for being such a romantic fool.

Carrie, a big, long-coated Lassie look-alike, with the same gentle and protective nature, whined her greeting. A little gray around the muzzle now, worried she might fall and break a leg, Jim no longer allowed her to climb the stairs. At one time she would scamper all over the big house, but not anymore; her movements now slower and more measured, Jim tried to forget she was nine years old. She too had fallen in love with Ian and Johnny, couldn't get enough of their attention, allowed the boys to brush her long fur, rewarding them with doggy kisses for gently removing her tangles. She sniffed disdainfully at Jim, looked up at his smoke-smeared face, and followed him out into the hallway where he sank down onto the stairs. Fondling her ears, he said, "The house seems so empty doesn't it, girl?" She let out a sigh and rested her head on his knee.

Jim looked around the familiar wood-paneled hallway of the old house: the dark well-polished wooden floor offset by a huge circular oriental rug. Above him at the top of the first flight of stairs hung the oil paintings so admired by MaryAnn when she and the boys had first come to the house on Monday, sharing a simple meal, treading carefully, and getting to know each other. Much to his delight she had accepted his fingers-crossed invitation to Thanksgiving at his brother Ben's. He happily introduced her to Ben, his wife, Jennifer, their four-year-old twins, Poppy and Daisy, Jennifer's sister, Elizabeth, and Jennifer's parents, Pat and Bruce. MaryAnn, Ian and Johnny had been welcomed with open arms, and even though Johnny had been spirited away by the twins to their pink world of Barbie dolls and nail polish, he seemed to have survived. MaryAnn, comfortable with his family, brought the two of them even closer together, making him love her even more. Arriving back at his house, he had asked her if she and the boys would stay the night. Reluctant at first, but getting the thumbs up from the boys, she had agreed. Grateful to be given the gift of opportunity to get to know her better, he assured her that was the only reason he had asked her and the boys to stay, but they found it almost impossible to ignore their mutual attraction. He admired MaryAnn's strength of character when she told him the boys had to come first, that she didn't want to do anything to confuse them. Happy to have her there under any circumstances, even if it was only for a little while, he respected her wishes.

He listened while she told him the sad story of her husband Sam's death three years ago and how she and the boys had been having a hard time making ends meet. That's when he understood why she drove such an old and dilapidated car and why she and the boys wore such shabby coats. "I'm going to help them, Carrie," but he knew it had to be on MaryAnn's terms. Giving the dog one last pat on the head, he wearily climbed the stairs to go take his shower to wash away the grime. His thoughts went to Jemma Morrison, not envying her the task of breaking the news of the fire to her grandparents.

Once back downstairs, he realized he was hungry but he wanted to talk to MaryAnn first. She answered on the second ring. "Hi," she said.

"Hey you."

"Are you all right? Was the fire truly awful?"

"Pretty bad, but no one was hurt and that's the main thing." He stifled a cough, decided not to tell her about the malfunction of his air pack; there was no need to worry her over the phone. "Fortunately, we get very few house fires that catch hold like that."

"I'm so glad you're okay. I was worried."

"I'm sure you were." No point in beating around the bush. He would have been frantic had the roles been reversed. "Thinking about you kept me going. What are the boys up to?"

"We were just playing a game of *Uno* and Johnny has been winning, much to his triumphant satisfaction."

"Wish I was there."

"I know. Can I call you back after the boys have gone to bed?"

"Sure. I need to go get myself something to eat. Tell the boys hi from me and tell them Carrie is looking a little lost without them. Talk to you later," and he hung up the phone.

Jim had known in his heart of hearts that she wouldn't invite him over, but he was still disappointed. He wandered into the kitchen, started a pot of coffee, scrambled some eggs and toasted an English muffin. His orderly world had been turned upside down, and even though he had worshipped Thea from afar and taken extreme measures by having parts of the house redecorated with Jennifer's help in the hopes Thea might one day see him in a different light, she had never created this kind of turmoil in his mind. Much as he had longed for physical contact with her, it had never happened, and that was where the difference lay—MaryAnn was tangible whereas Thea was not and never had been. Mounted on his self-created pedestal—seeing her as the perfect woman—had been nothing but a pipe dream. His love for MaryAnn on the other hand was true and deep and he was impatient to be with her, to start their life together. He had waited for so long, wanted to make an honest woman of her, have her in his bed. A wave of desire came over him with such intensity; the perfect fit of imagined spooning played in his mind. He cleaned up the kitchen, fed Carrie, took her out into the backyard, grateful for the cold air slapping him back into shape. He chastised himself for acting like a moonstruck teenager—for goodness sake, man, you're forty-five years old. But today he didn't feel a day over twenty-five.

Back in the house, he went off to the den, turned on the seven o'clock news as a distraction. Jennifer had helped him decorate this room too, made him throw away his old and decrepit, but much loved, recliner, replacing it with a deep burgundy chair that complemented the plaid couch in its shades of red, blue and yellow. It was still a manly room unlike the guest bedroom where MaryAnn had slept last night—incredibly feminine with its lilacs and deep rich creams—the boys in the room next door. Even though his bedroom was at the other end of the long wood-paneled hallway, well away from temptation, it had taken him quite a while to fall asleep.

The news droned on, full of all the normal doom and gloom, and soon he tired of it and picked up a book he seemed to have been reading for ages. It was one of Robert Ludlum's and just not grabbing his attention. The phone rang. "Hi Jim, it's Ben. I was just watching the local news and saw the house fire. Were you there? I thought I saw you, but it's hard to tell with all the gear you guys wear."

"I was there. Just got home about an hour ago. House is pretty much gone, but we were able to stop the horse barn from catching on fire. Do you know the family?"

"Yes, it's where Poppy and Daisy have been taking riding lessons. I'll give Jemma Morrison a call to see if there's anything I can do."

"That's why her name seemed familiar."

"Was there anyone in the house?"

"No, her grandparents are away visiting her sister in Portland. That's why the fire was able to get such a hold. Jemma only discovered it when the horses began to get restless. She called 911 right away, but we weren't able to save much."

"Do you know what caused it?"

"Possibly electrical or the furnace. I felt sorry for her having to call her grandparents and tell them."

"Seeing the house on the news, gutted like that, gave me the shivers. I don't think I've ever seen anything quite like it. It could happen to any of us."

"I know. The same thing crossed my mind when I was in the fire truck heading towards our end of town. I was so relieved when we turned off a couple of exits before."

"Glad you're okay, bro."

"I am, but I'm thinking of retiring from the fire department."

"You won't get any arguments from me. You know I could never have hacked it. You joined up for both of us and I don't know how you've done it all these years."

"It's taken its toll, Ben."

"Then, get out, leave it to the younger guys."

"Now you're saying I'm old."

Ben laughed. "That's not what I mean. You've done more than your fair share. I'm sure you scared MaryAnn half to death. She's already lost one husband and I'm sure she doesn't want to lose another . . ."

"So now you're marrying me off?"

"It's a foregone conclusion, isn't it?"

"If she'll have me."

"How is she, by the way?"

"She's fine. At home with Ian and Johnny."

"I like her a lot and those boys of hers are a credit to her. She's a great mom."

"I spent the day with them today while she was working and they're such good kids. We're going to build a tree house together and you should have seen their faces when I took them around the lumberyard and showed them all the different kinds of wood we could use. We also went online and looked at tree house designs and they loved the library here, especially the sliding ladder and I taught them some Cockney rhyming slang. Sorry, I'm rambling on . . ."

"I'd forgotten all about those rhymes. Granddad used to have us going up the *apple and pears* and taking off our *daisy roots*. He was a lot of fun that old man and he certainly enriched our lives."

"Yes, he did, and by the way, thanks for yesterday."

"We can do it all over again at Christmas!"

"Now that's going to be interesting and a lot more work, but it will be fun to have people to shop for besides you lot," Jim said.

"Well, thanks a bunch, and on that note . . ."

"Get lost, why don't you," Jim said. Ben hung up on him. His brother knew when he was beaten.

No sooner had he hung up and the phone rang again.

"Hi Jim, it's MaryAnn."

"Are the boys in bed?"

"Yup. Safely tucked up. Ian is reading, but Johnny nodded off as soon as I finished reading to him. He absolutely loves the book you loaned him and he was telling me all about the other Enid Blyton's in your library and he can't wait to get his grubby little hands on those. And, of course, I can't get Ian's nose out of the Harry Potter. You have an uncanny knack with kids, Mr. Hudson, and I thank you. You made two boys very happy today and they are so excited about all the plans you have for them. You won't let them down will you?"

"Oh, MaryAnn, of course not."

"That's all right then. I just had to get that off my chest and I'm afraid I do rather tend to speak my mind."

"You'd better be careful, lady, because you're likely to get as good as you give."

"That's okay then and now I have to tell you something and I am doing this for all of us so we can move forward in the right way. First of all I want to thank you for giving me hope . . ."

"I'd like to think I've given you more than hope."

"Of course you have, but don't interrupt, please."

"Yes, ma'am. Wouldn't it be easier to do this face to face?"

"Not necessarily, but in any case it's not possible, so please just listen. I decided today that it was ridiculous not to use some of the money I've saved from the checks Sam's parents have sent over the last three years. For one thing, we all need new coats, and secondly, we need somewhere decent to live. No, don't say anything." Jim sighed, buttoned his lip and remained silent. "I have been blind to my surroundings. It's amazing what you can get used to and I just haven't had the energy to make things better, but now thanks to you, I do. We are going to look at an apartment tomorrow." Jim's heart sank but he still didn't say anything.

"Jim, are you still there?" and he could hear a note of worry in MaryAnn's voice and he cursed himself.

"Yes, I'm here. You just took the wind out of my sails. I wish you'd all just move in with me."

"Jim, you know we can't do that. It would set a bad example for the boys and where would it leave us if things didn't work out? I have to get us settled in a place I can be proud of; somewhere you can come and spend time with us. This way you and I can build our relationship into something solid before we make any rash commitments. I will not be rescued. It would be wrong, at least for me, that is. I want to be around people, not isolated anymore, and up until this point, I haven't been ready. I've been hiding and this house has been my bolt-hole, dreadful as it is. Am I making any sense?"

"Yes, you're making perfect sense and I do understand what you are trying to do. I'm just impatient that's all. I had such a good time with Ian and Johnny today; I just can't wait for us all to be together."

"I will tell you a little secret and, hopefully, this will make you feel better. As soon as I mentioned moving, Johnny asked if we could go live with you. He was very upset when I said we couldn't, especially as I wasn't really able to explain why. Ian understands, but Johnny is just too little. You've really captured his heart and I told him that I wouldn't stand in the way of the plans the three of you have cooked up. They were talking all the way home about how much fun they had with you today. You've added a much needed dimension to their lives and it makes me very happy."

"It works both ways—they've added so much to my life already, and so have you. I'd like to take you out on a real date. I know Jennifer and Ben would be happy to look after the boys, but only if you're comfortable with that."

"We'll see. Baby steps. It's a lot to take in and we've known each other for less than a week. If it weren't for the boys, I would throw caution to the wind, but I can't do that. You do know I want to be with you, don't you?"

"I was beginning to wonder, Miss Practicality."

"I'm sorry. I don't mean to come across all stuffy and it's so good to have someone to talk to who has my true interests at heart. Sam and I used to talk all the time and I've missed that. We didn't always see eye to eye. We used to have healthy debates about everything under the sun, and I look forward to doing that with you. It's been a long time, Jim, since I've been this comfortable with another grownup and I must admit it's a huge relief to be able to share my thoughts with you. Oh, I talk to Will and he's a great friend, but I've missed the intimacy and I think I'd better stop before I dig myself into a hole I can't get out of."

"There's so much I want to talk to you about too. It's been quite an emotional roller coaster for me as well so I welcome the idea of having a close friend. I can't wait to lie in bed with you and just talk."

"Just talk!" MaryAnn said. She started to laugh. "Sounds awfully dull to me."

"Okay, okay, now I'm digging my own hole and on that note, I think we should quit while we're ahead, otherwise I will get in my truck and drive over there, even though I've no idea where you live."

"Don't you dare!"

"I give up. Give me a call tomorrow after you've seen the apartment and let me know what you've decided to do."

"I will and thank you. Goodnight and sweet dreams."

"Goodnight, MaryAnn."

Jim, exhausted but pleased with himself, had managed not to blurt out the fact there was a perfectly good apartment here over the garage, but MaryAnn would have told him it was too close for comfort and she would have been right. He wanted to ask her to marry him. He was in this for the long haul, but he had to bide his time and wait for the right moment. He was glad she was considering moving into town. Melford Point was a safe place and she would be close to Margaret and Bill Gilson at the Country Store if she ever needed help, rather than being isolated as she was right now. The solitary life she had created wasn't healthy, but he understood all about grief and the dreadful accompanying lethargy. He was no stranger to hopelessness and how it narrowed your world into a tiny cosmic space of pure survival, when just putting one foot in front of the other was about all you were capable of doing. The carving helped, enabling him to become immersed in an imaginary world where time just vanished while he shaped the fragrant wood into the little creatures so loved by all his lucky recipients. Escaping to his workshop with his dog at his heels had been his salvation; a way to deal with his grief after his mother died. If only MaryAnn had been around then to share his sorrow. He dragged his mind away from painful memories, thoughts of the boys and the day they had shared making him smile. He was looking forward to having a hand in bringing them up, and amongst other things, telling them stories about his grandfather, and showing them the photo albums. Ready to drop, yawning his head off, he settled Carrie down for the night, climbed the stairs, and went off to bed, but would he be able to keep the nightmares at bay?

∞

MaryAnn sat at the kitchen table, warm and loved after her conversation with Jim. She could have talked to him for hours and she suspected he felt the same. They were easy with each other and the fact he hadn't pressured her to let him come over had endeared him to her even more. It was comforting to know he respected her wishes. A little thrill of excitement ran through her at the thought of seeing him soon and she couldn't wait to call him tomorrow after she and the boys had seen the apartment. "Oh, Sam," she said. "I think you'd be happy for me."

She took herself off to bed, performed the nightly ritual of getting undressed in the warmth of the bathroom, filled a hot water bottle, made a mad dash across the freezing cold floor, and jumped into bed. She tugged open the drawer of the nightstand, the cheap wood warped, fighting its tendency to stick, and retrieved the letter Sam had written her in July 2002 one month before he died. She wanted to read it one last time. The cheap pockmarked brass lamp with its ugly frilly edged pink shade gave her just enough light to read the smudged words, the paper wavy, dampened so many times by her tears.

Dear MaryAnn

I am writing this letter to you while I still have enough energy because I want to tell you how much I love you and how much you have enriched my life ever since that day we bumped into each other at Orono College. We laughed then and even with this dreadful illness, we have still been able to see the funny side of things although it has been getting more and more difficult lately. You have been a tower of strength and I don't understand why this cruel twist of fate should have come to rest on our shoulders, but I can't believe how lucky I have been. My only regret is that I won't get to see the boys grow up, but I know they will both eventually be fine young men. With you as their mother, how can they fail?

MaryAnn paused, wiped her eyes with the edge of the sheet. "Yes, Sam, you would be very proud. I wish you could see Johnny now. He is such a sensitive and loving little boy." She read on.

I hope you will be able to make a life for yourself. Don't grieve for me too long. You're too young and beautiful to be on your own. I can just hear you arguing with me telling me you're not beautiful, but to me you are. I know I'm not the most romantic of men and maybe you wanted more from me, but I don't think so. There are very few marriages as good as ours. We built a good one didn't we? And I'm proud of us for that and I'm so sorry I'm going to be leaving the partnership. We are a good team, both in work, play and parenting. Oh, we had our disagreements, who doesn't, but we were always able to hash things out. We were a united front for the kids and this stability, even though it was short-lived—especially for Johnny—has given them a good start.

Remember the good times, won't you? Don't dwell on all this pain and sickness. It won't do and it won't help the kids, especially Ian who has been such a little man. Too much responsibility but please tell him how much he helped me. He is my carbon copy and I saw myself as the boy I had been through him, but he is stronger than I ever was. I had a charmed childhood without much to challenge me, not that I'm saying watching your father get sicker by the day is healthy for an eight-year-old and I wish I could have spared him this. Likewise for you too and Johnny, although I suspect he is much too young to understand, but I don't want to dwell on the bad stuff.

I just want to say I know you will always love me as I will always love you wherever I am going. Carry me in your heart by all means, but leave some space to let someone else in. I know you will find a good man and when you do, I give you to him. So dry your tears and be happy, MaryAnn, for my sake.

My love forever
Sam

MaryAnn sat staring down at Sam's handwriting, the tears coursing down her face. "Oh Sam, if my life with Jim is as half as good as it was with you, I will be truly blessed. To have two such loves in one lifetime is a miracle and Jim will be a good dad to the boys. I wish you could be here to help them build the tree house."

She wiped her face again with the sheet and took a long shuddering sigh. She wished Sam were there with all her heart and if she closed her eyes she could still see his neatly bearded face, feel the imagined softness beneath her fingers, but knowing it was impossible, her thoughts went to Jim instead. It was time to move on. "Goodnight, Sam," she said, folding the tear-stained letter, putting it back into its envelope and sliding it into the drawer of the bedside table. "I will always love you and thank you for letting me go."

CHAPTER EIGHT

❧❧❧

THEA—SATURDAY

Thea, after her conversation with Mr. Blunt, went into a frenzy of packing. Honey, mourning Ellie, lay on the floor, head resting on her paws, refusing to let her adopted mistress out of her sight. Thea talked to her, told her she was going on an adventure, that she'd have plenty of people to love her and not to worry about anything, attempting to comfort herself as much as the dog. She hated to admit she was scared: taking on the responsibility of Honey, wanting to give her a good home because of Ellie, she found the prospect daunting. Pushing her fear aside, her thoughts turned to Robert. Intimidated by his anger, the closeness of the night before gone up in a puff of smoke, they were now strangers. He'd burned his bridges; there was no way she was going to let another angry man into her life.

With the sky lightening, the clock by the bed registering six thirty, she suspected Izzie would be up soon. She finished all her packing, doing a double check in the bathroom to make sure nothing had been left behind. Nervous and anxious to be out of the house, she decided it would be best to go wake them all. She wasn't surprised to find Izzie and Jessica curled up together in the same bed, Izzie's soft reddish-brown hair a stark contrast to Jessica's dark curls. They were sleeping so peacefully and she hated to disturb them, but it had to be done. She dreaded the thought they might still be here when the mortician came, reason enough to lean over and kiss Izzie gently on the cheek. "I'm sorry to wake you," she said. Her daughter's beautiful gray-green eyes flew open and she looked at her mom, a frown of worry creasing her brow. "What's wrong, Mommy?"

"I'll tell you in a minute. Let me just go and wake Peter," she said, leaving the pretty room with its soft pinks and greens, Honey at her heels. Her son was deeply asleep, oblivious to his surroundings, in the rather juvenile room with its boyish decorations and much admired baseball posters. She paused and looked at him, so like Michael, his shock of dark hair falling over his forehead, the shape of his face more like her own, but even without the square jaw of determination, a Chamberlin trait, he still attacked life to the fullest. Bright, sensitive, and quick to anger, she worried about him constantly. She touched him on the shoulder; he groaned and turned over away from her. Honey took matters into her own paws, decided Thea needed help, walked around the other side of the bed, pushed her nose into Peter's face, giving him a big lick on the cheek. "Hello, girl," he said, his voice slurred with sleep. "What are you doing here?" Honey wagged her tail in reply, and satisfied she'd done her job walked back around the bed to sit by Thea waiting to see what needed to be done next. Peter's eyes followed the dog, looked at his mom in surprise. "Hi Mom. It feels like the middle of the night."

"I agree, it's early for you, but we need to have a family talk."

Peter, used to the unpredictability of their lives, didn't ask any questions, rubbed his eyes and shuffled along behind his mom to his sisters' room. Everything had been so bizarre since they had arrived on Thursday, he was prepared for another calamity, although he wished, for once, things could go smoothly.

Despite Izzie's coaxing, Jessica was only half awake. Propped up against a pillow, yawning and stretching, mumbling as if she had a mouth full of marbles, she said, "What's going on?"

"I could say *nothing* and we could just slip away from here, but I do owe you an explanation. This is going to come as a big shock to you all and I still don't believe it myself which is why I seem to be able to tell you without completely falling apart."

"What's going on?" Jessica asked again, now fully awake, her five-year-old brain working overtime, getting impatient.

"It's about Miss Ellie, isn't it?" Izzie said. "Is she very sick?"

Thea paused, choosing her words carefully. "Yes, she has been and finally it was too much for her body to take. She went to sleep last night and she won't be waking up anymore." Thea just couldn't bring herself to say the word "dead", but Jessica did it for her.

With her blue eyes as big as saucers, she said, "You mean she's dead, don't you?"

"Yes, pumpkin, she is, and I want us to pack all our things so we can leave."

Peter sat by his mother on the bed, didn't say a word. He felt bad about Miss Ellie, but he hadn't really known her, so apart from the fact he was in a strange house with a dead person, he didn't feel much of anything. His life was such a shambles, one jarring disappointment after another, and as far as he was concerned this was just one more rotten thing to deal with. He felt sorry for his mom because there would be no fresh start and she had lost her friend. They would all just go home with their tails between their legs and carry on, just as they always did. His ears perked up when he heard his mom say, "I do have one piece of good news though, especially for you, Peter."

"What's that?" he asked, jolted out of his self-pity.

"Ellie wrote me a letter and in that letter she made a request. She asked if we would take Honey home with us. What do you say to that?" and she turned to look at her son.

Peter, his face a picture of pure joy, threw his arms around his mom, squeezed her tight. "I take it you're pleased with the idea, then?"

"You know I am. Of course, I wish it hadn't been because Miss Ellie died, but Honey is such a wonderful dog."

Jessica, her expression a picture of indignation, folded her arms across her chest. "Why is Honey going to be Peter's dog?" she asked, her bottom lip a classic pout.

"She's not. She will be our family dog, but Peter will be the one taking responsibility for her care. He has wanted a dog for a very long time and I want to give him the chance to show that he can well and truly look after her. Of course we will all help, but under Peter's guidance."

"No fair," Jessica said, relapsing into brooding silence. Thea could only guess at the workings of her mind, knew she hated being the youngest.

Izzie, sitting next to Jessica, willing her not to go into a full blown tantrum, said, "I don't think Smokey's going to be very happy, do you, Mom?"

"Oh, my goodness, I hadn't thought of that. She's always been the queen bee so her nose is certainly going to be out of joint. We'll introduce them slowly and I'm sure eventually she'll be glad of Honey's company. Anyway, we don't have time to worry about that now because we need to pack. We'll say goodbye to Mr. Blunt and Robert and then we'll be off. We'll have breakfast at Grandma and Grandpa's; we'll pick up some bagels on the way. How does that sound?" she said, wondering how her parents were going to react to the sudden invasion. It couldn't be helped—driving back to Maine without stopping by to see them wasn't an option.

Always hungry, Peter spoke for them all. "Great, Mom," he said, sliding off the bed and going off to his room, Honey at his side. This pleased Thea no end. She didn't want the dog attached to her to the exclusion of the rest of the family. She knew that sometimes happened, but she sensed Honey would go with whoever needed her most, and in this instance, it was Peter, reinforcing the bond they had formed when they had first met. Listening to her son talking to Honey dispelled some of her misgivings, and with the realization a furry friend was going to be healthy for him she reached a turning point, flipping her initial reaction to Ellie's request from an imposition to a gift.

Izzie and Thea packed methodically. Jessica sat in bed ignoring both of them, taxing Thea's patience. Consumed with guilt, she lived an eggshell existence with her youngest daughter, always making allowances for her mood swings. Glancing at Jessica's miserable face, wishing with all her heart she could turn the clock back, she longed for the pre-abduction Jessica—the happy and uncomplicated child, safe and secure in her five-year-old world. Thea touched her forehead, rubbed away the beginnings of a headache, closed the lid on her suitcase, and pulled her mind away from depressing thoughts.

"Come on sweetheart, it's time to get dressed," she said, holding out Jessica's purple sweat suit. "Why don't you wear this? It will be nice and comfy and warm. Okay?"

"I want Honey to love me too," she said, looking at Thea with her eyes filled with tears. "It's not fair. Izzie has Smokey and now Peter has Honey, but I don't have anything."

It was all too much. Thea sat down on the bed. "I know it's very difficult for you right now and it's difficult for me too. I just lost one of my best friends and life isn't fair sometimes, but it will all work out. We need to help each other and be brave and I know you can do that. Just think about Johnny and how well you look after him."

Jessica nodded.

"Well, sometimes mommies need looking after, too," Thea said, appealing to Jessica's better nature.

"I'm sorry."

"No need to be sorry. Just give me one of your special smiles," and Jessica did just that, pushing the covers away and getting out of bed. Thea helped her get dressed, enjoying the feel of her daughter's small wide feet in her hands as she pulled on her socks. "You are my darling girls," she said, looking down at Jess and across at Izzie. "Let's go grab Peter and we'll go down and say goodbye to Mr. Blunt."

Thea noticed both of the girls glanced nervously at Ellie's door as they walked past, but nobody said anything. They traipsed into Peter's room, found he had done a pretty good job of packing his duffle bag, although there was a sleeve from a sweatshirt hanging out from between the zipper, but she didn't say anything. "Have you got everything?"

"Yup, and I double-checked."

"We're off to see Mr. Blunt if you're ready."

"I am."

When they got downstairs, Mr. Blunt's door was closed. She knocked and they all stood there waiting for what seemed an age. She expected Jessica to start complaining, but she was quiet for once. He opened the door, dressed in his pajamas and robe, his tufts of gray hair standing on end. "I hope we're not disturbing you," she said. "I know we said our goodbyes, but the children wanted to come and see you."

"Good thing I remembered to put in my teeth." They all laughed. "Come in, come in." They all trooped through the hallway, untidy and scruffy with hastily brushed hair, and in Peter's case, mismatched socks. "I see you've found a friend," he said, patting Honey on the head and looking at the kids. "I'm glad she's going home with you and did you know your mom has asked me to come visit?"

"Really?" Izzie said, finally finding her voice.

"Yes, and I'm seriously thinking about it."

"Oh, do come," Jessica said, bouncing up and down in excitement. "I'm sorry Miss Ellie died. She's with her guardian angel now." Thea cringed. Jess was not renowned for her tact, but Mr. Blunt recovered quickly, reached out and took the little girl's hands, and looked down into her face. "I'm very sorry too, but she's at peace now and she wouldn't want us to be sad."

Jessica stared up at him. "My guardian angel came to see me when I was sick. She sat at the end of my bed, but I wasn't ready to go with her. I think Miss Ellie must have been ready. She'll be all right, you know."

"I know she will," and he glanced at Thea over the top of Jessica's head, giving her a nod and a smile.

After Jessica's outburst, there was an awkward silence. "Well, I think we'd better be on our way. We have a long drive ahead of us so it's best if we make a start." Thea stepped forward to give Theodore a hug. "I'll call you when we get home."

Theodore put his broad rather plump hands on Thea's slender shoulders. "It was good to see you after all these years and you haven't changed a bit."

"I'm not so sure about that, but thank you. And let's make sure we see each other again real soon. Okay, kids, time to say goodbye."

Peter shook Mr. Blunt's hand; Jessica flung herself at him, gave him one of her exuberant hugs; Izzie stood shyly until he stepped forward and gave her a hug. She stood on tippy toes, whispered in his ear, "We all have to look for Miss Ellie in the stars. She will be the brightest one."

He leaned forward and spoke softly to Izzie. "You are absolutely right. That is a lovely thought." He stood straight and addressed the children. "It was a privilege to meet you all, and when I come visit we will be able to continue where we left off with my stories."

"We'll hold you to that. It will be something for us all to look forward to," Thea said. She found it hard to leave him; he seemed so lonely standing in the doorway watching them as they walked away. "Be safe," he called out. They turned and waved.

⧉⧉⧉

Thea went off to the kitchen, dismayed to find Robert sitting at the breakfast bar nursing a cup of coffee. He didn't offer her any. She needed to use the phone to call her parents, wished she'd used Mr. Blunt's instead. Trying to assess Robert's mood, she cleared her throat and swallowed. "Would it be all right if I used the phone?"

He nodded.

She listened to the ringtone, her hand damp around the receiver. She hated to disturb her parents this early, but it was better she call rather than arrive in a heap on Enid and Henry's doorstep without prior warning. She didn't think either of her parents would take kindly to being found in their pajamas. Henry answered the phone. "Good morning, Dad. I'm sorry if I woke you."

"No, no. You didn't. What's up?"

"Would it be all right if we came for breakfast? I'll pick up bagels on the way. Would you and mom like an egg and cheese?"

"That would be great and I won't ask you any questions until you get here."

Grateful for his sensitivity, she said, "Thanks, Dad. We'll probably be there in about an hour so if you could put on a pot of coffee that would be great. Bye for now." She replaced the receiver, and wiped off her sweat with a piece of paper towel.

She went into the mudroom to retrieve all their shoes and the cooler. Robert snuck up behind her, making her jump. "Let me help," he said. She handed him the cooler.

"There are some ice packs in the freezer which I brought with me and also some yogurts and fruit in the fridge. That should see us through until we get home. If not, we'll stop on the way. The kids will be thrilled to have another fast food meal; their last for a very long time." Making small talk to cover her nervousness in a futile attempt to break the tension between them, she decided to shut up.

Robert put the cooler on the floor and opened the lid. "Why don't you take what you need, and I'm sorry I've been such a bear. It wasn't fair to take it out on you."

"I understand, but you scared me," she said, opening the refrigerator.

"I know. I just couldn't help myself."

"Better you yelled at me than Mr. Blunt." She changed the subject. "Should we feed Honey before we leave?"

"I wouldn't give her too much food."

"Are you telling me she's not a very good traveler?"

"No, she's fine but she'll probably be nervous so it's best if she doesn't have too much in her stomach just to be safe."

She opened her mouth to say she was sorry she was running out on him, but changed her mind—it would be a lie.

"I have no right to ask this, but will you call me when you get home?" Robert said.

"Sure."

"I'm sorry we had to meet under such miserable circumstances," Robert said, rocking from one foot to the other, hands thrust deep into his pockets. "Could I come see you once all this is over?"

You have to be kidding me. No way. You've blown it, my friend. However, she wasn't totally heartless and said, "Perhaps."

"I'll just carry all this stuff out into the hallway for you."

Deciding to go out and start the car, she went off to find her coat, pulling on her hat and gloves, slipping her feet into her shoes, opening the front door and stepping outside. The cold took her breath away, the catch in her lungs welcome after the oppressive warmth of the house with its accompanying gloom; enveloped in a shroud of mourning all its own, Thea couldn't wait to make her escape. Even going to visit her parents would be a welcome relief.

A thick layer of frost coated the windows of the minivan, but the engine roared into life. Turning back to the house, leaving the heater to work its warm, breathy magic, going up the wooden steps onto Ellie's colorful porch, pausing to look at the whimsical Thanksgiving decorations, she walked through the door into the hallway for what she imagined would be the last time. The L-shaped house, skillfully designed by Mr. Blunt and Ellie, boasted a beautiful sheltered courtyard in the ell; living space at one end and bedrooms and bathrooms the other, but for Thea, it lacked heart. Even with the softly burnished honey-colored wooden floors, the brightly decorated rooms, the inviting fireplace, the homey kitchen, there was something missing. It was as if the house carried the burden of Ellie's sickness, creating an atmosphere that pressed down on Thea's shoulders like unwanted hands. She thought fondly of her house in Maine, and despite the trauma that had transpired under its sloping roof, it was full of love, wrapping itself around them, keeping them safe. Standing in the hallway, watching her children and Honey walking towards her carrying as much stuff as they could, made her realize how desperately she wanted to go home. It was silly to be sentimental about a house, but she was, and she suspected her children felt the same way.

They gathered everything, putting it into a neat pile. Thea ran back, did a last check in all their rooms, making sure nothing had been left in the bathrooms or under the beds. Peter, notorious for losing things, would be thoroughly ticked off if he discovered one of his CDs missing. The only thing she found was a sock that she stuffed into the pocket of her jeans. She didn't linger, glanced around the lovely room in which she had fitfully slept, hurried past Ellie's door, back to join the kids busily putting on their coats and shoes. Robert appeared out of nowhere and offered to help them carry stuff to the car. She said, "Thank you."

Peter stood next to Honey with his hand resting on her head, holding the leash, talking to her and telling her it was going to be all right.

Leaning into his leg, he could feel her trembling through his jeans. She sensed something was up, kept glancing over at her bed, nervously alert, watching intently when Robert picked it up. Peter followed Robert down the driveway, Honey walking by his side, the leash slack, unlike Lady, the crazy dog. He wondered whether Honey would dig holes in the sand, blow bubbles under the water as Lady had done. Probably not, but it didn't matter. What mattered was actually having a dog, even though he was anxious, afraid she would be unhappy. Haunted by nightmares, he was still angry with the man who had caused harm to his mom, Jessica and Lady. Pleased he was dead, but wished he'd had the chance to slug him, he unclenched his fist and shook his head to clear the memories.

Izzie went into an organizing frenzy with Robert's help, neatly stacking all their belongings in the cargo hold of the van, including Honey's bed. Peter climbed into the front seat and settled Honey firmly between his legs. A bit of a tight squeeze, he doubted they could do the whole journey that way, but it was okay for the short ride to his grandma and grandpa's. Izzie and Jessica scrambled in behind him, fastened their seat belts and dragged blankets over their knees. As on the outward journey, the cooler rested between them should they need a snack, the DVD player on top, headphones at the ready. Oblivious to their surroundings, Izzie sat with her nose in a book, and Jessica colored, her brand new box of pencils close at hand. Peter stared out his window, absent-mindedly fondled Honey's ears and watched his mom talking to Robert. He could only imagine what they were saying, and he turned his head away, unable to bear the look of sadness on Robert's face. His mom had that affect on men. They all fell in love with her and he could never really figure out why, just put it down to being some kind of grown-up thing. He still found girls annoying, but he knew one day he wouldn't feel that way. He was sure of one thing though, when he had a girlfriend he would treat her right—give her up immediately if things started to go wrong. He didn't see the point of spending time with people if you didn't like them and they made you angry.

Thea's farewell with Robert hadn't gone well. Despite his earlier behavior, she felt guilty for leaving him behind to deal with all the dismal details involved with his sister's death. Only slightly comforted in the knowledge he would have Mr. Blunt and Dorothy, Robert's grief pressed on her chest like an elephant's foot. Sorry she wouldn't be able to meet Dorothy, she was eternally grateful to this unknown woman for coming to the rescue.

She climbed into the van, glanced at Peter, and in an attempt to lighten her mood by continuing their nautical game, she said, "Okay, Mr. Navigator?"

"Yup," he said.

"So let's weigh anchor and be on our way." She lifted her hand, waved when she caught a glimpse of Robert in her rearview mirror, but he didn't wave in return.

After a quick stop at Barney's Bagels for breakfast sandwiches, they headed to her parents' house. Honey's nose, working overtime at the smell of the eggs and cheese, made Peter laugh. "Mom, I think we should have a rule right up front of no people food for Honey."

"I absolutely agree. It won't do her any good and a begging dog is never much fun to have around. I think we should give her something to eat before we leave to go home, but not too much. Do you agree?"

"Uh-huh. Do you think she knows any French words? I was going to ask Robert, but it seemed awkward."

"You could ask him when I call later. You'll probably have a list of questions by then. I think he did make a few notes and put them with her papers. We can check when we get to Grandma and Grandpa's."

With little traffic on the road, they were pulling into the Marchants' driveway in no time. Thea turned in her seat to look at the girls. "We don't need to bring in any games. We're just going to stay for breakfast because I'd like to get on the road as soon as possible." And, for once, there was no protest from Jessica. Peter gathered what he needed from the back of the van for the dog, putting it all in a plastic bag, and then all five of them were standing on the doorstep under the drab metal awning which had been there for as long as Thea could remember. She looked up at it. Was it her imagination or did it seem to be leaning down to the right even more than ever? Her parents, now in their early seventies, preyed on her mind, especially since her father's recent injury. It was a five-hour drive from Maine, rendering her useless in an emergency.

Henry opened the door, shuffled back out of the way, his sore foot and ankle encased in a special bandage inside a navy Velcro-fastened boot. Huddled together in the tiny hall, Peter looked at his grandma standing in the kitchen doorway, a shy smile of welcome on her face. Jessica, clutching the bag with the breakfast sandwiches, pushed her way through, thrusting the bag into her grandmother's hands. "Here," she said.

Henry, beaming, busily taking coats, hanging them in the hall closet, sliding the hangers to one side, tried to find space. Thea watched in amusement. With his obsession for orderliness, he had to make sure each hanger faced the same way. Addressing the children, he said, "Grandma set the table in the dining room because there isn't room for all of us in the kitchen, so let's go."

Peter looked at his grandmother, a blank expression on her face, still standing in the kitchen doorway clutching the food. "Grandma, would it be all right if I gave Honey something to eat?"

She came alive. "Of course. Silly old me, just standing here. Do you need any bowls?"

"No, I'm all set." He bent down, unhooked the dog's leash, and she followed him into the kitchen, her claws making little tapping noises on the linoleum. Filling one bowl with water and the other with a half-cup of dry food, he said, "It's okay, you can eat. I'm not going anywhere until you're done," and he sat down on one of the kitchen chairs. She looked at him as if she understood. He wondered when she had last been fed, sure she had been quite forgotten. As soon as she was done, she lapped up some water, looked at him as if to say, "What's next?" and happily followed him into the dining room.

Thea watched her mother's rather plain face, under its cap of crisp, permanently waved gray hair, come alive. She poured coffee for the grown-ups and milk for the kids, and made sure they each had a plate and a napkin before sitting down to eat her own sandwich. "This is very good," she said.

Jessica's mouth was full, but she chewed and swallowed rapidly. Thea knew she was about to say something inappropriate; she stared at her daughter and put her finger to her lips. Jessica scowled, but she was too hungry to get overly upset about having to wait. Thea knew she was on borrowed time, but she was determined to enjoy her sandwich. She stirred cream into her coffee, glanced over at Honey sitting with her head on Peter's lap waiting for crumbs.

"Don't forget to take those boxes with you."

"I won't, Mom, that's one of the reasons why we stopped by. You've no idea how much it means to me that you kept my little-girl things. I can't wait to show all my treasures to the kids when we get home. I'm sure they'll probably tease me unmercifully, but it will be worth it," and she gave her mom a big smile. If nothing else, this visit had brought her closer to her parents, giving her a new understanding of them. Her dad, sitting across from her, caught her eye. "Would now be a good time for you to tell us what brought on this impromptu visit?"

She nodded, nervously shredding the napkin in her lap, watching Izzie place a hand on one of Jessica's, and for once, her daughter remained silent. "I'm not sure where to begin and it's hard to talk about, but we're going home today."

"I thought you were staying until Monday. Did you and Ellie have a falling out?"

"No, Dad, it was nothing like that. I don't know if you realized she was sick."

"We thought she might be because it was Robert who stopped by after I hurt my ankle instead of Ellie and he ignored my question when I asked if she was all right. I thought it strange at the time but then forgot about it."

Thea couldn't go on with the children sitting around the table staring at her and Jessica bursting at the seams to say something. "Why don't you children help Grandma clean off the table while I talk to Grandpa. I won't be long and then we'll get on the road." Jessica, disappointed because she really wanted to be in the thick of things, nonetheless did as she was told. Thea got up, walked around the table to sit next to her dad, held his hand. "Ellie was very sick and she never told me. She invited me so she would have a chance to see me for the last time. Her body gave out and she died in the night."

"Oh, my goodness, my poor Thea. What a rotten situation for you and the kids. Now I understand."

"To be honest, it hasn't really sunk in and I'm just functioning on autopilot."

"Are you going to be able to drive all that way?"

"Yes, I'll be fine. I just felt so bad running out on Robert and Mr. Blunt, but I had to get the children away."

"Do you think there's anything your mom or I could do?"

"I think it would be kind if you called. You probably have Ellie's number and I'll give you Mr. Blunt's," and she reached over to the buffet to grab her pocketbook. Her father stood up and pulled open one of the maple-fronted drawers, took out a pen and an ancient address book, curled at the corners. "This way we won't lose it," he said, thumbing down the well-worn index until he got to the B's. Removing the top from the pen and finding an empty space on the page, he wrote down Theodore's number.

"Is that why you have Ellie's dog with you? I did wonder."

"It was Ellie's special request. She knew Honey wouldn't be happy with either Robert or Mr. Blunt because she's used to having lots of kids around. She also knew how much Peter wanted a dog and Honey does seem to have latched onto him and I'm thrilled about that. It's tough for Peter not having a dad and perhaps Honey will fill that gap, just a little bit. I wish you and mom lived closer."

"I guess the partnership is a thing of the past now."

"It was all rather strange. Mr. Blunt still owns Aladdin's Cave and he didn't mention anything about it to me. Maybe it was all part of Ellie's sickness, the tumor pressing on her brain. I'm not sure what will happen to the store now. It's all so dreadfully sad. She worked so hard, built it up to be somewhere special. You should see the craft room she created out of the old storeroom in back. It's amazing and kept Izzie and Jessica amused for much of the day on Friday. The tragedy is I could see myself there, but not without Ellie so it's back to Maine for us. Thanks, Dad, for listening and now I'd better gather the troops before they give Mom any trouble."

"I'll go retrieve those boxes for you."

"Can you manage with your sore ankle? Why don't you let me help you."

"I'm fine. It hardly hurts any more."

"You're sure?"

"I am. Go see to the kids."

Thea put her head around the kitchen door, surprised to see a happy domestic scene. Pretty sure Jessica had spilled the beans, she wasn't surprised when Enid said, "Jessica told me that Miss Ellie is now with the angels."

"Yes, she is. She was sick for a long time and now she's resting peacefully. I gave Dad Mr. Blunt's number and he said he'd call him later to see how he's doing." She turned to the children. "Well, gang, it's time for us to be going. Peter, why don't you take Honey out to the backyard for a quick pit stop."

"Already done," he said, beaming with pride. "Grandma gave me a plastic bag and Honey rewarded me with a prize! It sure was stinky!"

"That's the downside of owning a dog," Thea said.

"I know, but it's still worth it."

"Well, I hope you continue to feel that way because you are going to be Chief Pooper Picker Upper," Thea said.

"Sounds worse than Smokey's litter tray," Izzie said.

Peter agreed. "Ten times worse, but I don't care."

"Hah," Jessica said. "You will."

"I'll train her to go on the toilet!"

Jessica said, "Ugh!"

"While on the subject of toilets, we all need to make a pit stop before we leave. I'm going to run upstairs," and she was gone.

The kids all took turns to use the half-bath off the kitchen; now tightly packed in the hallway, coats zipped, hats pulled firmly down around their ears, they waited patiently. Peter clutched Honey's leash and the bag with her bowls and food. Thea looked at her mom and dad and swallowed the gathering lump in her throat. Surprised at how much they had enjoyed each other's company, and how well her parents had adapted to being invaded by her motley crew, she was finding it hard to leave. Never a physical threesome, she had a sudden desire to be a little girl again, to be able to weep in her mother's arms, but she knew her mother wouldn't be able to handle it. She'd just pat her on top of the head and say, "Never mind, dear. It will be all better soon." No good wishing for the impossible. Pulling herself together, she said, "Okay, crew, let's get you settled and I'll come back for the boxes." There were hugs all around. Thea watched Peter kiss his Grandma on the cheek, heartened by the special bond formed between this shy elderly woman and her quick-to-anger son.

Overcast, dark clouds hanging heavy, Thea prayed it wouldn't snow. Blessed with good weather so far, she hoped her luck would hold. She got the kids all settled. Peter, Mr. Navigator, sat up front, the girls behind, a blanket spread for Honey on the bench seat in the way back. Peter told the dog to stay and she obligingly stretched out. Thea understood the temptation to have her pressed against his legs in the front, but Honey's comfort came first and once they got closer to home she told him he could go sit with her. Ellie's death hung like a cloud over all of them with the exception of Jessica, but even she was behaving herself, not making a fuss. Admonishing them to sit exactly where they were, making sure the parking brake was engaged, she went back into the house. Her mom and dad's forlorn demeanor, standing exactly where she had left them, triggered her tears. "I'm sorry," she said.

Henry walked over to his daughter, put his arms around her, and much to her surprise, Enid came up behind her and put her arms around her too. "I wish you'd stay," she said.

Thea drew in a deep breath, swallowed the lump in her throat, and moved out of their embrace. "Oh, Mom, I wish we could too. Would you and Dad consider coming for a visit? That would make me feel so much better if you would at least think about it."

Henry wiped Thea's face with his spotlessly clean handkerchief and said, "We will definitely give it some thought as soon as my ankle is completely healed. Okay?"

She nodded, attempted a weak smile. "I guess I'll have to make do with that. Now I really must go. Sorry about the soggy farewell."

"Not to worry," Enid said. Henry held the door open for her, watched Thea carry first one box and then the other outside, placing them carefully on the step.

"I'll call you as soon as I get home. I love you. Close the door now, or you'll catch your death. It's freezing out here." Her dad blew her a kiss before disappearing from view behind the drab front door with the faded green paint.

Thea, bewildered by what had just happened, never having sought comfort from her parents before, sensed a connection, something on which to build a future. She had finally broken through the surface of their self-absorption and she was pleased they were no longer the polite strangers with whom she had lived as a child. She carried the boxes to the van, managed with a little reshuffling to stow them in the cargo space and pulled the door down, making sure it was securely closed. She turned around before getting into the driver's seat to see her mom and dad standing at the living room window, the net curtains pushed to one side, her dad's arm around her mom's shoulders. They were smiling and waving. At least they have each other, she thought, and I have my children; counting her blessings, she pulled out of her parents' driveway and headed for home. They all took one last look at Aladdin's Cave as they drove through Stockton—no pretty welcoming lights, the dark window a blank reflection of what might have been. She and the children could have made a life for themselves here, but not without Ellie. It obviously wasn't meant to be. She didn't believe in divine intervention but a hand more powerful than her own had certainly been at play. Did she believe that old cliché?— *Everything happens for a reason.* Not really.

Enid and Henry moved away from the window once the minivan had disappeared from view. Enid, overcome with sadness, said, "The house feels so empty."

Henry couldn't have agreed more. "I never thought I would say this, but I enjoyed being with the children. I always thought they would be too much trouble, and you know, Enid, how I hate to be out of my routine, but somehow it didn't matter. How would you feel about moving to Maine permanently?"

She looked at him in astonishment and said, her voice up an octave or two, "Oh my, now that's an idea. You've quite taken the wind out of my sails."

"Well, what do you think?"

"With you by my side, I can do anything." She blinked back her tears, stepping forward into Henry's arms. "I know I don't tell you very often, but I love you."

"I love you, too," he said, their kiss interrupted by the ringing of the telephone.

Enid hurried into the kitchen knowing she would be quicker than Henry because of his ankle. She plucked the receiver off the wall. "Hello," she said.

"Hi, is this Mrs. Marchant?"

"Yes."

"Please don't hang up on me. I'm not trying to sell you anything and this isn't a crank call. Will you listen to me, please?"

Enid, not curious by nature but nevertheless intrigued, wondered what else this strange day might bring. "I'm listening."

"My name is Christopher Morrison and I met your daughter in Aladdin's Cave yesterday when she helped me with a purchase. I'd like to get in touch with her."

"You've just missed her. Does she know you?" Henry had come up behind her and mouthed, "Who is it?" She held a finger to her lips.

"That's too bad," Christopher said. Enid could hear the disappointment in his voice. "And no, I don't know her, but I would like to. I was wondering if I could stop by and give you a letter I've written so you could get it to her. That way you wouldn't have to give me any of her personal information, and she would be free to contact me if she wanted to. I could give you my mother's phone number if you like so you could verify who I am."

"No, no, that won't be necessary. I believe you. You're welcome to stop by any time. We'll be here."

"I'll see you in about an hour then. Bye," and he was gone.

Enid stood staring at the receiver until Henry took it gently out of her hand and replaced it in its cradle. "Well, what was all that about?"

"You know, Henry, this is the strangest day. We are about to meet Christopher Morrison, a young man who wants to get to know our daughter better. He sounded very nice, but we'll be able to judge for ourselves in about an hour."

Henry had never seen Enid so animated. Always quiet, shy and unsure of herself, she seemed to have a newfound confidence. He hoped they would be able to maintain their momentum once the excitement of a prospective move had worn off and the practicalities set in—a huge step but the right one. He had a feeling in his bones that the housing market was going to tank. Henry recalled reading a recent article citing the cooling of the housing market, an eight percent drop since 2004, the declines widespread, seven percent in the Northeast; now or never the time to sell before the predicted "bubble" burst, with its accompanying certainty of falling prices. Even in retirement, he'd kept abreast of things. No longer in the banking business, but still well informed, he was aware of the cutting of the availability of subprime loans, and the timing certainly wasn't perfect. He straightened his shoulders and told himself they had nothing to lose so they might just as well give it a try even though the market wasn't as good as it might have been a year ago. Henry had maintained the house well and even though the furnishings were a little dowdy, Enid kept it sparkling clean. He decided to put it up for sale right away before they changed their minds, ask Thea to find a rental for them, sure there would be plenty at this time of the year even if they had to take a winterized cottage.

"Penny for your thoughts," Enid said.

"I was just thinking we should put the house on the market right away before we get cold feet. You know what we're like."

Enid didn't say anything. Henry peered into her face. "You haven't changed your mind have you?"

"No. It's just . . ."

"What's the matter, Enid?"

"I want to be closer to my daughter and I want to see that grandson of mine grow up, but it's such a huge step isn't it? I know I can't sit within these four walls feeling guilty for the rest of my life just because I'm afraid and I am trying to be brave, so let's do it."

Henry's mind was going a mile a minute. "That's my girl. It will be an adventure, you'll see."

"What do you think Thea will say? Do you think we should ask her first?" Enid briefly standing tall, her fleeting assertiveness replaced by her usual timid, shoulder-drooping approach to life, pulled a tissue from her sleeve and wiped her nose.

"Hm," Henry said, rubbing his chin. "Judging by the way she came to us for help today, I'm sure she'll be fully on board with the idea, but we could run it by her first if it makes you feel more comfortable. In the meantime, I could call a real estate agent today and at least make an appointment to have the house appraised. How does that sound?"

"It all sounds good," Enid said, a little enthusiasm returning. She turned to Henry. "You know, I think I'd like some new clothes. I'm tired of all my drab browns and beige."

Henry raised his eyebrows. "I always thought you would look lovely in blue."

"That's settled then. No more polyester. I want my daughter to be proud of me." Head high, shoulders back, she headed off to the kitchen; Henry watched her retreating figure in amazement.

Enid cleaned up, happily putting plates into the dishwasher, washing the floor where Honey had dropped little bits of dog food. She thought about what it would be like to be in Maine, the winters colder and snowier, a little longer than the winters here, but she and Henry didn't mind the cold. They'd be able to go to the beach and help Thea look after the children and Honey. Henry loved dogs, she not so keen. There had been no animals when she was growing up in the orphanage, and she was sad now that she hadn't allowed Thea at least a guinea pig or a hamster when she was a little girl. She reflected on the Thanksgiving she and Henry had spent at Ellie's, how Peter had made her day by befriending her, rescuing her from her awkward shyness. Living in the land of indifference for all those years—disappointment eating into her bones when no one stepped forward to adopt her—had taken its toll. She just didn't know how to reach out to people, gave up trying. She became completely institutionalized, a tiny shadowy figure following the rules, finally rescued by Henry the day she fell over in the Colonial Bank, her lucky day. Now she'd been given another lucky day, the beginning of many more, and she was going to make the most of life from now on. Busy wiping down the countertops when the doorbell rang, she flung the sponge into the sink and hurried out into the hallway. She opened the door and found herself staring up into the most amazing pair of grass-green eyes. "Hi, I'm Christopher Morrison," he said, hurriedly pulling off a glove and holding out his hand. Enid took the proffered hand in her slightly damp one and inadvertently almost pulled him into the hallway in a rare burst of enthusiasm. "Please come in."

Henry, appearing out of nowhere, said, "Why don't you take off your coat and we'll go and sit somewhere comfortable so you can tell us a little bit about yourself." Henry watched a brief flicker of alarm cross Chris's face. "It's all right," he said, smiling at the young man. "I promise this won't be the Spanish Inquisition!"

"There's not much to tell," he said, sitting down at one end of the drab sofa with its pale stripes of green and beige. The room was neat and tidy, with the exception of a large basket full of knitting needles, bright balls of yarn spilling over its edges, a stark contrast to the otherwise colorless furnishings. He'd never seen so much beige.

Henry came to the point. "Why do you want to contact my daughter, besides the fact she's quite beautiful?"

Chris decided to be honest. "I can't deny that I do find her very attractive and I just can't get her out of my mind. I should have asked this over the phone, and then I wouldn't have been wasting your time. Is she married, because if she is, then I have no right to contact her?"

"You can relax and I appreciate your integrity. She was, but she's been divorced now for about three years. You do realize she has three children: a son and two daughters?"

"I know she has a son because he was working the cash register at Aladdin's Cave, but I didn't know about her daughters, not that it makes any difference. I'd still like you to give my letter to her."

"I'm quite happy to do that. Now please tell me a little bit about yourself."

Chris relaxed a little and leaned back into the sofa. Thea's mother added nothing to the conversation, just sat summing him up, hands resting comfortably in her lap. "I've lived in the area all my life. My parents live in Lenox and my sister lives with her husband in New York City. I work as a computer programmer at a small company in Great Barrington and rent a loft apartment close to where the office is. I'm a sports nut, adapting each sport to the season. Currently, I'm running and will continue until the weather breaks."

"Thea likes to run," Enid said, breaking her silence. "I'm sure she still does when she can." She liked Christopher, thought how much better it would have been for Thea if she had married someone such as this young man—normal and down to earth—rather than the lofty Michael Chamberlin.

Chris continued, "Running's good. Get's out the kinks when you're having a bad day."

Enid nodded. "That's what she used to say," and then she fell silent again, leaving Henry to pick up the threads.

"Well, young man. As I said, I'd be happy to send your letter."

"Thank you, sir. It's in the pocket of my jacket." He stood up. "I can't help noticing you've hurt your ankle. Is there anything I can do for you, run an errand perhaps?"

"That's very kind, but we have a neighbor who has been especially good to us so we're all set for now and I should be able to start driving again in a few days."

"Let me give you my phone number anyway, just in case. Of course, I'm not much use to you during the day because I'm working, but I could run over after work. It wouldn't be any trouble."

"We both appreciate your thoughtfulness and we might just take you up on your offer." He turned to Enid. "Would you mind getting the address book?" She scurried off to the dining room returning seconds later with the shabby book and a pen. "We'll put your number right in here, Chris. That way we won't lose it." Enid found the M's and wrote Christopher Morrison and the number he gave her in her neat cursive handwriting.

"That's all done," she said.

"I'd better get going. I've enjoyed meeting you." Out in the hallway Enid handed Chris his jacket from which he retrieved the envelope. "It isn't sealed if you would like to read what I wrote."

"There's no need. In fact, I'd like you to seal it in front of our eyes," and Chris did just that, running his tongue along the glue and pressing the paper firmly together. "Here, Mr. Marchant," and Henry took the envelope from the young man's hand.

"Thea is going to be calling us when she gets home. Would you like me to tell her we've met you and that there's a letter on the way?"

"What do you think? Would it further my cause?"

"It might, especially when we tell her how much we enjoyed meeting you," Henry said, a twinkle in his eye.

Chris smiled. He was pleased. The meeting had gone better than expected. He liked these simple folks. "I hope I'll see you again real soon," he said, shaking Henry's hand. "Before I go, do you mind telling me where she lives?"

"Maine," Enid said, watching Chris's face fall.

"I was hoping it was close by, but I'm jumping ahead of myself. She may not want to have anything to do with me."

"We'll talk to her tonight so don't be too discouraged and I'll mail your letter first thing tomorrow morning," Henry said.

"Thank you."

Henry opened the door, watched Chris bounce down the steps, get into his ancient Jeep and drive away. "Well, Enid," he said after he'd closed the front door. "This has been quite a day. What a nice young man. Do you think he could be Thea's third time lucky?"

"He was so easy to be with, wasn't he? Not like that awful Michael. He gave me the creeps right from the start. He made me feel squashed like a piece of dirt on his shoe. You did a little better with him, didn't you?"

"Only because we could talk business. I had my misgivings right from the start, but what could we do?"

"Absolutely nothing, and in any case, it's all in the past now. Then there was the dreadful Kenny. Do you think she's learned her lesson, Henry?"

"Is it our fault she's had such a rough road?"

"Perhaps, but it's no good blaming ourselves. That won't do any good. All we can do is be there for her now."

"You're right, Henry. Are you going to call the realtor?"

"I think I'll wait until Monday. It's a bit late now and we can also run the idea by Thea before putting our plan into action. In the meantime, I'll go and make some of my famous lists," he said, putting his arm around Enid's shoulders, giving her a little squeeze. "Are you a teeny, weeny bit excited?"

"I am on the inside, but it's hard for me to show it on the outside."

"I understand." Henry went off to find a pad of paper; Enid went off to the kitchen to make a cup of tea.

CHAPTER NINE

MARYANN

MaryAnn was excited about the prospect of living in Melford Point, loving its quaintness and the seeming timelessness, happy to step back to a bygone era where history and loyalties ran deep. Not that she had spent much time there. She would glance at the storefronts when driving through but with no money to spend it was pointless being tempted by the merchandise in the window of Harry's Hardware or a book from A Good Read. Right after Sam's death she had taken some of her more stylish clothes to One Woman's Treasure, putting them on consignment in an attempt to raise some much-needed cash. Driving down Maine Street she found the empty store between Gems Fine Jewelry and the Scrapbook Nest, opposite It's a Fishy Business and slightly down from the Country Store on the other side of the street.

Managing to parallel-park without too much trouble, she remembered Sam's exasperation, bested by his wife who parked better than he did, surprised to find she could think about him with humor, rather than the habitual sadness. The boys were as eager to be out of the car as she, anxious to see the place where they might live—her only regret their shabby coats, offset by bright hats, scarves and gloves. The car a poverty-stricken dead giveaway sticking out like a sore thumb, MaryAnn hoped they would arrive at the door to the store prior to Georgie Simpson. They were in luck. A little early, they lingered outside A Good Read, itching to go into the bookstore, stopping to stare at all the books in the window before walking away. "When we're done," she said, "I'll treat you to a hot chocolate."

Standing in the doorway of the empty store out of the wind, stamping their feet to keep warm, they didn't have to wait long. Hurrying along the sidewalk coming towards them was this energetic woman about the same age as MaryAnn—dark curls escaping from a bright red hat, cheeks rosy from the cold. MaryAnn looked longingly at her fur coat, her knee-length scarlet leather boots. "You must be the Wilkinsons. Let's get inside out of the cold," she said, pulling a large ring of keys from her coat pocket and unlocking the door. "There's a back entrance which you would use most of the time, but we'll go in this way today." They followed Georgie into a large empty space; the freshly painted white walls crying out *rent me*, a perfect photographic studio for MaryAnn. She dispelled the idea, barely had rent for the apartment let alone anything else. Georgie noticing MaryAnn's interest said, "It used to be an art store, but the proprietor's idea of what he wanted to sell and what the locals and tourists are likely to buy didn't quite match, so he went under fast. Much as I would like the income, I don't hold out much hope of renting it before the spring." Unlocking a door on the right-hand side of the back wall, revealing a short hallway with a door at the end, Georgie led them up a set of wide sturdy stairs with a solid banister to a good-sized landing at the top where they huddled while she unlocked yet another door. Again, MaryAnn noticed how solid it was, and as if reading MaryAnn's mind, she said, "My husband, Paul, and I carried out a complete renovation when we bought the place three years ago as an investment. Unfortunately, it hasn't been very lucrative so far." She stepped to one side to allow MaryAnn and the boys to pass, and flipped on the light.

MaryAnn's eyes widened in surprise at the big open, airy space. She envisioned her bright rugs, longing to bring them out of storage, scattered across the deep chocolate wooden floor. She fell in love with the galley kitchen: the cabinets simple and light in color; the countertop not the ubiquitous, shiny granite but some kind of composite, giving the appearance of a pebble tumbled by the ocean to a soft charcoal gray. She ran her fingers across the matte surface and said, "This is lovely."

Georgie smiled at her. "Unfortunately, there's not a lot of light because there is only one window, but we tried to make it better by opening up the ceiling, adding supporting beams and putting in a skylight. It's hard to tell on an overcast winter day, but it does make quite a difference. The white walls and the track lights in the kitchen also help." MaryAnn didn't say anything. Her thoughts jumped to the dismal rental; the apartment a sunny day in comparison.

Two bedrooms, facing the street, ample storage in their built-in closets, were light-filled and spacious. The small adjacent bathroom—the lack of a tub making room for the luxury of a stackable washer and dryer—was fitted with a travertine tile-lined shower, the color reminding her of wet and shiny golden rocks once collected at the sea shore.

Georgie, brisk and business-like, said, "I'll leave you to yourselves for a little while so you can make up your minds. The door to the right of the window leads out to a small deck and the back stairs. You would have a set of keys for this door, and the back entrance."

"Was that the door I noticed at the end of the hallway downstairs?"

"That's the one."

MaryAnn walked over and looked out of the window at the parking lot, the garages across from the alley below. She rested her hands on the radiator; big and fat just like the ones in Jim's house. Pleased it had somehow escaped the Simpson's renovations, she couldn't wait to actually have some tangible radiant heat. The deck was small, but a safety gate at the top of the stairs alleviated her misgivings. "Is this south facing?" she asked.

"Yes, it is. You're much better off on this side of the street. The sun pours through this window on nice days. I'll leave you to it. Come downstairs when you're ready."

Ian and Johnny, silent during the tour, were full of questions as soon as Georgie left and shut the door. "What do you think, Mom? Do you like it?" Ian asked.

"I do. It's so clean and shiny and it will be so much fun to make meals in the galley kitchen. What about you Johnny? Can you see us living here?"

"Yes, but it will be kinda strange being upstairs all the time."

"This is a big space though so you'd have plenty of room to play."

"Do you think Jessica will like it?"

"I'm sure she will."

"And Mr. Hudson too?"

"Yes, and Mr. Hudson too. What about you Ian? Are you worried about having to share a room because if you are, I can sleep in the living room?"

Ian stood, pondered for a moment. "I think we should take it. We can figure out the sleeping arrangements after we move in. How does that sound, Mom?"

"Sounds like a very practical solution, young man, so let's go tell Mrs. Simpson the good news."

Georgie, waiting for them in the empty store, said, "Well, have you made a decision?"

"Yes, we have and we'd love to rent the apartment. Did you say there was an optional garage?"

"Yes, there's parking behind the stores and a road for deliveries, and on the other side of that there is a row of garages. The numbers correspond with the numbers of the stores and this one is Number 9. The garage is a little narrow, but it's quite long so there's plenty of room for bikes, skis, et cetera, at the end. It's an extra fifty dollars a month."

"It will be worth it to have my car under cover. It will be such a luxury after all the scraping and shoveling I've done over the past three winters."

"You'll be glad of it especially when there's a parking ban during a snowstorm. I have the lease agreement with me if you want to sign today."

"How does the lease run?"

"It's on a six-monthly basis. Does that work for you?"

"That's perfect."

"Why don't we go into the bookstore and find us a table and we can get this all settled."

MaryAnn opened the door of A Good Read, Ian and Johnny on her heels, and they stepped into a sensory experience, their nostrils assailed by the aroma of fresh and pungent coffee, their eyes feasting on books old and new crammed into floor-to-ceiling shelves. They walked between the shelves to the back of the store, the wooden floor creaking beneath their feet, coming across several round tables and chairs, strategically placed, filled with people sitting and chatting, or in some cases, just quietly reading. The boys grabbed the one remaining empty table. As soon as Georgie arrived, MaryAnn asked her what she would like to drink and she said she'd love a skinny vanilla latte. Of course, the boys wanted hot chocolate with whipped cream and she went to line up. How glorious to be out in the real world, throwing caution to the wind, spending money on four very expensive drinks—her life so small, so confined for so long, now finally seeing the light of day. She beckoned to Ian once the drinks were ready, watched him carefully pick up the hot chocolates and carry the big, fat, shiny white mugs back to the table. "Why don't you go get a couple of spoons? That whipped cream looks serious," she said, giving him a look of pure glee, a kid out of school.

Georgie, sitting talking to Johnny, had pulled off her hat—her dark curls an unruly but attractive mess. She had removed her arms from her coat, draped it over the back of the chair, revealing a bright blue turtleneck sweater. The prisms of her diamond rings caught the light and MaryAnn thought they must have cost a small fortune. She wondered what her husband did for a living to keep this lady in furs, albeit fake, and diamonds, which definitely were not. She even had diamonds twinkling in her ears, but MaryAnn liked her. For all her obvious wealth, she had no airs and graces. She was just a normal, if a little brisk, young woman who had walked the path of good fortune.

The table cramped, the boys drinks too hot, MaryAnn suggested they go browse. "Come back in a little while," she said. They didn't have to be told twice. No need to warn them to be careful; they would look after any books they chose to take from the shelves as if they were their own. Georgie pulled the rental agreement from her leather portfolio. MaryAnn read it line by line. As anticipated, she was expected to put down a month's rent and a security deposit, to be returned at the end of the lease, covered by the hoped for refund of the security deposit from her current landlord. She signed her name to the agreement, dated it November 26, 2005, wrote two checks from her meager money market savings account, and tried to keep her hand steady. "I won't charge you for these last remaining days of the month, so the lease will be effective December first, but you can move in whenever you like."

"Thank you. That will be helpful, but what about references?"

"I'm an excellent judge of character and I have a good feeling about you and your sons. My husband will probably give me grief for being impractical, and if he does, I'll contact you. Here, let me give you a set of keys. They are color-coded: the red one opens the back entrance; the green one, the inside door to the apartment; the yellow one the outside door, and the blue one the garage. I'm afraid there isn't an automatic door opener, but it's fairly easy to pull up so I don't think you'll have any trouble. You'll find us conscientious landlords so if there's anything that goes wrong, please don't hesitate to give us a call." She picked up her mug and drank the rest of her latte. "Thank you for the coffee," she said. "I must be going. My husband will be very pleased the apartment isn't going to sit empty over the winter months. The thermostat for the heating system is just inside the door on the left-hand side. You'll find it gets very toasty as there are radiators in both the bedrooms and radiant heat in the bathroom floor."

"Wow, you didn't spare any expense did you?"

"We wanted to do a proper job up front so we wouldn't be faced with a lot of repairs down the road. It is also an incentive for tenants to respect our property if they see how well we've cared for it. And it's not *that* luxurious. I'm afraid there's no air conditioning, but there are ceiling fans!"

"Oh, we'll manage. It is Maine after all."

"That's true." Georgie pushed her chair away from the table and unable to resist the temptation, MaryAnn picked up her coat and held it out for her, sinking her fingers into the soft fur.

"This is a lovely coat."

"I love it. I would never have a real fur and this is surprisingly warm and light and luxurious all at the same time. Well, MaryAnn, it was really nice to meet you and I'm sure we'll run into each other in town. Enjoy Number 9."

"We will, and I promise you we'll look after it as if it were our own," but Georgie was already gone. She went off to find the boys, caught up with Johnny in the children's section, and discovered Ian intent on a National Geographic Magazine. "Do you think I'll ever be able to go to any of these places?" he asked, pointing to a picture of puffins on the Galapagos Islands.

"I don't see why not if you work hard at school so you can get a good job eventually, but right now there are two hot chocolates waiting, plus I have the keys to the apartment," she said, jangling them from her fingers.

"Way to go, Mom." He gave her a high five. Johnny, reluctantly replacing the colorful picture book, followed Ian and his mother back to their table. MaryAnn sat with her boys, watching them with pride, whipped cream on their lips, declaring the hot chocolate delicious. Floating on air, bursting with impatience to call Jim, she drank the last of her coffee.

Johnny, attacking the remainder of his drink with a spoon, not wanting to miss a drop, said, "This was soooo good." Running his tongue over his lips, failing to remove his chocolaty mustache, MaryAnn came to the rescue with a napkin.

"Do you know what I'd like to do?" and before the boys could answer, she said, "I'd like to go across to the Country Store and tell the Gilsons we're going to be living in town. After all they did invite us for Thanksgiving, so I think it would be polite to tell them before they find out from somebody else. Is that all right with you?"

"'Course it is," Ian said, not wanting to burst her bubble of happiness by being disagreeable. He willed Johnny to cooperate, his worries unfounded when his brother nodded and said, "I like Mr. Gilson. 'Member how he laughed at Stanley's silly jokes when we were all at the Chamberlins' having dinner."

"Yes, I remember," Ian said. "He laughed so hard; his glasses filled up with tears."

"Oh, Stanley with his silly jokes. He set us all off didn't he, and then, Johnny, you and Jessica crawled underneath the table, giggling all the way. We had so much fun."

"It was too funny looking at everyone's knees," and Johnny started to laugh.

MaryAnn and Ian joined in. With no clue what they were truly laughing at, suddenly aware she and the children were beginning to attract attention, she muffled her laughter and said, "Why don't we clear the table and put on our coats." And then they were all helplessly giggling again as she ripped the lining of her coat and her arm got stuck in her sleeve. "Oh look, I've lost my hand. Where on earth has it gone?"

"It's in the lining, silly," said Johnny, running his hand along the bottom of the sleeve. "Now we really do have to go and get new coats, don't we?"

"Absolutely!"

MaryAnn, suddenly remembering how serious people from Maine could be, held a suitably dour expression on her way out of the bookstore. No doubt they'd go down in history for making a scene, but she didn't care. The boys were happy, she was having a good time, and that was all that mattered. Once outside, she grabbed her sons' hands as they crossed the road, Johnny's little legs going a mile a minute. The wind threatened to pull their hats off their heads and their scarves from their necks, but for once in her life, MaryAnn wasn't cold.

The bell jangled on the door of the Country Store. They walked past all the tempting jars of candy, the baskets with all the various items to tempt the kids such as plastic reptiles, erasers in animal shapes, balls that glowed in the dark, windup toys, jumping frogs and so much more. Behind the counter sat a large scale for weighing out the sweets. Shelves brimmed with tempting merchandise: tins of shortbread biscuits, boxes of crackers, bags of gourmet cookies, jars of jams and jellies, and Margaret's special chocolate fudge. Deep amber bottles of maple syrup and bags of pancake mix sat in amongst a collection of colorful bowls and tastefully arranged dishtowels.

They walked to the back of the store, found Margaret and Bill at the deli, both their faces lighting up with pleasure when they saw the

Wilkinsons. "Well, this is a nice surprise. What brought you into town?" Bill asked, wiping his hands down his apron.

"We are moving here," Johnny said, taking the words right out of MaryAnn's mouth.

"Is that right?" Margaret said. "Why don't the three of you sit down and I'll make you some lunch. How does that sound?"

"Yes, please," Johnny said. He was itching to sit at the counter on one of the round red stools with the silver edging, just as Jessica had described. She had told him how much fun it was to swing all the way around on them, except you had to be careful not to fall off.

"The sandwich menu is right in front of you on the counter tucked behind the napkin holder. Why don't you all look at it and choose what you would like."

MaryAnn looked at all the meats, the different cheeses and the bowls of salad. It all looked so appetizing and healthy compared with the greasy food at the diner. She helped Johnny read the children's menu. He chose peanut butter and honey on whole-wheat bread; Ian wanted ham and Swiss cheese on rye, and she decided on cheddar cheese and tomato with mayonnaise on a multigrain roll. She requested water to drink for all of them, explaining they'd just had hot drinks at A Good Read.

The boys, fascinated by the meat slicer, watched Bill's hand go back and forth, the other catching the sliced meat and cheeses, handing them to Margaret for the sandwiches. "How was your Thanksgiving?" she asked. MaryAnn watched her neatly and deftly put all the ingredients together, placing each sandwich on a plate when it was done, together with a handful of kettle chips. MaryAnn could feel her mouth watering. Why on earth was she so addicted to potato chips? They would be her undoing.

"We had a very nice Thanksgiving. How about you?"

"It was quiet and I'm sorry you couldn't come, but it was much more restful with just the four of us. It gave me and Bill the opportunity to get to know Stanley and I'm waiting now to hear from Nan when the wedding will be. I do hope she will decide to get married in the church here in Melford Point, but of course it's her decision. Here I am running on. What made you decide to move into town and where are you going to be living?"

"Just across the street in the apartment over the now empty store; the one owned by Paul and Georgie Simpson."

Margaret brought the plates over and set them down one by one. Both the boys said thank you before picking up their sandwiches. "This is so good," Johnny said, swallowing his first mouthful. "The bread is so yummy."

Margaret walked back behind the counter and over to the sink to pour their waters. "Are you going to have enough room? Our apartment here is large because the store takes up two spaces."

"Yes, we'll make do. It won't be forever, but it will be wonderful to be in town and there's even a garage. I'm thrilled about that."

"Sounds as though you're all set then, lass," Bill said, peering down at them, leaning on the top of the glass case, with its array of salads, meats and cheeses. "You'll be regular visitors, then."

"I hope so."

Intent on their lunch and conversation, they didn't hear the doorbell jangle and MaryAnn jumped out of her skin when Jim came up behind her and said, "Boo," resting his hands gently on her shoulders.

"You scared me half to death."

"Hi, boys." They both turned to look at him with huge grins on their faces. He sat down on the empty stool next to MaryAnn. "I was hoping I might find you here. I called the house and there was no reply so I just took a chance. You look lovely by the way."

"Thank you, kind sir. Are you hungry? Do you have time to have some lunch?"

"I do. Margaret, what's the soup of the day?"

"Chicken vegetable."

"Sounds grand. I'll take a bowl with a piece of your honey-wheat bread."

"Coming right up."

"How did the apartment hunting go?"

"It went well. I already signed the lease and . . ."

"Mommy already has the keys," Johnny said. "We can move in whenever we want. It's great."

"Well, I guess that answers my question. Will you show it to me?"

"'Course."

"Ian, are you on board with this?"

"Yes, Mr. Hudson. It's a great space and we get a garage too."

"And, we went to the book store and had hot chocolate with whipped cream and the lady who showed us the apartment had a fur coat," Johnny said.

"You've all had quite a morning and what are you up to this afternoon?"

"We're going to buy new winter jackets," Ian said.

"Ah, yes, I do remember your mom mentioning that." Jim took a spoonful of the soup, blowing on it to cool it down. Like all Margaret's soups, it was delicious, enhanced by the magic touch of her special secret seasoning. "Margaret, this soup's outstanding as always. Just what the doctor ordered on such a gray and chilly day."

Margaret smiled, heart warmed to see how much these four people enjoyed each other's company. She couldn't believe the change in MaryAnn in just a few short days. Transformed from a dull and colorless woman steeped in sadness to this joyous young lady with bright eyes and color in her cheeks, even her hair seemed bouncier and shinier somehow, the love between her and Jim blatantly obvious. Margaret couldn't be happier and just hoped everything would work out for them. She also wondered whether MaryAnn would like a job working in the store, but now was not the time to ask. She would wait and talk it over with Bill.

"Well, I have to get back to work," Jim said, wiping the last piece of bread around his bowl, not wasting a drop. The boys groaned. "It's okay, we'll get together later and you can show me the apartment. How does that sound?"

"Why don't we meet at Thea's as we have to go back there and feed the cat. What time would work for you?" MaryAnn asked.

"Let's say four thirty." He stood up, leaned over and kissed MaryAnn on the cheek, high-fived the boys, paid Margaret for the lunches and glared at MaryAnn when she opened her mouth to protest. She turned on her stool, her eyes following him until he was out of sight.

"Okay, boys, let's go get our shopping over and done with." They slid off the stools, carried their plates over to a receptacle for dirty dishes and cutlery, dropping their napkins in the trash. MaryAnn decided to ask Margaret where would be a good place to go for coats and she recommended a great store nearby called the Garment Outlet. "I'm sure you will all find something there. They carry good quality merchandise without it being outrageously expensive," she said, giving them detailed directions.

The shopping trip turned out to be a huge success with plenty of winter jackets to choose from. Even though the down-filled were out of their price range, the ones filled with man-made fiber were almost as good. MaryAnn chose a hooded, zippered, three-quarter length red coat, with soft gray cuffs—the bright scarlet complementing her silvery blond hair.

Ian chose a navy blue ski jacket in a style similar to the ones worn by the kids at school. Finally, he would feel as though he fit in, the jacket perfect if he ever had the luck to go skiing, and the way things were going, he thought it might just happen.

Johnny couldn't make up his mind and wished Jessica was with him. With her forthright manner and strong opinions, she would have known exactly the coat he should pick. It was a toss up between a dark green and a deep royal blue. MaryAnn knew which one she liked best, but it had to be his decision. He would try one on and then the other, standing looking in the full length mirror with a very serious expression on his face. Which one would Jessica choose? In the end, he opted for the blue and MaryAnn breathed a sigh of relief. She really detested green. "You look very handsome," she said. "You've made a good choice."

They all wanted to wear their coats home. Once paid for—well within MaryAnn's budgeted two hundred dollars—they walked over to the customer service desk, asked the clerk if she would be kind enough to cut off the tags, thrusting their old coats into the empty plastic bag. She was as excited as the kids to have something brand new to wear. Outside the store, after checking there was nothing in the pockets, and without a shred of regret, she shoved them into a providently placed dumpster. Holding hands, heads held high, Ian and MaryAnn marched, and Johnny skipped, across the parking lot. Oh, it was so lovely to be warm. They all piled into the car and sang *Ten Green Bottles* and *There were Ten in the Bed . . .* at the top of their lungs all the way to the Chamberlins' house. The only thing slightly, but only ever so slightly, dampening her spirits was the thought she was going to have to call her current landlord.

CHAPTER TEN

❦

THEA—SATURDAY

Thea decided coming home from a trip was much worse than planning one—the journey tortuous, the last couple of hours in the dark. They had stopped at a rest area so all of them could go to the bathroom, including Honey, the poor dog becoming more and more disoriented. Much as she loved her newfound family, she was perplexed and mourning Ellie. The familiar pressure of dread in Thea's chest dragged her down, a headache niggling. Now she had absolutely nothing to look forward to, and she blinked away threatening tears, concentrated on the road ahead. Peter sat in the back with Honey, trying to reassure the poor animal. She alternated between resting her head on his legs and sitting up to look out the window in total bewilderment. The dog's distress was his distress, and Thea felt for her son.

Jessica finally fell asleep after a bout of whining when Thea thought she would scream and Izzie's plea for help, saying she couldn't amuse her sister any longer, made Thea feel even worse. She longed for another adult to be with her, to help with the children, so she could just concentrate on her driving. She was so tired of being a single mom.

Just to make matters even worse, it started to snow when they were still about an hour away from Melford Point. The hypnotic swirl of the flakes in the oncoming headlights made her feel dizzy and sick. Unable to leave the dog on her own in the van, they hadn't even stopped for a decent meal, just snacks from a vending machine, and yogurt from the cooler. Anxious to be on the road, she hadn't prepared well for the return journey, and now they were all suffering from her lack of planning.

She had never been so pleased in all her life to pull into her driveway, almost running into the side of Jim's truck. Even though it was parked well over to the left-hand side, she wasn't expecting it. She said, "Shit," wrenching the wheel hard to the right, narrowly missing the bumper by a hair's breadth—already jumpy and tense from the drive, this was the last straw. She also realized why Jim hadn't pulled the truck closer to the house—MaryAnn's car was there too. She wondered where they were because with the exception of the porch light, blurred by the falling snow, the house sat in darkness. Of course Jim and MaryAnn had no way of knowing she and the kids were on their way back from Ellie's, and her brief burst of anger immediately turned to relief to finally be home. She undid her seat belt, and rolled her shoulders to release the tension. Happy at the thought of sleeping in her own bed, but unable to shake the sense of let-down with no one to greet her except the cat and a virtually empty refrigerator, she swallowed her anti-climatic disappointment and watched her dream go up in a puff of smoke.

Turning around in her seat, she looked at her sleeping daughters. "We're home," she said. Honey let out a howl; Jessica and Izzie woke up, sat blinking in the semi-darkness like a couple of owls.

Peter, much too concerned about Honey to even question why Mr. Hudson's truck and the Wilkinson's car were in their driveway, didn't even comment on his mother's near miss and her momentary lapse into bad language. "What's wrong with Honey, Mom?" he asked, almost in tears. "Why is she so unhappy?"

"She's missing Miss Ellie. It's going to take her a few days to settle, but she'll be all right eventually, so don't take it to heart. It's nothing to do with you. Let's go inside. Leave all the stuff. I'll come out and get it later, and before you all ask, I have no idea why Mr. Hudson's truck and Mrs. Wilkinson's car are here. No doubt, we'll find out."

Honey seemed to recover a little when she saw the snow, happily pushing it along with her nose, making little snuffling noises. Peter clung to her leash tightly, knowing it would be fatal if she got loose on a night such as this. Mighty pleased to find her family home, Smokey wove her way between their legs, purring, tail held high. Peter stayed back, Honey behind him. Izzie grabbed the cat, tucked her under one arm, and hurried off to her bedroom. Peter took Honey into the back yard, armed with a plastic bag. In the safety of the fenced in area, he let her off the leash, watched as she ran around, relieved that she seemed calmer, coming readily when he called. Back in the kitchen, the dog promptly shook herself off, fur flying, the snow falling all over the floor, melting with the growing puddle from Peter's boots. Izzie, always the practical one, grabbing an old towel, rubbed Honey down and mopped up the floor. "You'll soon get organized, you'll see," she said, looking at Peter and giving him an encouraging smile.

"Where's Smokey?"

"I shut her in our bedroom. Jess said she'd stay and keep her company. She's not a very happy cat, and we'll introduce them later. I think she may be spending a lot of time in high places for a while."

Thea bustled around the kitchen, prepared a meal, glanced at the clock, turned on the radio, listened to the weather report and the six o'clock news. She pulled a large container of beef stew from the freezer, ran the container under water to loosen the frozen clump, dumped the contents into a large saucepan, set the heat to medium and stuck a lid on the top. Fortunately, because they'd only been gone since Thursday morning, the two containers of organic milk hadn't turned sour. She set about toasting and buttering honey-wheat English muffins, sticking them in the oven to keep warm. Keeping an eye on the stew, absentmindedly stirring the rapidly thawing liquid with a wooden spoon, she picked up the phone to call her parents. Henry picked up on the second ring.

"Hi, Dad. I just wanted to let you know we're home safe and sound."

"Thank goodness. Is it snowing there? Your mother and I were worried."

"Yes, it is, but according to the weather forecast, it isn't going to amount to much, but the last bit of the journey was a bit hairy. We're all tired and glad to be home as you can well imagine. I'm in the middle of making supper, so could I call you back later?"

"Of course."

"Say hi to Mom for me."

"I will," and he was gone.

Thea attacked the stew, cut up the now semi-frozen chunks with a knife. Peter and Honey had disappeared. Relieved the dog had stopped howling, she thought it would be quite cathartic to stand on the top of a hill somewhere and just howl to one's heart's content; this weekend would have been enough to put anyone over the edge. Her stomach growled, the herb-laden aromatic stew, mouth watering; not wanting to ruin her appetite, calls to Mr. Blunt and Robert would have to wait until after the meal.

Peter put his head around the door, said he was going to go out to the van to fetch Honey's food and bowls. Thea told him to be quick. He went out the back door telling Honey to stay. Used to sitting on the round rug in Ellie's hall, she decided to try and fit her body onto the doormat. Thea, amused no end, watched her circle, attempt to sit in the center of the tiny mat, body overlapping. Stroking the top of her silky head, rewarded by the twitch of her tail when she told her she was a good girl, Honey didn't budge until Peter came back in.

"Where would be the best place for her bowls?"

"There's a space there to the right of the back door. I think that will work because it's well away from where we feed Smokey, and you can put her food in the bottom of the pantry."

Peter filled Honey's water bowl, put a cup of kibble in her other bowl, watched her devour her food and lap up most of the water. He kept away from her, concerned she might be protective of her food, but he needn't have worried; a great big teddy bear of a dog, with a huge capacity for love, she didn't have a mean bone in her body.

Thea went off to find the girls, opened the door a crack, found them both trying to console Smokey, Izzie obviously upset. The poor cat, confused at being confined, tried to make her escape. "Do you want to introduce the two of them and get it over with, or would you rather wait until after supper?"

"Let's do it now. I don't want to leave her in here all by herself while we're eating."

"All right. I'll warn Peter to hang on tightly to Honey's collar. I suggest you put Smokey on the floor rather than trying to hold her because of her back claws. I have a feeling it's going to be all right. After all, she never took much notice of Lady."

"You're right, Mom. I'd forgotten. We just never made much of a fuss about it and they pretty much ignored each other, didn't they?"

Smokey followed them into the kitchen making her usual attempt to weave herself between their legs; this time she chose Jessica who wasn't in the mood. "Oh stop it, you stupid cat," she said, but Smokey took absolutely no notice. When they reached the kitchen door, Thea asked Peter to hold onto Honey. On high alert at the sight of the cat, her ears shot up, her tail wagged madly and she strained against her collar but Peter hung on tight. Smokey blew herself up to twice her size, arched her back, performed a funny sideways unique cat dance, and hissed madly.

"Uh-oh," Jessica said.

Peter told Honey to sit, pushed her haunches down with his spare hand; she did as she was told. Smokey ceased her dancing, inched her way closer, one tortuous paw at a time. Honey quivered under Peter's hand. Smokey, unable to reach the dog's nose, batted one of her legs. Peter let go and they all held their breath. Honey slid to the floor, a wary eye on the cat. Smokey's affectionate nature got the better of her, and placing Honey on a par with her human companions, she proceeded to rub herself all over the dog, purring like mad. None of them could believe their eyes.

"Well, I'll be darned," Thea said. "Who'd have thought. I really believed the fur would fly. I'm so pleased because they'll be good company for each other, especially when we're not home. Okay, let's eat."

The stew was hearty and sustaining and they all felt much better after they had eaten. The kids seemed to have made a remarkable recovery and seeing as both Izzie and Jess had slept, there was no need for them to go to bed right away. She and Peter were the exhausted ones, but she could see he was okay now that Honey seemed to be enjoying herself. He kept a watchful eye on her and Thea said, "She's going to be all right now, you know. You've done a good job and she knows you love her. She's the kind of dog who needs people to look after and she will be very happy looking after you, with the rest of us as backup. I want to thank you all so much for being so well behaved this weekend. It was tough for all of us, but you made it bearable and you've all made a huge hit with Grandma and Grandpa. In all the time I was growing up, I never saw them like that. They're good people once you thaw them out."

"You make them sound like a frozen dinner," Jessica said.

"I think they've been frozen for years and we defrosted them!" They all started laughing, their imaginations running riot, making them sillier and sillier. Even though she realized they were being a little disrespectful, she thought her parents would appreciate the humor, go along with the gentle teasing.

Supper over and done with, Thea made a couple of trips out into the snow to retrieve all their belongings from the van. Izzie went off to the basement to do some stretches and practice her steps for *The Nutcracker.*

Peter asked if he could have Honey's basket in his room, and even though Thea suspected the dog would probably end up on his bed in the night, she hadn't the heart to refuse. Perhaps it would encourage him to keep his room tidier, but she doubted it. At least Honey was past the chewing stage, even though she did like her rawhide bone. She ran a bath for Jessica, tying her hair up into a knot onto the top of her head to keep it dry, let her play for a while, finally dragging her out before she turned into a prune. Wrapping her in a towel, she rubbed her dry, and Jess lifted each foot to rest it on Thea's knees so she could dry thoroughly between her toes. "Are you doing all right, Jess?"

"Ooooh, that tickles and, yes, I'm all right. I guess we won't be moving to Mass-a-chu-setts now," she said, carefully sounding out the difficult word the way Thea had taught her. "Are you sad, Mommy?"

"A little bit. To tell the truth, I feel a bit let down if you know what I mean," she said, holding Jessica's pajama bottoms so she could step into them, pulling them up around her waist.

"I do. It feels like the day after Christmas," Jessica said, struggling into the top half of her pajamas.

"Yes, that's exactly what it feels like, but it's good to be home isn't it?"

"Yes, it is and I can't wait to tell Johnny all about our adventures."

"Perhaps he's had some adventures of his own while we've been gone."

"I 'spect he has."

Thea undid the ribbon holding up Jessica's hair, let the water out of the tub and hung up the towel. "Go choose a book and I'll be there."

Izzie eventually emerged from the basement, her face quite pink from exertion. Totally immersed in the wonderful music for the past hour, exhilarated by her dancing, pushing herself harder and harder, she couldn't wait until she was old enough to dance en pointe. Fortunately, for the role of Clara, there was no need. Her ballet school's production of *The Nutcracker*, a less sophisticated version of the Boston Ballet's annual show, gave Clara a limited role in the second half. Miss Beauchamp's pupils, in collaboration with dancers from a larger and more sophisticated ballet school, reaped the benefit of spending time with older children further along the path in their ballet careers, capable of dancing the more complicated and strenuous routines. Izzie loved meeting the more experienced dancers. Inspired and excited by just watching them, she couldn't wait to be on stage in front of an audience.

Izzie took herself off to the bathroom, stopping by her bedroom to grab her nightgown, saying hi to Jessica sitting cross-legged on the floor, elbows on her knees, amidst a pile of books, trying to make up her mind which one to choose. Izzie let her be, ran her shower, undoing her knot of silky hair, leaning forward to shake it out. The water felt good, and pleased to be home in familiar surroundings, she hummed contentedly while rubbing the fragrant shampoo into her scalp, squeezing her eyes tightly shut. She wondered how her mom was feeling. It was such a let down for her, and Izzie was sure she must be sad, especially as Miss Ellie had been her friend. She remembered how terribly upset she had been after Lady died, and if her mom was feeling even half as bad as that, then she must be hurting real bad.

Izzie stepped out of the shower, wrapped herself in one of the big fluffy towels hanging on the back of the door, twisted her hair inside a turban, slowly and methodically rubbed herself dry, especially between each toe. Her precious feet needed to be massaged and pampered and rubbed generously with lotion. If she was going to be a professional ballerina, it was important she keep in shape, and while her slender frame and long legs were just right, she was a little concerned about her height. Her mom said she would stop growing when she reached puberty, and although she didn't relish the idea of becoming a woman before her time, it would be all right if it stopped her getting too tall. She ran her hands over her chest, flat as a pancake, giving her hope it would be a while before she'd have to worry about all that stuff. Her mom said she had an old soul and she didn't have a problem with that. She was quite content with who she was. She had just never been one of those giggly, silly girls, and she always gave one hundred percent to each and every activity she undertook, large or small. She wanted to be the best she could be and make her mom proud. After all, she had enough to worry about with Jess and Peter, and Izzie didn't want her worrying about her, too, and if that meant she was old beyond her years—a little girl in a grown-up skin—then that was just the way it was.

She wondered how Peter was making out with Honey. She thought the dog a great addition to the family and she was pleased for her brother. It was tough for him not having a dad. She wished her mom would meet someone really nice. She thought about Grandma and Grandpa and how much she had enjoyed spending time with them and she did hope they'd come and visit. It would be fun to have them around at Christmas, including Mr. Blunt, and it made her sad to think of him being all by himself without Miss Ellie. Too much sadness she decided, busily cleaning up the bathroom before heading off to bed.

CHAPTER ELEVEN

❦

SATURDAY—4:30 PM

After their very successful shopping expedition, MaryAnn and the boys stopped at the Chamberlins' house to feed Smokey just as it started to snow. Both Ian and Johnny lingered in the driveway, holding out their arms, turning in circles, sticking out their tongues to catch the snowflakes. Johnny, absolutely fascinated by the fact the snow just sat on top of his new jacket rather than sinking into the fabric, stretched his arms out sideways. "Look, Mom, I can blow the snow right off!"

"So, I see. We shall have to buy you snow pants as well if this keeps up."

"Then we could make snow angels without getting cold."

"You and Ian are my snow angels," she said, gathering them to her just as Jim's truck rolled into the driveway. MaryAnn loved snow, even when it was inconvenient. She felt a momentary pang that the boys wouldn't have a yard in which to make a snowman, but then there was the park and Jim's yard, problem solved. And there he was, large as life, walking towards them. Johnny pulled from her embrace and ran to him. "Mr. Hudson, look at my new coat."

"You look very handsome, young man, and it looks nice and warm."

"It is, it is, and Mommy said we could get snow pants so we can make snow angels," Johnny said, moving his arms up and down frantically.

"Is that right?" Jim looked up to see MaryAnn standing in the snow, with tendrils of her silvery blonde hair escaping from her hood. "The scarlet suits you," he said. "You look beautiful." Dragging his eyes away, he glanced over at Ian. "You made a good choice with the dark blue. That's one of my favorite colors."

"Thank you, sir," Ian said, a slow smile creasing his face.

"Come on you knuckleheads, let's get inside." Warmed by Jim's compliment, MaryAnn retrieved the keys from beneath the flowerpot and unlocked the door.

"Jim, I'm a bit worried about the snow. I'm wondering whether the boys and I should just go straight home."

"Don't even think about it. I listened to the forecast and there's only going to be a couple of inches. I thought perhaps we could walk into town, have dinner at Mario's Restaurant, after which you could show me the apartment, and if you and the boys don't want to walk back, I could come get the truck and go back and pick you up. How does that sound?"

MaryAnn wasn't going to argue; the look of delight on her sons' faces a joy to see. Being with Jim made anything possible, besides which she wanted to spend time with him, the tantalizing idea of a meal in a restaurant too much of a temptation to resist. She just didn't want this day to end.

"Would you mind if I made a couple of phone calls?"

"You go ahead. We'll go into the living room and see what we can find on TV."

"Thanks, it won't take long."

She unhooked the receiver from the wall, called her landlord with fingers crossed, hoping there would be some shred of humanity in his scrawny frame, but she doubted it. He answered on the third ring. "Yup," he said.

"Mr. Murdoch, it's MaryAnn Wilkinson. I hope you're well."

"I've bin better. What's up?" he said, coughing wetly down the phone.

She swallowed and nervously bit her lip. "I wanted to let you know I won't be renewing the lease on the house in January."

"You could've given me a bit more notice. I've got no way of rentin' it this time o' year."

"I know and I'm sorry. It wasn't planned."

"No good bein' sorry. Don't help me. You'll have to pay for December."

"I realize that, but if you could send me back my security deposit . . ."

"I'll have to think on that. Technically, you should give me three months' notice. That was the agreement."

"I know and I'm sorry, but I've been a good tenant haven't I?" She was clutching at straws, knowing he had the upper hand.

"I suppose ye haven't asked for much, but what's the point of an agreement if ye don't stick to it?"

MaryAnn attempted to pull an ace out of the hole. "It would help to give the boys a nice Christmas. That extra five hundred dollars would make all the difference to us."

"I'll think on it. When are ye movin' out?"

"In about a week. As soon as I can get a truck arranged. I'll call you when I know."

"Goodnight, Mrs. Wilkinson," and he hung up.

Miserable old curmudgeon and it serves him right if he can't find any more tenants. Nobody in their right mind would live in that dreadful hole unless they were desperate. She wasn't that disappointed about the security deposit because he was right about the three months' notice and his penny-pinching nature just wouldn't allow him to be generous. He definitely needed a dose of Christmases past and scary ghosts—she only wished.

She dialed Will's number, hoping she'd picked a good time, the diner slow because of the snow. "Will, it's MaryAnn. Do you have a minute?"

"Sure. What's up?"

"I have a huge favor to ask."

"Oh yeah, and what's that?"

"I was wondering whether you know someone with a truck who could help me move."

"Why don't you ask Jim?"

She lowered her voice so Jim wouldn't hear her. "Because I don't want him to see where we live. I don't want him to have a mental picture of the boys and me in that dreadful house. I do have some pride, you know. And don't think he hasn't offered."

"I'm sure he has, but I'd be happy to help you. When are you planning on doing this and where are you movin' to?"

"As soon as possible and we're moving into town into an apartment over one of the stores."

"Won't that be a bit of tight fit?"

"No worse than living in two rooms, and besides which, it's a beautiful space and it's warm!"

"All right, MaryAnn, I won't ask you any more questions. Let me make a couple of phone calls and I'll get back to you."

"Thanks, Will. We should be home by about eight o'clock and I owe you one."

"No, you don't. I'm just happy you asked because I know what an ornery person you are sometimes."

"Takes one to know one."

"Hah! Bye, MaryAnn," and he was gone.

She went off to the living room, found Jim and the boys all sitting together watching a rerun of *Friends*. "There's not much on," he said, "but I thought this would be fairly harmless."

"It's fine," she said. "I'm ready to go if you are." Jim turned off the TV, Ian pushed himself off the couch, Johnny picked up Smokey and carried her to the kitchen, dangling from his arms; she made no attempt to escape. Talking away to her, in a world of his own, he put her down on the floor, no harm done. Huddled together in the hallway, enjoying being together, they laughed as they bumped into each other, tying shoes and putting on coats. MaryAnn, making sure Johnny's hat was down over his ears, Ian old enough to take care of himself, pulled up her hood. She was ready for anything.

"Are we on a 'venture?" Johnny asked once they were out on the sidewalk, reaching out his hands, grabbing one of MaryAnn's and one of Jim's. Much to his delight, they swung him forward, letting him land, and then doing it all over again.

"We should all sing the song I taught you yesterday. Do you remember?" Jim said.

"'Course," Johnny said.

"Ready, gang? We need to puff out our chests and get marching," and Jim started to sing in his deep, and surprisingly good, baritone. *"The Grand Old Duke of York he had ten thousand men. He marched them up to the top of the hill and he marched them down again. When they were up, they were up, and when they were down, they were down, but when they were only half way up, they were neither up nor down."*

MaryAnn's quick mind and phenomenal memory soon got the hang of it. Her voice rang out pure and clear, in tune with Jim while they marched through the snow, snug and warm in their new winter coats. Jim swung Johnny up onto his shoulders, and the little boy sat resting his mittened hands on top of Jim's hat. "I can nearly touch the top of the street lamps," he said.

"Is that right?" Jim said, wrapping his arms around Johnny's legs so he wouldn't fall.

They walked for about fifteen minutes, the snow falling steadily, catching on eyelashes, covering the brick sidewalk, creating a magical world. They passed Harry's Hardware. "We're not competitors," Jim said. "In actual fact, we complement each other. Harry carries fancier goods. He has a whole kitchen section with every imaginable gadget and we have nothing like that." The lights from the Country Store shone brightly, in stark contrast to the darkness of the adjacent real estate agent and fish store, both shut up for the day. The old-fashioned street lamps lit their way. MaryAnn walked in front with Ian, her arm hooked through his, keeping pace with each other, every now and again doing a little skip when they lost the rhythm, Ian's heart doing little flip-flops of happiness. He kept glancing at his mother and she was smiling, her big pale blue eyes appearing to sparkle with the snow.

"Where's the apartment?" Jim asked. MaryAnn and the boys pointed up to the windows above the empty store. "I can't wait to see it."

They crossed the street. Jim gently lowered Johnny to the ground before opening the door to Mario's, and the pungent smell of herbs and garlic wafted into their nostrils as soon as they stepped inside. It wasn't a fancy restaurant, but welcoming and homely; the tables set with red-checkered cloths and bright red napkins. The glasses and the silverware sparkled in the light of the candles and MaryAnn couldn't wait to sit down and eat.

A large wood-framed sign on a pedestal asked them to wait to be seated, and despite the weather, the restaurant was busy. They hung their coats on the rack just inside the door while the hostess searched for a vacant table, running her scarlet fingernail down the list in front of her. Shown to a booth by a young and energetic waitress with a mass of red curly hair tied back from her face, she recognized Jim. He asked after her family; she said they were all doing well. She looked at Johnny, asked him if he would like a booster seat to which he replied, "Yes, please." She scurried away returning a moment later with the seat in one hand and a tray with four glasses of water in the other. "Wait 'til I tell Manny you're here. He'll be out in a flash," she said, placing the waters on the table and making sure they each had a straw. "Can I get you anything to drink besides the water?" They all said water was just fine, and she was gone, leaving them with the menus, which to MaryAnn's dismay, were large, and when she glanced at the meals, expensive. She had already blown her budget for the day, had no way of paying and sat in worried silence.

Jim, sitting opposite her, his uncanny ability to read her mind, said, "I have coupons. What would you boys like to eat? Manny makes a mean pizza."

"*Si, si*, the best pizza in town," and there was Manny in his fake Italian glory putting on a show for the boys. He stood looking at the four of them, plump hands resting on his ample belly, his apron stretched to the max; his once dark and luxurious hair, much to his distress, now thinning and gray; his nose a blob of molded dough, under which he boasted a neatly trimmed mustache. He smiled to reveal two rows of pearly white teeth, too perfect to be real. "*Benvenuto*, welcome to my *Ristorante*. The meal, how you say, is on zee house, per *la casa*. Mr. Hudson he has made many kindnesses to me and this is way I say *grazie*, so you look at menu and order what you like. No worry about *denaro*. Manny generous man," and he spread his arms wide to prove his generosity.

MaryAnn suspected a conspiracy, but she didn't care. She thought Manny quite extraordinary and both Ian and Johnny were enthralled by the spectacle of this larger than life character putting on this show for them. He gave a little bow. "I go to the *cucina* now and soon you will send orders and I will prepare the most *deliziosa* food for you." He put his fingers to his lips and kissed them. "*A presto*," he said, walking away from them, waving to the other patrons, greeting them with a flamboyant, "*Buona sera*," as he went.

Johnny looked at Jim and said, "Mr. Hudson, this has been the most 'mazing day."

"I agree," Ian said. "But I have a question," pausing to take a sip from his water. "If the owner is called Manny, why is the restaurant called Mario's?"

"That's all part of the mystery. Manny doesn't have an Italian bone in his body. He calls himself Salvatore, but his real last name is probably something like Smith. He pretends Mario was his father, but he's a fictitious character too. He does know Italian though and loves the language. He also goes to Italy for holidays and has learned all about authentic Italian cooking, so I suggest we choose something from the menu and in the meantime here's our waitress with a basket of bread to keep the wolf from the door."

MaryAnn threw caution to the wind and ordered Sole Florentine; the boys asked for pizza, and Jim chose the Chicken Parmesan. The bread was indeed delicious—warm and fragrant, with butter to spread and olive oil to dip. She took a piece and placed it on her side plate, pulling it apart with her fingers, dipping it into the peppery and garlicky olive oil. It was heavenly. She declined Jim's offer of wine, deciding she was relaxed enough without it. She helped Johnny spread some butter on his bread and asked Ian whether he wanted to try the olive oil, but he shook his head, taking a pat of butter instead. "Mr. Hudson, can I ask you another question?"

"Sure, go ahead."

"What made you decide to be a volunteer fireman?"

"Do you rescue cats from trees?" Johnny asked.

"In answer to Ian's question, I kinda followed in my father's footsteps, although he was reluctant to sign the necessary papers because I was only eighteen and, Johnny, we don't rescue cats from trees. That's more of a job for the police with just a regular ladder. You don't really need a fire truck to do that. I hope you're not disappointed."

"No, not really."

"Was your dad in the fire department for a long time?"

"He stayed in until he was forty and then he had to stop because his health wasn't good. You have to be fit and it's not a job if you scare easily because it can be difficult at times."

MaryAnn, sensing Jim was struggling with what he should tell the boys, was much relieved when their meals magically appeared. The waitress placed the pizza on a four-legged metal trivet to keep the heat away from the table and gave each of the boys a plate. MaryAnn breathed in the garlicky odor of the succulent roll of fish, resting on a nest of golden-crusted mashed potatoes, surrounded by spinach. Jim's Chicken Parmesan was swimming in sauce and the smell of the cheese and seasonings wafted across the table. She reached over and took a piece of pizza for Johnny and left Ian to help himself, warning both boys that it was hot. Her fish was done to perfection; chewing slowly, she savored every fragrant mouthful. She looked at Jim and smiled. "Thank you for bringing us here."

Manny appeared as if from nowhere and said, "You like?"

"We like. This is one of the most delicious meals I've ever eaten," MaryAnn said, giving Manny one of her lovely smiles.

"*Buona, buona.* You make Manny one *uomo felice*, happy man. I leave you in peace now. *Buonanotte*, and you come back soon."

Jim spoke for them all. "We will and thank you, Manny, very much."

The rest of the meal passed in pleasurable silence. Jim asked for a box for the remainder of the pizza and left a hefty tip for the waitress. The boys and MaryAnn made quick trips to the bathroom, meeting Jim at the coat rack. Standing behind her, holding her coat, he lingered a little longer than necessary, enjoying their closeness. The boys peered through the doorway, fogging up the glass. "I think it's stopped snowing," Johnny said.

"See, the weatherman was right, and let's go see this apartment of yours," Jim said.

"Unfortunately, I don't have a key for the store, so we will have to go round the back. There's an alleyway just before the Scrapbook Nest so we can go through there," MaryAnn said.

Jim picked Johnny up, holding him firmly. Johnny wrapped his legs around Jim's waist. "You're getting heavy, young man."

"It's all the yummy food I ate today," he said, putting his arms around Jim's neck.

They made their way down the moonlit alleyway, watching their footing, huddled close together, the boys jumpy and afraid of the inky shadows. "I should have brought a flashlight," MaryAnn said.

Jim glanced up and said, "We have heaven's flashlights. Just look at all those stars."

They rounded the corner, noticed a light by the door, which didn't appear to be working. "Perhaps the bulb's blown," MaryAnn said.

"It's probably on a sensor," Jim said, setting Johnny down. "I think we need to dance up and down and clap our hands." The kids, always looking for an opportunity to be silly, jigged about, giggling helplessly, and MaryAnn and Jim joined in. The lamp came alive. After a little fumbling, MaryAnn found the keyhole; still laughing they jostled their way through the door and into the hallway. They made their way up the stairs, waited on the landing while MaryAnn, yet again, fumbled with the keys. She flung open the door, flipped on the light switch, wondering whether the apartment would now be a disappointment. Would she regret her earlier impulsiveness? She didn't think so, but she was tentative in her question to Jim. "What do you think?"

"I like, and I can see why you fell in love with it." He walked into the kitchen and ran his hand down the smoothness of one the cabinets. "They've done a great job with the renovations. I'm impressed."

"There's even a heated floor in the bathroom. Can you believe that?"

"Right now, I'd believe anything. You've turned my life upside down. But are you sure this is really what you want to do? You know my offer still stands."

MaryAnn turned away from Jim and walked towards the window. The boys had gone off to explore the bedrooms and she could hear them discussing which bedroom they should choose. She put her hands on the radiator, disappointed it was only lukewarm, only radiating just enough heat to take the chill off the room. She felt, rather than heard, Jim come up behind her. "Have I upset you?"

"I'm afraid, Jim."

"Not of me, I hope."

She turned to face him, her arms hanging limply by her sides. "No, I could never be afraid of you. Afraid of losing you, yes. Afraid to make another commitment, only for it to end in loss, yes. I couldn't believe how lucky I was when I met Sam and I felt the same when I met you, but what if I bring you bad luck? Sam's parents still blame me for his death, at least his mother does."

Jim made no attempt to touch her and MaryAnn was grateful. They both knew they wouldn't be able to control their emotions and neither of them wanted to scare the boys. "Now's not the time to talk about this. Let me just say we can't predict the future. Life is one great big gamble and, yes, the stakes are high, but we're only going to be half alive if we don't take the risk."

"I know," she said, giving him a watery smile. "I didn't want the day to end like this," and she looked down to see Johnny staring up at her. He glared at Jim. "Did you make my mommy cry?"

MaryAnn made a quick recovery. "No, Johnny, Mr. Hudson didn't make me cry. He would never do that. I think it's time for us to be heading home as we all have some packing to do. Did you choose which bedroom you and Ian would like?"

"Not really," and MaryAnn realized how very tired he must be.

"MaryAnn, would you like me to go get the truck so you and the boys don't have to walk?"

"No, we'll be fine. We can carry Johnny. How about you, Ian, can you make it back?"

"Sure."

Sad and deflated, they walked back downstairs and out into the alley-way. MaryAnn had a dreadful lump in her throat that wouldn't go away. She and Jim needed time to themselves without the boys. The emotions she had stuffed for so long kept resurfacing and she felt raw and vulnerable. Jim carried Johnny and she heard her son whisper in his ear, "Sorry I was mad at you."

"You can be mad at me anytime."

"You're not cross with me, then."

"No, Johnny, I'm not cross." The little boy wrapped his arms tightly around Jim's neck. Jim hugged him close. There was so much love between them, between all of them, in fact, but they just didn't know what to do with it. MaryAnn tucked her arm through Ian's and said, "Okay, champ?"

"I'm okay, Mom. A bit tired."

"We all are. It's been quite a day."

They were all surprised to see Thea's rental car in the driveway and her house ablaze with lights. "Uh-oh, I thought she wasn't coming back until Monday," MaryAnn said. "We'd better go knock on the door and offer her an explanation."

Jim hung back once they reached the bottom of the porch steps. "Why don't you go talk to Thea. I think I'll just head off home," he said, his tone somber.

MaryAnn was at a loss. She didn't want him to leave without resolving the tension between them. She knew she wouldn't get a wink of sleep, and she suspected neither would he. Thea saved the day by flinging open the front door and saying, "Look at the lot of you. Why don't you come inside; there's someone I want you to meet."

"Jim has to head home, but if the boys could come in for a minute, that would be great." Thea wasn't stupid so she hustled the boys into the hallway and closed the door.

Jim held out his hand. "Would you please come and sit in the truck with me for a minute?" MaryAnn followed meekly. He opened the passenger door for her and she sat sideways on the seat so she could bang her shoes together to get off the snow. She swung her legs inside the cab, closed the door and watched the snow slide down the window. She shivered. Jim sat in silence, making no attempt to touch her, unsure of himself, taking his time and choosing his words with care. "I'm sorry if I upset you. My insides are tied in knots, and I don't know what to do."

It was all too much for MaryAnn. She could no longer hold back her tears, the lump in her throat threatening to choke her, she forced out the words. "We need a good roll in the hay, don't we?"

"That would certainly help, but it's more than that."

"I know."

"How is it going to be better if you and the boys move to the apartment? I love you. Now I've said it, so there's no turning back. This probably isn't the most romantic marriage proposal you've ever had, but would you please put me out of my misery and marry me?"

MaryAnn sat with tears coursing down her cheeks, twisting her wedding band. She had never taken it off from the day Sam had slid it gently down her finger. Now she slowly removed it, felt the engraving on the inside of the band for the last time and put the ring in her pocket. She swallowed, fumbled for a tissue, wiped her face and blew her nose. "Yes, Jim Hudson, I will marry you, but there are two people we have to ask first before it's official."

Jim turned to look at her with tears in his eyes. "Look what you've reduced me to," and he leaned over and kissed her. "Does that mean you and the boys will move in with me?"

"Yes, we will, but there's to be no hanky-panky until after the wedding—separate rooms and all that."

"Yes, ma'am, I'll take you on any terms I can get."

"Let's go rescue Thea from our rug rats."

"Oh, so now they're *our* rug rats."

"You bet and I'm still not having you help me move. That is one last thing I have to do on my own."

Jim held up his hands in mock surrender. "I give up and I suspect this isn't the first or the last time I won't win." He turned off the engine and they reluctantly left the intimacy of the cab. Jim tucked her arm within his own and they retraced their steps to Thea's front door in a much lighter frame of mind. Peter, dressed in his pajamas, opened the door, a large teddy bear of a dog glued to his side. "This is Honey," he said, "and she will shake paws with you if you hold out your hand." Jim hunkered down and took hold of Honey's lifted paw. "Peter, she's a beautiful dog. Is she yours?"

"Yes, she was an early birthday present. I'm sure my mom will tell you all about it. Izzie and Jessica are asleep, and they're going to be mad in the morning—especially Jess—to think they missed you."

Thea appeared with Ian and Johnny in tow, expressions of concern creasing their faces. Johnny ran to MaryAnn and clung to her; Ian hung back awkwardly, his eyes darting between his mother and Jim. She looked down at Johnny, held out her hand to Ian, asked Thea if she could use her living room and said, "Come with me."

"What's going on?" Ian asked, slumping down in the chair by the fireplace, resting his head in his hands, his elbows on his knees. Johnny—a limpet, refusing to be pried from MaryAnn—sat next to her on the couch.

"Mr. Hudson has asked me to marry him," she said, waiting for their reaction.

Johnny perked up immediately. "Does that mean we can move into his house?"

MaryAnn ignored his question, asked Ian, "How do you feel about this, champ?"

He rubbed his hands over his face. MaryAnn sat quietly. "It's going to take some getting used to," he said.

"Yes, it is."

"Do you love Mr. Hudson?" Ian asked.

"I do. Not the way I loved your dad. Nothing could ever replace that, but Mr. Hudson is a generous and warmhearted man. We will have a good life together. You do like him don't you?" she asked, fighting back the tears, resisting the temptation to go over to Ian and take him in her arms.

Johnny, after his initial burst of enthusiasm, looked at his brother, and out of kindness, said, "It will be okay, Ian."

"I know, but it's just that I miss Dad so much."

"We all do," MaryAnn said, "And I won't marry Mr. Hudson if it makes you unhappy."

"It doesn't make me unhappy, just all mixed up inside."

"I'm all mixed up inside too, so what should we do? It's your call."

Ian sat for a moment. MaryAnn held her breath, her happiness hanging by a thread. Finally, staring down at the floor, he begrudgingly said, "I guess, it's okay with me, and if Mr. Hudson makes you happy, that's what's important."

"And don't forget we're going to build a tree house," Johnny said, his five-year-old mind focusing on more practical things, not understanding why his brother was putting up such a fuss.

Ian brightened considerably, and remembering the fun time spent with Mr. Hudson and Johnny, he switched gears as only kids can do. "I'm okay, Mom, I really am. Sorry I gave you a hard time."

"You didn't. It's important to be honest and respect each other's feelings, and Mr. Hudson isn't going to get in the way of that. I want both of you to come to me right away, anytime, if there's anything you want to talk about, just as we've always done."

"Even in the middle of the night?" Johnny asked.

"Especially in the middle of the night. That's when our fears are worse. Ready to go now?"

<hr />

Abandoned in the hallway by MaryAnn, Thea raised her eyebrows and looked at Jim. "You and MaryAnn look like the cat that caught the canary. Is what I think is going on, going on, if that makes any sense?"

Jim nodded, looked awkward; twisted his hat in his hands. "You don't mind do you?"

Thea didn't hesitate in her response. "I'm absolutely thrilled. It's the best news I've heard since Nan and Stanley's engagement."

"It's rather taken us by surprise. It's going to be an adjustment for all of us."

"The boys will come around if that's what you're worried about."

"I know Johnny is already on board, but I am concerned about Ian," Jim said, on tenterhooks, his eyes on the living room door.

"Don't be. Just be yourself. Don't try too hard and everything will fall into place. Kids' antennae are permanently tuned to anything fake. If you are the genuine article, and I firmly believe you are, you have absolutely nothing to worry about. Those boys are lucky to have you."

"Thanks, Thea, for straightening me out. Makes a lot of sense. Sorry we barged in on you like this. You must be tired."

"It's okay. I'm used to the unexpected."

"How did things go in Massachusetts?"

"Let's just say, we won't be moving," she said, the finality of her tone putting a stop to any further questions. The silence hung like a heavy cloud between them; Jim cleared his throat.

"I'm almost afraid to broach the subject, but what's happening with Kenny these days?" Thea asked.

"Still healing, I guess. I haven't seen hide nor hair since I let him go."

"Your patience finally ran out, then?"

"Yup. His attempted break in here was the last straw."

Thea, about to voice her fears, lost the chance when the living room door opened. She watched MaryAnn nod at Jim. "All is well," she said.

Thea sensed the conversation hadn't been an easy one. Johnny yawned, Ian appeared subdued; Jim stayed where he was leaning against the wall, still worrying away at his hat. MaryAnn broke the silence. "We have to be going. Johnny is running on fumes. It's been quite a day."

Huddled in the hallway, the Wilkinsons donned their much-admired new coats. Jim shrugged into his jacket and re-laced his boots. MaryAnn said she would call her. Thea offered to help her pack, hoping she might just take her up on the offer, giving them both the opportunity to get to know each other better.

Jim went over to talk to Peter, hanging back in the kitchen doorway, staying out of the way. "I think our families are going to be spending a lot of time together and I will definitely have you, your mom, and the girls over for dinner. You can bring Honey because I'm sure you won't want to leave her behind. She's a fine dog and we'll have to introduce her to Carrie. A walk on the beach with both the dogs would be good, wouldn't it?"

"It sure would, Mr. Hudson."

"Goodnight, Peter."

After they'd all said their goodbyes, Thea stood at the door watching the Wilkinsons and Jim walk down the driveway. She waved to them, closed the door and turned to her son. "Well, what do you think about what just happened?"

"Is Mr. Hudson going to marry Mrs. Wilkinson? Is that why she took Ian and Johnny off to the living room?"

"Yes. Do you and Ian ever talk about his dad?"

"He's mentioned him a couple of times. He was eight when his dad died so he remembers him. He doesn't say much and I think it will be harder for him than for Johnny, but I'm sure he's pleased to see his mom so happy. It was awful quick, though."

"How does it make you feel?"

"A little bit jealous. Mr. Hudson is a very nice man and he'll make a great dad, but having Honey helps me a lot and I'm so pleased for the Wilkinsons. They need some good luck."

"I like MaryAnn and I believe I've found a friend. It feels good because with Nan so far away, it will be great to have someone to spend time with. We all need at least one good friend and I know you've found one in Ian." Thea paused, mentioning friends bringing Ellie to mind. She looked at Peter. "I can't believe we're still standing in the hallway; your feet must be freezing."

"To tell the truth, I hadn't even noticed. Too much going on, but now I'm going to bed."

"Can I have a hug?" Thea asked. Caught off guard, he stepped into her embrace. "You've grown over the weekend," she said, placing her hands on his upper arms, holding him away from her. "You're as tall as me."

"Must have been all that turkey!"

"Thank you for being such a help with your navigating. We did well didn't we, despite the circumstances?"

"We did. We got through another Chamberlin trauma."

"At least this one wasn't my fault, and hopefully, my track record will improve." She smiled, ruffled the top of his head. "Now off to bed with you young man, I have phone calls to make."

Thea, in a much better frame of mind than she had been earlier, actually looked forward to making her promised phone calls. She decided some of Jim and MaryAnn's happiness had rubbed off on her and she wasn't about to waste the little pool of sunshine they had left in her hallway. Calling her parents first, her dad answered on the third ring. "Hello," he said.

"Hi, Dad."

"Can I ask you something?"

"Sure. Fire away."

"After you left today, your mom and I realized how much we've missed by not being closer to you and the kids. I know we're not getting any younger, but we were wondering what you thought of the idea of us moving to Maine."

Thea sat down on the nearest kitchen chair. "You've certainly taken me by surprise. I think it's a wonderful idea. I was hoping you'd come visit, but having you close by permanently would be fantastic. Is Mom on board with this too?"

"Yes, she is. I've never seen her so excited. And there's something else."

"You are certainly full of surprises."

"We had a visit from a young man today by the name of Christopher Morrison . . ."

"And who is he?"

"Now, don't interrupt your old dad."

"Sorry."

"Do you remember waiting on a man in Aladdin's Cave? He said you helped him with the purchase of a pendant for his sister and choosing a birthday card."

"Yes, I do remember him. He had the greenest eyes I've ever seen."

"He would like to get to know you. He's written you a letter, and I'll put it in the mail first thing Monday morning. It was his idea in order to maintain your privacy. This way he has none of your details, and it will be up to you whether you contact him or not. I will tell you, both your mom and I liked him very much. He was most considerate and when he noticed my sore ankle offered to help us out and gave me his phone number so we could call if we needed anything."

"Are you matchmaking, Dad?"

"Of course not."

"Well, I'm intrigued and once I've read Mr. Christopher Morrison's letter, I will make up my own mind. Now, do you have any more surprises up your sleeve?"

"I think that's it. So are you really okay about us moving? We don't want to be a burden. We'd like to put the house on the market right away before we get cold feet and we hoped you could find us a rental when the time is right."

"I can certainly do that and you and Mom could never be a burden. The kids will be thrilled. Did you call Mr. Blunt?"

"I did. He's going to stop by with a list of folks for me to phone. He said it would take the pressure off him and Dorothy because poor Robert is in bad shape and of little help."

"Thanks, Dad. That's really kind of you and I'll offer to do the same thing. I'm sure Ellie knew lots of people. I'll go call him now and thanks for your news. It's giving me something to look forward to and I sorely needed that. To tell you the truth, I'm feeling letdown as you can well imagine. Say hi to Mom for me and I'll talk to you soon. Goodnight."

"Goodnight, Thea, sweet dreams."

Thea, unaware she was still holding the telephone receiver, startled by the annoying beeping noises, stood up and replaced it in its holder. Thrilled by her father's news, she went into planning mode. Hopefully, she'd be able to find a ground-floor apartment in town. Of course, it all depended on how long it took her parents to sell the house, but she was excited at the prospect. Life, with its never-ending unpredictability, sometimes turned up trumps, and despite the tragedy of Ellie's death, something good had come out of the trip after all.

Eventually finding the scrap of paper on which Mr. Blunt had written his number, she was disappointed when she got a busy signal. She dialed what she still thought of as Ellie's number, wondering whether Robert would actually pick up. She was about to hang up when she heard his sad "Hello."

"Robert, it's Thea. How's it going?"

"Not so bad, I guess. How was your drive home?"

"Tedious, especially the last hour because of the snow. Is it snowing there?"

"A little. How's Honey doing?"

"She seems to have settled and her meeting with Smokey the cat was uneventful. No flying fur, thank goodness."

"*Bon*, that's very good. I miss her and I miss you too."

Thea, taken by surprise, unable to lie about missing him, out of kindness, hoping it would never happen, said, "You'll have to come visit when things have settled down so you can see how Honey is doing."

"I'd like that."

"Do you need me to do anything for you? I could make some phone calls."

"I think Dorothy and Theodore have taken care of that, but if I think of anything, I'll give you a call."

"Please do, and take care of yourself. I'll talk to you soon."

"*Au revoir*, Thea."

"Bye, Robert."

This time she firmly placed the receiver in its cradle and made a cup of tea before trying Mr. Blunt again. She wished she could have been more of a consolation to Robert, but she just didn't have it in her, and had no wish to be sidetracked by a relationship doomed to fail. She had neither the will nor the wherewithal to be dragged down by his guilt, a reminder of her own, and she hoped he would be smart enough to seek professional help. Still in a state of disbelief over the loss of Ellie, she'd had no time to analyze her feelings. Right now she was light-headed with fatigue after sleeping fitfully last night, and drained of energy by the drive home. She sipped her tea and tried Mr. Blunt's number one more time. A female voice answered.

"Is this Dorothy?" Thea asked.

"It is."

"This is Thea Chamberlin. I told Mr. Blunt I'd call after I got home. Did he tell you about me?"

"He did. Hold on a second and I'll get him for you," and she was gone before Thea could say thank you.

"Hello, Miss Thea."

"Sorry I didn't call earlier, but it's been a little crazy to say the least. How's it going?"

"Better now that Dorothy is here. She is going to organize a local memorial service. We're not quite sure where yet, but we may do it at Aladdin's Cave. It will be an opportunity for all of us to say goodbye to Ellie. Since we started calling people, the phone's been ringing off the hook. It's very comforting for me to know how much folks care. How are you feeling?"

"I'm exhausted and nothing has sunk in yet. Do you need me to make some phone calls for you? There must be quite a list."

"I appreciate the offer but Dorothy has it well in hand, and I'm going to give a list to your dad in the morning, so it seems as though everyone is rallying around. It's Robert who worries me."

"I know. I talked to him briefly, but I don't think I was much help. Will he or any of Ellie's family come to the memorial service?"

"I mentioned it to him, but he has no interest and said the family would be unwilling to travel, so there's nothing more we can do, my dear. He'll be leaving soon, and once he is back with his family, I am sure he will begin to feel better."

"I do hope so. Are you okay?"

"It's good to be busy and I have to keep reminding myself of how hard Ellie struggled to get better, but the hand of fate was cruel. We could spend the rest of our lives asking why somebody as gracious and selfless as Ellie should be taken when there is so much evil in the world, but it wouldn't do us any good, would it? Of course I miss her, but I'm thankful she's not suffering any more."

"Are you *sure* there's nothing I can do?"

"Not that I can think of right now, but I will phone you if I need you and I haven't forgotten about coming to visit. It's a bright spot on my horizon."

"That makes me happy, and as I said before, I'm sure I can find you a ride. I'll give you a call in a couple of days and you know where I am if you need me."

"I do. Goodnight, Thea."

"Goodnight, Mr. Blunt, and make sure you take care of yourself."

"I will."

She put her tea mug in the sink, turned off the light and went to say goodnight to Peter. He was sitting up in bed reading; Honey, to Thea's surprise, was lying in her bed. She thumped her tail but made no attempt to get up. "Looks as though Honey is out for the count," she said, sitting down on the end of Peter's bed.

"She's been very quiet. I do hope she's all right."

"I'm sure she's just exhausted and you'd better get a good night's sleep because I'm sure she's going to wake you up bright and early."

Peter just pulled a face and Thea wondered how conscientious he was going to be about getting up earlier in the mornings to take Honey out when it was dark and cold, especially before school. They would have to work out a routine, but she was much too tired to think about it now.

Thea coaxed Honey out of her bed for a final pit stop and with a little persuading, the dog eventually dragged herself out of her bed, stretched and yawned. "I know how you feel. Come." She tapped her thigh and the dog padded along behind her, sat waiting while Thea thrust her feet into her boots and put on her jacket. She stood outside the back door looking up at the stars, breathing in the cold ocean-scented Maine air, pleased to be home. It was so quiet and still, just the odd car going down the road, an owl hooting somewhere in the distant pine trees. She watched Honey by the light of the moon wandering around the yard, leaving paw prints in the snow. Thea hugged herself, accepted the loss of Ellie, made easier because they had spent so little time together. They had lost touch, never turned to each other for help, her love for Ellie less intense, made her death easier to bear. Perhaps Izzie was right in her fanciful belief that Ellie was one of the bright stars hanging low in the inky black sky. Honey walked over and sat by her side, nudging Thea's gloved hand with her nose. "You know, Honey, Ellie was very wise when she asked us to look after you. We need you as much as you need us. It's much easier for me to love you than it is for me to love a man." Was Honey their therapy dog? Even though she wasn't trained to turn lights on and off, or help people in wheelchairs, Thea decided each member of her family had his or her special needs, so she rubbed Honey's ears, looked up, and whispered, "Thank you," to the biggest star she could find.

CHAPTER TWELVE

~~~~~~~~~~~~

SATURDAY EVENING

After the excitement of the day, MaryAnn's euphoria threatened to desert her as soon as she arrived in her driveway, but she held onto it, grasped it with both hands and refused to let it slip away. Back to her current reality, the dismal rental a reminder of the past three years of putting one leaden foot in front of the other in order to survive, but now with the prospect of a bright future, she allowed herself to hate the house. Downtrodden and miserable, with its sagging porch and broken railings, the curtainless windows staring back at her like sightless eyes, she decided how right she had been to stick to her guns in not allowing Jim to see where she and the boys lived.

Opening the backdoor of the car she found both Ian and Johnny fast asleep. Tugging Johnny's blanket aside, undoing the belt of his car seat, wrapping him as best she could, she lifted him into her arms. She gently nudged Ian. "Sorry to wake you, but we're home and I don't have enough arms to carry you too."

"It's okay, Mom," he said, getting out of the car, stumbling with weariness. Trudging across the driveway, the snow sliding over the sides of their unsuitable shoes, MaryAnn said, "Ian, could you please get my keys?" His hand inside MaryAnn's pocketbook, he rummaged around, eventually finding them right at the very bottom under her wallet.

Enveloped by the air in the hallway—cold, unwelcoming and damp— she was glad of her new coat. Ian, not wanting to be parted from his, hung it over the back of the chair in his bedroom. Johnny, out for the count, didn't even come to when she sat him on the toilet. Had he been awake, he would have told her she was "making him pee like a girl!" She tucked him up in bed, kissed him on a cheek still cold from the night air, relieved to find he was breathing peacefully, his little lungs working normally, despite all the time they had spent outside today. Convinced Johnny's well-being the result of all the laughter, the singing, all the good food they had eaten that day, she counted her blessings—a welcome change from all her usual worrying about her shortcomings as a provider for her boys. She put her head around Ian's door, thinking he might like to talk, but he was fast asleep so she whispered, "Sweet dreams," pulled his door shut, and headed downstairs.

Removing her coat, she gathered it to her, pressing her face into the fabric, breathing in the newness. She left it hanging in the hallway, a splash of color, in contrast to the stark green wall. "I think you're my good luck charm," she said. "My cloak of enchantment to give me courage." Always a lover of fairytales, it had been easy to get caught up in the magic of today's falling snow sprinkling down on them like fairy dust, but of course, like all good fairytales, there was a modicum of fear to keep her on her toes.

She turned up the thermostat in the kitchen, unhooked the receiver off the wall and called Jim's cell phone. "Hi, future wife," he said, his voice light with happiness and satisfaction, a battle won.

"Hi," she said, suddenly shy, her commitment a huge leap of faith.

"Are the boys asleep?"

"Yup, absolutely dead to the world. Thank you for taking us out to dinner and thank you for sparing my pride, but I'm sorry, I saw right through your little ploy."

"I'm not saying a word."

"I'm assuming you went back and settled up with Manny on your way home."

"Not telling."

"Okay, I give up, and I'm going to go now because I want to start packing. Unfortunately, I'm not very organized so I shall have to make a superhuman effort to stay on task."

"I have plenty of room here where you can store your stuff until you decide what you want to keep. There's a nice dry apartment over the garage which I was very tempted to tell you about, but I knew you would turn it down."

"You're absolutely right, but because of my wish to be independent, I am now stuck with a six month lease on an apartment I don't need!"

"Serves you right," he said, chuckling down the phone.

"Can I go now?"

"If you must. Please call me in the morning and we'll decide what we're going to do for the day and there's also the small matter of a wedding date."

"Am I dreaming? I don't want to wake up in the morning and find myself in rags again."

"You won't, and I love you."

"I love you too," she said, meaning it with all her heart.

Should she call Georgie Simpson or wait until tomorrow? Opening her bottomless pocketbook, she pulled out the envelope with the lease agreement and the card with her number. She decided to get it over with. The phone rang for quite a long time and she was just about to hang up when she heard her say, "Hello."

"Georgie, it's MaryAnn Wilkinson and I'm sorry to disturb you."

"You're not disturbing me. What's up?"

"Something rather wonderful happened today and I'm not going to need the apartment after all. I'm not asking to get out of the six month lease because I will honor the commitment, but if you should hear of anyone who would like the apartment, perhaps we could do a sublet."

"Please satisfy my curiosity."

"I'm getting married."

"Congratulations. Who's the lucky fella?"

"Jim Hudson from Hudson's Hardware and Lumber."

"I know who he is. He's a nice man."

"It seems as though all the townsfolk know and like Jim."

"I'm very happy for you, but sorry we're going to lose you as a tenant. Something will turn up, it always does, and Paul and I will keep our ears to the ground. Unfortunately, as you know, this isn't the best time of the year for finding renters but you just never know, stranger things have happened."

"Thank you for being so understanding."

"Goodnight, MaryAnn, and I'm very pleased for you."

"Goodnight."

She then called Will because she was bursting to tell him her news. He immediately said, "No, I don't have any news about a truck, yet."

"That's not why I'm calling."

"Now what?"

"Jim and I are getting married. He proposed to me today and I said yes."

"Well ain't that a turn up for the books. You two don't waste any time, do you?"

"Guess not."

"Does that mean I'm going to lose a waitress?"

"No, not right away. I'm not sure what I'm going to be doing, so I'd like to keep on working for the time being. I don't want to leave you in the lurch."

"Okay. I'm gonna miss havin' you around. Do you still need the movin' truck?"

"Yes, we're going to be moving into Jim's house. Now that we're getting married I can do that in all good conscience, plus it's going to be so much better for the boys."

"Are they on board with all this?"

"Yes, at least Johnny is. Of course, I know it's going to be an adjustment for Ian, but Johnny is already saying Jim is going to be his new daddy."

MaryAnn heard Will blow his nose. "You're gettin' me all sentimental," he said. "This is the best news I've had for many a long year. I'm not much for marryin' myself, but when it's right, there's nothin' measures up. See you on Monday bright and early, and in the meantime, I'll find you a movin' truck and some movers, even if I have to do it myself. Take care and say hi to Jim."

"For sure, and thanks, Will. See you Monday."

MaryAnn, flying high, not in the least bit tired, decided to go down into the basement to see what was there in the way of empty boxes. Deathly afraid of spiders, she hated the basement, had no idea of the origin of her irrational fear, had sucked up many of the ugly hairy insects with the vacuum cleaner, always convinced they were going to crawl back out again and bite her. Unfortunately for her, the boys didn't share her fear. They thought the spiders cute, studied them with scientific eyes, no matter the size, putting them in glass jars when she wasn't watching. Armed with the vacuum cleaner, nozzle at the ready in her right hand, canister in her left, she opened the basement door and flipped on the light switch with her elbow. With visions in her head of spiders running for their lives away from her, she could overcome her fear; she didn't want to think about the ones that might drop on her head, especially Cyril, a particularly large and fuzzy one, named and vividly described by the kids. She shivered.

Despite the age of the house, the basement was thankfully dry, aided by the lumbering furnace giving off its winter heat. Will had managed to find a dehumidifier for her that she ran in the summer months, otherwise everything would have been ruined, and she was thankful all her belongings—some of which were covered with old sheets—had survived their three years of forced hibernation. She spied what she was looking for, some boxes which she had flat-packed leaning against the wall to the left of the stairs, together with a large plastic bag full of packing materials. Plugging in the vacuum cleaner, she cleaned off the dust, and made a couple of hasty trips up the basement stairs until she had all she needed stacked in the hallway. Lustily sneezing the dust out of her nose, she took one of the boxes into the kitchen, assembled it, and secured the bottom with packaging tape, cringing at the noise. Rummaging around in one of the kitchen drawers, a catchall for junk, she found a marker tucked way in the back, but much to her annoyance on removing the lid discovered it was bone dry. Now what? A decision would ultimately have to be made about what to keep and what to store so each box needed to be clearly marked.

MaryAnn hated packing: a two-man job, no fun on her own. Disorganized, without a methodical bone in her body, she gleaned no satisfaction from seeing empty cupboards and full boxes, all carefully marked. She needed Ian. He was single-minded when it came to tasks and consistent in the way he did things, but he was in bed and asleep, so she should at least make a start. Turning on the radio, hoping the music would make the chore less painful, she told herself to begin on the left and work her way around the room. Using one of Johnny's crayons, she wrote "1" and "KITCHEN" in big bold writing on top of the box, went down on her hands and knees and started removing pots and pans.

While she worked, she asked herself whether she was disappointed about not moving into the apartment and decided her only regret was the missed opportunity of living in town. Jim's house, like the current rental, wasn't within walking distance of anything and she wondered why she hadn't moved into town after Sam's death, but she knew the answer to that question—she had been hiding from the world. It was the best she had been able to do at the time; it was a poor best, but they had all eked out an existence and survived. Her mind buzzing, she wished she had someone to talk to, someone to ask whether they thought she was absolutely out of her mind to be moving into Jim's house and saying yes to his marriage proposal when she had only known him for such a short time.

She paused, resting her hands on the kitchen table, peering down into the box she had just filled. This packing was proving harder than she thought because all the items she was nestling carefully one within the other reminded her of Sam: the big pot in which she'd cooked her first stew; the frying pan she'd used to make their breakfasts—his hands on the wooden spoons when she'd asked him to stir something for her. Unlike Jim, he hadn't really liked to cook, but he had loved to spend time with her in the kitchen while she was preparing meals. She used to tease him, telling him he was the typical only son, had to be taught how to do chores, but he wasn't a lazy man and they had quickly formed a partnership, each with their allotted tasks. They had fallen into an easy rhythm, but once Sam became sick, all the household chores fell upon her. Resentful and angry—not at Sam—but at the injustice of it all, she had longed to turn the clock back. Crumpling up some newspaper, cramming it into the top of the box with her memories, little wet dots of her tears darkening the paper as they fell, she taped the lid shut, and set the box on the floor against the wall. She paid little attention to the radio humming away in the background until she heard Celine Dion singing *All By Myself*, and although some of the words didn't really fit her life, they nevertheless reinforced her desire to no longer be alone. Turning up the volume, reveling in the raw emotions the song evoked, realizing her good fortune, she sang along with the powerful and haunting lyrics, her sweet voice brightening each corner of the dingy room.

She fell into a kind of rhythm, taped and marked each box sadly but symbolically, sealing her life with Sam away, ready to move on. Eventually, too tired to do anymore, but reluctant to leave the warmth of the kitchen, she decided to make herself a hot chocolate. Sitting at the kitchen table, surrounded by boxes and packaging materials, emotions raw, her mind wandering into those keep awake places, she thought about the people who were part of her life, realizing those with whom she was truly connected were few and far between. She would always be grateful to Will, her salvation and true friend in her hours of need. He had given her solutions when she had none and a shoulder to cry on. Working at the diner had been so hard in the beginning when she had been so grief-stricken, but it had given her a place to go, a reason to get up in the morning. Will had also good-naturedly solved the babysitting dilemma by allowing her to take the boys with her.

She thought about Sam's dad, how much she liked him, still saddened that Sam's mother had broken the link between them. She had watched him being torn apart, his loyalty lying with his wife even though being estranged from MaryAnn and his grandkids broke his heart. MaryAnn, totally disconnected from her own family, loved her mother but barely tolerated the rest of her relatives. Totally self-sufficient, determined to make her mark on the world, she learned through Sam how good it was to be truly connected to another human being, to not have to go it alone. And because of Sam, she was now able to build a connection with Jim, albeit shaky—the nagging fear of loss her constant companion. The last three difficult years had given her and the boys time to grieve, but deep down she didn't believe she would ever truly get over Sam's death. She pushed the now empty mug away, folded her arms around herself looking for comfort, thought about Thea and their developing friendship, pleased she would eventually be able to repay her for her hospitality. "Oh, Sam," she said. "It's not healthy for me to be on my own anymore. I do hope you understand my love for Jim. I'm weary from the fight, and so are the boys, but I will always love you."

MaryAnn pushed the chair away from the table, went over to the sink, rinsed out her mug, and tugged her mind back into the present away from Sam. Lightening her mood by concentrating on thoughts of Jim, her body ached for physical closeness, the missed intimacy of just lying in bed and talking, having someone to share all her fears and joys. She couldn't wait. After turning down the heat, shutting off the light, and closing the kitchen door, she tiptoed up the stairs, totally oblivious to the wobbly banister and the chill of the hallway.

CHAPTER THIRTEEN

THEA—SUNDAY

Thea, waking early, her bedroom illuminated only by the light of the moon, tossing and turning for a little while, her mind going a mile a minute, decided it was useless to try and go back to sleep. Donning her robe, pushing her feet into her slippers, making her way downstairs, she walked past the children's rooms into the kitchen to make a pot of coffee. Glancing at the two boxes in the hallway, overcome by a sudden desire to take a trip down memory lane, she picked up one of them and carried it into the living room, setting it down on the coffee table, upsetting a pile of magazines that toppled and slid to the floor. "Darn," she said. She wished her mom were with her now, enabling them to continue the welcome intimacy recently shared. Thea, surprised by the realization of how much she truly loved her mom, longed to hear stories about her life. With her revelation of her orphanage upbringing came understanding for her daughter, casting her mom in an entirely different light and giving Thea the reason for her reticence and rather distant parenting. Carefully scoring the packaging tape with a utility knife, she lifted the cardboard to reveal a wealth of childhood treasures.

Setting a roll of paintings to one side, she removed two hand puppets: Freddy, a once gaily colored parrot, and Mandy, a tattered gray squirrel. She seemed to remember her falling in the toilet, but couldn't recall why. Putting a hand in each, her fingers moving inside Freddy's wings and Mandy's arms, she brought them alive, transporting her back to the land of childish make-believe and all the imaginary conversations with these two old friends. Laying them gently on the sofa, she pulled out a clay pot carefully wrapped in tissue paper. Cupping her hands around the rough surface, she closed her eyes. As if only yesterday, she recalled the heaviness and the earthy smell of the slick wet clay; her attempt, with tiny untrained fingers, to shape it into a bowl and render it smooth; the anticipation while waiting for it to come out of the kiln and her "Oh," of disappointment at the dullness of the color—the bright blue absorbed into the clay, lost in the firing. But she had still proudly taken it home. Despondent from both her mom and her dad's half-hearted enthusiasm, she had taken it to her bedroom and tucked it away in a drawer. She carefully rewrapped it. Reaching into the box she pulled out two tousle-haired, beautifully dressed Barbie dolls. Lost in her emotional time warp, she failed to notice Izzie until she sat down next to her. "Are you all right, Mommy?" she asked, placing her hand on Thea's knee.

"Yes, I'm fine. These are happy tears. I'm having a trip down memory lane and just realizing how much your grandma cared for me. These clothes on the Barbie's were all knitted by her." Izzie took one of the dolls out of her mother's hand and fingered the tiny garments. "These are quite something."

"There's a whole box full. Here," Thea said, handing Izzie a red satin box with a treasure trove of Barbie clothes. Izzie sorted through them taking in every detail, the most amazing of which was a jacket with a tiny zipper. "There seems to be sweaters and pants for Ken as well."

"Oh my goodness, I'd completely forgotten about Ken. He must be in the box somewhere. The games I used to play." Thea pulled a tissue from the pocket of her robe, wiped her eyes and blew her nose. "I didn't expect to get this sentimental and I can't believe Grandma saved all this stuff for me." She leaned back into the sofa. "I think I'm done for now and I have some news. Mrs. Wilkinson and Mr. Hudson are getting married."

"What! And how did you find out?"

"They stopped by on their way back from town to pick up their vehicles. If you remember they were parked in the driveway."

"Yes, I remember."

"I'm sorry you and Jessica missed all the excitement."

"It's awfully soon, isn't it?"

"It is, but you know, sometimes it just feels right, although it's not something I would ever recommend for one of my daughters." She leaned forward and put her arm around Izzie's shoulders, giving her a gentle squeeze.

"Oh, Mom, I'm so pleased for them, especially Johnny."

"There's something else."

"There is."

"Yup. Your grandpa completely blew me away by telling me he and Grandma want to move to Maine, to Melford Point, so they can be close to us."

"That's awesome. How do you feel about it?"

"I'm thrilled. Of course, they have to sell their house so it won't be right away and it's not the best time of the year, but it will all work out, I'm sure of that."

"Where will they live?"

"I thought I would try and find them a ground-floor apartment in town, but they could always stay here, at least temporarily, even though it would be a bit of a tight squeeze. I'm truly excited about having them close by. That way I can keep an eye on them because they're not getting any younger, and who knows, they might be able to help out at the Country Store."

"It will be nice to have family around. Most of the kids at school have grandparents to do things with and now I will too and I like the idea of that."

"Will you tell Jessica all the news when she wakes up? Peter already knows. Mr. Hudson was very taken with Honey and said we will have to get her and Carrie together. That should be interesting. Now what do I need to do for you, young lady?"

"Check your email to see if there's a rehearsal schedule from Miss Beauchamps, and then we need to make sure all the dates are on the calendar."

"How are you feeling? Not too overwhelmed, I hope."

"I have butterflies, but I've been looking at the video of last year's show and going over what I need to do. It's pretty simple and I can make myself become Clara, and once I go into that land of make-believe, I can do anything."

"You are remarkable and I'm so proud of you."

Izzie smiled and looked at her mom. "Are you okay after all that's happened?"

"Do you know, I truly am. The great thing that's come out of all this is that I've found a friend in Mrs. Wilkinson and that was something I desperately needed, especially since Nan is so far away. Of course, I can always talk to you, but sometimes we need a friend of our own age. Don't you miss that?"

"Not really because I have Jess and we talk about lots of stuff, but I will make an effort to find a friend once *The Nutcracker* is done and I have more time."

"That's a good idea. Thank you for being such a star over the weekend and especially with helping out with Jess. I'm sorry if I ask too much of you sometimes because I know how difficult she can be. Sometimes I forget that you're only eight and a half."

"I know. You're always telling me I have an old soul. That's just the way I am and I will be perfectly happy as long as I don't grow too tall."

"Unfortunately, there's not much we can do about that."

"It's still my wish."

"It's so good to be home and I was so happy to sleep in my own bed."

"Me, too. How are Mr. Blunt and Robert doing?"

"I talked to both of them last night and Mr. Blunt seems to be coping with Dorothy's help, but poor Robert is having a hard time, but as Mr. Blunt said, he will feel much better once he's back in Maine with his family."

"It's all so sad isn't it, Mommy?"

"Yes, sweetheart, it is."

"Are you sad you won't be able to work with Miss Ellie in Massachusetts?"

"I did enjoy working in Aladdin's Cave when we were there on Friday. It brought it all back to me, how much I love being surrounded by all that wonderful merchandise and being able to help customers. Ellie and I had such a great time together and I can't quite believe she's gone. I also wonder what Mr. Blunt will do with Aladdin's Cave and that makes me sad to think he might have to close it, or find a stranger to run it, but there's nothing I can do. There's no way I am going to disrupt our lives and hike us all off to Massachusetts without Miss Ellie being there, even though it would make it easier for Grandma and Grandpa. How do you feel about our staying here?"

Izzie frowned. "I didn't really want to move, but I do worry about Kenny and the fact he might try and break in again."

"I know, but Mr. Hudson and Kenny's brother, Phil, are really keeping close tabs on him now and if he causes any more trouble, the police will be called and then he will go to jail."

"That's good to know. Having Honey will help, although I don't think she's much of a guard dog!"

"You're right about that and speaking of her, I think I'd better go check she doesn't need to go out. Then I'll make us some breakfast. How does that sound?"

"Sounds great, Mom."

Izzie went off to her room to see if Jessica might be awake, and as luck would have it, her sister was just beginning to stir. She couldn't wait to tell her all the news and see what Jess's reaction was going to be. Knowing her sister, she was sure she would be very happy for Johnny and Ian. Izzie didn't really miss having a dad and she was pretty sure Jess felt pretty much the same way. She hoped for her mom's sake she would meet someone one day who would be good for the whole family, but that thought was a little scary because her mom didn't seem to be able to choose good men. Izzie liked her family the way it was with just the four of them. They all got along and they understood their mother and the way she chose to discipline them. Things had always gone wrong when her father was around and then after he left there was Kenny and they never knew which way to jump when he tried to tell them what to do. It would be nice if her mom could find a man who didn't make them nervous and was fun to be around, like Mr. Hudson.

Izzie decided to get into bed with Jessica and she turned and whispered in her ear, "Are you awake?"

"Am now."

"I have such news," Izzie said and proceeded to fill Jessica in on all that her mother had told her. They lay side by side with both their heads on Jess's pillow, staring up at the ceiling, and Jess didn't say a word until Izzie had finished.

"Do you wish Mr. Hudson was going to be our dad?"

"Not really. I like him a lot and I think Ian and Johnny are very lucky as he will make a great dad, but I don't really want a dad. It just complicates things."

"That's for sure."

Izzie reached for her sister's hand. "I love you, Jess, and we don't really need a dad because we've got each other, but I do wonder if mom might be a bit lonely."

"Hm. There's Peter, too. I know he'd like a dad, but it will be good for him to have Grandpa close. Now we've defrosted him, I think he's a lot of fun."

Izzie started giggling and Jessica joined in. It didn't take much to start them off. "Did you know Mom has two puppets: Freddy, the parrot, and Mandy, the squirrel? She found them in one of the boxes Grandma packed. They're pretty ratty looking, but I guess she used to play with them a lot and you should see the Barbie doll clothes Grandma knitted. They're amazing."

"You know, I think we're really lucky. I'm glad we went to Mass-a-chu-setts because it made coming home so much better and we've got Peter's birthday to look forward to and then it will be Christmas and I love Mom's Christmases cuz she makes them so special."

Thea put her head around Peter's door, not in the least surprised to find he was still asleep. Honey, all curled up in her basket, rewarded Thea with a thumping of her tail. "You're such a good dog," she said. Peter rolled over in his sleep and yawned. Honey stood up, stretched, walked across the floor and thrust her nose into Peter's face. Thea backed silently out of the room, deciding to put Peter's dog care to the test. Her worries, however, were unfounded. His jacket thrown hastily over his pajamas, he and the dog appeared in the kitchen; all beams and smiles, he said, "Hi, Mom." Honey patiently waited while he slipped his bare feet into his boots and tucked a plastic bag into his pocket. She stood watching through the window, smiling at the dog's crazy attempts to catch Peter's snowballs, her face covered in snow. Shaking her head and sneezing, she stood waiting for Peter to throw another one. It did Thea's heart good to hear him laugh, surprised Honey wasn't barking in her excitement over the game, but then she remembered Ellie saying she wasn't much of a barker. Thinking of Ellie, knowing Honey would always be a constant reminder, she wished the dog had come to them in less tragic circumstances.

Peter waved, his hands red with the cold and called to Honey to come. Once inside, Honey shook herself vigorously; Thea handed Peter an old towel. He removed his boots, wished he hadn't, his feet freezing on the wet floor while he dried Honey off. Lapping up all the attention, she promptly sat down on the mat by the door as if to say, "What next?"

Peter went in search of Robert's hastily written notes, ran his finger down the list, found how much food Honey should get each day. Worried, he said, "We didn't feed her enough yesterday, Mom."

"Look at her. I don't think she suffered, do you? Plus the fact she was a little out of sorts and probably didn't have much of an appetite. Anyway, it's always better to under rather than over-feed."

"You're right. Oh look, here's a list of all the words she knows. I'm not going to read them out loud because it will just confuse her but have a look." He handed the list to Thea.

"I don't see any French words."

"Probably just as well, because I'd have a hard time saying them."

Peter looked at Honey. "You really are a silly dog trying to fit yourself onto that tiny mat. Here's your breakfast." He dumped a cup of dried food into her bowl, but much to his dismay she didn't move.

Thea looked at the list in her hand. "I think you have to say *come eat.*" Honey's ears perked up, and she headed for her bowl. "There, what did I tell you?"

"I just want to do everything right." Sensing Peter's nervousness, she said, "Come sit down for a minute." He dragged out one of the kitchen chairs, sat down, looked at his mother apprehensively, and rubbed his hands together. She took one of them in her own, and he made no attempt to pull away. "Listen," she said. "If we had decided to get a dog of our own, it would have been a rescue dog just like Honey and each rescue dog has a past. It's not like getting a puppy where you virtually start from scratch and in a way that's easier because the puppy grows with you and understands you. But in the case of a rescue dog, he or she may have had more than one home and more than one owner before finally being adopted by someone who really cares. In Honey's case, it was Miss Ellie. We are lucky because Miss Ellie did all the hard work and we are benefitting from the fact she trained her so well. What I am trying to say is that Honey is a lot more adaptable and forgiving and loving because she is a rescue dog. I firmly believe she knows how fortunate she is, so please don't worry about doing anything wrong. Am I making any sense?"

Peter nodded and looked at Thea with tears in his eyes. "Thank you, Mom, for letting us bring Honey home."

"No crying, now," she said, squeezing his hand, now nice and warm.

Peter got up to refresh the water in Honey's bowl. "Do you think I could walk to the park with Honey after breakfast?"

"Now that's a great idea. Would you like me to call Mrs. Wilkinson to see if Ian would like to go with you?"

"That would be awesome." With the resilience of youth, all his worries instantly forgotten, he went off to his bedroom to get dressed with Honey following close behind.

CHAPTER FOURTEEN

MaryAnn—Sunday

MaryAnn and her boys were in high spirits. She had sent them down to the basement to retrieve more boxes and Johnny had come back with a dirty face and cobwebs in his hair. "What on earth were you doing?" she asked.

"Trying to find Cyril," he said, looking at her mischievously and giving her an evil grin.

She shuddered. "I hope you didn't find him."

"We didn't, but we found his sister and she was even hairier!" Ian said, jumping on the bandwagon.

"Stop it, you two. You're giving me the heebie-jeebies, and as a punishment for all your teasing, I'm going to set you to work." She gave Johnny the task of cleaning out the catchall drawer admonishing him not to throw out anything unless it was true rubbish, such as a broken rubber band, without asking her first. She had Ian stand on a chair and hand down items from the top cupboards; once the table was full, they both started wrapping and packing. Ian sealed and happily labeled each box with a bright red marker he'd stashed away in his room for safekeeping. They were making great headway until the phone rang. MaryAnn, expecting Jim, was surprised, but not disappointed, to hear Thea's voice.

"How are the Wilkinsons this morning?"

"Fine and dandy, and we're having a packing marathon."

"This might upset the apple cart. I was wondering whether you could spare Ian for a couple of hours. Peter wants to take Honey to the park and I would be happier if he had company, but only if you're comfortable with them going off on their own."

"I think it's a grand idea. It's such a glorious day, and it will be good for Ian to get out of this house. He's already been a great help, so I can

139

certainly give him time off for good behavior." She winked at her son. "Let me ask him."

"You can drop Johnny off here to play with Jessica if you'd like."

"Hang on," and she put her hand over the mouthpiece. "Ian, Mrs. Chamberlin wondered whether you'd like to go with Peter and Honey to the park and, Johnny, she's invited you over to play with Jessica. Are you on board?" Ian said, "That rocks," and Johnny said, "Yes, please."

"Okay, you've got yourself a couple of extra kids. They can't wait to get away from me. I'm not half as much fun! We'll be over in about half an hour, or is that too soon?"

"No, that's perfect. See you in a little while."

MaryAnn combed the cobwebs out of Johnny's hair and washed his face. "Do I look okay?"

"You look very handsome," she said, standing out of the way so Ian could brush his teeth.

"I'll help you later, Mommy," Johnny said, worried because he hadn't finished his task.

"I know you will and thank you both for helping me." She glanced at their three faces reflected in the pockmarked mirror, their happiness bouncing off the flawed surface. She wished she could catch that happiness, an elixir in a bottle, a golden spoonful to be swallowed on those days when the clouds rolled in. MaryAnn hugged the boys to her and said, "I love you so much." Leaving the ancient bathroom, the three of them marched down the stairs and out into the bright sunlight, singing *The Grand Old Duke of York* all the way.

CHAPTER FIFTEEN

PETER AND IAN

Thrilled to be out on their own, Peter and Ian thoroughly enjoyed the freedom and each other's company, Peter content to do most of the talking. Peter looked down at his leather hiking boots—perfect for a day such as today—protecting his feet from the residue of snow on the sidewalk. He glanced sideways at Ian's well-worn high-top sneakers, his faded and baggy jeans; Peter's, almost brand new, fit him just as they should. But at least Ian had a new jacket and he just knew things were going to get better for his friend.

More or less the same height, there was plenty of room on the sidewalk for the boys to walk abreast with Honey snuggly between them, her leash clutched tightly in Peter's hand, happy to be going off for an adventure without a moment's hesitation, boosting Peter's confidence.

"So what do you think of our news?" Ian asked, scuffing the snow with the toe of his sneaker.

"I think it's great and I'm a little bit jealous if you want to know the truth."

"It's going to take some getting used to because it's just been me, Johnny and Mom since my dad died, but I think it's going to be okay. I'm not angry anymore."

They paused at the corner and turned to cross. Ian pressed the button at the light and they waited for the icon of the walking man before setting foot in the street. Honey sat, and Peter said, "Come," as soon as it was safe to cross and she walked obediently staying level with her two charges.

"I wish I wasn't so angry," Peter said, picking up the thread of the conversation. They walked past Harry's Hardware and the Country Store, neither of which was open. Sunday was a day of rest in Melford Point, and with the exception of Mario's Restaurant, all the shops were closed. "What did you do when you got angry?"

"Went outside and kicked a soccer ball around or shot hoops until I wasn't angry anymore and I'd do that every time I felt like lashing out. I'd sit in the bottom of my closet with my pillow over my face and cry so my mom wouldn't hear me. It was terrible. Why are you so angry?"

"I don't really know. It's usually triggered by something though, like when the kids at school, Marty especially, were teasing Izzie because they thought Kenny was our dad. I saw red that day and we had a terrible fight."

"I remember. That was rough. I'd have done the same thing if someone had been teasing Johnny."

"It's funny though, because I've never really been angry at my Mom," Peter said, pausing at the light opposite the park. Again, they waited for the white walking man. Once in the park, Peter allowed Honey to go from him as far as the leash would allow. "It's a shame we can't let her off, but it's not safe because she might run away and then I'd never forgive myself."

"I'm glad you have a dog because I know you've wanted one for such a long time. When we go and live with Mr. Hudson, we'll have Carrie, which is great."

"Do you think you'll ever be able to call Mr. Hudson 'Dad'?"

"I don't know. My dad was great and I wish you'd known him. He was just how a dad should be, so it's going to be hard, but I'd do anything to make my mom happy and we can't bring my dad back."

"We're awful serious aren't we?"

Ian laughed. "Yup, like a couple of old men," and he started to run across the snow-covered grass, not caring that his feet were getting soaking wet. Peter ran after him, with Honey gamboling along beside, her feathery golden ears flapping up and down. He bent down, scooped up some snow, formed it into a ball, tossed it after Ian's retreating figure. Out of breath, needing a break, they went to sit by the pond, brushing the snow off one of the benches. Eerily quiet, no sign of ducks or geese, the edges of the water beginning to freeze, Peter's breath vaporizing in the frigid air, he asked, "Have you ever come here to skate?" Leaning forward, resting his elbows on his knees, he received a wet kiss on his cheek from Honey.

Ian sat back, looked across the pond. "We haven't done much of anything. There's never any money, but I think that'll change now. I'm tired of being poor and having the other kids look at my shabby clothing, but my mom's done her best. It's been rough for her, but she's a good mom."

"I like her a lot."

"I like your mom too. She's very pretty."

"I know and that's part of the problem. Men fall in love with her all the time. I don't understand it, but I suppose I will one day. How do you feel about girls?"

Ian raised his eyebrows, turned down the corners of his mouth. "I haven't really thought about it. Anyway, we're too young to think about girls—ugh!"

"You're right." Peter turned to give Ian a high five. "I think we should call in on Aunt Margaret and Uncle Bill on the way back, seeing as we have to walk right past. They don't know about Honey, or your mom and Mr. Hudson either."

"Great idea. They still think we're moving into town."

"Huh?"

"My mom signed a lease to an apartment yesterday. I'd forgotten all about that. Now we don't need it."

"I'm glad I'm a kid. This is all much too hard to understand."

The three of them jogged out of the park, Ian and Peter too out of breath to do any more talking. Reaching the side entrance to the Country Store, Peter removed his glove, pushed the bell, stood back out of the way of the door when he heard footsteps on the stairs. Uncle Bill grinned at the trio. "How did you manage to escape? I thought they kept you under lock and key so you couldn't cause any trouble. And who do we have here?" he asked, looking at Honey who was waving her plume of a tail in absolute delight at having yet another human paying her attention.

"This is Honey, Uncle Bill."

"You'd better come inside and tell me all about her." They followed Bill up the stairs, leaving a little trail of snow as they went. "Margaret, look who I've found."

Margaret appeared from the living room. "What a lovely surprise. Take your boots and coats off otherwise you're going to get too hot. And who is this gorgeous dog?"

"Her name is Honey," Peter said, all puffed up and proud. "And she's mine. At least she's mine to look after, but she belongs to the whole family really." He wondered if telling Aunt Margaret Honey was a rescue dog would be enough to satisfy her curiosity, rather than having to go into the whole sad story of Miss Ellie's death.

Margaret, a puzzled expression on her face, said, "What are you doing home? I thought you weren't coming back until late tonight or even tomorrow."

Uh-oh, this wasn't going to be easy. He was just beginning to wish they hadn't come when Ian came to the rescue. Peter flashed him a look of pure gratitude. "We're not going to be moving into town after all, Mrs. Gilson."

Peter, not sure how long Ian was going to be able to keep Aunt Margaret off track, was nonetheless grateful to his friend for creating a diversion.

"How come, Ian?"

"Because my mom is going to marry Mr. Hudson and we're going to move into his house."

"My, oh my," Margaret said, sitting down on the sofa. "You boys are certainly full of surprises, and judging by the look on your face, Ian, you think it's a good idea."

"Yes I do. Mr. Hudson is a nice man and he makes my mom happy."

Bill reached over and shook Ian's hand. "Congratulations, young man. Margaret and I like good news, don't we, lass?"

"We sure do."

Bill, sinking down into his favorite chair, said, "Come, Honey." Forever compliant, she wandered over and put her head on his knee. He caressed her ears, looked up at Peter and said, "If you ever need a dog sitter, lad, I'd be happy to look after her for you. You know how I feel about dogs."

"Thank you, Uncle Bill. I'll remember that. Anyway, we must be going otherwise Mom will be getting worried. I just wanted to stop by and introduce Honey to you."

"Thank you for doing that. You've quite made my day."

Margaret, almost bursting with unasked questions, sensed there was something Peter didn't really want to talk about, but she was sure Thea would tell her. In any case, it wouldn't be fair to grill the boys. She gave them both a hug, said she hoped to see them again soon and stood at the door watching them go down the stairs. "Mind how you cross the road."

"We will," they said in unison, turning to wave goodbye.

Once outside, the door firmly closed, Margaret and Bill out of earshot, Peter said, "Thanks, Ian, for rescuing me. I didn't really want to answer a lot of questions and your news took Aunt Margaret by surprise so you got me off the hook. I owe you one."

"I'll remember that," Ian said, looking sideways at his friend and giving him a wicked grin.

"Boy, am I hungry," Peter said, and with the thought of food in their minds, they hotfooted it for home.

Thea persuaded MaryAnn to stay and have coffee, and seeing as there was no pressing need to get the packing done because she had the house until the end of December, she took Thea up on her offer. She asked Thea if she could call Jim to let him know where she was and Thea told her to go ahead and use the phone in the living room to give her some privacy. She dialed his landline rather than his cell and he answered on the fourth ring. "Hello," he said and his deep voice sent a little shiver of pleasure up her spine.

"Hi."

"I was just going to call you. What are your plans for the day?"

"Right now, I'm at Thea's. Ian and Peter are walking Honey to the park and Johnny is playing with Jessica. As soon as Ian's back, I'm planning on heading home. We started packing, but we still have a long way to go."

"I won't keep you if you're at Thea's, but I had an idea. You know, you don't have to do all your packing before you move in with me. Why don't you pack what you need and you and the boys could move in today if you liked."

"Can I think about it and call you when I get back to the house?"

"Of course. I miss you and I know this isn't easy for you, so don't feel pressured into doing anything you don't want to do."

"I won't and I miss you too. I'll talk to you in a couple of hours."

"I'll be here. Love you."

"Love you too."

MaryAnn replaced the receiver and walked back into the kitchen. Thea looked at her face. "You look worried," she said.

"I feel as though I'm living somebody else's life. It's all happening too fast. Jim just suggested we move into his house right away and do you know what went through my mind?"

"Tell me."

"Here's this wonderful man offering to share his house and his life with me and all I could think about was my underwear and how dowdy it is, and the boys' too. It's not that Jim's going to be seeing me in my underwear until after we're married, but I'll have to do laundry and I just can't bear the thought of him seeing all our ratty underwear. Am I being ridiculous or what?" and she started to laugh.

"You'll have to come clean, no pun intended!" Thea said, holding her stomach, doubled over with laughter. "Please stop laughing, my face is killing me."

"I can't stop. On the one hand, I'm so happy, and absolutely panic-stricken on the other, and this combination is making me slightly hysterical. Here I was yesterday signing a lease to an apartment," and her voice rose again in an attempt to control her laughter, "and now I don't need it."

"You did what?" Thea started laughing all over again and she looked at MaryAnn with tears running down her face.

"Oh," MaryAnn gasped, "I signed a six month lease for an apartment in town. It seemed like such a good idea at the time and then when Jim asked me to marry him, it seemed pointless, so now I'm stuck with a dismal house until the end of December and this absolutely lovely apartment."

"Where is it?"

"Over the empty store between Gems Jewelry and the Scrapbook Nest."

"Now that's given me an idea. Are the stairs easy to negotiate?"

"They're wide and sturdy. Why?"

"I was wondering whether it might be suitable for my parents, but probably not, because I'd hate to have them move again when they become too frail to climb stairs. Sorry, I'm not making much sense. They're relocating from Massachusetts to be close to me and the kids, but they have to sell their house first and I said I'd find a rental for them, but it really does need to be ground floor," Thea said, placing a steaming mug of coffee in front of MaryAnn. "What used to be in the empty store? I can't remember."

"Georgie Simpson, the owner, said it was an art gallery, but the guy hadn't a clue about the local market so he soon went under. It would make a lovely photography studio. That's what my husband and I used to do."

Thea sat down opposite MaryAnn, added cream to her coffee and absently-mindedly stirred. "You've given me another idea . . ." Interrupted by the ringing of the phone, she grabbed the receiver.

"Thea, it's Michael." She cupped her hand over the mouthpiece and mouthed, "My ex," and indicated with her hand that MaryAnn should stay.

"Are you sure?" Thea nodded.

"How are you, Michael?"

"I'm well, and you?"

"Pretty good," she said, thinking please get on with it. She looked at MaryAnn, did winding motions with her hand!

"I had an idea for Peter's birthday. It's a little outrageous and if you don't agree, he need never know."

"Okay, out with it."

"From what I remember, the Bon Jovi rock band was always one of his favorites. Am I right?"

"Yes, and it still is."

"They're playing in Boston on the ninth of December and I can get tickets. He could bring a friend and we could drive up really early Saturday morning, stay overnight and come back on Sunday morning."

"Wow, that would be quite a birthday present. Let me think about it. Can I call you back in a little while?"

"Sure, but don't leave it too long."

"I won't. Bye, Michael."

Thea sat back down at the kitchen table and looked at MaryAnn. "Now I have something to ask you."

"Go ahead."

"Michael has just asked whether he can take Peter to a Bon Jovi concert as a birthday present and has said Peter can bring a friend, and of course, I know he'll want to take Ian. It's on the ninth of December in Boston and they would leave early on the Saturday morning, stay overnight in a hotel and then come back on the Sunday. What do you think?"

"What a fantastic birthday present. How many eleven-year-old boys are given the choice to go to a Bon Jovi concert and I know Ian will be over the moon, especially to be going with Peter, but, and of course there are always 'buts' when you're a mother, would they be safe with Michael?"

"You and I don't know anything about each other do we except what we've learned through our children. Let me tell you at least a little bit about Michael. Basically, he's a troubled soul and he can be an arrogant bastard at times, but he would never let anything happen to the boys. He is a very good, safe driver and he has an expensive and reliable car—in fact probably more than one from which to choose for every season. If Peter wants to go, I don't have a problem with it, but I completely understand if you're not sold on the idea and we will say no more."

"Does Jim know Michael?"

"Not well, and he didn't see him in a very favorable light I'm afraid because Michael didn't behave himself very well when Jessica was hospitalized after her abduction. He was frightened, although he would never admit it, and when he's threatened in any way he becomes obnoxious and impossible to deal with, but Jessica's accident changed all of us, including Michael. Unfortunately, Peter was the only one who wanted to spend any time with his father, but it never happened and Michael just faded into the background. He did fairly recently make an attempt to come back into the children's lives, and this threw Jessica into a panic, but he's not a bad man. He's generous to a fault when it comes to child support and he would give you the shirt off his back if you were in trouble. He's a mass of conflicts and difficult to understand, but I would trust him with Peter and Ian, so why don't you run it by Jim and see what he says. You could always suggest he go along too!"

"Now that's a thought, but it doesn't sound as though he would relish the idea of being in Michael's company for any length of time, but I bet you he'd do it for Ian," MaryAnn said. "Let me talk to him and I'll let you know."

"The other side of the coin is that Peter may not want to go now that he has Honey. He may not want to leave her, but find out what Jim's reaction is first, and if he thinks it's an okay idea, I'll talk to Peter because ultimately the decision rests with him."

"Now what was this other idea you had?" but no sooner were the words out of her mouth when they were interrupted yet again by Peter, Ian and Honey arriving in the kitchen in a burst of cold air and snowy footprints. They brought the clean fresh smell of the outdoors with them and they looked bursting with health and well-being. "Did you have a good time?" MaryAnn asked and Ian said, "Yes," and Peter said, "We're starving. We stopped by to see Aunt Margaret and Uncle Bill because I wanted them to meet Honey. Now Aunt Margaret is bursting with questions so, Mom, I'm sure she'll call you."

Ian looked at MaryAnn. "Mom, I told them you and Mr. Hudson are getting married and that surprised them, I can tell you. Mrs. Gilson had to sit down on the sofa."

Peter leaned over, took off Honey's collar, scratched her neck where the leather had been and one of her back legs started to twitch. "She's in heaven, just look at her face. You are such a silly dog," he said. "She was so good and we had so much fun running around with her in the park, didn't we, Ian?"

"We sure did. Peter said there's ice-skating on the pond once it truly freezes over. Do you think I'll be able to go?"

"I'm sure you will. Now, I'm going to go off and find Johnny because we need to get home. Please don't give me that face. I'm sure Mrs. Chamberlin has things to do and so do we."

"I'm afraid it's a trip to the grocery store for us because the cupboard is pretty bare after our few days away."

Peter pulled a dreadful face. "Aw, Mom, you had to go and ruin my day, didn't you."

"Actually, I was going to suggest you stay here because I know you wouldn't want to leave Honey on her own or, alternatively, we could bring her in the van with us. It's up to you."

Peter's face lit up. "Thanks, Mom. We'll probably stay home."

MaryAnn found Jessica and Johnny in the living room playing *Sorry*, and for once, Johnny was winning. "Can we finish our game? We're nearly at the end." MaryAnn was sympathetic. She knew what it was like to be rushed by a grownup. Her whole childhood had been like that, so she sat back, and said, "Sure." Johnny only had two remaining men to get home and they were both in the safe zone so it was just a question of being lucky enough to get the cards with the right scores. She hoped he wouldn't pick too many fours because it would be bad luck to be forced to go backwards and out of his safe zone. As luck would have it he pulled a seven and was able to split the number exactly the way he needed to get his men home. Jessica pulled a face, but she wasn't a sore loser, and because she loved to mother Johnny, she was happy he'd won. She looked at MaryAnn. "Does he really have to go home?"

"I'm afraid so, Jess, and I have a question. How do you know what the *Sorry* cards say when neither you nor Johnny can read?"

"I 'member them cuz I've played the game so many times with Peter and Izzie. They teached me and I know my numbers and so does Johnny, so it's easy."

"I must say you are very clever, both of you."

"Thank you," Jessica said, and started to put the game away in the box, and with Johnny's help, it was soon done. She carefully placed the game back on the shelf where it belonged and MaryAnn was quite impressed.

She thought how lucky she was to have found a friend in Thea and to also have friends for her children who she truly enjoyed. They were wonderful kids, bright and friendly, and like Ian and Johnny, seemed to have weathered the hard knocks of life without any lasting ill effects. She suspected it was because the Chamberlin children had an anchor in Thea and her kids had an anchor in her. She might have been depressed at times, but she had always been there to love them when they needed it and it was this consistent love that had pulled them through.

She reached out and took Jessica's hand. She was looking a little forlorn. "Don't be too sad, Jess. You'll see Johnny in school on Tuesday and maybe even tomorrow, who knows?"

"Uh-huh. I like you Mrs. Wilkinson."

"Well, thank you. I like you too. I couldn't wish for a better friend for Johnny."

Ian, Peter, Honey, Thea and Izzie were all crowded in the kitchen. Johnny went over to Honey and stroked the top of her head. "She's great," he said, turning to look at Peter.

"I think so."

"Come on you two, here are your jackets. Slip your shoes on and we'll go out the back way. Thanks, Thea, for everything and I'll give you call."

"It was great to see you. Talk to you soon. Bye Ian, bye Johnny."

The boys said their thank-yous, Jessica gave Johnny a hug, and finally MaryAnn was able to pull herself and the boys away, and the thought that buoyed her up on the drive back to the house was that she wasn't going to have to do it for much longer. Now she just had to figure out how she was going to be able to call Jim and talk to him about the Bon Jovi concert without Ian overhearing their conversation.

CHAPTER SIXTEEN

THEA

The mention of the empty store jump-started Thea's thought process, set her to wondering how much the monthly rent might be, wished she could help MaryAnn out with a sublet, but it was no good putting her parents in an apartment which wouldn't work in the long-term. They really did need a place all on one floor. But the store was another kettle of fish altogether. A brilliant idea forming in her mind while she was driving to the grocery store, barely acknowledging her daughters, she absent-mindedly pushed their requested CD into the slot. Their singing in their sweet, slightly out of tune, little-girl voices didn't even penetrate her consciousness until Izzie tapped her on the shoulder and told her she'd missed the turning to Hannaford's. "Whoops," she said, reversing into someone's driveway, turning back, and parking the van outside the store.

Izzie was puzzled by her mother's behavior. Normally so with it and organized, she seemed to be miles away. "What are you thinking about, Mom?"

"It's just an idea I had about something. I'll tell you all about it later after I've had more time to think it through. Do you have the shopping list?" Izzie nodded.

The three of them clambered out of the van, walked across the parking lot, Izzie firmly holding Jessica's hand. Once in the store, they went into a frenzy of activity and all went well until Jessica dropped a container of blueberries. "Uh-oh," she said, staring down at the rolling berries, looking at her mother in dismay.

"No worries," Thea said. "It won't take us long to pick them up." They set to work, soon refilling the container, much to Jessica's relief.

"I'll be more careful next time."

"Jess, it's all right. No harm done. Izzie, what's next on the list? Do we need to divide and conquer, or should we stick together?"

"Me and Jess could get the rest of the fruit and veggies while you go off to the meat counter."

"Good idea, Iz."

Izzie and Jess went into a frenzy of activity, making sure they picked out the best produce. Thea had taught them well; they made sure the tomatoes were firm, the apples crisp and without bruises and the broccoli stiff, not rubbery. Izzie's arms, wet from the mister, reached for a bunch of fresh carrots. Jess attempted to stuff them into a plastic bag, but the green feathery stalks kept trying to escape. "I'm not having much luck, am I?" she said, looking at Izzie and giggling.

"We're getting it done, though," Izzie said, grabbing a bag of potatoes, scrutinizing them intently to make sure they weren't green or growing sprouts, carefully placing them in the cart. Jess went to get bananas while Izzie checked off the items they had already gathered.

"Well done," Thea said, arriving with packages of chicken breast and ground beef. Standing at the checkout, she mulled over her concept, excited about putting her plan into action, but wondering at the same time whether she was completely mad to even consider it. Pigeonholing her plan for now, she turned her attention to her daughters, helping them unload the cart, removing the items beyond their reach, Jessica nearly standing on her head determined not to be outdone. "How do you think Peter and Honey are making out? I was a bit nervous about leaving them on their own."

"It will make Peter feel 'portant," Jessica said.

"I agree," Izzie said, placing the bag of tomatoes on the belt. "Anyway, even though I love my brother, shopping is much easier without him."

"Don't let him hear you say that otherwise he'll wriggle out of it every time," Thea said, pushing the cart through, smiling at Tony, one of their favorite baggers, his slow and methodical packing of their produce making the wait worthwhile. She handed the cashier her coupons, lifted Jessica up so she could slide the credit card through the slot and waited for the receipt. Izzie checked it over carefully. "We did well, Mom. We saved over ten dollars."

"That means five dollars for each of you. Remind me to give you the cash when we get home."

CHAPTER SEVENTEEN

MARYANN

MaryAnn, sitting in the partially packed kitchen surrounded by boxes, mulled over Jim's suggestion about moving in right away. A no-brainer as far as the boys were concerned, she knew exactly what they would say, but morally it didn't sit well. She trusted Jim, that wasn't the issue, so why was she hesitating? Brought down to earth with a bump by the nagging inner voice of her conscience, she unhappily realized what her decision must be.

"What are you thinking about, Mommy?" Johnny asked.

"All the things I have to do," she said.

"We'll help you."

"I know you will." She turned sideways in the kitchen chair, hugged Johnny to her, and looked at Ian standing with his back to the sink. "You boys are the best. Let's have some lunch and we can talk about our battle plan. How does that sound?"

Moving around the kitchen, helping the boys make peanut butter, honey and banana sandwiches helped alleviate the knot in her chest. She hated the decision she was about to make, the accompanying disappointment for Jim and the boys. With little appetite for food, she decided the only way out of her dilemma was to have a heart-to-heart with Jim, tell him exactly how she was feeling.

She cranked up the heat and sent the boys off to their rooms to do a little packing of their own, but she doubted they'd accomplish much. In high spirits, playfully punching each other, she listened to the dragging of a box along the floor of the hallway and their fading laughter. Standing in the kitchen, hands poised over the telephone, she imagined Jim sitting by the phone waiting for her call; he picked up on the second ring. She swallowed, hoped he would understand and wouldn't be hurt by what she had to say, but first she had to broach the Bon Jovi concert.

"Hi," he said. "What are your plans for the afternoon?"

"More packing, I guess. I sent the boys off to their rooms, but I turned the heat up and it's all your fault I have this devil-may-care attitude."

"Is that a good or a bad thing?"

"It's a great idea, at least until I get the bill, but I have something much more important to talk to you about. I have a question."

"Go ahead."

"Michael Chamberlin—"

"That arrogant son of a bitch."

"I gather you're not a fan."

"No, I'm not, but I'm sorry, MaryAnn, I interrupted you."

"He has invited Peter to a Bon Jovi concert for his birthday. Apparently, the band is playing in Boston on December ninth. The plan would be to leave Saturday morning, attend the concert that night, and then drive back on the Sunday. Michael told Thea Peter is welcome to bring a friend, and even though he doesn't know anything about his father's invite at this point, we both know Peter will choose Ian. Thea is in favor of the idea, but says the ultimate decision rests with Peter and I said I would run it by you because I value your opinion."

"Hm," Jim said. "It is a wonderful opportunity, but are you comfortable letting Ian go with a man you know nothing about?"

"No, of course not, but then how many eleven-year-old boys receive an invitation to go to a Bon Jovi concert. It may, however, be a moot point because Peter may not want to go because of Honey, but I told Thea I would run it by you."

"If Peter says yes, would you like me to swallow my pride, thrust my fists into my pockets and go with them?"

"Do you actually enjoy Bon Jovi?"

"I'll suffer through it, and if I have selective deafness after the concert, you'll have nobody but yourself to blame."

"Thanks a lot, but you've no idea how much better you've made me feel."

"That's my job from now on, making life easier for you and the boys, and while on that subject, have you given any thought to moving in right away?"

Interrupted by crashing and giggling coming from the hallway, she asked Jim to hold on a second, putting off the inevitable, welcoming the diversion. Opening the kitchen door she saw the boys staring at the contents of a recently packed box. "Whoops. What happened?"

Doubled over and in stitches, Ian said, "I guess we didn't use enough tape. The bottom fell out!"

Their giggling was infectious and MaryAnn found herself laughing helplessly. "I'll help you in a little while, once I get off the phone with Mr. Hudson."

"It's okay, we can manage," Johnny said, attacking the roll of tape and getting into a sticky mess.

"Sorry, Jim, you probably heard all that. We're all so much more light-hearted these days; it doesn't take much to set us off into fits of giggles. In answer to your question, I keep asking myself whether I am just being tempted because it would be so much better for the boys, but I am wondering whether it would be awkward for you and me. Suddenly, it doesn't seem such a good idea."

Jim took the bull by the horns. "Let's just set a wedding date. How does a Christmas wedding sound?"

MaryAnn sat down on the nearest chair. "I would love that," she said and burst into tears. "Could we have a simple ceremony at the house?"

"If that's what you truly want, and no more crying."

"They're happy tears, and yes, that's exactly what I would like. I can just imagine us all gathering in your hallway by a Christmas tree. I'm assuming there will be a tree."

"You'd better believe it. You realize, of course, at some point we will have to have a large party of some kind otherwise I will be ostracized by all the folk in Melford Point. They've been waiting a long time for someone to make an honest man of me."

"I love you, and I don't want to hurt your feelings, but I am going to choose to stay here until our wedding day. I just don't feel right moving in with you. I hope you can respect my decision."

"Of course I do, and I should have known better than to ask you, but it's going to be a long month. Would you and the boys please come over this afternoon? I've got a couple of things I want to show them, and while they're occupied, you and I can talk about our plans. I know it's no good my asking if I can pick you up."

"You know that's a lost cause and I'm sorry if my pride gets in the way, but I hope you understand."

"I do and I love you. Bye for now." She hung up the phone and went off to find her sons.

CHAPTER EIGHTEEN

❦

THEA—SUNDAY

Thea was about to pick up the phone to call Theodore Blunt when it rang. She listened to MaryAnn, thrilled at her news, joining in her excitement about a Christmas wedding. She wasn't surprised to hear Jim had agreed to be an added chaperone for the Bon Jovi concert outing—a man in a million, but not the man for her. She told MaryAnn she would let her know the outcome of her discussion with Peter.

Still with her idea buzzing around in her mind, curbing her impatience she decided to go talk to Peter first before calling Mr. Blunt. Honey, tired after her morning walk, lay in her basket; Peter sat on his bed reading, earphones plugged. She gestured for their removal, mouthed, "I need to talk to you."

"What's up?"

"I had a call from your dad."

"Why?"

"He wanted to run something by me concerning your birthday."

Peter raised his eyebrows. "This has got to be good, *not.*"

"Don't be such a Doubting Thomas. He called to ask whether he could take you and a friend to a Bon Jovi concert."

Peter's jaw dropped. "Are you serious? When?"

"In Boston on December ninth."

"Are you okay with it?"

"I am and I made the assumption you would want to bring Ian so I discussed it with Mrs. Wilkinson. She talked to Mr. Hudson and he has agreed to go along too. Would you like me to leave you to think about it for a little while?"

"Of course I want to go. I'd be crazy not to, but I'm worried about leaving Honey. She might not like me when I come back."

"Oh, Peter. She will always love you best. Dogs aren't fickle like humans. They don't switch their loyalties and the only way you would be second best is if Miss Ellie were still around, but because she isn't with us anymore, you are Honey's number one best pal."

"Are you sure?"

"Yes, I am, and we will look after her while you're gone. She will get plenty of exercise so she will be too tired to miss you too much. Anyway, the concert's a little ways away by which time the bond between the two of you will be even stronger."

"Do you think it would be all right with Dad if I asked Marty as well?"

"I'm sure it would be fine, but I think you should call your dad and ask him yourself. I know he would like to hear from you directly. You don't need to say anything about Mr. Hudson. I'll handle that. Once you've talked to him, I'll call Mrs. Wilkinson and Marty's mom. Okay?"

"Thanks, Mom." Thea left him sitting on the floor by Honey's basket, fondling the dog's ears, deep in thought.

She called Michael just to get it over and done with. His reaction to Jim Hudson being part of the concert party was begrudgingly accepted. She sensed he knew better than to make any disparaging remarks and had, hopefully, learned his lesson well during Jessica's hospitalization when he was less than charitable to Jim and Bill Gilson. She doubted he would have felt the same parental protection towards his son had the positions been reversed and Peter had been invited to a function by someone Michael didn't know. But she was long over worrying about Michael's reactions to anything. Picking up the phone again, she finally called Mr. Blunt. He answered on the second ring.

"My, that was quick," she said.

"Hello, Thea. I was sitting dozing in my chair—a favorite activity on a cold winter afternoon."

"How are things going?"

"Dorothy and I spent the morning making phone calls. We put our heads together about the remembrance service and have come up with a good plan. Robert, apart from working with the mortician and talking to his family, has been laying low. The burial in Maine will just be a family affair."

"Thank goodness for Dorothy. I would have found it impossible to leave you if you hadn't had her help. I'm pleased things are getting resolved, but I do worry about you being all by yourself."

"Please don't concern yourself, my dear, I'm used to it, and I'm not going to be on my own for much longer. I think I told you Dorothy is a widow, so she has offered me a room in her house. There is no romantic attachment, but we do enjoy each other's company and share similar interests."

"That's fantastic news. Now I can stop worrying about you."

"I know, and bless you, young lady, for your kindness, but I suspect by the intonation of your voice that you had another reason for your call besides wishing me well."

"This is probably horrible timing, but I just had to share a proposal with you and you can tell me if you think I am completely mad."

"Go on."

"Being back at Aladdin's Cave was like coming home for me and I realized running such a store is my passion. Unfortunately, we can't come back to Massachusetts, even though that would be the perfect solution, so I was wondering if I could find a sponsor whether it would be possible to purchase the inventory of Aladdin's Cave. I'll tell you why. There's an empty store in Melford Point which would be perfect and I thought it might help you out of a bind if I could offer you some small consolation by carrying on with Aladdin's Cave in Ellie's memory. What do you think?"

"My, you have taken me by surprise. I think it's a splendid idea. Much as I would like to keep the store going here, my heart isn't in it without Ellie. I hate to see its darkened window and I just can't envision some unknown person in there running it. Obviously, I don't have any energy to deal with this now, but go ahead and see if you can find your sponsor. I'm not sure how much all the merchandise is worth, but I am sure I can find someone to help me with that and arrive at a fair price. Thank you for this idea. It has given me something else to think about and I love the thought that Aladdin's Cave will keep going and be run by someone who truly knows and loves the business. Good luck with your money raising, but I do feel as though this might have to be a spring project."

"I agree, but if it all works out, I can at least get the space ready. I haven't even looked at the store yet, so I'm not sure whether it is even suitable. Anyway, enough about that and thank you."

"No, *thank you*, and let me know how you get on."

"Also, could you let me know when the memorial service is because I might be able to make it down. It would also give me the option of taking some pictures of Aladdin's Cave. Even though I have a pretty good mental image, some actual photos would be really helpful."

"If you are unable to come, I can always take some for you."

"Well, thank you. Now, you take care of yourself and I'll talk to you soon."

"Bye, Thea."

Thea, although overjoyed by Mr. Blunt's reaction, was a little horrified at herself for breaking into his grief in such a way, but the conversation had gone well and she believed she had helped rather than hindered him. Now, she had to put her plan into action.

CHAPTER NINETEEN

MaryAnn

Ian, Johnny and MaryAnn arrived at Jim's at about three thirty. The boys chattered on the way over, still giggling about the box mishap, and it seemed to MaryAnn that Ian was finally coming to life. He would always be a boy of few words, but he did appear to be shedding some of his self-imposed responsibilities, behaving appropriately for an eleven-year-old. Being in a warm house had also lifted all their spirits. MaryAnn, unable to completely throw caution to the wind, and still concerned about the oil consumption, listened with trepidation to the lumbering old furnace kick on more than usual. Wrapped in their warm coats, rendering the journey in the old car less arduous still did little for MaryAnn's frozen feet. The boys, wondering what Mr. Hudson's surprise could possibly be, were tingling with anticipation by the time they reached the mailbox with its ridiculous ducks.

Needless to say, Jim greeted them with open arms, his face wreathed in smiles. Carrie, equally enthusiastic, wagged her tail until Johnny thought it might fall off. MaryAnn hung back while Jim greeted the boys, giving Johnny a hug and Ian a knuckle punch. Glancing around the kitchen, a room she already loved, having a hard time believing this fantastic space was going to be her space too, she imagined rolling out dough on the scrubbed pine table. She looked forward to cooking on the big shiny stove, a stark contrast to the ancient relic in the rental house, with unreliable burners and sporadic heat, the oven an inherited blackened and grease-coated nightmare totally beyond her cleaning powers. She sensed Jim watching her. "I was just thinking how nice it's going to be when I can use your kitchen."

"Our kitchen," he said, kissing her gently on the lips.

Johnny pulled himself away from Carrie and stood staring at Jim. "I'm glad you're going to marry my mommy," he said, and switching topics entirely, asked Jim what the surprise was. He just couldn't wait any longer.

"Here, let me take your coats, and I'll show you. I'm going to take you up into the attic, but don't worry it's not scary. There isn't a mad woman hidden away up there. Have you read *Jane Eyre* at school yet, Ian?" When Ian shook his head, Jim said, "I'm sure it will happen. It's a real classic, but maybe you're still a little young."

"Can you tell us what the story is about?"

"Sure I can, but first let me show you what I have in store for you. Follow me." Trailing along behind, up the stairs and along the hallway, Jim went into one of the bedrooms. "I'm afraid this room needs redecorating, but Jennifer and I only got as far as doing three of the six bedrooms. See why I need you to help me fill this house up?" The wooden floor creaked beneath their feet. Jim opened the closet door and Ian said, "This is just like the *Chronicles of Narnia.*"

"Ah, so you do know those stories and what wonderful tales they are. Here, in our own story, we have a staircase that leads to the wonders of the attic. Are you ready?"

The stairs were narrow and MaryAnn was relieved to see a railing running along the left-hand side. Jim pushed open the door at the top and flipped on the light switch. They all stood, glued to the spot with their mouths open—it was a child's paradise, an enormous lofty space, a place to play, sit calmly listening to music, or bounce on an enormous mattress. "This is where Ben and I used to hang out and our father before us. You will probably find some of the toys rather old-fashioned," he said, running his hand along the mane of a large dapple-gray rocking horse. He walked towards a train set assembled on a huge table at the far end of the room, the boys following closely. He pulled out a wooden box for Johnny to stand on; the little boy's face a picture of amazement at the sight of all the trains—some with passenger cars and some with freight. There were stations with people standing on the platforms; level crossings with levers that actually worked; tunnels and bridges; houses with fences; a small town with a bank, a post office and a country store; roads with cars; fields with horses and cows; even a group of children at the bottom of an embankment waving at a train, and so much more. Jim touched a switch, setting one of the trains in motion and the boys were transfixed; they had never seen anything like it. "The trains were my grandfather's and they were modeled after some famous engines, such as this one here—*The Flying Scotsman*. There's a history of all the trains in a book in the library and it has some fantastic pictures so we can look at that later. In the meantime, let me show you how it all works."

"Aren't you afraid we'll break something?" Ian asked.

"No, it's meant to be played with and if something happens we'll just fix it. You don't ever need to be worried about telling me about anything— the punishment will fit the crime," and he winked at MaryAnn. The remark went over Johnny's head, but Ian looked concerned. "Sorry, Ian, I was only teasing and that wasn't fair."

MaryAnn sat down on a nearby trunk, resting her hands on the smooth surface wondering what mysteries it contained. She listened in perfect contentment as Jim explained all the intricacies of the various switches that would enable the boys to change the tracks, work the warning lights and the gates on the crossings, as well as the trains themselves. He was enjoying himself and she was momentarily forgotten as he shared his much loved trains with her sons. It made her realize how lonely he must have been, always living in the hope that one day he would have a kid to share all these treasures with, and now she had given him two, and she was glad. She heard him say, "Now you've gotten the hang of it, I'm going to go and talk to your mom for a little while." But they barely acknowledged him, engrossed as they were in the art of moving freight and passenger trains along the tracks so they wouldn't collide.

Jim took MaryAnn's hand, led her over to a couple of beanbag chairs, pulling them close together so that once they were sitting down, he was able to reach over and take her hand. "Are you all right?" he asked. "You seem awful quiet."

"It's a lot to take in. You are a man of surprises. I never quite know what you are going to pull out of your hat next."

"Oh, I'm not done yet. I plan to always keep you on your toes. On nights after the boys are in bed and fast asleep, we'll be able to come up here and dance. The floor is double thick and it was designed that way because of the room being a play area for boys, but it's easy to clear a space in the center so we can waltz and there's a gramophone and a stack of old records. All very romantic."

"So, it's just like Will said—I do fit the glass slipper. I never truly believed in fairy tales, but I do now."

Jim turned MaryAnn's hand over and studied her slender fingers and neatly trimmed almond-shaped nails. "You have beautiful hands," he said, lifting her palm, resting it against his cheek. "And so soft."

"I feel as though I could sit here forever which may be the case because I'm not sure either of us is going to be able to get out of these chairs without a great deal of difficulty."

"We'll have to enlist the help of the kids, then."

"That could be hours, just look at them. What a wonderful gift you have shared. You know, the one good thing about us living hand to mouth, there's never been any money for electronic gadgets and I would hate to have to fight with my boys about not spending hours playing solitary computer games. This is so much healthier."

"Wait until I show them the toy soldiers, but we'll save that for another day. Would you like to talk about the wedding? If we have the ceremony the day after Christmas, I'm sure I could persuade the local minister to come to the house."

"I was thinking Christmas Eve because getting married to you would be such a wonderful gift."

"A gift I'd get to unwrap. Now I really like that idea."

"Oh, Jim. What am I going to do with you?"

"It's just everyone will be so busy Christmas Eve with church services and their own traditions, but the day after Christmas is pretty quiet so I thought that would be the best day."

"I can see you're a force to be reckoned with, so I agree—just this once, mind you."

"I thought we'd limit guests to just immediate friends and family and then have a big celebration in the spring. Melford Point has been trying to marry me off for a long time so it wouldn't be fair to deprive them of a party, but we don't have to think about that right now. I just wanted you to be prepared. I'm afraid you'll be getting the once over."

"I went through that with Sam's parents. Admittedly, it wasn't a whole town, but I can hold my own, especially when I have a stake in something as important as my life with you."

"I'd like to ask you something and it doesn't make any difference if you say no, but it's been nagging at me. Would you ever consider having another child?"

"You'd like me to say yes, wouldn't you?"

"That's not why I'm marrying you."

"What would you say if I told you I was incapable of bearing any more children? Would you be terribly disappointed?"

"No. It's you I love, MaryAnn, the person, warts and all."

"Let's just take each day as it comes and if I fall pregnant, something I don't accomplish very easily, then so be it and I will happily bear our child. Does that answer your question?"

"Yes, you've more than answered my question," and he turned to look at her, his eyes moist. "I know we're responsible for our own happiness, but sometimes that self-help jargon is a load of old claptrap. I was reasonably contented with my lot before I met you, but it was a life without purpose, a life without touch, and I am an extremely tactile man. Just sitting here and holding your hand gives me more pleasure than you can possibly imagine."

"I know. That was the hardest part about losing Sam. He would always come up behind me when I was standing at the sink and put his arms around my waist and nuzzle my neck. Sometimes we would just sit side by side on the sofa close enough so we could feel each other's warmth. I never thought a woman was able to have that easy touch with a man without the man wanting to jump her bones, but it was like that with Sam. Of course, sometimes, it ended in lovemaking, but I was never afraid to touch him because sex would always be the end result. Am I making any sense?"

"Yes, and I promise I will never pressure you into anything you don't want to do."

"I'll hold you to that, Mr. Hudson, and judging by the way Johnny is fidgeting, I think he needs to go to the bathroom and he's too polite to ask, so a rescue mission is in order," and she rolled sideways out of the chair and landed on the floor on her hands and knees. Jim sat there, watched her in amazement as she ignored him completely and made a mad dash for her son. "Come, Johnny, and Ian please go pull Mr. Hudson out of the beanbag. I think he's stuck."

Ian grinned at his mom, walked over to Jim and held out his hands. "Do you need some help?" he asked.

"I'm not sure you're strong enough, but you can try."

Ian leaned back, dug the heels of his sneakers into the floor and pulled like mad, but Jim couldn't get any leverage. "It's no good," he said. "I'll have to roll like your mom did." Ian stood to one side and watched Jim lean over sideways, eventually pushing himself to his feet. "Remind me not to sit in those anymore. Come on, champ, let's go downstairs. You must be getting hungry."

"What were you and mom talking about?"

Jim, caught off-guard by Ian's question, but pleased he was being less reticent, wasn't quite sure how to respond. "Mainly wedding stuff," he said as they started down the stairs with Ian in front.

"Did you choose a date and will there be lots of people?"

"We decided on December twenty-sixth, and no there won't be many, but there will be a party in the spring so a lot more people can celebrate."

"Are you a very important person?" Ian said, turning to look at him as they reached the bottom of the stairs and made their way out of the closet.

"Not important like the President or the Queen of England, but I do know a great many people because my family has been here for three generations and Melford Point is a small town."

"When my mom marries you, will that make us important too?"

"You're important now."

"Yes, I know, but it will be different, won't it?"

Jim sat down on one of the beds and looked at Ian. "What's on your mind, son?"

"I don't know. It's hard to explain. I had one world with my dad, and then I had a world with just my mom and Johnny, and now there's going to be another world with you. I worry that people will treat me different, I guess. It seems I just get used to things being one way and then they change."

"Would you rather I didn't marry your mom?"

"No, that's not it." Ian shuffled his feet, looked at the floor and burst into tears. Jim held out his arms and he walked into his embrace.

"We'll figure it out together, I promise you. I know how difficult it has been for you and you can still look out for your mom. I'm not going to get in the way of that." He held Ian by the shoulders and looked into his tear-stained face. "I love you very much and you can talk to me about anything. I will never be able to replace your father and I am not even going to try, but I will be good to you and your mom and Johnny and I will look after you."

Ian moved back, wiped his sleeve across his face, gave Jim a tentative smile. "Sorry about the waterworks," he said.

Jim stood up and put his arm around Ian's shoulders. "Let's go find your mom." Surprised by Ian's outburst, he considered the boy's willingness to confide a step in the right direction, more confident now that he and Ian could make their relationship work. Sympathizing with him, he understood Ian's confusion, knowing full well what it was like to have the rug pulled from under your feet.

CHAPTER TWENTY

ENID AND HENRY

On Sunday morning, Henry spent a great deal of time in his study happily writing "to do" lists, not quite believing he and Enid were about to disrupt their lives. He finally leaned back into his comfy leather chair, removed his glasses and rubbed his eyes, tired and scratchy from all the concentration. He heard the doorbell and Enid saying hello to Theodore Blunt, asking him to come in; he went to join them, glad of the distraction, eager to tell their visitor all about their idea. Theodore, ensconced comfortably in one of the armchairs, rested his plump hands on his rounded belly and listened intently to what Henry had to say. "I think it's a grand idea. If Thea were my daughter, I wouldn't hesitate to find a way to be closer to her."

"You don't think we're too old?" Enid asked, looking nervously at Theodore, giving him one of her shy smiles.

"You're only as old as you feel and you and Henry look spry and healthy to me. In any case, it's a good thing to be close to family especially when we get older. My wife, Jenny, was my family and then Ellie became my adopted daughter, but all I have now are cherished memories. I would wish more than that for you."

"We've missed out on an awful lot because we've been so self-absorbed. Of course, I've only been retired a couple of years but that's a poor excuse. Thea's done a fantastic job of raising those kids virtually single-handedly and we can't wait to be a part of their lives. Right, Enid?"

Enid nodded. Sitting on the edge of the sofa and clutching her mug of coffee tightly in her tiny hands, staring down into the milky liquid, she looked up and said, "I'd like to think it will be helpful to Thea to have us around."

"I'm sure it will," Theodore said.

"Thank you for listening to us. It's always helpful to have another opinion, but we're taking up your time and distracting you from the true purpose of your visit. Do you have the list of people you'd like us to call?" Henry asked.

"Certainly." Theodore reached into the inside pocket of his tweed jacket, pulled out a folded sheet of paper. "Here," he said, holding it out to Henry, suggesting he look it over just in case he was unable to read his writing.

Henry picked up his reading glasses from the coffee table, and holding them in both hands, slid them up his nose. Carefully unfolding the piece of paper, he perused the list intently, the handwriting shaky, a little dismayed to see there were about thirty names. He walked over to Theodore, asked him to clarify a couple of the names and numbers just to make sure he was reading them right. "I hope I haven't given you too many to call," Theodore said, "and I'm sorry about my chicken scratch."

"It's fine," Henry said, returning to his chair, "and a wintry Sunday afternoon is probably a good time to catch people in. What is it you would like me to say to them?"

"I'm sorry, this isn't very pleasant, is it? Just tell them you are calling on my behalf and that Ellie passed away in her sleep Friday after a long illness. Please tell them there will be a notice in the paper giving all the details about a memorial service and where to send charitable donations in lieu of flowers. You can tell them the burial will be a private family-only affair in Maine, but that there will be a memorial service here, the details of which will also be posted in the local newspaper. I'm sorry, I appear to be repeating myself. It's hard to think straight sometimes. Do you have any other questions?"

Henry sat silently, rubbing his chin up and down with his fingers. Finally, he said, "I wish your coming over to visit had been for a happier reason. I am truly sorry . . ." and he was unable to continue. He glanced at Enid sitting knitting, the soft clicking of her needles comforting in the sudden and awkward silence. Theodore leaned forward, pushed himself out of the chair. "I think I had better leave before I make a fool of myself."

Enid thrust her knitting to one side, held out her arms to Theodore and moved towards him. He stood motionless, tears rolling down his face, one arm hanging limply by his side and the other searching in his pocket for his handkerchief. She stopped in embarrassment, surprised at her desire to comfort this poor man. She turned to Henry, "I think we all need a stiff drink."

"I couldn't agree more," Henry said, limping off to the dining room, still favoring his injured ankle.

Enid put her arm around Theodore's shoulders. "This has been an emotional time for all of us. Please stay and have a drink with us. I can't let you leave like this."

"Thank you," he said, removing his glasses, wiping his face and polishing the lenses with his handkerchief. "I'm sorry you and Henry have been the ones to witness my falling apart. I just realized when I was talking how clinical I sounded about one of the most beloved people in my life. I just can't believe she's gone. She was so young and I don't understand why someone as good as Ellie had to get sick. It's just not fair."

Enid didn't say anything, removing her arm from his shoulders and taking the tumbler of whisky from Henry's hand, she gave it to Theodore. "Here, drink this. It's the best medicine, I know."

"You are both very kind." He put the glass to his lips and sipped the amber liquid, feeling the warmth slide smoothly down his throat softening the edges of his grief. He looked up into the concerned faces of Henry and Enid. "I'm sorry. I'm feeling a little embarrassed as you can well imagine."

"There's no need. You're among friends," Henry said.

Henry sat sipping his drink. There were a million questions on the tip of his tongue, but he didn't dare voice them and run the risk of upsetting Theodore again, so he talked about the real estate market and how he was concerned about the length of time it would take to sell the house. He concurred with Enid when she extended an invitation to dinner one evening next week; he too worried about Theodore being on his own. Henry, delighted to hear Theodore had a friend in Dorothy, offered to help with the arrangements for the memorial service. He watched Theodore relax, noticing the whisky had brought a little color back into the old man's cheeks. Enid produced crackers and cheese. Surprised to find he was enjoying the conversation made him realize how much he missed the comfortable bantering he had once had with his business colleagues. Theodore was a smart and well-educated man and Henry broached the subject of whether he played chess. The old man shook his head. He would have liked to build a friendship, but decided it was rather futile seeing as he and Enid would be moving away.

Eventually, Theodore stood up to leave, saying he was feeling fine now and seeing as he seemed steady on his legs, they let him go. He and Henry shook hands, and sensing Enid's earlier boldness had deserted her, stepped forward and gave her a hug. "Thank you, good friends. You have no idea how much you helped me today." Henry opened the door. He and Enid, standing side by side, oblivious to the wintry air's icy breath seeping into the house, watched Theodore as he climbed into his car and drove away.

Henry declined Enid's offer of lunch, and went back to his study to start making phone calls. Feeling mellow as a result of not only the whisky, but also for reaching out to a fellow man, he embarked on his task with a sense of well-being, realizing how much easier it was for him to be dispassionate because he hadn't known Ellie very well. Had it been Thea, he would never have been able to make any of these phone calls. With the effects of the whisky wearing off, he found himself becoming more and more depressed but he soldiered on, barely acknowledging Enid when she brought him a sandwich and a very welcome steaming hot cup of tea. His throat was dry and his voice almost reduced to a croak, but he decided if he stopped now with only five names left on the list, he'd be unable to continue. He sipped the tea, forgot the sandwiches, and turned on the desk lamp to dispel the gloom. Fortunately, Theodore had given Henry Dorothy's number as well as his own in case there were questions he couldn't answer, but for the most part, the people he called were well mannered and respectful, took the proffered information with appropriate sadness and thanked him for calling. He only had to give out Dorothy's number twice and Theodore's not at all.

Eventually, he was done; the last name on the list crossed off. Slumped in relief, he ran his hands through his sparse head of white hair, turned off the desk lamp, picked up his abandoned sandwich and empty mug, and went off to find Enid. Not by nature a physically demonstrative man, he was surprised to find how badly he wanted a hug. Finding her standing at the kitchen sink peeling potatoes, he went up behind her, put his arms around her waist and rested his chin on top of her hair. "That was one of the hardest things I have ever had to do," he said. "I'm so glad we've made the decision to move. Having to make those phone calls really brought it home to me about the importance of being close to our daughter. I can't wait to call the real estate agent in the morning."

Enid, surprised by the depth of her own feelings, firmly believed she had her grandson to thank for her newfound awareness. Reaching out to her when she was feeling lost and overwhelmed by shyness, Peter had stirred up the buried emotions within her orphaned heart. She now found herself fascinated by her grandchildren, wanting to spend time with them, and she knew Henry felt the same way. Finally, she could feel herself turning into a human being brave enough to weather a new life. She turned as Henry stepped away from her, looking up into his much loved and familiar face. "I love you, Henry Marchant," she said, putting her hands on his shoulders, standing on tippy-toes to kiss him and he bent over and returned her kiss.

CHAPTER TWENTY-ONE

THEA

Thea had one more day to get through before the kids went back to school. Together virtually non-stop since early Thursday morning, she was desperate for some time to herself. Exasperated, she shooed Honey and Peter out into the yard; attempted to placate Jessica who, whining and bored, pulled faces at any of Thea's suggestions, and became really cross when she said she couldn't invite Johnny over to bake cookies. Stamping and pouting, she went off to her room. Only Izzie seemed tranquil, quite content to be at home practicing her ballet, writing her stories or drawing.

The house was a mess, the kitchen floor dirty, especially where Honey went in and out, but it was pointless trying to clean today. In any case, she wasn't in the mood and it wouldn't be fair to the kids on their last day of vacation.

Thea called MaryAnn to find out the name and phone number of the owner of the empty store, and suggested a walk on the beach while Izzie was at practice to which MaryAnn readily agreed. Thea said she would pick the three of them up, saying it would be a bit of a tight squeeze because she had to return the rental car. Delighted to find Georgie Simpson at home, and deciding to curb her impatience knowing it would be easier without the children, she set up an appointment for ten o'clock Tuesday morning. Should she call Michael now, or wait until after she had seen the space and found out what the rent would be? She chose to wait.

They all piled into the van for the last time to make the drive to Yarmouth to pick up her much loved but ancient Volvo. She also realized, even without Izzie, four kids and a rather large dog would not be able to fit in the back seat. Oh, well . . . she would worry about it when they got to MaryAnn's. Fortunately, the Volvo—cleared of snow by the rental company—roared into life, energized by the new battery replaced a few weeks ago. Leaving the car running, she, the children and the dog wandered into the Enterprise office and waited while one of the employees carried out a thorough examination of the van. All was well, but she swallowed when she saw the cost, and even though she'd already worked it out in her head, the reality of the figure on the receipt hit home. Pulling out of the parking lot, the car cumbersome and sluggish in comparison to the smoothness and luxury of the minivan, tempted her into the fantasy of a new vehicle, but she would have to make do with the Volvo, at least for now. She dropped Izzie off at the studio, making sure her daughter was safely inside before pulling away.

MaryAnn's directions to the house made it easy to find. Appalled at the rundown state of the place, it gave her the creeps, but she changed her horrified expression to one of delight when she saw the Wilkinsons coming towards her warmly dressed in their new coats. Thea thought how good MaryAnn looked, and even Johnny seemed to have more color in his cheeks. Ian's face lit up at the sight of Peter and Honey; he seemed more youthful somehow and Thea was glad. She explained the predicament of not being able to fit four kids and a dog into her back seat, so they had no choice but to take two cars. Jessica and Johnny went with MaryAnn, and Ian and Peter clambered into the back of the Volvo, Honey sitting between them, panting her excitement.

Thea parked in the lot above the beach and MaryAnn pulled up alongside. MaryAnn tugged the little ones' hats firmly down over their ears, checked their gloves were on and their jackets snugly zipped. Struggling over the pebbles to the sand below, Thea thought about the last time they had been there on that Indian summer day in September when Peter had nearly drowned. MaryAnn tucked her arm through Thea's and said, "Penny for your thoughts. You were miles away."

"Oh, I was just thinking about the last time the kids and I were here, that's all. How are things going with you and Jim?"

"We're ironing out the kinks and we've picked a wedding date—December twenty-sixth—at Jim's house. He must be fed up with me changing my mind, but I've decided not to move in until after the wedding. It just didn't sit right, but things aren't so bad because I've thrown caution to the wind and turned up the heat! We can stand that awful house if we're warm and I'll worry about the bill later. It also means I'll have time to buy new underwear!" and MaryAnn laughed. "Did you call Georgie?"

"I did. I'm going over tomorrow at ten." She stopped walking, watched the children running up and down the sand. Their voices and Honey's barking carried on the breeze. Running after pebbles thrown by the kids, the dog lunged towards the ocean, the waves calm for her initiation, jumping back when one came too close to her paws. Thea took a deep breath, looked up at the wispy fair weather clouds softening the harsh winter sunlight. "I love the beach," she said. "Just look at how much fun they're all having. Right this very minute life is good and I'm able to count my blessings rather than dwelling on all the bad stuff. How about you? I'm sorry, that was rather a silly question. Obviously, things are better for you."

"We'd better keep walking otherwise we're going to get cold, and yes, I feel as though I am living the most amazing fairy tale."

"I'm a little jaundiced when it comes to fairy tales because my glass slipper never truly fits, but I know yours does."

"That's what Will told me. I can't believe how lucky I am and the best thing of all is how Jim's and my happiness is affecting the boys. Even the boy in Ian is beginning to emerge, but I have no illusions about how hard it is going to be for him. Johnny accepted Jim right away because he doesn't really remember Sam. But that's enough about me. Tell me all about this plan of yours."

Thea thrust her hands deep into her pockets. "I'm actually feeling a little selfish because I let my enthusiasm get in the way of my compassion."

"How come?"

"Our reason for going to Massachusetts was to see my friend Ellie with a view to us moving to take up a partnership in a retail store called Aladdin's Cave; a partnership she had no right to offer me as it turns out." Thea swallowed. "This is hard to talk about. Let's just say the weekend was full of unpleasant surprises."

MaryAnn remained silent, tucked her arm through Thea's once again. They held onto each other, walked along the rapidly disappearing sand, oblivious to the waves lapping at their feet.

"The store is owned by a man named Theodore Blunt and he, Ellie and I worked together for two years until I married Michael and moved to Maine. We both knew, even though we promised to get together, that it would be virtually impossible with her having to run the store and me busy having babies. Consequently, we had very little contact over the years, so imagine my surprise when she called out of the blue and offered me a partnership in Aladdin's Cave. It seemed too good to be true. I discussed it with the kids, and eventually talked them into making the trip." Thea took a deep breath. "Ellie didn't tell me she was sick with an inoperable brain tumor, and had I been aware, I would not have taken the kids. I still have mixed feelings about what happened and I know she wanted to see me one last time before she died, and to be fair, she had no idea she was going to die this past weekend, but . . ." She paused. Keeping her promise to Robert, she omitted to tell MaryAnn that Ellie had taken her own life, although she would have loved to share the burden of her own guilt.

"You don't have to say anymore if you don't want to," MaryAnn said.

"It helps to talk. She wrote me this beautiful letter telling me how much she loved me; how she'd never wanted to get married because she had seen what it had done to her mother, but I could read between the lines. I honestly had no idea and I'm glad I didn't and I would never have known had she lived. We ended up with Honey at Ellie's bequest."

"That's a lot of responsibility for you."

"Anyway, I called Mr. Blunt because as soon as I heard about the empty store, I thought I could open up an Aladdin's Cave here in Melford Point in Ellie's memory and I asked him if I could buy the inventory if he decided to close the store in Massachusetts. He jumped at the chance without so much as a moment's hesitation, and now I have to find a sponsor. So, if the space is suitable, I am going to swallow my pride and ask my ex as he's not short of a dollar or two."

"I'm pleased something good has come out of all this tragedy for you. You certainly deserve it."

"I'm not so sure. I still feel bad about leaving Mr. Blunt and Ellie's brother behind to deal with all the funeral arrangements, and I would have stayed if it hadn't been for the kids, but I had to get them away. I'm sorry, this is thoughtless of me; you and the boys have already been through all this."

"That was different. We knew it was going to happen, but let's change the subject. You know, when I saw the store, I immediately thought how ideal it would be for a photography studio because that's what Sam and I used to do for a living. But I put the thought out of my mind because I barely had enough money for the apartment, let alone a studio."

"Well, if this all comes about, you can have a nice big corner," Thea said, squeezing MaryAnn's arm and pushing her sleeve back and looking at her watch. "My goodness, is that the time? I need to round up the troops and go get Izzie. Thanks for listening to me."

The kids, amazed at Honey's boundless energy, stood in a circle and watched her dig a hole, scooting backwards, pushing the sand out of the way with her paws. "See, see," Jessica said. "She digs holes just like Lady did."

"So, she does," Thea said, "and I hate to break this up, but it's time to go."

Once they reached the parking lot, Honey stood patiently, distracted by the gulls flying high above her head, while Peter rubbed a towel from side to side underneath her belly. Even with his diligence, Thea had no doubt the car would be full of sand, but a little discomfort was a suitable trade-off for the enjoyment the trip to the beach had given the kids and one ecstatic dog. They said their goodbyes, climbing into their separate cars, Thea promising she would let MaryAnn know how her meeting with Georgie went and her subsequent phone call with Michael. She said she also wanted to hear about her wedding plans and apologized for monopolizing their conversation. MaryAnn just thanked her for rescuing her from her interminable packing.

Dark by the time Thea reached the studio, she sat in the car and observed the dancers through the studio window. Gathered together doing their final stretches, she loved to watch their lithe bodies and graceful movements. Miss Beauchamps appeared to be exceedingly animated, smiling and gesticulating wildly; Thea assumed the rehearsal had gone well. She got out of the car once she saw Izzie putting on her coat. Unable to leave Jessica and Peter alone, she willed Izzie to hurry up, moving from one foot to the other in an attempt to stay warm. Eventually, she emerged from the studio, walked over to her mom, all beams and smiles. "I gather the rehearsal was a good one," Thea said.

"It was. I actually got to dance with a Nutcracker and that helped so much."

Thea looked at her daughter, positively bristling with good health and excitement with roses in her cheeks and stars in her eyes. "How lucky you are to have such a passion and now let's get you home." She waved to Miss Beauchamps, clambered into the car, made sure Izzie's seat belt was securely fastened, her much-loved ballet shoes clutched in her lap. Glancing around at her precious cargo, she headed for home, hoping she'd be able to realize her own passion in creating a Melford Point Aladdin's Cave.

CHAPTER TWENTY-TWO

MARGARET AND BILL

On Monday night, Margaret and Bill had just finished supper and she was sitting at the kitchen table reading the local paper, reluctant to tackle the dishes, when the phone rang. Margaret was tired, her ankles swollen from standing all day, and she didn't feel much like talking, unless it was Nan, of course. Bill, ensconced in the living room watching the news, didn't pick up the phone; evenings were quiet time for him. Pushing herself to her aching feet, she walked a couple of steps and unhooked the receiver from the wall.

"Hi Mom," Nan said. "How are you?"

"I'm fine. You?"

"Are you sitting down?"

"I can be," and she slumped down onto the nearest chair. "Go on. There have already been quite a few surprises around here, and now are you going to add your own?"

"I don't know quite how to tell you this."

"Please get it over with. I only hope you're going to give me good news."

"For me and Stanley it is, but I hope you and Dad will think so, too."

"For goodness sake tell me," Margaret said, beginning to lose patience.

"Okay, here goes. I'm pregnant."

"Oh, Nan," Margaret said, visions of the fairy tale wedding she had planned in her head vanishing into thin air. "How are you feeling?"

"Are you all right? I'm sorry to drop this bombshell over the phone, but I just couldn't wait any longer, and in answer to your question, I feel really good. Luckily, no morning sickness."

"You take after me, then. What's going to happen about your wedding plans?"

"We thought we'd come home and have a small wedding at Christmas."

Margaret could hear the hope in Nan's voice and she put her daughter out of her misery. "I'd like that and I'm truly happy I'm going to be a grandma, even if it is a little sooner than I expected."

"Oh, Mom, thank you. What do you think Dad's going to say?"

"As long as you're happy and safe, that's all he'll care about and you know how much he loves kids. You know if you bear a son, he's going to be summing him up to eventually run the store."

Nan chuckled. "Too right. I'm so glad I've told you. I've wanted to for a while now, but I wanted to make sure I was pretty safe. Didn't want to jinx it. I hope you understand."

"Of course I do, now that I'm over the initial shock. How did Stanley's parents react?"

"Absolutely nothing fazes them. They love me, and as far as they're concerned, we are just adding another family member to their already huge brood. I must admit it is all a little overwhelming for me at times because there's so many of them, but I couldn't ask for better in-laws. I'm sorry if you had visions of a big wedding."

"I won't lie to you, I have wondered what kind of wedding you would have, hoping it would be in the church here, but as long as you are happy and healthy, that's all that matters. I also have some news of my own concerning weddings. Jim Hudson and MaryAnn Wilkinson are getting married."

"Wow. That was fast."

"You should see the change in MaryAnn and in her youngest son Johnny. It's quite remarkable. Also, the Chamberlins have a dog. I don't know how that came about, but it seems as though she's Peter's primarily. Your dad offered to dog sit. He was very taken with her. Her name is Honey and she's got a lot of retriever in her and is a little bigger than Lady was."

"I'm pleased for Peter. Chances are I'll find out the story behind it before you do because I plan to call Thea," Nan said.

Margaret chose to ignore her teasing. "I wish you weren't so far away, especially now, and I never asked you how Stanley has reacted to the news."

"He's thrilled, of course, but like me he would have liked us to have some time to ourselves before having a family, but we shall make the best of it. We love each other very much and that's all that really matters. He will be a great hands-on dad."

"Do you want to tell your dad yourself, or shall I?"

"It's okay, you can tell him."

"I'm assuming you will be house hunting. I don't suppose there's any way you could persuade Stanley to take up a position with a veterinary practice in this area."

"We have talked about it, but he loves his job at Tufts, plus he gets very good medical coverage. He likes having all the latest scientific and technical procedures at his fingertips, something he says he wouldn't get in private practice, so we're stuck in Massachusetts, at least for the time being."

"Well, that's that, then. I can't say I'm not disappointed. Makes me wish I weren't so tied to the store because I'd love to be able to drop the whole kit and caboodle and come help with the baby, but I'm jumping ahead of myself."

"I know, Mom, but unfortunately, it is what it is."

"Have you had any thoughts on how you would like to plan the wedding?"

"I know for sure I'm not going to be sailing down the aisle in a white dress trying to hide my bump, so I'm undecided. If you've got any great ideas . . ."

"How about a private room at The Crooked Inn? If you remember, Thea gave your dad and me a gift voucher and we had a lovely meal there."

"I think that's a great idea. Do you think Reverend Matthews would still marry us?"

"I'm sure he would. I can talk to him if you'd like. I'm not sure whether the laws in Maine have changed, but I could find out about blood tests, et cetera."

"Thanks, Mom, that would be great."

"Do you think any of Stanley's family will come?"

"I don't know. I suppose it all depends on the date, the weather . . . If we chose New Year's Eve, that would mean Christmas was out of the way."

"Now that sounds like a really good idea. What time of day, do you think?"

"I would like late afternoon for the ceremony and then dinner afterwards at the Inn. I'm so glad I talked to you. I've really been floundering, what with work and being tired all the time."

"You know what they say, a problem shared is a problem halved."

"Talking to you always makes me feel better. Anyway, I'm going to let you go now so you can talk to Dad. I love you."

"I love you, too, and you make sure you take care of yourself and Little Bump."

"I will, Mom. Bye."

Margaret heard the click as Nan cut off. She stood up, replaced her own receiver, and choosing to ignore the dishes, went off in search of Bill who, predictably, was napping in front of the TV. But this wasn't the time to let him sleep. She nudged him gently on the shoulder with the palm of her hand and sat down beside him. "Bill, wake up. I have something to tell you."

"What is it, lass? You look mighty pleased with yourself."

"Nan called, and guess what? You are going to be a grandpa a little earlier than planned."

"Well now, ain't that a right turn up for the book."

"You don't sound very surprised. Here am I dropping a bombshell and I might just as well be telling you it's going to snow tomorrow," Margaret said, looking at him with disappointment.

"Did you see the way Nan and Stanley were with each other when they came for Thanksgiving? They couldn't keep their hands off each other, so I'm not the least bit surprised."

"I guess I didn't pay much attention, but now that you mention it . . . Anyway, are you pleased?"

"Of course I am. This is the best news I've had for a long time. My own grandchild—how absolutely wonderful that will be. Love is definitely in the air, what with Jim and MaryAnn and now Nan and Stanley. Life should always be this good," and he put his arm around Margaret's shoulders, squeezed her tight and gave her a kiss on the cheek. "I am one very lucky man, and I'm assuming we have a wedding to plan."

CHAPTER TWENTY-THREE

THEA

The vacant store in Melford Point was all Thea hoped it would be. Standing next to Georgie Simpson, she absorbed the atmosphere of the white-walled space, visualizing all the colorful merchandise of Aladdin's Cave beautifully displayed. Armed with a tape measure, a pencil and a notepad, she measured, made notes on where to put a book corner; shelves and a cutting table for fabric; an area for items from local craftsmen; racks for greeting cards, leaving one whole wall for art supplies. The possibilities were endless. Delighted to discover a storage area with a bathroom out back to the left of where the stairs climbed to the apartment above, she imagined a craft room such as the one in Massachusetts, but smaller.

Thea asked Georgie all sorts of questions, found her easy to talk to, and was delighted to learn there would be very few restrictions when it came to making alterations. With the freshly painted walls and refinished floor, there was little she would have to do other than fill the empty space. "I can't thank you enough. This is perfect for what I have in mind. The only snag is confirmation of monetary backing, but I promise I will get back to you as soon as I can."

"Of course. I understand. There's unlikely to be any interest at this time of the year, but I will call you if anything comes up. Give you the right of first refusal."

"Thank you. That's only fair." They shook hands and Thea waited while Georgie locked the door, taking one last peek through the window.

Thea crossed the street heading for Down East Real Estate. Marjorie Franks looked up as Thea walked through the door, instantly recognizing her. Thea was no fool. Marjorie seemed friendly enough, but there was little warmth in her smile. Immaculate and business-like, salon-bleached neatly trimmed hair, scarlet lipstick and nails to match her sweater, she said, "How can I help?" Thea, feeling like a country bumpkin in her jeans and comfortable but well-worn boots, explained her parents planned move to Melford Point from Massachusetts. Marjorie's eyes shrewdly appraised. Unfazed by the scrutiny, Thea asked about the possibility of a ground floor rental apartment within walking distance of town.

"Why don't you sit down and I'll see what we have."

Thea perched on the edge of the chair, unzipped her jacket, pulled off her gloves, and stuffed them into her pockets. Beads of perspiration broke out on her upper lip. Marjorie stared at her computer screen. "There are a couple of possibilities. A ground floor, two bedroom, in a converted Victorian house actually in town just past the park on the left-hand side, and one in a small apartment complex just past the library. I'm sure you're familiar with it."

"Yes, I do know where you mean. I've never paid much attention to it, but this is encouraging news. Do either of them have garages?"

"They both do."

"This gets better and better."

Marjorie printed off details for both properties and Thea looking at them briefly, asked Marjorie how long she thought they would remain vacant.

"They are both long-term rentals. This time of the year, I think they will be available for quite some time, but you never know. Do you have any idea of the time frame of your parents' move?"

"They have only just made up their minds and I think my dad was contacting a realtor today. Let me discuss these properties with him and see if he's happy with the monthly cost. Of course, this is a terrible time of the year to sell a house, but miracles do happen and there might be a buyer just around the corner."

"If you need any help, let me know. I have contacts in Massachusetts and I'm sure I could find a good real estate agent for your parents."

"Thank you. You've been very helpful and I'm glad I stopped by. I'll let you know what my dad says and how he wants to move forward."

Marjorie stood up, walked around her desk and held out a business card. "Here," she said.

Thea glanced at the clock on the wall, noticed with horror she was going to be late picking up Jess. "I must dash," she said, "and thank you again."

Jess, sitting with Miss Simms on the bench outside the Kindergarten class-room, looked a little forlorn. "Where were you, Mommy?" Thea bent down, took both of her hands. "I'm so sorry, I stopped at the real estate agent to see if there were any apartments available for Grandma and Grandpa and I lost track of time."

Monica Simms stood up, tendrils of her neat dark hair beginning to escape from the bun at the nape of her neck. "No harm done, but we were concerned. Jessica told me you don't have a cell phone. We did try to call you at home, but it just rolled into the answering machine."

"I'm absolutely mortified to have worried Jessica and inconvenienced you like this. It won't happen again, and Jess is quite right, I don't have a cell phone, but I guess it's time."

"In situations like this, it's reassuring for the school to know they can reach you."

"Of course, I understand. Come, Jessica, let's go home." She held out her hand. Consumed with guilt, worried she might have damaged her rela-tionship with Monica Simms, crucial for Jessica's well being, she was mad at herself. She had also created an awkward situation for her daughter and this bothered her more than anything. Routine was so essential to Jess and being let down like this was not good. She wasn't sure how to make amends.

Monica Simms, after watching them walk away, went back into her class-room. She would never forget the look on Jessica's face when she realized her mother wasn't there to pick her up. The little girl, standing with all the other children, saw them leave one by one, until she was left all by herself. She had looked up at Monica, her lip quivering, her eyes filling with tears. "Why isn't my mommy here?" Now the little girl was always going to be worried her mom would be late, just when she was getting back her self-confidence. "Darn it," Monica said, sitting down at her desk, wishing this had happened to any other child but Jessica.

Thea, worried about Honey, was eager to get home. Of two minds about taking her in the car with her, but deciding it was too cold, she had left her in the house with Smokey for company. When she and Jessica arrived home—their ride short but emotionally charged, Jessica refusing to be placated—they found the dog sitting in the middle of the hall mat, tail swishing back and forth, shivering in excitement. Jessica bent down, gave Honey a gentle hug. "I'm so pleased to see you," she said. "And you too," turning her attention to Smokey, giving her mother the cold shoulder.

"Why don't you take Honey out into the back yard."

Ignoring Thea, standing up, looping her gloved hand through Honey's collar, tugging her gently, Jessica said, "Come." Honey dutifully walked with her through the kitchen, sat waiting until she opened the door. Running across the snow-covered lawn, Jessica found the tennis ball Peter had left by the stone bench in the rose garden. Her underhanded throws didn't send the ball very far, but Honey still ran and picked it up, dropping it at Jessica's feet, looking expectantly at her to throw it again. Jessica giggled, some of her natural buoyancy returning, but she was still mad at her mom. Eventually with her enthusiasm over the game waning, her hands cold, Jessica admitted defeat and marched back into the kitchen. Sitting down on the floor, she attempted to pull off her boots, teeth gritted in her determination to be independent. "Are you still mad at me?" Thea asked. "Don't you think I've been punished enough?"

Jessica, sticking both legs out in front of her, leaning back on her hands, looked up at her mother. "I suppose. My boots are stuck."

"Thank you for forgiving me," she said, taking hold of each of Jess's boots by the heels, tugging them off. Jess leaned forward to rub her toes; Honey came over to investigate, pushing her nose into Jessica's ear.

Jessica giggled. "I'm so glad we have Honey. She makes me feel happy. Even though I love my teddy bears, she's a real one because she has a heart. I feel safe with her around cuz I know she would take care of me if there was a bad man."

Thea swallowed. "I agree," she said, a catch in her voice. "She makes me feel safe too. Why don't you give her a biscuit for being such a good dog?"

Jessica didn't need to be told twice and held out her hands so Thea could remove her gloves. Pulling off her hat, she stood up and shook off her jacket. Honey, deciding Jessica was her charge for the afternoon, followed the little girl to the pantry, and gently took the biscuit from Jessica's outstretched hand.

Thea idly flipped through the mail. It was mostly junk, a couple of bills and the letter from Christopher Morrison, the envelope addressed in her dad's neat and tiny handwriting. Christopher's handwriting also neat, but firm, bold and well formed seemed to imply determination. She read:

Dear Thea

I know this is presumptuous of me, and of course you have no clue who I am, but hopefully, you will remember me as the guy who came into Aladdin's Cave and bought a silver pendant for his sister. You also helped me choose a card—the cat with the bird sitting on its head. You said it was "whimsical and cute."

I didn't want to invade your privacy so I called your dad, explained who I was, and asked if he would get this note to you. I know nothing about you except your first name and if you wish to keep it that way, I will completely understand.

I will tell you a little bit about me. I'm a computer programmer and work at a small company in Great Barrington. I love to exercise and be outdoors so I run, hike, bike, ski, depending on the weather. I'm also an avid reader—makes a pleasant change to stare at the printed page rather than a computer screen. My parents live in Lenox and I have a sister named Madeline (Maddy) and she lives in New York City with her husband, Colin.

I do hope you will either write back to the address above (snail mail, a novelty in this electronic age!) or shoot me an email. I've also listed my phone number, so please feel free to give me a call.

Best wishes
Christopher Morrison

It was a nice letter, but she had no idea what she was going to do about it. She did remember him, their brief encounter no more than a passing thought. Pushing the letter to one side, she decided to talk it over with MaryAnn. No more snap decisions for her.

Thea went off to see what Jessica was up to and found her sitting in the beanbag chair in her room—Honey laying at her feet—pretending to read one of her favorite books, *The Problem with Chickens* by Bruce McMillan. The story, set in Iceland, was all about chickens who forgot they were chickens and started acting like ladies. Thea, enchanted by the bright oil paintings when she had first picked it up at A Good Read, bought it for Jessica's fifth birthday.

"Are you okay?"

"Uh-huh. I'm reading to Honey."

"I see that. I need to make a couple of phone calls, but come find me if you need anything."

Thea took a deep breath, cleared her throat, plucked up the courage to call Michael first, but it rolled into voicemail. Frustrated, she left a message. Her dad was home, though, and answered on the second ring. "How are you? How's the ankle?"

"Much better. Another few days and I'll be driving again."

"I just wanted to let you know I found a couple of ground floor rentals within walking distance of town. I haven't looked at them, but I can if you'd like me to. Should I send you the specs? Did you call the realtor? Sorry, I'm getting carried away here. I'm assuming you and Mom haven't changed your minds."

"Absolutely not, and the real estate agent came over yesterday. She didn't seem to think we'd have any problems selling, but realistically, we won't be able to move until the house is sold and that's not going to happen overnight."

"I understand. Do you think you could at least come for Christmas? That way you'd be able to see Izzie in *The Nutcracker* and she would love that."

"I don't see any reason why not. Let me talk to your mom, and in the meantime, why don't you send me those specs."

"I will. I have another piece of news."

"You do?"

"I am hoping to be able to open up an Aladdin's Cave here in Melford Point in Ellie's memory. I talked to Mr. Blunt and asked him, if I can get the financial backing, whether I could buy the inventory. He thinks it's a great idea. I'm going to ask Michael if he would like to invest in a business venture."

"Do you think that's wise?"

"I don't know what else to do. Besides which, he has more money than he knows what to do with."

"I don't like to think of you being beholden to him. It's one thing to take money for the children . . ."

"I know, but do you have any better ideas?"

"Do you have a mortgage because, if not, you could take out a loan against the house? I could look into it for you if you'd like."

"It's hard because I have no idea what the inventory is worth, so at this point, I don't know how much I need. There's also the question of the monthly store rent and I'm going to be paying that for a while before I have any income, but I just know I am doing the right thing. I know the winter months will be slow, but the area is hopping in the summertime and I have to believe it will be successful."

"Well, with that attitude, you can't fail. I guess going to Michael isn't such a bad idea, and it sounds as though you will be able to pay him back fairly quickly. Let me know how you get on, and in the meantime, I'll talk to your mom and get back to you about Christmas."

"Okay. Oh, by the way, I received Christopher's letter, but I really don't know what to do about it. You know my luck with men . . ."

"I do, but he's a cut above the rest, and that's all I'm going to say."

"Thanks, Dad. Talk to you soon and I'll put the apartment details in the mail."

"Bye, Thea."

Thea wandered off upstairs to find an envelope in what used to be Michael's desk. Standing looking at the heavy, cumbersome piece of mahogany furniture, with its inlaid green leather top, she wondered why she had kept it. The room had become a dumping ground and it bothered her, but there was no time to do anything about it now. Sidetracked by her mental list, the number one priority a shopping trip with the girls for Peter's birthday this coming Saturday, she almost forgot the envelope. The desk drawer was as muddled as the room. Sitting down on the dust-covered wooden chest, a storage place for all their Christmas decorations, her thoughts jumped to MaryAnn. With Nan so far away, it was good to have a friend close by. Her musings cut short by the ringing of the telephone, she made a mad dash to her bedroom.

"Hello," she said, slightly out of breath.

"Thea?"

"Yes."

"It's Mr. Blunt."

"Oh, hi. Are you okay?"

"We're fine. I just wanted to let you know when Ellie's memorial service will be in the hopes you might be able to come."

Thea's heart sank and she sat down heavily on the edge of the bed. She had been full of good intentions, but now that it was a reality she wasn't sure she would be able to get away. "When is it?"

"Sunday, December tenth at eleven."

"This is divine providence," she said.

"How come?"

"My ex-husband is taking Peter to a concert in Boston on the ninth which means I would be able to bum a ride, so it looks as though I will be able to make it."

"This is excellent news. Even though it's going to be crowded, we've decided to do it at the house. That way it will be less formal and I know Ellie would have liked that. I plan to read the eulogy and if you would like to say something, please let me know. We have quite a few people who want to be part of the program, including some of the older kids. There will be music and food, and even though it will be sad, I think it will be a fitting tribute to someone who gave so much. Also, no dark and dismal clothing—Ellie would have hated that. Sorry, I'm rambling on, and before I forget, you're welcome to stay over if you'd like."

"I would like to write about how Ellie and I first met and how good she was to me during those two short years when we worked together. And I agree with you, it should be a celebration of Ellie's life. Thank you for including me. I wish I were closer so I could help you out."

"I know, but Dorothy is a tower of strength and your mom and dad are splendid. I can't tell you how much I have enjoyed getting to know them. They are so kind and helpful. We are going to have the food catered, a notice will go into the local newspaper, and we will make a few back up phone-calls, so we are all set."

"It certainly sounds as though you've thought of everything. Thank you for the offer of a bed, but I will stay with mom and dad. And if you do think of anything I could do, please let me know. Bye for now."

"Bye, Thea. I'm looking forward to seeing you."

Thea replaced the receiver, sat thinking about how life had the habit of working out sometimes. She also realized with a start, it would solve the Christopher Morrison dilemma because meeting face-to-face would make the decision for her as to whether he was the kind of person who would add, rather than detract from her life. She most definitely was not going to get into a relationship with yet another unsuitable man, and if she didn't like him she could just put the whole thing to bed. Now all she had to do was contact him, pray for good weather and find out from MaryAnn whether she would stay with Izzie and Jessica after she had cleared it with them. And she still had to talk to Michael.

CHAPTER TWENTY-FOUR

MaryAnn

Life settled into a comfortable pattern for the Wilkinsons. MaryAnn continued to work at the diner, and Jim would sometimes stop by, whisking Johnny off with him away from Will's dismal office. The wedding constantly on her mind, she had more or less decided on what she would wear and her dress certainly wasn't going to be white. She and Jim discussed the details, including whom they should invite and Thea had graciously designed and printed invitations. MaryAnn asked Margaret whether she knew of anyone who specialized in wedding cakes. She didn't, but Jennifer came to the rescue.

MaryAnn had listened to Thea when she had called to tell her about Ellie's memorial service, instantly putting her mind to rest by saying she would be happy to stay with Izzie and Jess. They both agreed their friendship was the best thing that had happened for either of them for a very long time, with the exception of Jim of course, and they had both laughed. Thea had told MaryAnn about Christopher Morrison and how he had the stamp of approval from her parents. She had said, "Uh-oh," and that had set them off laughing again. She and Thea were good for each other, and much as she loved Jim, she liked the reassurance of a female confidante, plus having a reciprocal babysitting service was a blessed relief. They had discussed whether they thought Jim still needed to go on the Bon Jovi concert excursion seeing as Thea would be in the car with them for part of the journey each way, plus the fact it would be a tight squeeze with three adults and three children. MaryAnn decided they were being over-protective, and if Marty Johnson's mother was comfortable with the boys just being with Michael, it was okay with her, and Jim had agreed.

Jim had wisely not said anything about her continuing to work at the diner. She had told him about Thea's plan to open a store in Melford Point;

that she was trying to get financial backing, and had offered MaryAnn a corner to set up a studio, presenting her with the possibility to bring her photography business back to life. But she wasn't sure she was ready to go down that road—there were just too many memories. Knowing her days at the diner were drawing to a close, it was hard to let go. Will had been so kind to her and the boys, had thrown her a lifeline when she was drowning. He was a good and honest man with a generosity of spirit. He truly cared for her and the boys, and she had clung to him, not in a physical way, but as a life raft in a stormy sea. Taking the Wilkinsons under his wing, offering her shelter in her time of grief, she just couldn't give those kindnesses up lightly. She also suspected that deep down he had strong feelings for her, but he had never acted on those feelings for which she was eternally grateful. The diner had become her world—a world of people with whom to connect but who demanded nothing in return. Now all that was going to change.

She and Jim had talked at length about their wedding vows, deciding they were quite happy with something traditional. The minister, Reverend Tim Matthews, a warm and charismatic character, a long-time resident of Melford Point, had many stories tucked up his sleeve. Jim warned MaryAnn to be prepared. In love with Jim and the idea of being welcomed into his solid world where roots ran deep, she was really looking forward to their intimate ceremony. She planned to walk down the lovely, elegant staircase, her mind already conjuring up images of all the guests gathered in the spacious hallway.

MaryAnn couldn't get over the change in her boys, and she was pleased she had decided not to move in with Jim until after they were married. This way, it was a gradual transition, and even though they spent a great deal of time in Jim's house, the three of them still spent time together at home. Jim had been true to his word and invited the Chamberlins over for dinner the Sunday after Peter's birthday. She had helped him cook the meal. Ian and Johnny, eager to show off the attic, had taken Peter, Izzie and Jessica up the secret staircase into their magic kingdom and the Chamberlin kids found it hard to hide their envy, but Ian and Johnny placated them by saying they could come over anytime.

Growing up with constant bickering, MaryAnn reveled in the friendly and animated chatter around the dinner table. Thea, once supper was done, needing to satisfy her curiosity, asked Ian if he would show her the attic. He was as proud and as pleased as punch to be able to act as tour guide. Even Carrie and Honey took to each other immediately. Both gentle dogs by nature, Honey sensed Carrie could no longer participate in boisterous games, so she was tentative in the way she approached her. MaryAnn just sat back and watched all this interaction, pleased that both Thea and Jim seemed comfortable together, relieved to see how he treated her with no lingering looks of longing. Always in the back of her mind, even though she trusted him, she hadn't been convinced until she had seen them together that he had actually been able to extinguish the flame he had carried for so long. She breathed a huge sigh of relief; her happiness now complete.

CHAPTER TWENTY-FIVE

THEA—MASSACHUSETTS

Thea, keeping an eye on the weather pattern all week, thanked her lucky stars there were no major snowstorms in the forecast, only flurries. She was nervous about leaving Izzie and Jessica behind, but they kept telling her they were going to be fine. MaryAnn had assured her she would make sure Izzie got to her rehearsal on Saturday afternoon and that she would take Jessica and Johnny to the library. Thea had listened to her talking to Peter, promising walks in the park for Honey, easing Peter's separation anxiety. Thea hugged her daughters and climbed into Michael's shiny black BMW SUV with Peter, Ian and Marty safely strapped in the back, their belongings stashed in the rear, except for their CD players and discs from which they could not be parted. Peter introduced his two friends to his dad and they both politely said thank you for taking them to the concert. Michael just nodded and smiled, the boys a little in awe of his towering presence, his expensive cologne and obvious wealth. She settled herself into the luxury of the leather passenger seat, prepared to enjoy the journey come what may.

"Thank you so much for doing this, Michael, and especially for taking a detour for me. I really appreciate it. Here are a couple of numbers where I can be reached, just in case." She handed him a slip of paper which he tucked into the inside pocket of his navy blazer.

"Still no cell phone, then?"

"Afraid not."

"What time do you think the memorial will be over tomorrow?"

"It starts at eleven and I'm not sure, but if you stopped by Ellie's anytime after one o'clock, I'm sure that would be fine."

"I was thinking about taking the boys to the Aquarium before we leave, so that should work."

"They would love that. They're good kids and I'm sure you are going to enjoy them." She wanted to say, "If only you would come down off your high horse," but she didn't voice her thoughts. "This will be a rare treat for them, especially Ian, and he deserves a little spoiling. I am sure this trip will probably be something they will all talk about for a long time to come."

"I booked a suite at the Residence Inn so we could have two separate bedrooms and it's only a quick cab ride to the concert from there. I trust they'll all be able to sleep in a queen size bed together."

"I'm sure they will. After all it's only one night. Not quite your usual five star, is it?" she said, believing a motive lay behind Michael's choice, fearing the boys would embarrass him at the fancier Boston Harbor Hotel.

"You know me too well. No, it isn't, but the boys will be more comfortable there and will enjoy choosing what they'd like from the buffet breakfast."

"I hope you can get them down from their high place after the concert and please make sure they stay off the soda. That will help." Secretly, she wished him luck!

"Yes, ma'am."

"Thank you for offering to give me a loan."

"Do you have any idea how much you are going to need?"

"Not yet."

"Give me a call as soon as you do and we'll work out the terms and I'll put a legal document together."

There was nothing more to say. Michael didn't ask her any questions and appeared to have little interest in Thea's business venture so they lapsed into silence. She turned in her seat to glance at the boys. She winked at them and they grinned in return. She sat looking out at the overcast day, lost in her own thoughts. Michael drove carefully and expertly, making one stop at a rest area with services after they had been on the road for about three hours. He gave the boys some money and they headed straight for the vending machines. Both Ian and Peter knew better than to get candy, but not so Marty. Thea just watched them, didn't say a word. A little unhealthy eating over the next couple of days wouldn't do any harm.

Back on the road, Michael appeared undaunted by the darkening sky with its threat of snow and pressed on—the luxurious vehicle purring along, eating up the miles. They pulled into Ellie's driveway just shy of four o'clock. Not wanting to hold them up, she said goodbye to the boys, told them to be good, took the slip of paper from Michael with the hotel's phone number, and grabbed her bag from the back. He waited until the front door opened and then he drove away. Thea felt a sense of loss and she hoped she had made the right decision in not having Jim go along. She had given strict instructions to each of the boys to make sure they called home as soon as they arrived at the hotel and she hoped they wouldn't be too intimidated by Michael to do that.

Mr. Blunt welcomed her with open arms and said in his customary fashion, "Come in, come in." She stepped into the beautiful hallway with its highly polished floor, thinking it odd not to see Honey sitting in the center of the rainbow colored rug.

"You're looking well," she said.

"Can't complain. I'm sorry, but you just missed Dorothy. She made lasagna for us and it's bubbling away in the oven. I hope you're hungry."

It felt strange to be back in Ellie's house and she was glad she wasn't sleeping over because the bad memories would just be too close. She and Mr. Blunt talked while they ate and he told her that Robert had called after the funeral in Maine and said taking Ellie back there to be buried had been the right thing to do. He also said he was coming to terms with his sister's death, and even though it was going to take a long time for the Tetreault family to get over their loss, it was good to be home. "He was so much a part of our lives during those last few months of Ellie's illness it's hard to believe I may never see him again, but he is where he's meant to be," Mr. Blunt said.

"He did seem a bit of a square peg and I think he was terribly lonely. Ellie left her French-Canadian roots behind, but I don't think Robert ever did."

"You're absolutely right. So, what have you been up to?"

"Michael is prepared to back me and set up a loan so I can get the store going. It's going to be all very business-like with properly drawn up papers, and of course I will get a much better rate of interest because he's always looking for investments. I did a really good job of convincing him I could make a go of it, but he's no fool. I did want to tell you I felt bad calling you to ask about the inventory, especially when you had so much on your plate."

Theodore looked up from his plate of food and smiled at Thea. "You did me a big favor actually. I think opening a store in Ellie's memory is a wonderful idea. Closing the store here will be sad, but I have my life with Dorothy now and that will ease the heartache."

"I can't wait to meet her. She sounds like a lovely lady."

"Oh, she is, she is," he said, his face breaking into the biggest smile. "We're going to have a good time together, do a little traveling, and check off a few items on my bucket list."

"Good for you. You are an inspiration. Ellie would be happy, you know."

"I believe so. She certainly wouldn't want us to sit around being miserable. I won't be sorry to leave this house now. Having the memorial here tomorrow will help me say goodbye. It feels so empty without her."

"Are you going to put the house up for sale?"

"Yes, when I'm ready. It's not going to be easy."

"I don't know what to say."

"Sometimes there are no words, but I'm so pleased you came," and he pushed his chair back from the table and took his empty plate over to the sink. "Let me show you the program we put together. Come with me." He shuffled off towards the sitting room and Thea was surprised to see most of the furniture had been pushed against the walls. "We'll set up the food in the dining room and bring out all the chairs into the hallway. When we designed this spacious entryway, it certainly wasn't for an occasion such as this, but it will serve us well. At least some of the older folk will have chairs and the children will be quite content to sit on the floor."

Thea glanced down at the program in her hand and read the list of music alternating with the names of those who wished to speak. There were about ten people in total and she was fourth on the list. "Mr. Blunt, I don't see your name. I thought you were planning on reading the eulogy."

"I changed my mind; it would be too much for me," and he looked at her, his lips a grim line. "Tania, one of the older children, is going to read what I wrote. That way I won't make a fool of myself."

"But nobody will mind."

"I will. It's going to be difficult enough as it is."

"I noticed there aren't any flowers."

"Dorothy and I decided if we didn't ask people not to donate flowers, the place would have begun to look like a funeral parlor and that's the last thing we wanted. We requested donations instead to go to cancer research, with an emphasis on brain tumors. This is what Ellie would have wanted. I'm sure there were flowers at the funeral in Maine, but tomorrow is a celebration, not a funeral, so no flowers."

"I think what you are doing here is going to be a wonderful way to say goodbye."

"I think so," he said, looking into her face, taking her hands. "Ellie loved you very much, you know."

This was not an emotional road Thea wanted to travel. "She loved you very much too," and pulled her hands away.

But Theodore wasn't to be sidetracked. "She talked about you all the time."

Thea stared down at the program in her hand, the nervous dampness of her fingers warping the edges of the paper. She just didn't know how to respond, not quite sure what Mr. Blunt expected her to say. His words had made her sad. In the end she just said, "I'm sorry if you feel I let her down."

He just nodded, wandered off towards the kitchen. She followed him, wondering how she was going to ask him if she could use the telephone. She placed the now smudged and wrinkled program on the table and took her plate over to the sink. Mr. Blunt seemed to have withdrawn into a solitary world of hurt and he sat on one of the chairs with his elbows resting on the table and his head in his hands. It seemed as though Ellie's ghost had suddenly appeared and Thea shivered. She sat down next to Theodore and put her arm around his shoulders. The wool of his heather-green cardigan felt soft beneath her fingers and he smelled of shampoo and a faint lingering of mothballs. "I'm sorry I'm not Ellie," she said, blinking rapidly to stop her tears.

"Oh, my dear, please don't take any notice of an old man. I didn't mean to get melancholy on you and I apologize. It's just that Ellie really taught me how to love, to give without asking anything in return. I loved Jenny, but I nursed her out of a sense of duty, always more concerned about myself, how I would manage when she was gone. Ellie made me see things differently." He leaned back in the chair, took out his handkerchief and blew his nose loudly. Thea squeezed his shoulder, removed her arm.

"I know what you mean." The silence dragged on. Unable to stand it any longer, she asked, "Would it be all right if I used the phone?"

"Of course. I think I'll go downstairs to my apartment for a little while." He pushed himself out of the chair and shuffled away. Thea wished with all her heart that Dorothy would appear to cheer things up.

Thea called home, longing to talk, a temporary respite from grief. MaryAnn picked up the phone. "Please tell me all's well at your end."

"A little chaotic, but we're all as happy as clams. Izzie's rehearsal went well—she was positively glowing. I had a hard time getting Johnny and Jessica to leave the library, mainly because, as you know, Jess can never make up her mind. Jim took us to the diner for supper and Will put on quite a show. The girls loved it. In fact, we just got back. Have you seen Christopher yet?"

"No, not yet. Being here is much harder than I thought it was going to be, and that's all I can say. I'll give you a call tomorrow and thank you so much for looking after my girls. Please tell them I called and give them each a hug from me."

"I will. Hang in there. I'll be thinking of you."

"Thanks, MaryAnn. Bye."

She had a quick conversation with her dad, told him she was going to spend a little time with Christopher, that she would ask him to drop her off, but that she wouldn't be late. She hung up, wandered off towards Mr. Blunt's apartment, past Ellie's bedroom, unable to summon up enough courage to go inside. She shivered, imagined a ghostly apparition seeping from beneath the door, and chastised herself for being ridiculous.

Down the stairs to the basement she went, glancing into Robert's bedroom, now empty of all his possessions. It looked clinical, unlived in, totally uninviting and it seemed surreal to her now that they had once sought solace in each other's arms. The door to Mr. Blunt's apartment slightly ajar, she knocked tentatively, walked into the hallway, calling out his name. She found him sitting in his faded brown recliner, a mug of rapidly cooling coffee at his side. He still seemed out of sorts, just sat silently staring into space.

"Mr. Blunt, I will be going out in a little while. A friend is coming to pick me up." He didn't respond.

"Are you unwell?" she asked, kneeling down and placing her hand on his knee. "Would you like me to call Dorothy? I don't like to leave you like this." He made no response.

Finally, he drew in a long shuddering breath and said, "I am feeling rather overwhelmed."

"Please let me call Dorothy, and if she can't come, Christopher and I will stay with you. I'm not leaving you by yourself when you're feeling like this."

"Her number is on the fridge."

Thea's conversation with Dorothy was brief. "I guess giving you two some time alone didn't work out too well. I'll be right over." Practical and matter of fact, she immediately put Thea at her ease.

The doorbell rang. She told Mr. Blunt Dorothy was on her way, said she would be right back, dashed madly up the stairs and down the hallway, arriving at the front door quite out of breath. She heaved it open, the weatherstripping holding it tight, and looked up into two bright green eyes.

"Please come in," she said, stepping out of the way. "I'm in the middle of some kind of crisis."

"Do I have time to take off my coat?" Thea nodded. Catching her breath, she watched Chris stuff his gloves into his pockets and unlace his boots. He smelled of the cold, the outdoors, and a subtle hint of *Old Spice*. She had never been so relieved to see anyone in her life.

"How can I help?" he asked, removing his jacket, laying it on the floor next to his boots.

"Just come with me and I'll introduce you to Mr. Blunt. Perhaps meeting you will bring him out of his despondency. We need to stay with him until his friend, Dorothy, arrives. Once she's here, we can leave and I'll explain."

Back downstairs, Thea stood in front of Theodore. "Mr. Blunt, there's someone I'd like you to meet. This is Christopher Morrison."

"Good evening, sir. Please call me Chris." He extended his hand. Mr. Blunt's good manners popped to the surface and he bent forward in his chair, grasping Chris's hand, shaking it vigorously. Thea breathed a sigh of relief and sank down on the sofa, grabbing the edge with her fingers. She observed Chris while he politely answered Mr. Blunt's questions. He sat on the sofa next to her, leaning forward slightly, listening intently to the old man. Impressed by the fact he had just adapted to the situation without asking questions and without any thought of himself, he scored high on her people assessment meter. Coiled tight as a spring, she relaxed, thankful to have someone else take over.

All thoughts of going to Aladdin's Cave and taking pictures, doing a few sketches and making notes went up in a puff of smoke. There was no way she was going to ask Mr. Blunt for the keys to the store in his current frame of mind, figuring it might truly push him over the edge.

In the end, Thea never did meet Dorothy because Mr. Blunt insisted he was now fine and that there was no need for them to wait. "Are you sure?" she said, worried about leaving him.

"I am. You've both cheered me up. Go off and enjoy yourselves."

She leaned over and kissed him on the cheek. "I'll see you tomorrow and if there's anything you need, you can reach me at Mom and Dad's." He nodded and squeezed her hand.

As she and Chris walked out of the apartment and up the basement stairs, she wondered what Chris had planned for their brief date and decided there and then to just let the evening run its course.

CHAPTER TWENTY-SIX

THE CONCERT

Peter, feeling a little awkward now that his mom had left, glanced at Ian and Marty who had become very quiet. Dark outside now, he could barely make out the top of his dad's head; the only light the reflective headlamps of oncoming vehicles and the brightly illuminated dashboard. He longed for his dad to say something and he suddenly wished Mr. Hudson had come along after all. He was also starving and he was sure his hollow-legged friends were too, but even had there been any food to eat, he would have been afraid to make crumbs in his father's car. He decided the best way out of the dilemma was to close his eyes and try to sleep for a little while, probably a good idea seeing as they would be having a really late night. Not wanting to break the silence, he placed both his hands together and put them up against the side of his face, indicating a nap to his friends. He breathed a sigh of relief when they took the hint and closed their eyes.

Peter awoke to the sound of his father's voice and a blast of cold air from the open car door. "Hi boys," Michael said. "Come on you sleepy heads, we're at the hotel." Peter glanced at Ian and Marty blinking owl-ishly, struggling into their jackets. Marty's spiky blonde hair seemed even spikier than normal and Ian's dark curls were flat where he had been leaning against Peter's shoulder, cheeks flushed from sleep. Peter didn't know about his friends, but he really needed to go to the bathroom. Marty slid out of the car, wriggling off the edge of the seat, jumping to the ground, followed by Ian and then Peter. Their nylon duffle bags, sitting side by side on the pavement along with his father's smart leather holdall, illuminated by the lights from the hotel, looked sad and dilapidated. Awkwardly huddled together, Peter watched his father speaking to a man in a navy-blue uniform with a matching flat-topped peaked hat, who appeared out of nowhere. His father handed him a ten-dollar bill and the man got into the car and drove it away. "Valet parking," he said, leaning down and picking up his bag. "Let's go inside." Peter and his friends grabbed their own bags and followed his dad's tall, broad-shouldered, camel-coated figure into the hotel.

Peter, wide-eyed, glanced around the lobby at the green leather chairs, the swirly-designed beige and green carpet, the welcoming glow of the three-sided gas-logged fireplace, and the multiple-shaded light fixtures hanging from the ceiling. A detailed model of an old-fashioned sailing ship sat on one of the deep golden-brown side tables just begging to be picked up, but he didn't dare. The view of the city lights across the harbor was a magic movie-land—an awe-inspiring spectacle for three boys from a small town in Maine. The man at the desk gave them a wink and a smile. Peter smiled back, tentatively lifted his hand to wave, his eyes drawn to the glass container of complimentary candies sitting tantalizingly on the counter. He was so hungry, but he didn't dare ask for one.

Michael's commanding voice brought Peter back to earth with a bump. "Our room's on the eighth floor and we should have a grand view of the harbor so let's go see, shall we?" They all stepped into the elevator. Peter, never comfortable with his father, found their close proximity awkward. Ian and Marty didn't appear to be suffering from the same emotions, but even so, Peter yearned for a jolly dad who would joke with his friends and make them feel at home.

Relieved to be out of the close confines of the elevator and the comparative spaciousness of their suite, Peter was able to finally go to the bathroom. He felt so much better after that. He washed his hands and face, ate some crackers his mom had thoughtfully packed, sharing them with Ian and Marty. The three of them sat on the queen-sized bed and Ian said, "This rocks." Marty bounced up and down until Peter scowled at him to stop.

"Come out here and look at the view," Michael said, ordering them into the sitting area. Huddled beside him, they looked with amazement at the inky black water and the sparkling reflection of the city lights. "To the left over there is the USS Constitution, old 'Iron Sides,' and she fires her cannon twice a day, so in all likelihood, the noise will wake you up at eight o'clock! I'm sure we can find a leaflet in the lobby about the ship's history. It is very old and has fought many battles." Michael lapsed into silence. Peter wondered what he was waiting for. Finally, he said, "I'm sure you boys are hungry and I hope you like Italian."

Peter would have eaten anything, even old shoe leather at this point, and speaking for all of them said, "We just love food."

"Well, let's go then." Peter, intimidated by his father's demanding tone, guiltily decided against asking if they could all phone home and the opportunity was lost. Perhaps his father would allow them to use his cell phone later, and he put the piece of paper with Miss Ellie's and his grandparents' number into his jacket pocket just in case.

A cab waited outside, engine running. The boys piled in the back; Michael sat up front. The driver, a cheerful looking gray-haired man, who reminded Peter of Uncle Bill, said, "Where to?"

"Massimino's," Michael said.

"That's a great place to eat. I hope you boys are hungry because the portions are huge."

"We sure are," Marty said.

"Well, it won't take us long to get there, so hang on tight." He pulled away from the hotel and into the traffic. "Now we're going to be doing lots of twists and turns. Boston's like that."

Peter sat back in the seat and looked out the window. From what he could see from the lights flashing by, everyone seemed to be driving very fast, but the skillful taxi driver forced cars out of his way. He seemed to remember someone telling him that Boston was a difficult place to drive around because of all the one-way streets, but the cabbie seemed to know exactly where he was going, pulling up in front of the restaurant in no time. In any case, it would have been hard to miss. A large neon sign saying, *Massimino's Cucina Italiana* sat above the first floor windows of the elegant brick building. While his father paid for the cab, the boys checked out the menu in the glass case to the right of the door, but soon gave up. They hadn't even heard of half the foods.

This time his dad held the door open for them and they trooped inside ahead of him. The aroma of food immediately made Peter's mouth water. Always with a good eye for detail, he photographed the decor with his mind so he could tell his mom all about it when he got home: the old-fashioned frosted windows at the front with their etched designs; the deep rusty-red of the upper part of the walls, the lower an intricate diamond pattern of cream and black ceramic tiles. Beneath his feet, large square tiles in a rusty-orange, with the odd black tile set in the same way as the walls. Bright red and yellow inverted glass cones hung from the ceiling above the polished black tables, lighting up the sparkling glasses and silverware. He couldn't wait to sit down and eat.

Peter had never known Marty to be so silent. Normally talkative, always in trouble at school, in awe of his surroundings, his friend was speechless for once. Ian, his best friend, so grownup in comparison, had nothing to say either.

A waitress with dark olive skin, long hair tied back in a neat bun, showed them to their table. There weren't any other kids in the restaurant and this made Peter nervous. But the waitress welcomed them enthusiastically, said even though there wasn't a kids' menu, the chef would be happy to do smaller portions. She asked them what they would like to drink. Both Peter and Ian said water would be fine, but Marty asked for a coke. Peter didn't think this was a good idea for his already hyperactive friend, but he didn't say anything. His dad ordered a glass of wine and handed each of them a huge menu. Marty and Ian, sitting opposite Peter and his dad, shared one between them. Marty started to giggle and Peter resisted the temptation to kick him under the table. In an attempt to avert disaster, Peter took charge. "Dad, what do you think we should order?"

"I think you would like the Chicken Parmigiana which is just breaded chicken with tomato sauce and cheese over pasta and then if you look down on the left-hand side under Primi/Pasta there's a linguine marinara and also a baked tortellini. What do you think?"

Peter liked the sound of the chicken and so did Ian; Marty chose the linguine. The waitress returned with their drinks, a basket of bread covered with a snowy white napkin, and a little blue ceramic dish with pats of butter. The yeasty odor seeping from beneath the napkin was almost more than Peter could bear, but he sat on his hands and decided his father had forgotten what it was like to be eleven. He fully expected Marty's hand to dive in and snatch a piece, so he glared at him and he just stuck out his tongue. The waitress was pretty and he could see his dad eyeing her up and down. She was soaking up the admiration, but still managed to take their orders in a professional manner and he listened to his dad ask for two small portions of the Chicken Parmigiana, one small portion of the linguine marinara and the Scrod Pizzaiola for himself to which she replied, "Good choice," giving him a coquettish look from beneath her long dark lashes. She managed to drag her gaze away from his dad long enough to ask whether the boys would like a small salad each, but they all said, "No thank you."

"Just a salad for you then, sir? And what kind of dressing would you like?"

"The house, on the side."

"Very good," she said, gathering up the menus and walking away. His dad watched her until she was out of sight and Peter wondered whether this was how he had behaved when he and his mom were still married. He thought it was rude not to pay attention to the person or people you were with, but he decided there and then he was going to have a good time, despite Marty's unpredictable, and possibly, embarrassing behavior. Overlooked at home, he always made up for it by constant attention-seeking and playing the class clown. Peter liked Marty's mom who was loving and warm, but she was worn out from trying to bring up seven children. Even though Marty had a dad, he was a shadowy figure and never seemed to be around when Peter had gone over to his house. Peter had long ago come to the conclusion he was no worse off than Ian and Marty in the dad department.

Michael picked up the basket of bread, took a piece and then passed it around the table. He sipped his wine and asked the standard questions about school, sports, hobbies, et cetera. Peter wondered whether there was a book called *How to Talk to Eleven Year Old Boys* because he sounded as though he had rehearsed all the topics. At least he was talking to them and Peter found himself relaxing and enjoying the delicious chicken, lightly breaded and juicy. He was having a bit of a problem controlling the strings of mozzarella cheese, as was Ian, and Marty had tomato sauce all over his mouth and chin. He glanced sideways at his father who was eating his fish fastidiously with a knife and fork. He didn't offer any of them a taste and when they were finally all finished, declined dessert when the waitress came back to clear away their plates. "There will be snacks at the concert," he said by way of explanation as if reading their minds.

Back outside in the dark and cold, Peter wished he had brought his hat. "It's only a short walk," his father said, making a right out of the restaurant. Peter decided to link arms with Marty and Ian and they all skipped until they were walking in sync, Marty lengthening his stride to keep up with his two taller friends. Once they'd made a left onto Causeway, they could see TD Garden in the distance—vast and brightly lit.

Without any word of explanation, his dad took them into North Station. They unlinked their arms and looked at each other with puzzled expressions. Seeing their concern, his dad said, "We have Club Seats and the way in is through the station. We just have to find one of the Premium Club entrances, so stick close." They didn't need to be told twice. The station was mobbed. Peter could hear the distant rumble and screeching of trains—the smell metallic and dusty. Tamping down his excitement, he kept a watchful eye on Ian and Marty, especially Marty. Fortunately, they didn't have to walk far and almost immediately found the escalator leading to the ticket turnstiles. Riding the escalator was an adventure in itself and his father made sure they were in front of him. Of course Marty jumped straight on, but both Ian and Peter, a little more hesitant, paid close attention to their feet, worried about making fools of themselves. Once through the ticket turnstile, they quickly found the private entrance leading to their section. Peter stopped in his tracks and Ian and Marty bumped right into him, realizing immediately why he had ground to a halt. They gaped at the enormous awe-inspiring auditorium. His dad chivied them along. "You're holding people up."

"Oh, sorry," Peter said, looking behind him, but nobody seemed to mind and they still had plenty of time to find their seats. Climbing a few stairs, sliding into a row on the left, they sat down. They had a grand view of the stage to their right. "Dad, these are great. What an awesome birthday present. Thank you so much." Peter let his excitement rip, hitting his thighs with the flat of his hands. A member of the auditorium staff appeared with programs for each of them and his dad asked for some bottled water, but nothing else until the intermission. The three boys sat in the plush seats with Michael to the left of them. With about ten minutes before the concert started, they each opened their programs, read the order of the songs, pointing out their favorites. As soon as the lights dimmed, they lapsed into silence, absorbing every little detail of their experience, knowing the chance of doing it again was pretty slim. His dad had settled into his seat and Peter couldn't tell from his expression exactly what he was feeling. He, personally, couldn't stop grinning.

As soon as Bon Jovi appeared on stage the auditorium was in an uproar. People were already standing and the moment the music started and the spotlight was on Jon Bon Jovi, the audience screamed. Peter looked up at the video screen, drank in every detail: Bon Jovi with his messy blonde hair, his black leather jacket open at the neck, his chest bare except for a gold medallion, gray sparkling pants and black leather shoes; Tico Torres on drums and percussion, center stage behind Jon, dressed in a black tank top, his bare arms keeping to the beat like no other; Richie Sambora to

Jon's left, his long dark hair falling to his shoulders beneath his customary Stetson, the best guitarist out there, and David Bryan on keyboard and piano, flinging his long curly blonde hair madly to the rhythm of the music. Peter couldn't work out who the other guitarist was. Compared with the rest of the band members he was conservatively dressed in a gray shirt and jeans, clean-shaven, wearing glasses and Peter thought he looked a little like Elton John, at least from a distance. The bright bars of neon lighting surrounding the drummer and the keyboard players illuminated the stage, changing color, fading from blue to pink. He watched Jon work the stage, grab the microphone, his black and white guitar hanging down his back. The opening song, *Last Man Standing*, was one of Peter's favorites and he hummed along to the chorus. He was lost. Seeing one of his favorite bands actually in the flesh a dream come true.

When Jon started to sing *Story of My Life*, Peter just closed his eyes, let the lyrics take him. A song close to his heart, it had helped him through many a bad day. They stood up for *It's My Life*. Peter looked at all the people around him and below him standing and swaying to the music. He didn't care what his father thought, sitting hunched in his seat, looking as though he wished he were a million miles away. His friends were having a good time and that was all that mattered.

Michael was miserable, uncomfortable in his surroundings, a stuffed shirt, a polite stranger. He cursed his elitist upbringing, his inability to let his hair down. Always full of good intentions, his attempts at reconciling with his children a dismal failure, he had wanted to try one more time with his son, overcome his dislike of the boy. Needy, always trying too hard to please, Peter grated on his nerves. Downhearted in his loneliness, a recent breakup with Maggie, work no longer a challenge, he had thought the concert would be a welcome diversion. Now, surrounded by thousands of screaming people having the time of their lives, he wallowed in a mire of self-pity. You're a self-centered bastard, Michael Chamberlin. You can't even rise to the occasion for your son.

Intermission came and went. His dad supplied snacks, but Peter wasn't really hungry. He sipped some water, waited for the show to start again. "Isn't it great?" Marty said, grinning from ear to ear, revealing his evenly spaced white teeth. His dad had asked them if they wanted to stay to the end and they looked at him as if he'd lost his mind. Michael held up his hands. "Just wanted to make sure you weren't getting too tired." Tired, they didn't know what tired was, all three of them on an adrenaline high. The rest of the concert, just as fantastic, included the encore with yet another of Peter's favorites, *Welcome to Wherever You Are*. The words just seemed to fit sometimes when Peter was feeling unsure of himself. He knew some of the words of Bon Jovi's songs were inappropriate for an eleven-year-old, but he knew he would understand them all someday, especially when it came time to date girls. But for now, he just let them go over his head.

The audience went mad clapping to *Captain Crash and the Beauty Queen from Mars*—Peter, Marty and Ian included. When they realized it was the last song, understood the band was leaving the stage for the final time, they were disappointed. Peter felt sure Bon Jovi and all the members of the band must be exhausted from all the expended energy, but exhilarated at the same time. He decided he was going to ask his mom for guitar lessons; it would be something to put on his Christmas list.

Sitting in the cab on the way back to the hotel, Peter reflected on the experience, knew it was something he was going to always remember. His dad might be a bit stuffy, but at least he had put his own likes and dislikes aside for once. Peter still didn't like him much and nothing was going to change that, but he appreciated the treat he and his friends had been given. Going out into the world like this didn't make Peter feel disappointed with his simple life in Maine, and now the concert was done, he was anxious to go home and see how Honey had managed without him.

CHAPTER TWENTY-SEVEN

THEA

Thea sat silently in Chris's Jeep, hunched in the seat, her overnight bag tucked between her feet. Now they were alone, she was tongue-tied and a little embarrassed by the way she had greeted him. Emotionally drained, dreading tomorrow's memorial service, she asked herself why she had come.

"Earth to Thea."

"I'm sorry."

"Don't be sorry. You look as though you could do with a drink. I know just the place."

"That would be great," she said, stretching out her legs, relaxing into the worn leather seat. Having Chris take charge was just what she needed and she wondered where they were going. Dismayed to find they were heading towards Stockton, she hoped with all her heart he wasn't going to take her to the Colonial Inn. There were just too many memories and she didn't want to be reminded of where she and Michael had met, but she needn't have worried. He turned into the parking lot of a restaurant well before they reached town.

"The Peppermill is one of my favorite places to eat," he said. "And when I show you the menu and you taste the food, you'll know why, but if you're not hungry that's fine too. Let's get you inside."

The restaurant, situated in the lower half of a gray wood-shingled house with red-painted window frames, looked inviting. Chris ushered her through the door into the warmth, and standing in front of him, she took stock of her surroundings. A shiny wooden-surfaced bar, dozens of wine glasses hanging from the ceiling above, took up much of the small room. Rows of fairy lights strung along the ceiling, together with the candlelit tables, created a magical atmosphere. The dark-planked wooden floor creaked a little as they made their way across the restaurant, the smell of food tantalizing, garlicky and spicy. Even though she had eaten supper with Mr. Blunt, she was suddenly hungry again. Thea looked around for an empty table, didn't see any, but Chris knew Ray, the owner—they went way back. He found them a small table tucked into a corner, appraised Thea, asked Chris how he was and handed them two menus.

"It's wonderful in here," Thea said. "So quaint and different."

"Ray and his wife, Patty, opened the restaurant about five years ago now. We all went to school together. They were the high school sweethearts, the first to get married. We always kept in touch, followed each other's career paths, and they fulfilled their dream, but I'm still looking for mine." Abruptly switching subjects, not wanting to bore Thea, he said, "I nearly always order the tapas, but of course, you can have anything you'd like."

"I've never had tapas, but it looks intriguing. I'd love to try it."

"I'm not keen on calamari, especially in squid ink, so I usually order the first or the third out of the set menus."

"I agree with you," Thea said, pulling a face. "It's so rubbery and the suckers are creepy."

They each ordered a glass of wine and decided to split the third tapas menu. She sipped the rich, smooth merlot slowly, allowing the flavor to linger. Comfortable with Chris, she relaxed. Being here in this warm and hospitable place was fun and she smiled at him. "Thank you for bringing me here. I am truly enjoying myself. And what did you mean when you said you've never realized your dream?"

"I envy people who have a real passion for what they do. I enjoy my job, but that's what it is, just a job. How about you?"

"I tend to be rather single-minded so I've put my dreams on the back burner for now. I'll bring them out when I'm ready. And you will find yours as long as you never get complacent, or take off your explorer hat."

"Are you good at taking your own advice?"

"Now that's not a fair question."

"Okay, I'm going to change the subject for now," he said, locking eyes with her. "I had to make an effort to see you again, but of course, I was disappointed to find out you live so far away."

"There's not much I can do about that, I'm afraid," she said, saved from saying anymore by the arrival of their meal. Ray placed three long platters on the table on which rested six small individual dishes filled with steaming food, a serving spoon in each. He returned with two very hot plates, warned them to be careful, refilled their water glasses and walked away. Thea spread her napkin on her lap and looked at Chris. "Where do I start?"

"Just put a little of each on your plate."

She had never tasted food quite like it. It was absolutely delicious: the chorizo and potato, buttery and spicy; the lamb chop in its red wine sauce, sweet and succulent; the beef stroganoff, rich and creamy; the salmon crispy, complemented by the aioli, and finally, the seared strip steak melted in her mouth. "This is food from the gods," she said, taking her napkin and carefully wiping her mouth. "Now I definitely wish I didn't live so far away."

"I see, you only want me for my food. Now that's not fair," he said, teasing her, drinking down his last sip of wine.

"Do you know, I don't remember the last time I've enjoyed a meal so much. You've no idea how much of a treat this is. Thank you."

"No, *thank you*. Do you have room for dessert?"

"Just coffee for me, but you go ahead."

Thea, sure Chris must have a million questions for her, was reluctant to say anything for fear of breaking their bubble of contentment. Their coffees arrived. She added cream, stirred the fragrant liquid with a long handled spoon, wrapped her hands around the tall glass mug and looked at Chris across the table. He smiled at her. "What makes you happy?"

"You go first . . ."

"I like to fix things, especially my ancient Jeep and I'm a bit of a grease monkey at times. Her name is Jasmine, by the way. Your turn."

Thea chuckled, "Jasmine the Jeep. I like that. Walking on the beach. You next."

"Physical exertion and how it makes you feel afterwards."

"Curling up with a good book on a rainy day."

"Going to bed in the winter time in flannel sheets."

"The smell of baking."

"Definitely the smell of baking," Chris said. "Reminds me of my mom. I'd like you to meet her. What else? Any pet peeves?"

"Rip-out ads in magazines. I compulsively tear them out because otherwise the pages don't lay flat. Spitting. I played tennis indoors once and the guy on the next court spit into the corner. I'll never forget it. You?"

"While we're being gross, people who don't clean up after their dogs. Being kept waiting in doctor's offices."

Thea was enjoying herself so much, reveling in the lightheartedness of their conversation; it took her mind away from the sadness for a while, Chris a breath of fresh air. He seemed such an uncomplicated person and she was drawn to his easy self-confidence.

The restaurant now almost empty, Chris said, "I'm afraid it's time for us to leave. Ray shuts up shop at nine thirty."

Thea nodded, stood up, retrieved her jacket from the back of her chair, shrugged into it and picked up her purse from the floor. Chris refused her offer to help pay for the meal. "You can pay next time," he said, leaving a generous tip. "Let's get you to your parents." On their way out he thanked Ray for another great meal and asked him to say hi to Patty.

Thea and Chris walked side by side across the parking lot and he made no attempt to touch her, but the lack of physical contact heightened rather than diminished her awareness of his masculinity. He opened the passenger door and she climbed into Jasmine's interior, carrying the smell of Chris's aftershave with her. "I feel quite differently about your car now I know she has a name."

"It's probably silly to be so fond of a car."

"I don't think it's silly at all. I'm quite fond of my ancient Volvo; I just never got around to naming her. She's only let me down once and that was my fault when I didn't pay attention to her whining sluggishness, warning me she needed a new battery. It's odd to think of an inanimate object giving solace, but she has on many occasions."

"I'm glad you understand."

"I do," and they lapsed into a comfortable silence. Chris drove well without any male recklessness and it was such a relief to be with a man without a huge ego. He appeared not to need to prove himself to her in any way and she couldn't quite believe her luck.

It was just shy of ten o'clock when they reached Thea's parents' house, the lights still on. She turned to Chris. "Won't you come in and say, hello. Mum and Dad will be disappointed if you don't. You made quite an impression on them."

"It was easy. I like them."

Thea stood on the top step under the drab green awning and pressed the bell. Her dad opened the door. "Thea, how lovely to see you and Chris. Please come inside."

Huddled together in the tiny entranceway, Thea glanced over at her mother standing in the kitchen doorway. She walked over, gave her a hug, surprised when her mom hugged her in return, coming to the realization they should have done this years ago. She stepped back and they looked at each other and smiled. Chris, shaking his dad's hand, asked him about his ankle. "It's good as new," he said.

Henry went to take Chris's jacket, but Chris shook his head. "I just came to drop Thea off. I really should be going."

"Please stay for a little while," Henry said, barely concealing his disappointment.

Gathered in the living room, Thea asked how the sale of the house was going. "Nothing, so far, but it's early days," Henry said. He turned to Chris. "We've decided to move to Maine so we can be with Thea and the grandchildren."

"That sounds like a great idea. Do you have a good realtor because, if not, I'm sure my mom knows of someone?"

"I'll bear that in mind if things don't appear to be moving along smoothly and thank you for the offer."

"Did you look at the info on the rentals I sent?" Thea asked.

"We did and they both look good and within our price range, but I think we are just going to stick it out here in the hope the house will sell fairly quickly. If push comes to shove, we'll just rent it out, but Carol Stevenson, the realtor, seemed reasonably optimistic so we'll keep our fingers crossed."

"You will come for Christmas though?"

"We will unless we are in the midst of real estate transactions. Well, Enid, I think it's time we took ourselves off to bed and let these young people have some time to themselves," and he winked at Thea.

Chris immediately stood up. "It was good to see you both again."

"Likewise," Henry said. "Don't be a stranger."

"Please don't hesitate to call me if there's absolutely anything I can do. I'd be happy to pick up boxes for you and help in any way I can."

"We will definitely call you," Henry said, meaning his words; he didn't want this young man to slip through his fingers. He liked him tremendously and he knew Enid felt the same. "Goodnight to you both," he said, kissing Thea on the cheek.

Chris sat back down in his chair and looked at Thea. "I'm sure you're tired so I won't stay long, but I did want to ask if it would be all right if I came to Maine for a weekend. I've really enjoyed being with you this evening and I would like to see you again."

Thea sat in silence thinking things through, rubbing her chin with her forefinger, not wanting to say the wrong thing and Chris waited patiently. "If you come to Maine, there will be little or no possibility of us spending any time alone. Are you prepared for that?"

"If you are worried about your kids, please don't be. I love kids."

"Even feisty, stubborn, little ones?"

"Yup."

"And how about dogs and cats?"

"Yup to that too."

"I believe you. I don't want to spoil our evening by talking about my life. What I would like to do is write you a letter when I get home. Once you have read it, you can judge whether you think our friendship is worth pursuing. This evening turned out to be more than I ever expected it would be and I will treasure the memory. You made me forget all about my responsibilities just for a little while and I thank you for that. You've made me realize how important it is to dwell on the things that make us happy. It's been hard for me to do that and that's all I am going to say."

Chris leaned forward in his chair and rested his elbows on his knees, his head in his hands. "You don't need to write me a letter. I don't care about your past. I have one too, but it's not relevant. If you would rather I didn't come for a weekend, then please say so and I will back unhappily, but silently, away. I promise you I won't ever pressure you into anything you don't want to do and if you think I am running away from Massachusetts—doing the grass is greener thing—I'm not."

Thea, emotionally drained, was close to tears. "It's been a long day," she said. She and Chris stood up at the same time.

He opened his arms. "Come here." She stepped into his embrace. He rested his chin on top of her hair and breathed in the faint scent of roses. He made no attempt to kiss her, although it took all his willpower not to. Eventually, she stepped back and looked up at him. "Yes, you can come to Maine, but only for a weekend," she teased.

"That's enough for me," he said, and reluctantly let her go.

CHAPTER TWENTY-EIGHT

ELLIE'S MEMORIAL SERVICE

It seemed so strange to be waking up in her childhood bedroom. The room so familiar, the sheets smelling of the same economy-brand, powdery-fresh laundry detergent her mother had always used. Just able to make out the utilitarian pieces of furniture in the early morning light, the room had never been a place to lift her spirits, but it had once been her sanctuary; now bare of all her belongings, it was only a place to rest her head. Staring at the ugly popcorn ceiling and the fly-infested frosted glass light fixture, she attempted to gather her thoughts for the day ahead. She understood why Mr. Blunt had asked people not to send flowers, fearing large funereal arrangements, but Ellie had loved flowers. Why hadn't she suggested she bring a couple of bright bouquets with her today? She wondered whether he would mind if she did. Perhaps Chris could take her to get some. Thinking about Chris and the evening they had spent together helped lift her mood; she liked him and wanted to get to know him better. The way he had hugged her, intuitively knowing that was just what she needed, only served to deepen her regard. She decided life was like a flower garden that had to be tended well. She had seriously neglected hers, let the weeds grow out of control, and now it was time to step back—take the time to pull those weeds and fertilize and nurture those flowers. She thought it an interesting analogy, but a good one to live by. Michael and Kenny had definitely been weeds, but Chris was a flower—a vibrant and loving one, but not invasive as far as she could tell. She was the thorny one and that was something she would have to work on.

Breakfast with her parents was much as it had always been, although Enid and Henry had a lot more to say these days, full of talk about moving to Maine, being close to Thea and the kids. Her mother's scrambled eggs, consistently overcooked and dry, the white toast lacking in flavor, reminded Thea of her childhood. Growing up in an orphanage, the institutional food had doused Enid's desire to cook, dulled her taste buds and her imagination. Thea had taught herself to cook, using the kitchen in Ellie's apartment to experiment and learned to love it. Would her mother like to learn how to make more flavorful meals once she and her dad lived close by? She was chewing on the last dry mouthful when the phone rang. Peter, full of apologies, said, "I'm sorry I didn't call yesterday."

"It goes both ways because I could have called you. As long as you're all right, that's all that matters."

"I'm okay. We didn't get much sleep though."

"I'm sure you didn't. How was the concert?"

"It was awesome," Peter said. She could hear Michael's voice in the background. "I have to go now, Dad's calling me."

"I love you. See you later."

"Love you too," he said, the final click of the phone cutting off their conversation. Thea hated that.

Once showered and dressed in the bright and colorful clothes selected with great care for the occasion, she asked her dad to please run her over to Ellie's house. Making sure she had the speech—if *speech* was the right word—she had written safely in her pocket book, she packed her overnight bag, took one last look around her old room and went off to find her mom. "Thanks for breakfast," she said, kissing her on the cheek. "It was just like old times. I'll call you when I get home."

"Good luck with everything this morning. Mr. Blunt invited us, but seeing as we really didn't know Ellie that well, we decided it would be inappropriate to come."

"I understand."

✺✺✺

Thea, while waiting on Ellie's porch, noticed all the Thanksgiving decorations had been cleared away, and it seemed so bare without the whimsical scarecrows, pumpkins and Indian corn. Mr. Blunt answered the door, seemed to have reverted to his usual cheerful self, and greeted her with his customary, "Come in, come in."

"Are you all right?" she asked, looking at him with concern.

"I owe you an apology, young lady, and by the way, you look lovely. I'm sorry if I upset you and where's that nice young man of yours?"

215

"I don't really know. Yesterday was only the second time we'd met, so he's not really mine."

"Ah."

"What would you like me to do?"

"Come into the kitchen with me. Both Dorothy and I decided we should have a few flowers around and she picked up a couple of colorful bouquets, but they need arranging. Are you up to that?"

"I'd love to, and you must have read my mind because I was thinking this morning that Ellie loved flowers, but I wasn't sure I'd be able to find any close by on a Sunday. Is Dorothy here?"

"No, she stayed with me for a little while last night and then as soon as she realized I was all right, she went home. She will be here soon in time to meet the caterers. The kids who are playing the music for us will be here soon too so they can set up their area. The aim is to keep it informal so if we don't start on time it doesn't matter."

Thea set to her task using the two vases Mr. Blunt had found. "Do you have any scissors?" He pulled open one of the cabinet drawers and handed her a pair. "Thank you," she said. "These flowers are perfect and just what I would have chosen." She spread them out so she could see what she had to work with, judging the various lengths needed to fit into the squat round glass containers. She had a good eye and skillfully arranged the yellow roses, the pastel-shaded lily-shaped alstroemeria, the pale pink button spray chrysanthemums, interspersing them with red miniature gerbera daisies. She then inserted the white asters and the purple sea lavender, moving the vase around as she worked to make sure all the flowers were evenly spaced. Finally, she poked the pieces of fern all around the edge. Mr. Blunt sat at the kitchen table watching her in comfortable silence without the unease of the evening before. In any case, they weren't on their own for long and Thea was just tidying up when, just as Mr. Blunt had predicted, Dorothy arrived with the caterers in tow. The kitchen went from being a peaceful place to a room full of people with a purpose. She stood by the sink, well out of the way, taking it all in, listening to Dorothy giving instructions to the Harvest Bakery staff, waiting for the right moment to introduce herself. Mr. Blunt saved the day, attracting Dorothy's attention by tapping her on the shoulder. "Dorothy, I'd like you to meet Thea."

"Of course, how rude of me. I didn't see you standing there in all the confusion. You've done wonders with these flowers."

"Thank you. It's so good to finally meet you."

"I'm so pleased you were able to come. Now I must get on. We'll have time to chat later."

"Where would you like me to put the flowers?"

"Wherever you think best." Feeling a little like a dismissed schoolgirl, Thea took the bouquets one by one, weaving her way through the chaos, placing one in the living room on the mantel and the other in the center of the table in the dining room. At loose ends, she wandered into the hallway almost bumping into a beautiful dark-haired girl carrying a guitar case who had just walked through the front door. "Whoops," Thea said, stepping out of the way. "Let me take your coat."

"Thank you, that would be helpful. Do you know where we are supposed to set up our instruments? My name is Shana," and she smiled shyly at Thea, her features completely symmetrical with a fine straight nose and almond-shaped eyes slightly tilted at the corners. Before Thea could introduce herself, an extremely tall, wild and disheveled young man burst through the front door holding a microphone in one hand and a music stand in the other. Thea looked at him in astonishment. His shoulder-length flyaway curly blonde hair appeared to have a life of its own; he wore no coat, just a navy scarf hastily and untidily wrapped around his neck. Compared with Shana's quiet elegance, he was a train wreck. She said, "Hi, Tony," in her sweet, kind voice, looking up into his intense blue eyes. "This lady here was just going to show me where we can set up, so why don't you take a deep breath and follow us."

Once in the living room, Thea indicated the designated space and asked them if they had enough room. "We'll make it work," Shana said. "Thank you."

Thea walked into the kitchen, asked what she should do with coats once people started arriving and Dorothy suggested the first bedroom on the left. She walked along the hallway into the room in which she had slept during her brief visit and dropped Shana's coat on one of the beds. Uncomfortable lingering, she hurried back to see how she could help, but preparations were well in hand and seemed to be under control. The Harvest Bakery staff, calmly efficient, had set up hot chafing dishes along the breakfast bar; placed bowls of salad and covered plates of bread on the kitchen table. The desserts had been carried to the dining room together with the urns for coffee and hot water with instructions to turn them on as soon as everyone started eating. They had thought of everything: napkins and serving implements, plates, mugs and cutlery. As soon as their white van disappeared out of the driveway, people started arriving and Thea began to get nervous. Never comfortable with crowds and the added stress of having to speak, especially on such a sad occasion, threatened to get the better of her, but the music helped. Shana strummed her guitar and Thea wondered whether she had written the haunting melody herself. Once the children from Ellie's after-school program arrived, accompanied by a rather haggard-looking woman, she relaxed, talking to them and asking their names, taking their coats, stuffing hats and gloves into pockets. They were quite a raggle-taggle bunch, but she got them settled on the floor in front of the couch by the slider and they sat patiently waiting, their hands resting in their laps. She nearly lost her composure when a little boy with dark brown hair looked at her with a puzzled expression and asked where Honey was. "I'll tell you later," she said, putting her finger to her lips.

When Mr. Blunt took up a vantage point in the living room doorway, she realized he must have changed his mind, decided to speak after all. Her admiration went up a notch and she crossed her fingers. He looked around with a vestige of a smile at all the expectant faces. "I want to thank you for coming today to give what I think will be a fitting tribute to Ellie, something that I believe Ellie herself would have enjoyed. Thank you also to Tony and Shana for providing our music. Dorothy and I put together a program, but we certainly don't have to follow it. Ellie was the daughter I never had and I loved her dearly. She brought me solace in my old age, gave me companionship and the will to keep going after my wife died. Without Ellie, I would not have had the energy to run Aladdin's Cave or the imagination to build this lovely house. Ellie will always be in my heart and I am trying to dwell on the good times because I know she wouldn't want any of us to be sad, but I know that's asking the impossible. I came across a quote the other day written by a man called St. John Chrysostom. Even though it was written in the fourth century, I believe the beautiful message is still appropriate today. The words are a gift for all of us and I used a little poetic license and changed he to she: *She whom we love and lose is no longer where she was before. She is now wherever we are.*"

Theodore paused, swallowed hard, blinked a few times and continued, "Now it's Corinne Baxter's turn to say a few words and after that we'll have some music."

Thea watched the bedraggled woman who had accompanied the children stand up: her dirty blonde hair severely pulled back into a ponytail, her tired face completely devoid of makeup, deep shadows beneath her unremarkable brown eyes. Thea wondered what her story was. Corinne cleared her throat, looked down at a piece of much-creased lined paper in her hand, and started to speak in a voice as clear as a bell. "Ellie was a remarkable person and these children's salvation," she said, pausing to rest her hand on the hair of the child on the floor in front of her. "The town is severely lacking in after-school programs and Ellie came to the rescue. She gave the kids a safe haven either here in her home or in the craft room at Aladdin's Cave and something to look forward to at the end of the day instead of an empty house. Because of her inspiration and her tireless working with the school authorities, I will be able to continue the program in her name. Mr. Blunt has kindly donated all the supplies from the craft room at Aladdin's Cave and they will be transferred to a designated room in the middle school. I will never forget her for all that she gave me and the children." She sat back down and everyone clapped, including the kids.

Shana raised her guitar, strummed a few chords, adjusted the tuning and nodded to Tony who placed his fingers on a portable keyboard resting in his lap. "We're going to play Carly Simon's *Coming Around Again/ Itsy Bitsy Spider* song and I know you kids can join in the chorus. I'm told it was one of Ellie's favorites so here we go." Shana's sweet voice filled the room and the children sang along at Shana's cue. Thea could tell they had sung the old nursery rhyme to Carly Simon's tune many times before because they sang out strong and loud and only slightly out of tune:

"The itsy bitsy spider climbed up the waterspout
Down came the rain and washed the spider out
Out came the sun and dried up all the rain
And the itsy bitsy spider climbed up the spout again."

"Thank you everyone," Shana said, smiling and acknowledging the applause, extending her arms to include the children.

It was Thea's turn to say something and she had no need of the written words on the neatly folded piece of paper in the pocket of her skirt—she knew them by heart. Nervously, she stepped into the living room but stayed near the doorway so she could be seen and heard. "I first met Ellie in June of 1991 when she interviewed me for a job at Aladdin's Cave. As soon as I met her, I knew I wanted to work with her and she immediately became not only my mentor but my friend too.

Unfortunately, we only had two short years together before I married and moved away, but they were the best two years of my life. Ellie was such a no-nonsense, honest person. She had an incredible ability to get inside people, to get to the root of their problems, to know when words were useless. She also had enormous energy and drive and it was contagious. Everything she touched turned to gold and I am humbled to have known her. I only wish we could have had longer. I took it for granted she would always be here in Massachusetts." She swallowed, blew her nose. "Had I known she would be taken away, I would have made more of an effort to stay in touch and now it's too late. Let that be a lesson to all of us, never put off until tomorrow what you can do today." Thea stepped back and wished with all her heart she could just fade away, longed for some of Alice's shrinking potion. There was a hush in the room, the sound of fidgeting and throat clearing. No one clapped. Corinne leaned forward and tapped one of the older children on the shoulder. "Jimmy, it's your turn now."

He stood up, a tall, gangly child with a body that hadn't quite caught up with his large hands and feet. His ears stuck straight out and his mousy brown hair fell across his forehead, obscuring his eyebrows. "We all got together and wrote a poem for Miss Ellie because we know how much she likes—liked—poetry, although some of this doesn't rhyme." He blushed and nervously unrolled the piece of paper in his hand.

> "My friends and me had nowhere to go
> Until Miss Ellie came along
> The boys thought crafts were sissy
> So we worked in the store
> And she trusted us not to steal
> And we didn't think she was for real
> Because we were always in trouble
>
> She taught us to care for each other
> Even my stinky little brother
> And that's how she was
> Never pulling any punches
> And not putting up with our guff
> Even when sometimes it got rough

She held us together and made us laugh
She told stories, played music
And was never ever mean
We believe she's an angel
And watching to keep us in line
So, Miss Ellie, we miss you
And we promise to help each other
And try to be good and make you proud."

"Thank you, Jimmy. You can sit down now," Corinne said.

Two more people stood up to say a few words: one of the quilting ladies—small, gray-haired and wizened, with ill-fitting teeth, and a man in his mid-forties, plump belly hanging over his belted waistband, who said Ellie had been helpful and kind to him when his wife had been unwell.

The well-known Christian hymn *Morning Has Broken*, another of Ellie's favorites, was the final song. Ellie, a fan of Cat Stevens' earlier music, would have loved Shana's rendition. Shana sang as Cat Stevens would have done, her beautiful guitar playing a wonderful accompaniment to the melody. Her soft and slightly husky voice filled the room, the children joining in with the first and last verse. This was the song that brought the tears, tears of peace, at least for Thea they were—a fitting ending to a wonderful tribute to her friend.

Mr. Blunt seemed to be holding up well. Dorothy, taking charge, suggested all the guests form a line so the soggy Kleenex were tucked away and people started to talk to each other. Thea, always of the opinion food was a great icebreaker, commended Mr. Blunt for providing a meal rather than sending the teary faces of Ellie's friends out into the cold. This way their grief could be shared, knowing they were not alone in missing someone who had died before her time.

Eventually, folk began to drift away and she was beginning to wonder where Michael and the boys were. Mr. Blunt and Dorothy looked exhausted and she asked what she could do to help. "There's nothing to do, my dear," Mr. Blunt said. "The Harvest folk will be back to clean up. We don't have to do a thing. They will even box and refrigerate the leftovers for us. I'm going to bid you farewell because I need to go lie down for a little while. I haven't forgotten about pricing Aladdin Cave's inventory just in case you were afraid to ask."

Thea walked over and gave him a hug. "Just as long as you're all right. That's all that matters."

"I will be fine. No one is ever prepared for all the things that have to be done after someone dies and there are just too many memories in this house. I will be moving out soon and then I won't expect to see Ellie every time I turn a corner. I'm an old man; my mind plays tricks and sometimes the dreams I have are all too real. I keep imagining she's here, especially when I think I've turned off a light only to find it's still on, leading me to believe that she really is still here after all. Anyway, enough of my ramblings, and thank you so much for coming; despite what you might believe, your being here meant a lot to me and to Ellie too I'm sure."

Thea, having a hard time holding herself together, said, "I hope so."

"Goodbye, my dear. Have a safe journey back and I will call you once the dust has settled." He turned and walked away.

Just as she was leaving the kitchen in search of Dorothy, Michael arrived, a frown between his eyes, impatient to be gone, declining her offer to come in. "I'll wait in the car," he said.

"I won't be a minute," she said, closing the door on his retreating regimental figure. She ran into the bedroom, grabbed her coat, overnight bag and pocketbook; put her head around the dining room door to find Dorothy turning off the urns. "I'm sorry to leave so abruptly. Thank you for being such a wonderful helper. I would love for you and Mr. Blunt to come visit."

"He did mention it to me and it sounds like a lovely idea. I know he would like to see your daughter in *The Nutcracker*. We'll talk about it and let you know. Thank you for coming. It meant a great deal to Theodore."

"Bye then," and Thea made a mad dash out the front door and across the driveway just as Michael began to beep the horn. She opened the rear door, asked the boys whether they were all right and if they needed to go to the bathroom before continuing their journey. They said they were good, but she could see by the relieved expressions on their faces they were pleased to see her. Once settled in the passenger seat, she turned and asked Ian whether his mother knew what time they had left and he said they had called her. Pleasantries out of the way, she looked at Michael's taught profile and wondered what had put him into such a foul mood. Boy, was she glad she wasn't married to him anymore and she said thank you silently seven times and immediately felt better. She was looking forward to getting home and promptly fell asleep.

CHAPTER TWENTY-NINE

THEA AND MARYANN

MaryAnn, extremely pleased to get Ian's brief phone call, heard the tiredness in his voice and wanted him home. Even though she had enjoyed looking after Izzie and Jessica, the separation from Ian preyed on her mind. Johnny didn't seem to miss his brother at all. In seventh heaven in the company of Jessica, his best pal, with Smokey curled up at the end of his sleeping bag on an air mattress between Izzie's and Jessica's beds, he was one contented little boy. Honey, missing Peter, sat in silent vigil outside the girls' bedroom until MaryAnn, taking pity on her, dragged her bed onto the one remaining piece of floor space. She ignored the kids' giggling; they were having just too much fun for her to play the bad guy and after about thirty minutes they dropped off to sleep.

After arriving back from the diner the evening before, they had all played *Sorry*. Jim chose to sit out the first round, perfectly content to settle back in the chair by the fire and watch. Honey, with her head on his knee, tolerated Smokey playing with the end of her tail—dancing sideways, back arched, pouncing, batting it with her paws. The cat's silly antics had them all in stitches until, eventually, Jim took pity on Honey and lifted Smokey onto his lap where she finally settled down. Having the opportunity to spend time with the Chamberlin girls was a gift and he was pleased MaryAnn had found a friend in Thea. It was kudos to MaryAnn that Jessica had actually agreed to stay with her. Jim knew how fragile she was, especially after Kenny's attempted break-in, and what amazed him even further was Thea's confidence in leaving her children with MaryAnn. She must have sensed just as he had that she was a rock; one of the calmest people he had ever known, relaxing to be around, but fun at the same time, the reason why the children wanted to be with her. To him, she became more beautiful every day. The shadows beneath her eyes had disappeared, together with the deep well of sadness she had been carrying around for the past three years. She was contented and it showed. The MaryAnn of old was beginning to emerge and he was pleased for all of them, especially Ian and Johnny.

The two of them, sitting by the fire after she had put the kids to bed, talked about their plans, about going next weekend to cut down a Christmas tree, and the rituals they would create as a family. MaryAnn stressed she didn't want their Christmases to be too materialistic, wanted the boys to continue to have good values, and now that things were good for them, she didn't want them to forget those less fortunate than themselves. Jim told her they did a great deal for the community through the store and she and the boys could certainly help. Contented with that, she told Jim he was full of surprises and always seemed to have an answer no matter the question. In the end, she had to send him home otherwise they would have talked all night and when she kissed him goodnight, the twenty-one days to their wedding seemed like an awfully long time.

Now it was Sunday evening and the kids were fast asleep. She scurried around making sure the place was tidy and the kitchen clean of dishes; unable to settle, anxious for Ian to be home, she sat at the table idly turning the pages of a magazine, listening for the sound of tires in the driveway.

Even though Thea dozed on and off most of the way home, thus avoiding having to interact with Michael, she was much relieved when they eventually pulled into her driveway. The boys, eager to be out of the car, subdued by the oppressive atmosphere, including the irrepressible Marty, thanked Michael, gathered their bags from the way back and Thea watched them hurrying away towards the welcoming lights of the house. She turned to Michael, noticed the tension in his jaw, his well-manicured hands clenched around the steering wheel, and said, "I gather you won't be doing this again anytime soon. Why the face of doom?"

He glanced at her briefly, tilted his chin down and frowned. "Thea, I tried, but I failed. Peter isn't comfortable with me, and to be honest, I just don't know how to be around kids."

She had little tolerance for Michael's moods. Impatient to be gone, she said, "Why are you always so hard on yourself? You gave those boys a wonderful treat, something they will talk about for a long time to come."

Michael unclenched his hands, leaned back into the seat. "Please tell Peter I'm sorry if I came across as being a bit stuffy. He and Ian were really well behaved, but it was difficult to keep the lid on Marty."

"You really are your own worst enemy and you're over-thinking this whole weekend. Kids don't dwell on things like adults. They are so much better at living in the moment. Anyway, I must go and see how MaryAnn made out, but I do want to thank you for being so generous and especially for helping me out with a ride to and from Ellie's. Goodnight Michael."

She stood in the driveway, clutching her overnight bag, watching him drive away. She shrugged her shoulders and immediately dismissed him from her mind; he was no longer her problem.

MaryAnn and the boys were in the kitchen. Honey, overjoyed to see Peter, had attached herself to his side and that was where she was going to stay. Thea held up her hand saying she was sorry, but they would have to save all their news until another day because it was late and time for bed. MaryAnn said she and Ian would go home and she would drop Marty off on the way. She and Thea agreed it was best to leave Johnny where he was and she would take him to school in the morning. "I gather all went well," Thea said.

"We had a great time and thank you for trusting me with your girls. That's the greatest compliment anyone could ever pay me. Are you all right?"

"I am, and I'll talk to you tomorrow and thanks again for being a true friend. It was good to get away and you gave me the chance to stop being a mom just for a little while."

"We all need that and I was glad I could help. Come on boys, time to go."

Thea stood at the kitchen window to make sure MaryAnn's car started and as soon as she had gone, she turned to Peter who was sitting at the table gently fondling Honey's ears. "I'm glad we're home, Mom."

"Your father asked me to apologize to you for being so stuffy. Was it truly awful?"

"No, but he makes me nervous and I was beginning to wish I hadn't asked Marty, especially when he forgot to spray the waffle iron at breakfast this morning and the waffle got stuck. I thought Dad was going to burst a blood vessel." Peter giggled and Thea joined in.

"I wish I'd been a fly on the wall."

"But the concert was amazing and it didn't matter Marty was a little crazy because we were standing a lot of the time, waving our arms above our heads or clapping. We just needed to slip Dad a happy pill and then everything would have been perfect."

"What was the hotel like?"

"Super-nice. And we all loved the breakfast buffet—you know me and food. Sleeping with Ian and Marty wasn't the best, and we didn't really get much sleep. Marty is such a giggler and being overtired made it worse, especially when he tripped over his bag in the dark. Fortunately, our door and Dad's door were shut and we eventually managed to stop laughing."

"It's good to be silly, but I'm glad you didn't get into too much trouble. Did you make it to the Aquarium?"

"We did. Do you know there's a pool full of stingrays and you're allowed to put your hand in the water. The rays swim right up under your hand and you can touch them. It was so great, but we had to whisper and keep our hands really still otherwise they would go away and hide. We saw so many things, but I loved the seahorses; I could have watched them all day. Some of the fish are so beautiful and some of them are really ugly. The giant ocean tank with the sharks was awesome. We saw penguins and sea lions and a giant octopus, which can change color and move up to seven hundred pounds. Dad bought a book for each of us about the Aquarium and I can show it to you if you'd like."

"I think we'll have to save that until tomorrow. I know you had a nap in the car, but it really is time for bed and I do have to make a couple of phone calls. Why don't you go take Honey out." For once, Peter didn't argue.

Although Thea was pleased to be back under her own roof after her brief respite, there was now a multitude of things that needed to be done. She wished the weekend had gone better with Michael for Peter's sake, but pleased she'd had the opportunity to thank Michael for agreeing to give her a loan. Now all she had to do was wait for Mr. Blunt to give her a firm figure for the inventory. In the meantime, the Christmas preparations took precedence: designing her annual card, writing a poem, and making cookies and English toffee for the kids to take in for their teachers. She called her mom and dad to let them know she was home safe. Her thoughts went to Chris but now she was back in Maine, it seemed like some fantastic dream. They had parted without making any firm plans, but no doubt he would reach out to her. Was she worried about him coming to Melford

Point for the weekend? She wasn't really sure. Again, it was another bridge to be crossed.

MaryAnn, thinking as she drove how strange it was to be going home without Johnny, was pleased she had given him a heads up about possibly staying overnight. Completely unfazed, he had given her a big hug, told her not to worry because he was a big boy now and happy to be with Jessica and Mrs. Chamberlin. Was she ready for the untying of the apron strings, to let the kite string out just a little bit? Not really. First Ian and now Johnny, what a weekend of firsts. Marty chatted a mile a minute all the way home, but Ian, as usual, said little.

"Do you know, Mom," Ian said, once they were in the house. "I'm so lucky."

"How's that?" MaryAnn asked, taking his jacket from him and hanging it up.

"Because I don't have a dad like Mr. Chamberlin," he said, walking into the kitchen and sitting down at the table.

"How come?"

"He makes Peter nervous and made me realize having all the money in the world doesn't make you happy."

MaryAnn, not wanting to jump on the negative bandwagon, just said, "But don't you think it was nice of him to take you to the concert?"

"Yeah. He's very generous, but when I think about how much fun we have with Mr. Hudson, I can't help feeling sad for Peter because he doesn't have a proper dad."

Listening to her son singing Jim's praises, MaryAnn wanted to shout from the rooftops, run a victory lap, but she sat quietly, silently thanking Michael for setting a bad example. It was so like Ian to worry about other people's feelings and she was quite sure he had been keeping a tender eye on his friend all weekend. Ian and Peter, forced to grow up much too quickly, had a great deal in common—their friendship mutually beneficial—and even had she gone looking, she couldn't have found a better companion for her son. "Did you have a good time anyway?"

"It was fantastic." His whole face lit up. "The concert was awesome and the auditorium was enormous," he said, extending his arms out wide. "I've never seen anything like it. We didn't have to sit still, which was good because Marty always has the fidgets. Even riding the escalators in North Station and the elevator in the hotel was an adventure. Our suite was on the eighth floor and there was a great view of the harbor and Boston. The buildings were so tall and all lit up. It looked like something in a movie. We went out to dinner at an Italian restaurant and the food rocked but it wasn't half as much fun as the meal we had at Mario's. And the Aquarium blew us away. We laughed so hard when we watched the penguins waddling about and I wished I could go walk around with them. The sea lions were funny too, coming up to look at us, pulling themselves along with their flippers, and then diving back in the water. I'd love to go back someday and spend more time. Because of Mr. Chamberlin, we always felt as though we were being rushed and I just don't think he remembers what it was like to be a boy."

"I think he sounds rather sad and lonely and we should probably feel sorry for him. Did you go swimming?"

"No. We had to check out of the hotel by eleven o'clock and we wouldn't have had time. In any case, Mr. Chamberlin wanted to get us to the Aquarium as soon as possible after breakfast and I'm glad he did because we did spend about three hours there and even that wasn't enough."

"It sounds to me as though you've had quite the trip, but it really is time for bed otherwise you won't be fit for school tomorrow. By the way, I missed you."

"I know. I missed you too and both Peter and I wished at one point we had stuck to the original plan to have Mr. Hudson come along. He could have helped with the whole Marty thing because he really is like a wind up toy with a battery that never runs out, but I don't think having Mr. Hudson there would have made Peter feel any better. It would have just shown his dad up even more."

"Oh well . . . there's nothing we can do about it now. So off to bed with you and I'll come and say goodnight in a little while."

MaryAnn lingered in the kitchen, quiet except for the hum of the refrigerator and the distant rumble of the old furnace. It had been fun listening to Ian, her normally reticent son animated for once, and she was glad she had put her misgivings aside and allowed him to go on the trip. She filled the teakettle, set it on the stove and hummed happily while she waited for it to boil. She had to admit she had been glad of the distraction of looking after Izzie and Jessica over the weekend with Ian so far away. But she had trusted Thea in her decision and Michael *had* cared for the boys and kept them safe, even if he hadn't been any fun, and she, like Ian, did feel sad for Peter. The teakettle whistled; she poured the steaming water onto a chamomile flavored tea bag in her favorite mug and went off to see what Ian was up to. She found him sitting up in bed. "Did you unpack your bag?"

"Uh-huh and here's a book about the Aquarium and the concert program if you'd like to see them." He reached over and pulled them off his bedside table, holding them out to her.

"I'd much rather read them with you after school tomorrow."

"I'd like that."

"Goodnight, champ. I wouldn't worry too much about Peter. I'm sure you gave him lots of support."

"I tried my best because we are best buds."

"He's lucky to have you as his friend."

"Thanks, Mom."

"Okay, time to snuggle down." She waited until he was well under the covers, gave him a kiss on the cheek and said, "I'm glad you're home."

CHAPTER THIRTY

❦

CHRISTMAS TREES

On the morning of Sunday, December seventeenth, Jim went up into the attic to unearth all the Christmas decorations. The gracious hallway had been without a tree since his mom had died in 1998. The holiday had initially saddened him and then he had become indifferent, although he enjoyed shopping for his family, especially his nieces. Ben had always rescued him from his loneliness and the empty house, but Christmases away from his home had never been the same. His mother had never really recovered from the shock of the tragic accident that took his dad's life. It was one of those freaky things that should never have happened, and as always, Grant Hudson was doing a good turn for an elderly neighbor cutting tree limbs that were too close to his house, sure to fall in the next heavy snow storm. Grant had all the right equipment, but he wasn't paying attention; distracted by lowering rain clouds and a distant rumble of thunder, he was working too quickly. The ladder slipped sideways, and the neighbor, Old William, too frail to be of any use, watched Grant tumble to the ground, chain saw in hand. He cracked his head on the driveway and never regained consciousness. Kneeling on the floor, peering into the trunk, staring at all the decorations, brought back memories best left buried. Jim pulled himself together, hurried downstairs when he heard Carrie barking. It was time to make new memories; he'd been living in the past for far too long.

MaryAnn and the boys, standing huddled on the doormat in the kitchen, tolerated Carrie's greeting. The way she thrust her long nose into places where it really shouldn't have been always made them laugh. Laughing so hard, oblivious to the sound of knocking until Carrie started barking, MaryAnn opened the door to find Thea standing there, warmly dressed in sensible boots with a bright turquoise hat pulled down over her ears. MaryAnn looked down at her own legs now encased in the pair of boots she had always wanted: a warm brown suede lined with sheepskin from top to bottom, right to the tips of her toes and she loved them. The boys had new boots too and were all kitted to go on their adventure. "The kids are waiting in the car," Thea said. "Are you ready to go?"

"I just have to grab the saw, some rope, and a couple of old blankets to protect the top of your car," Jim said.

"We brought Honey just as you suggested and I hope that's still okay."

"It sure is. Why don't you bring your car around to the other side of my truck and then you can follow me out. It's not far."

MaryAnn sat in the front with Jim, Carrie nestled at her feet, and as usual, the boys were tucked into their cozy space in the back of the cab. Jim drove past the entrance to the hardware store and turned left onto a dirt road about a half-mile further on. He glanced in his rearview mirror to make sure Thea was right behind him, and concerned about her car on the rutted and uneven road, he drove slowly. Fortunately, there was only one giant crater that she managed to drive around and then they all arrived in a small open field with plenty of room to park. "Now, let's have a plan of action," Jim said. "We don't have to stick together, but let's make sure we are all within shouting distance. If we go in pairs, one person can stay with the tree they've chosen and the other can come find me so I can cut it down. Does that sound okay?"

There was much nodding of heads. "Come meet Mr. Andy Ferguson. He's the owner of the tree farm. He came from Scotland many years ago, but he's never lost his accent so you might find him a little difficult to understand." They all walked behind Jim with Honey tugging on her leash, having forgotten her manners in all the excitement. Peter, making an attempt to calm her down, wasn't having much luck.

Andy Ferguson, a short, bow-legged man wearing laced rubber boots to his knees, saw them coming and stepped out of the warmth of his hut to greet them. Piercing blue eyes peeked out from beneath bushy gray eyebrows and his ruddy cheeks and red-tipped nose heralded his liking for a *wee drop o' whisky*. "Och," he said, "I canna believe it's you, Jim, after all this time, and who are all these bairns?"

Jim named each of them in turn and when he introduced MaryAnn as his future wife, the old man's face lit up in a beaming smile, revealing the worst teeth any of them had ever seen. "Aye, you're a bonnie wee lassie that's for sure. And when's the great day?"

"The day after Christmas. And that's why we need a rather splendid tree."

"Oh, aye. Well ye've come to the right place. So off with ye all now. There'll be mulled cider, hot chocolate and shortbread when ye're done and a wee nip for the grownups," and he winked at them and sent them on their way.

The trees, tagged with different ribbons according to their height, were Scotch pines, Douglas firs, Eastern White pine and Fraser firs—Jim knew them all. The frost-covered grass crunched beneath their feet and in shaded places there were pockets of snow. Peter, deciding to run the risk, let Honey off the leash, treats in his pocket to lure her back. She and Carrie ran around in absolute doggy heaven. Jessica and Johnny walked off hand in hand after Jim's warning to be careful not to fall over the tree stumps; Thea and Izzie stuck together; Peter and Ian paired up, which left Jim and MaryAnn to themselves. They stuck close to each other, entering one of the rows. "How's this for our first Christmas tradition?" he asked.

"I think it's wonderful, but it's going to be hard to agree on a tree, isn't it?" He grabbed her arm as she tripped.

"Now I did warn you about the stumps."

She looked down at her feet. "As long as my boots aren't damaged, I'm okay. Now what were you saying about trees?"

"This one here, a Fraser fir, is a more traditional shape. The others tend to be bushier."

"What kind did you use to pick?"

"It was different every year. My mother always used to say there had to be a good point on the top for the angel."

"Well, that's a good way to start."

As with all Christmas tree hunting, each one was discussed with the usual criticisms—this one's too fat, this one's lopsided, this one's too short and so on and so forth. Eventually, they heard a cry from Peter saying they'd found one and Jim marched off, brandishing the saw above his head; Izzie appeared to show him the way. They had found a Fraser fir, about four feet tall, and he made the children laugh by walking around it and inspecting it. "You've picked a real beauty. Now if you will hold her steady, I'll cut her down for you." He lay his considerable length down on the ground and was immediately attacked by Honey who decided he was fair game. Carrie, old-lady-tired, just sat at Jim's feet, familiar with the ritual. Peter pulled Honey off and firmly held her collar while Jim sawed through the trunk with firm, even strokes. "Now we have to drag her out and then you are all going to have to help us find a tree. Mrs. Wilkinson and I don't seem to be having much luck," he said, pushing himself to his feet and brushing pieces of dry grass and pine needles from his pants.

Eventually, they found a seven foot Eastern White pine, bushier than the Chamberlins' tree but with enough space between the branches for ornaments and, of course, the perfect spike at the top for the angel. Ian and Johnny declared it was just right and Jessica agreed. Having already selected their own tree, she now considered herself an expert and she stood with hands on hips, her dark unruly curls peeking out from her bright red hat, cheeks flushed from the cold. "It's just right for Mr. Hudson's house," she said.

The lot was beginning to get busy and Jim kept running into people he knew. There were kids and grownups all over the place moving around in their bright winter clothing all saying that it was a picture-perfect day. "I couldn't agree more," Jim said, grabbing hold of the trunk of his tree, dragging it back towards the car. Peter managed to pull theirs, sorely tempted to harness some of Honey's energy by tying her leash to the trunk. In the end, they were able to fit both trees in the flatbed of Jim's truck, making life a great deal easier. He told Thea he would bring her tree to her house and help her set it up.

Andy Ferguson's pretty granddaughter, Kirsty, a thick braid of coal black hair hanging down her back, was helping him serve the customers. Jessica whispered to Johnny, "She looks like Snow White." She was friendly and spoke without any trace of her grandfather's Scottish accent, just a hint of a Maine brogue. There were benches on which to sit and a brazier burning brightly, sending pine-scented smoke and sparks into the frosty air. The sky was as blue as could be; the day without the normal biting wind. "Och, Kirsty, dinna forgit to put a wee dram into them drinks."

"I won't, Granddad," she said, using the same word Jim had always called his own grandfather. He wished his mom and dad were still around to meet MaryAnn. He sat silently cradling his hot cider, trying to keep his emotions at bay, longing for his mom and dad who had both died too young. He glanced at MaryAnn and she too was deep in thought. They both had their own memories to deal with and he was sure it was just as hard for her, but they had each other and that's what counted. He reached sideways and took her hand. "I love you," he said and her eyes sparkled with unshed tears.

Setting up the Chamberlin tree had been chaotic, but fun, Thea's house bursting at the seams with three adults, five children and two dogs. Gathered around the dining room table, eating Thea's homemade chicken noodle soup, reminded Jim of the day he had met MaryAnn, both guests at Thea's table. Ravenous after their morning in the clean, crisp Maine air, happy to be together, they all talked over each other, and passed platters piled high with thick slices of the Country Store's crusty bread, slathering them liberally with butter. The soup, fragrant and delicious, full of vegetables and chunks of tender chicken with just the right amount of seasoning, truly hit the spot. Once they were satiated, the dishes done, and before they could fall asleep, Thea produced the tree holder. The corner of the living room where they always put their tree was going to be a tight squeeze: this tree so much bushier than their standard pre-cut one. Jim, suggesting it would be easier to fit it into the holder outside, asked Ian and Peter to come help him. Negotiating Thea's narrow hallway was difficult, but by pulling the tree in backwards, they maneuvered it into the living room. "We only ever manage to decorate it on three sides and we may have to trim the branches just a little," Thea said. "But, Jim, it's the most beautiful tree we've ever had. Thank you so much."

"I'm pleased you were able to come with us and it will probably be a good idea if you give it some water right away."

"I'll do just that."

"I think it's time for us to get out of your hair."

"Let me give you your tickets for *The Nutcracker* before I forget and how much do I owe you for the tree?"

"Let's call it even, shall we? After all, you gave us lunch and I haven't paid you for the ballet tickets."

Thea held her hands in the air. "I admit defeat."

Jim, MaryAnn and the boys were fairly quiet on their way back to Jim's house. "You boys must be tuckered out," he said.

"No, sir," Ian said. "We have to put up our tree now."

"Are you sure you're up for it?"

"You bet. Right, Johnny?"

"Uh-huh."

Ian and Jim made a masterful job of removing the tree from the bed of the truck and between them carried it through the front door. Setting it into the holder, Ian and Johnny steadying it, Jim lying prone beneath the branches told MaryAnn her job was to stand back and make sure the tree was straight. "Okay," she said, and Jim madly went to work turning the screws all the way in.

"Are you sure it's still straight?"

"I think it is leaning a little to the left."

"Ian, why don't you turn the bolts—loosen the right-hand ones just a little and then tighten the ones on the other side while I hold it steady," and he crawled out from underneath. "How does it look now, MaryAnn?"

"It's perfect. You have it just right."

"Okay, Ian. Tighten the bolts evenly and that should do it. I'm going to tie it to this hook in the wall, which has been here for as long as I can remember, just to be on the safe side." He retrieved a piece of string from his pocket, looped it over the hook, around the tree about three quarters of the way up and tied it securely. "There, that should do it," he said, standing back to admire his handiwork. "Now it's time to do our decorating and we need Christmas music for this," and he went off to the library.

MaryAnn and the boys admired the tree, truly magnificent in its pine-scented glory. The trees she and Sam used to get from the local lot paled in comparison, but it hadn't mattered. Forcing herself back into the present, she wondered what Ian was thinking. Johnny, too little to remember much, which was probably just as well, certainly made it easier for him to move forward. She turned to look at Ian just as the most beautiful rendition of *Away in a Manger* filled the hallway and made her heart soar.

Jim snagged Ian and Johnny, taking them up to the attic to help bring down the lights. "We need to start with those first," he said. MaryAnn went out to her car to fetch their meager box of special decorations she and the boys had packed earlier. Walking back towards the house, she wondered how Jim was feeling. Christmas was such an emotional time of the year anyway and she was sure he was also flooded with memories. They really hadn't talked too much about his family, but she knew how deeply he had loved them. She remembered the day he had pulled a little wooden box from one of the kitchen drawers, opening the lid to reveal neatly categorized, well-thumbed index cards, a little stained and yellowed with age. "This box holds all my mother's recipes. Here are the Christmas ones.

Perhaps we could make some of my old favorites," he said, taking out the one for plum pudding, holding it in his hands and gazing at his mom's neat handwriting.

"I'd love to," she said, but he had replaced the card and returned the box to the drawer.

"Next year, perhaps," he said, his voice subdued.

MaryAnn consoled him by saying, "We'll get through this together."

He had just nodded and pulled her gently into his arms. "Thank goodness you're here."

MaryAnn, having a hard time keeping her mind in the present, took a deep breath, carried the box of decorations through the kitchen and out into the hallway. Jim was standing on a stepladder and Ian and Johnny were trying to straighten out the lights while singing *Jingle Bells* at the top of their voices. Her arms wrapped around the cardboard box, she stood there looking at the three of them, and came to the realization that it was going to be all right. A few tears would be shed for those they had lost, but it would be short-lived and her overactive imagination visualized Sam and Jim's parents standing in the hallway and she decided she had watched *A Christmas Carol* one too many times.

CHAPTER THIRTY-ONE

THEA

Thea, beginning to hit the panic button because she was running out of time, attempted to stay in the Christmas spirit and not get annoyed with the kids. There was just so much to organize with Chris, her parents and Dorothy and Mr. Blunt all arriving on Thursday in time for the evening performance of *The Nutcracker*, and she wasn't quite sure how she was going to keep them amused as well as buy gifts for them all and plan her menu. But at least she and the kids had had a great time decorating the tree, laughing over the strange ornaments which came out every year: the faded pictures in the foam frames; the strange red and purple feathered birds which Jessica hated and always hid at the back of the tree; the angel with the sequins pinned onto her polystyrene body, becoming balder every year; the misshapen felt Santas, snowmen and gingerbread men, and the angel at the very top with the lop-sided halo. But still the tree looked pretty with its tiny colored lights and the sparkling crystal ornaments collected over the years mixed in with the unlovely sentimental ones. They all decided it was the nicest tree they had ever had and Honey, absolutely exhausted from all her running around earlier in the day but wanting to be in the thick of things, lay on the floor with her nose resting on the colorful quilted skirt Thea had hand-sewn many years ago while she was pregnant with Peter.

Thinking through the logistics, she had contacted Sally Connolly at the Harbor Inn bed and breakfast to see if she could accommodate her guests, and breathed a huge sigh of relief when Sally said that wouldn't be any problem at all. She gave Sally their names, arrival and departure dates and secured the whole lot with her credit card. Chris, getting a little lost in the shuffle, appeared to be undeterred; he and Jasmine were riding solo, whereas her parents, Mr. Blunt and Dorothy had pooled resources and decided to rent a minivan. This pleased Thea no end, especially as

Dorothy, the youngest of the four, and her dad would be sharing the driving. They planned to return home on the morning of the twenty-sixth, and even though both MaryAnn and Jim had said they were welcome to come to the wedding, they had all felt it would be an imposition and had politely declined. With Chris an unknown quantity at this point, Thea decided to play that one by ear.

After the tree decorating, Thea had put the kids to work wrapping toffee after breaking up the three chilled, chocolate and nut-covered slabs. Even though the job was tedious, there wasn't too much complaining because they were allowed to eat the pieces too small to wrap. They devised quite a system whereby Peter cut the pieces of plastic wrap, Jessica measured and cut the ribbon and Izzie did the tying. It was one of their traditions—Thea's standard gift for teachers, friends and family—the crunchy, buttery toffee so delicious, people had been known to hide away in dark closets to eat their stash secretly, unwilling to share.

Once the kids were in bed and the house was quiet, she sat at the kitchen table and made herself a list going day by day of what she needed to accomplish. Planning always stilled the anxiety, and this way she would have the satisfaction of being able to check things off and, hopefully, not forget anything. She still had three mornings in which to do last-minute shopping and wrap the remaining gifts while the kids were in school, and once that was out of the way, she would breath easier. She always set up a wrapping station in Michael's old office and this made it easier for all of them without having to constantly hunt for tape, scissors, paper and tags. For her, organization was the key; it was when things got out of hand that she began to fall apart and she couldn't afford to do that this year. Then there was the time-consuming added complication of Honey, and even though they loved her and wouldn't be without her, both she and Peter came to the conclusion she was a lot of work, but they both agreed it was a labor of love and definitely worth it for the pleasure she gave in return.

She grabbed her pocketbook and pulled out the children's wish list from her wallet. Jessica still believed in Santa, although she was always worried about how he could possibly get down the chimney because the gas logs were in the way. Thea always said he was probably like Alice in Wonderland and that he had a magic shrinking potion, and she seemed satisfied with her mom's answer. On Christmas Eve, Jessica left carrots for the reindeer and cookies for Santa where he could easily find them and Thea made sure the cookies were gone before morning with a few crumbs remaining. Jessica was convinced Santa just put the carrots in his pocket and gave them to the reindeer when he got back on the roof. Peter and Izzie went along with the fantasy remembering their own disappointment when they finally realized Santa wasn't real.

List in hand, Thea climbed the stairs and going to her closet where she had stashed all the gifts, decided to take inventory. She laid all the items out on the bed and discovered, as far as the kids were concerned, she was in pretty good shape. Michael always sent a hefty check and this certainly helped with expensive things like skis for Peter and ice skates for the girls, items they would purchase after Christmas. Other than that, the gifts were low-key because she didn't believe in going overboard and the kids knew better than to ask for anything extravagant, but Peter was definitely due for new skis; his current well-used secondhand ones much too short. The girls had outgrown their ice skates and they would be thrilled to have new ones with smooth, sharp blades to skate on the local pond. Thea went off happily to start wrapping the books, CDs, art supplies and the inevitable socks and underwear. Stocking stuffers were always identically wrapped to continue the Santa tradition, and she hid the roll of paper in the back of her closet so it wouldn't get used by mistake. She suspected this was probably Jessica's last year to believe, but she might be wrong.

While she wrapped, she thought about Chris and wondered whether she was making a mistake in allowing him to come to Maine, but her mind always took her back to how much she had enjoyed spending time with him. She believed he was a truly good person and what was it Nan had always said about going with your intuition? "If you truly listened to your inner voice, it would never steer you wrong." She had certainly never listened before, turning a blind eye, leading her into one mess after the other. Having Chris come and meet the children, to just be introduced to them as a friend without any romantic involvement, would be the way to start; she would then be able to see their reaction and take it from there. Being able to tap into Nan and MaryAnn's wisdom and go to them for advice would, hopefully, keep her on the straight and narrow.

Nan's pregnancy had taken her by surprise and she had echoed Margaret's words by wishing she lived closer to help with the baby when the time came. She was looking forward to the wedding at the Crooked Inn on New Year's Eve and told Nan it was the perfect place. She was also helping MaryAnn with her wedding, going with her tomorrow morning to pick out a dress. Her life was beginning to take shape, and being jolted out of her solitary existence with only the children for company was just what she needed. It gave her no time to brood and become melancholy, and even though there was always the fear of Kenny lurking in the shadows, she was glad she had decided to stay in Maine and tough it out. Besides which, there was too much about Maine that she would miss: the smell of the ocean; the cry of the gulls; the sandpipers darting erratically across the sand; the pungent salt marshes; the boats in the harbor; the distant mountains; the rocky shoreline with the flying spray of the pounding waves; the stars that shone so bright in the inky black sky on clear nights. There was so much more than this, but Maine was in her bones and for the first time she felt settled. Had she finally grown up and lost the desire to flee when things went wrong? She hoped so with all her heart.

CHAPTER THIRTY-TWO

THEA AND MARYANN

Sometimes MaryAnn thought she was in someone else's life, bobbing along on a tide of inevitability, new experiences appearing on the horizon regular as clockwork—today's a shopping trip with Thea. She applied a little makeup, brushed her winter-static, flyaway hair and went downstairs to wait for her friend. Thea was late and apologized to MaryAnn as soon as she got in the car. "I'm sorry. I forgot Jessica's lunch and had to go back. It's a good thing Jim is picking Jessica and Johnny up from school."

MaryAnn, relieved to finally be on the move, said, "I'm just glad you're here."

"Well, I am too. I've been looking forward to going shopping with you so much. This is such a treat for me. Did you have a particular kind of dress in mind?"

"Nothing bridal that's for sure. I was thinking red, not scarlet, more a deep burgundy and if that fails, a midnight blue. Do you think that's appropriate?"

"Of course it is. You must wear what makes you feel comfortable. It is your day, after all. I know just the place with knock-off prices just in case you're worried. I'm assuming you want to go new."

"I do. I did look to see if there was anything in One Woman's Treasure when I bought the rhinestone clips, but I would really rather have a dress that no one else has worn. I'm a bit superstitious and would spend my time wondering about the previous owner, whether she was happy or whether the dress had brought her bad luck. I'm kinda done with secondhand."

"I know exactly what you mean, besides it wouldn't smell right. There's nothing like the clean scent of brand new clothes."

"It's wearing out of my coat a little," MaryAnn said, bringing the sleeve to her nose, "but you're absolutely right."

Thea turned down a side street and parked alongside a row of cars outside a one-story building with barred windows, cement block walls and a corrugated iron roof. "Don't be put off by appearances. You will be pleasantly surprised." She opened a dark green door, and they stepped into a dimly lit hallway, pausing to blink and adjust their eyes after the outdoor glare. "Follow me," she said.

Walking down the narrow passageway on the well-worn linoleum they passed a men's and a women's restroom, a green encrusted water fountain, a hair salon and a gym—the light from the windowed doors, the sound of music and the thud, thud of feet on a treadmill, spilling into the corridor. "Here we are," Thea said, reaching a solid wooden door with the name Frannie's Fashions painted in bold black letters across the top. She pushed it open to reveal a woman's paradise.

"How on earth did you know about this place?" MaryAnn said, eyes wide.

"It's a well-kept secret. Actually, it was Nan who put me onto it. She's the best bargain hunter around. The dresses are in the back, but it's one-stop shopping because there is everything here you could possibly want except shoes."

"I can see that. Let's get started," MaryAnn said, fingering a silky peach negligee as she walked past, glancing at the jewelry locked safely inside well-lit glass cases, and the bottles of expensive perfume nestled in amongst artfully draped, vibrantly patterned silk scarves. She and Thea weren't the only shoppers.

Half way down the store they heard a voice say, "Good morning, ladies. How can I help?" MaryAnn turned to see a young woman peering around a rack of bright sweaters, her blonde head spiked, her brown eyes black-rimmed, lips scarlet. Could this be Frannie?

"We're here to look at dresses," Thea said.

"Well, you're headed in the right direction. Have you been here before?"

"I have, but this is a first for my friend."

"Welcome to both of you. Our pricing system hasn't changed," and she pointed a shocking pink fingernail at a large notice on the wall behind the cash register. "Each item is color coded, and the longer the item has been sitting in inventory, the greater the discount. We hate to see stuff gathering dust. Just give me a holler if you have any questions."

MaryAnn, finally finding her tongue, said, "We will."

They climbed three well-scuffed wooden stairs and found themselves in a small square room with clothes on three sides and two floral-curtained changing rooms on the right with a mirror in between, one curtain pulled tightly across, a pair of bare feet visible beneath. "What size are you?" Thea asked.

"It varies, but usually a ten. What are you—a six? I feel like an elephant next to you."

"A giraffe more like it, or a gazelle, but no way are you an elephant!"

MaryAnn headed for the larger sizes, slid the full-length dresses along the rod looking at each of them until she found one in just the color she had in mind. Unable to believe her eyes, she unhooked it, walked over to the mirror and held it up against her. "What do you think?" Thea came up behind her; a sage green dress draped over one arm.

"I think it's perfect. Why don't you try it on?"

MaryAnn, pushing the curtain to one side, stepped into the vacant cubicle, thankful for the subdued lighting, and keeping her fingers crossed the dress would fit, got undressed. She managed to get the zipper half way up and then asked for Thea's help. "Wow," Thea said. "You look stunning. That color is so right for you." The simple deep burgundy silk dress complemented MaryAnn's slender figure and accentuated her curves: the neck scooped but not too low, the sleeves long, the dress falling in soft folds to her ankles. MaryAnn twirled in front of the mirror. "What shoes should I wear?"

"Hm. How about some sexy silver sandals? And while on the subject of sexy, we need to find you some fabulous underwear to go underneath."

"Now you're making me blush," she said, realizing they had been overheard by the woman in the other changing room who suddenly appeared. Brown-haired, overweight, middle-aged, favoring one hip, dressed in a white top and navy pants, she was all smiles. "Don't mind me," she said, looking MaryAnn up and down. "Your friend is right about the dress. You look spectacular."

MaryAnn said, "Thank you," and watched her walk cautiously down the stairs, leaning heavily on the rail.

"Turn around and let me unzip you," Thea said.

"Are you going to try on the sage green?"

"Do you think I should? I wasn't planning on shopping for me today, but this caught my eye."

"I don't mind waiting."

Thea held the dress away from her. "It is tempting."

"Go on. Spoil yourself."

MaryAnn loved the dress; the soft sage green a perfect complement to Thea's coloring, the style flattering to her petite figure. "It suits you," she said

The girl with the spiked blonde hair magically appeared. No taller than Thea she bubbled over their choices. "Let me take those and hang them at the cash desk for you while you finish your shopping." She marched away, her black high-heeled boots making sharp tapping noises on the old wooden floor; her tight, bright pink, bum-hugging skirt barely reaching the top of her mesh-tighted thighs. MaryAnn found her clothing quite astonishing and said a silent thank you she didn't have a daughter to raise.

They spent the next thirty minutes or so hunting for underwear. MaryAnn was sold on ivory with just a hint of peach, with smooth lines to go beneath her dress. She shook her head when Thea held up a garter belt and stockings; she only wanted the silky feel of a full-length slip. She also chose a powder blue negligee with a matching lace-trimmed wrap just because, knowing full well it would probably stay in its box on her wedding night, but it was elegant and sensual, too beautiful to resist.

MaryAnn had purposely avoided looking at any of the prices and stood nervously waiting for the total. The girl draped a plastic bag over each of the dresses and tied knots in the bottom to protect them. Producing a box from beneath the counter, she nestled the negligee within layers of tissue paper, wrapped the slip and underwear and placed them at the bottom of a black bag with Frannie's Fashions emblazoned in fancy gold lettering. Handing them each a complimentary phial of perfume, she said, "It's a new scent called Just a Hint," dabbing a little on the inside of her tiny white wrist, holding it out for them to sniff. MaryAnn, not a user of perfume, surprised to find she liked the clean yet subtle fragrance, asked if there was body lotion to match. The girl added it to the bag. The total came to one hundred and twenty-three dollars and ninety-five cents, and when she produced Jim's credit card—pressed into her hand the night before, a no-arguing expression on his face—the girl said, "I'm sorry we only take cash or checks."

"No problem," MaryAnn said, tucking the credit card back into her wallet, desperately afraid of losing it, digging down to the bottom of her pocketbook and retrieving an envelope of cash removed from her dwindling savings account. Thea wrote a check for her dress and a pretty pink sweater she had chosen for her mom. Back out in the hallway, MaryAnn said, "I can't believe how many beautiful things I have for so little money and what a fun way to shop. Thank you for bringing me here."

"You are quite welcome."

"Where to now?" MaryAnn asked, laying her dress along the back seat, stowing her packages in the trunk and hanging Thea's dress from the handle in the roof of the car.

"DSW has the best selection of shoes around or would you rather try Payless? I'd also like to stop in at Barnes & Noble if you don't mind."

"I don't mind at all and let's try DSW first."

MaryAnn hesitated inside the door, overwhelmed by the rows and rows of shoes and the piles of boxes stacked underneath. Thea grabbed her hand and pulled her towards a display of sandals. "How about these?" she said, picking up a silver pair with a sensible but elegant heel. "What size are you?"

"An eight." Down on their hands and knees they hunted through the boxes, initially disappointed, eventually finding a box marked with an eight right at the bottom of the pile. "This is my lucky day," MaryAnn said.

Giggling like a couple of schoolgirls over the nylon shoe protectors, MaryAnn tugged them over her feet. She slipped the sandals on, buckled them around her slender ankles, and wiggled her toes beneath the delicate silver straps. "You'd better walk up and down just to make sure they fit and are comfortable enough to wear for at least a few hours," Thea said.

"Yes, ma'am," she said, standing in front of one of those silly foot mirrors before walking away. Thea followed her friend, grabbing MaryAnn's pocketbook absent-mindedly left behind. "They're not the most comfortable shoes I've ever owned, but actually not bad for sandals."

"Are we sold?"

"We are. I'm having a hard time believing all this is real. Is it possible to be too happy?"

Thea sat down on one of the measuring footstools. "I don't know. I'm not sure what happiness is. I'll let you know if I ever find out. Come on, let's put these magical shoes back in the box and go pay for them." This time MaryAnn handed over Jim's credit card, knowing he would be disappointed she had only used it for a pair of sandals costing less than twenty dollars.

Once inside Barnes & Noble, they split up. MaryAnn headed for the mystery section to look for a book for Jim, and Thea went off to find the

New York Times crossword puzzle calendar for her dad. She picked out a novel for her mom, one she had read and hoped her mom would like because it was light-hearted and fun. She was stumped when it came to Mr. Blunt and Dorothy and she wandered aimlessly up and down the shelves until she ran out of time. MaryAnn had found the *2005 Compendium of American Mysteries,* a couple of books for the boys and a thousand-piece colorful jigsaw puzzle of candy wrappers that looked challenging, but fun. "Well, you've certainly been a lot more successful than me," Thea said as they stood in line waiting to pay.

"I guess, I have," MaryAnn said. "I'm hungry. How about you?" Clutching their packages, they lined up for coffee and sandwiches. MaryAnn chose an egg sandwich with cheddar cheese and ham and Thea went for a salad. MaryAnn took her coffee black and Thea added calories by ordering a vanilla latte.

Purchases at their feet, they sat at one of the round tables and looked at each other. "I've had the best time today. Outings like this almost never happen for me, and much as I love my kids, it's nice to have a breather," MaryAnn said.

"Let's drink to Jim for coming to the rescue," Thea said, raising her coffee mug and tapping MaryAnn's.

"I was surprised you actually agreed to let Jim pick up Jessica."

"Jess made up my mind for me. She was completely sold on the idea. She trusts Jim and so do I, and I decided in this instance it would be safe to let her go. It's a huge step for both of us but the right one."

"Well, you made Jim's day. He was quite overwhelmed when you accepted."

"He is a remarkable man, but you already know that. I don't need to sing his praises to you." MaryAnn smiled and took a bite of her sandwich. "What do you think you will do once the dust has settled? Are you going to continue at the Diner?"

"No. I'm currently reducing my hours, but it's hard. Will has been so good to me, but I really want to put my college education to good use. It's been idly sitting on a shelf and so has my brain. I also don't want to be totally dependent on Jim, not that he would care, but I like earning my own spending money. Something will turn up when the time is right. In the meantime, I will enjoy playing wife, at least for a little while."

"I don't play wife at all well."

"Maybe because you have never found the right husband."

"That could be part of it, but it's my temperament. I can only stand so much togetherness and then I have this terrible urge to flee. It's an only child syndrome. Solitude is as necessary to me as the air I breathe and anyone coming into my life would have to understand that without getting all bent out of shape."

"In a way I understand. I am the oldest of seven and the only one to leave the nest and seek a college education. My siblings resented me always having my nose in a book, said I didn't do my fair share of the chores which wasn't entirely true, but I did spend a great deal of time in a corner of the local coffee shop because there was no private space at home. I had such a thirst for knowledge, and still do, and I have no idea where it came from. I stay in touch with my mom, send her a little money when I can, but I've little interest in the rest of my unpredictable, alcohol-dependent family, including my father. Once I'm settled, I would like to have my mom to stay, and if she won't come, I will go visit her."

"Where do they live?"

"Upstate New York and I would have to borrow Jim's car because my old bone-shaker won't make it, or, on the other hand, perhaps we'll just go together."

"I'd be happy to take the kids," Thea said, forking up a mouthful of salad, holding it in mid-air, looking at MaryAnn, a frown creasing her forehead. "I know I'm completely changing the subject, but I worry about my inability to feel. I just seem to plow on regardless. Why am I not more affected by Ellie's death? I can't figure it out."

MaryAnn didn't know what to say, but sensed Thea's need to talk. Never one to give advice, remembering all the useless condolences after Sam's death, she chose her words carefully. "We all react differently. There's no right or wrong way to feel."

"But even at the memorial I felt detached somehow. I looked at all the grief-stricken faces and hardly shed a tear. Do you think there's something wrong with me?"

"Oh, Thea, of course not. You can shoot me down if I'm wrong, but I think you're angry at Ellie right now."

With a look of surprise on her pretty face, she said, "You are spot on. Thank you. Sometimes living alone is tough, not having another adult to talk to and I do tend to bottle things until I explode."

"I'm more than happy to listen to you if you want to voice your thoughts, but I'm not much good on the advice front."

"You've helped me more than you could possibly know. I've been neglecting my journal, and now you've pinpointed the problem, I'll be able to work things out by writing it all down."

"I find it strange now we've gotten to know each other that I never formed any female friendships over the years and now I realize what I've been missing," MaryAnn said.

"I only wish I'd met you sooner. I think you would have helped to straighten me out and I could have given you some solace in your grief, but at least we have each other now and that's good enough for me. It's comforting to know you are just a phone call away."

"You can call me anytime except on my wedding night."

"Aw, you're no fun," and they both laughed.

Riding home in the car, Thea asked MaryAnn if she needed any help with her wedding preparations. "I don't think so. It's going to be really simple," she said, "and Jennifer, my sister-in-law to-be, is taking care of the caterers, the flowers and the cake. I'd love your help with my hair, though."

"Done deal. What about music?"

"Jim is going to rig up a speaker in the hallway and there's a stereo in the library. We just have to pick out the CDs we want to use and find someone to man it. I haven't quite decided on the music for when I walk down the stairs, but it won't be the wedding march. I can't do the *Here comes the bride, all fat and wide* thing," and she chuckled. "Then the plan is to gather around the piano in the library and have a carol sing just before everyone goes home. The lady who plays the organ at the church—I can't remember her name, Lily something, I think—will play for us."

Thea picked up on MaryAnn's excitement. "You're positively beaming, and quite rightly so."

Thea turned into MaryAnn's driveway. "Oh, Thea, I shall be so glad to leave this place. I never want Jim to see where we've been living, but for some reason I don't mind you knowing."

"I'm not quite sure what to say, but I believe you have just given me the gift of true friendship. Thank you."

MaryAnn gathered up her purchases. Draping her dress over her left arm and holding the Barnes & Noble bag and her shoes in her other hand, she watched Thea drive away. Climbing the sagging porch stairs, fumbling as always for her keys, she was full to bursting with anticipation and joy and began to sing. She had so much to look forward to. With her ear for music and her ability to sing a melody after only hearing it once, she quickly remembered lyrics. Shyly asking Jim one day whether it would be all right if she learned how to play the piano after they were married, he immediately unearthed all the well-thumbed sheets of music from which his grandfather and his mother used to play. Her fingers itched with anticipation when she saw some of the scores—the Oscar and Hammerstein show tunes she loved so well—but she curbed her impatience. In the meantime, Jim had promised to get the piano tuned. She knew he was excited about having family sing-alongs just like the old days and she hoped she wouldn't disappoint him. He was unable to give her a reason why he and Ben had never learned to play. She had teased him by saying, "Now's your chance; we can learn together," but he was non-committal although she knew he was pleased the piano would no longer be sitting in the library, lost and forgotten.

MaryAnn walked up the stairs with her precious packages, ignoring the scratchy sound of mice in the wall. She'd have to set the trap again, but not for much longer, thank goodness. Before hanging her dress in the closet, she undid the knot at the end of the plastic bag, putting her hand inside, feeling the softness of the fabric, and resisting the temptation to try it on, she retied the knot. Opening the shoebox she gazed at the pretty silver sandals, her heart doing a little flip-flop of happiness. She stashed them safely away together with the gifts she had purchased and went outside to meet Ian from the school bus.

CHAPTER THIRTY-THREE

THEA

Thea checked the long-range weather forecast. Of course there were no guarantees—predictability always a little shaky—but she nevertheless took comfort in the promise of a precipitation-free few days. Things were beginning to come together and she was looking forward to the arrival of her visitors. Taking advantage of her last free morning to gather her thoughts, she sent Peter and Izzie off with gifts for their teachers—festively decorated tins filled with the much sought after English toffee—admonishing them not to eat any! Jessica, in possession of her own tin for Miss Simms, could hardly contain her excitement, especially as she had, with Thea's help, labored over a special card to go with her present.

Thea solved the gift problem for Mr. Blunt and Dorothy by assembling a basket of goodies, and satisfied with how it had turned out, created a similar one for her parents. With all the gifts wrapped and the house decorated, she was in a festive mood even if a little overwhelmed, and being busy kept the darkness away. Always an only child at heart, solitude a necessity, she constantly struggled when surrounded by people, but she was determined to rise to the occasion. She had mixed feelings about Chris coming into her life, mainly because she wondered if it was fair to him and she asked herself whether she should have nipped it in the bud before any friendship had a chance to take shape. But she kept coming back to the evening spent together, unable to quash the pleasant memories, and she wanted more of the same.

"Am I being selfish?" she asked Honey. Sitting on the mat by the door, the dog tilted her head to one side, making every effort to understand. "You don't know how lucky you are not to be a human because it's terribly complicated, and here I am talking to you when I have a million things to do. You are such a distraction." Honey got up, padded over to Thea and placed a paw on her knee. Thea looked down at her and placed her hand on top of Honey's head. "You're really smart. We could all take a leaf out of your doggy book, and I don't know if you realize it, but because you demand so little and give so much you end up getting more attention that way."

In the end, the morning was a complete loss and she achieved nothing; she shrugged it off. She and Honey hopped in the car and went off to pick up Jessica. Honey, delighted to "go for a ride" because those were four words she did understand, sat on the passenger seat leaning to the left or the right depending on the way the road curved. As always, it made Thea smile.

Thea waited outside the school, watched the double doors open and release the excited kindergarteners; they scurried down the steps. Jessica was in a muddle as usual and as soon as Thea reached her she grabbed her backpack, leaving her daughter to carry a bag filled with Christmas loot. "Wait until you see what I got," she said, grasping hold of the handles and opening the bag wide.

"Oh, my," Thea said. "How many Secret Santas did you have?"

"Only one, but we played games and there were prizes. It was so much fun."

"I bet. How many cookies did you eat?"

"Miss Simms only allowed us to eat two. I brought the rest home."

"That was smart."

Jessica prattled on and Thea tried to listen so she could answer her questions, but her mind was on Izzie as she drove home. She decided she was probably more nervous than her daughter about her performance in *The Nutcracker*. Yesterday's dress rehearsal had gone well, Izzie all lit up like a Christmas tree, and now the pretty white dress with its blue satin sash was hanging in her closet waiting for tonight's performance, together with the simple nightdress. Worried about projecting her own nervousness onto her daughter, she decided a run on the treadmill the best remedy to ease her tension. She went over the order of events: Izzie had to be at the theater by six o'clock and she would stay; Bill and Margaret the only ones attending this evening would find their own way for the seven-thirty performance, and MaryAnn would arrive to babysit at five thirty. With the realization she seemed to have all her ducks in a row, Thea began to feel a little better.

Once in the house, Thea assured Honey Peter would take her for a walk when he got home, told Jess she was going for a thirty minute run, and to please come and get her if the phone rang. The run and a shower worked miracles and she coped with the afternoon, back in her festive spirit. As soon as Peter and Izzie arrived home, Peter and Honey disappeared and Izzie went up to Thea's room and lay down to relax for a little while.

Izzie lay on her back doing her belly breathing and going through the dance steps in her head, a technique that worked well and renewed her energy. She didn't understand why she wasn't nervous, unlike some of her fellow dancers who were sometimes physically ill before a performance, but she knew she was lucky to have the ability to completely immerse herself in the role. Once on stage, she became Clara, only recognizing the stage faces of her fellow dancers, and she never worried about the possibility of an occasional mistake from either herself or the other kids; she just adapted accordingly. She knew her mom was nervous for her even though she tried to hide it by being extra calm, but Izzie wasn't fooled. She sat on the bed in the darkening room and gently massaged her feet. The time was beginning to drag and she was impatient to be gone. She stretched her slender arms above her head and rolled her head to relieve any tension in her neck before sliding off the bed and making her way downstairs.

CHAPTER THIRTY-FOUR

AN EVENING OUT

Margaret wasn't used to getting dressed up, but it made a nice change to be going out. She and Bill, by other people's standards, lived a rather insular life, but they'd never had any desire to travel, which was just as well because there was no one to mind the store. Bill put a notice on the door saying they would be closing at five o'clock sharp to give Margaret the time to rest for her "forty minute power nap" as she called it. "Makes all the difference," she told Bill, and he had to agree with her because she looked the picture of vitality. "You look grand, lass," he said.

"You don't look too shabby yourself," she said, and indeed he did look sharp in his neatly pressed gray flannels and tweed jacket. She had ironed a cream shirt for him and she could still smell that fresh-ironed scent when she stood close to straighten his dark green tie. He leaned down to kiss her. "Even after all these years, you're still my bride. I love you so much."

"I love you too." She stood there looking at him; her ample figure snugly encased in a navy blue dress, her mother's pearls in a glistening circle around her neck. "It's time for us to go."

The theater is just as Margaret and Bill remembered it from the year before: the dark red plush seats inviting them as they walk down the aisle, and the discordant music from the orchestra tuning up filling their ears. The lights from above shine down on the stage; the dark blue curtain hangs richly in shadowy folds, and the sconces on the side walls temper the severity of the modern angular decor; this is no opera house with a gilded and painted ceiling, but the acoustics are superb. They spot Thea, pause at the end of the row, wait for the people already sitting to stand up, their seats making thudding noises, flipping into their upright positions. Margaret and Bill squeeze past, saying sorry as they go, trying not to tread on anyone's toes. Thea turns and smiles as soon as she sees them. "Boy, am I glad to see you. I'm so nervous, I've nearly ripped my program to shreds." The lights flicker to remind the members of the audience to find their seats and with just ten minutes to go, the conductor arrives to the sound of applause and the music from the orchestra pit swells and tugs at their emotions. Margaret, thumbing through her program, finds a picture of Izzie, and her heart swells with pride. She shows it to Bill and he smiles and squeezes her hand.

The lights dim and for a moment the audience is in complete darkness, but it serves to stem their restlessness while they wait, holding their breath, watching the curtain rise, rustling as it folds and glides upwards. Nothing exists for Thea except what is happening on stage and she hugs herself in excitement, her nervousness forgotten, eyes focused searching for her daughter.

The stage is in darkness, except for a spotlight on the right-hand side, where people gather, festive in their party clothes, greeting each other and disappearing through a doorway. Now the stage is empty. The lights go up to reveal the Stahlbaum's living room decorated with Christmas ornaments, wreaths, stockings, mistletoe and filled with guests, young and old, strutting about in their finery, greeting one another gracefully and fluidly as only ballet dancers can: the women nodding, skirts swaying; the men bowing; the majestic Christmas tree the main backdrop, skillfully painted to appear three-dimensional, decorated with gold and silver apples. The children run and dance and Thea watches in awe as Izzie, so slender and elegant, immersed in her role as Clara, interacts with the other children as they excitedly receive their gifts, and Clara, especially delighted with a pair of pointe shoes, holds them up for all to see. The party picks up with dancing and celebration until a mysterious stranger enters from the right-hand side and Fritz, Clara's brother, and some of the other children look scared, but Clara knows who he is—Herr Drosselmeier, her favorite uncle. All the children dance and carry on with laughter while he strides around the stage, swirling his magnificent blue cape around him. A puppet theater is wheeled in and then two life-sized boxes, and when the doors are opened, a mechanical ballerina and a harlequin emerge, and the delighted children eagerly ask for more. Thea waits knowing that Drosselmeier will soon produce the Nutcracker and watches as his face falls when the children are not interested with the exception of Clara, who takes it from her uncle. She and Drosselmeier dance with the Nutcracker and he lifts her and twirls her around. "Don't drop her, please," Thea whispers. Clara dances alone with the Nutcracker, alternately holding him up into the air and then resting him gently against her cheek. Disenchanted with his gift, Fritz grows jealous, snatches the Nutcracker from Clara and plays a game of toss with the other boys. Clara looks on in horror and it isn't long before the Nutcracker breaks. Clara is upset, but Drosselmeier fixes it with a handkerchief, and his nephew offers Clara a small makeshift bed under the Christmas tree for her injured Nutcracker. She smiles up at him and nods, laying the Nutcracker gently down.

It is getting late and the children become sleepy. All the guests generously thank the Stahlbaum's before they leave and the stage empties with the exception of Clara who checks on her Nutcracker one last time, blows out the lights on the Christmas tree, and ends up falling asleep under the tree with the Nutcracker in her arms. The lights dim.

At the stroke of midnight, Clara wakes to a frightening scene. The house, the tree and the toys seem to be getting larger. Thea watches as the tree cleverly expands, rising higher and higher. It's the same set as last year, but she still can't figure out how it's done. Clara looks around in horror and dances across the stage in alarm. Life-sized mice scampering around the room surround her and she runs and sits in an enormous chair. She is agitated and hides her face. The Mouse King appears in a cloud of smoke and is carried around in triumph by the other mice—yellow eyes blazing, red cape shining. He owns the stage. Fritz's toy soldiers, resplendent in their blue gold-braided uniforms, come to life and march towards Clara's now life-sized Nutcracker. A battle is soon underway between the mice and the soldiers, led by the giant Mouse King. The Nutcracker and the Mouse King enter an intense battle. Clara watches in alarm and throws her shoe at the Mouse King, stunning him long enough for the Nutcracker to stab him with his sword. The army of mice rapidly carries their King away and The Nutcracker leaves the stage.

When he returns, he has been magically transformed into a handsome prince and he bows before Clara, takes her hand in his and leads her to the Land of Snow. The backdrop changes; the tree slides away to be replaced by a scene of snow-topped trees and white rooftops with a church tower and brightly lit windows. The stage is filled with blue light; snow falls in the background.

Thea sits transfixed as Clara dances with the Nutcracker prince. It's hard to believe Izzie is only eight years old because of her stage presence and her height. The dance isn't complicated, but it is beautiful and the emotion between the two dancers projects out to the audience and as the music soars, so does Thea's heart.

Their dance is finished and they come forward to take their bows, and even though Thea wants to get up, she will save her standing ovation until the end. In the meantime, she claps until the palms of her hands sting with pain. "Oh, well done," she wants to cry, but she restrains herself, not so her tears which fall uncontrollably down her cheeks. The curtain comes down, and the lights go up, and she fumbles in her pocket for a tissue, but Margaret saves the day. "Here," she says, and Thea gratefully accepts the proffered Kleenex. Both Bill and Margaret have tears in their eyes. "Wasn't she splendid?" Margaret whispers. "Bill and I are going to walk around and stretch our legs. Do you want to come with us?"

"No, I'm just going to sit here, but thank you."

"Would you like something to drink?"

"A bottle of water would be great."

Emotionally exhausted, Thea is left sitting in the row alone. She has danced every step, holding her breath when Izzie was raised high above the stage. She hadn't felt like this when Izzie had just played a minor role, as one in a group, but now that she is performing solo, it is nerve-wracking. One slight twist of the ankle and her daughter's dreams will be shattered.

Margaret and Bill make their way to the lobby bumping into people they know, pausing to make a greeting, shake a hand and comment on how much they are enjoying the ballet. Of course, there is the inevitable talk of the weather and how lucky for the performers it didn't snow. "Nothing worse than putting on a show and then having to cancel," they all agree. Bill hands over a five-dollar bill to the man behind the bar and receives two bottles of water in return. The lights flicker and he and Margaret go back to their seats, hand Thea her water and settle in for Act II. Bill pulls Margaret's coat up around her shoulders and she shuffles around until she is comfortable. They listen to throat clearing, a lot of whispering and candy wrapper rustling from the row behind.

Thea sips her water and relaxes into her seat. Clara's part in the second half is minimal in this particular version of *The Nutcracker* and this means she doesn't have to vicariously dance through the second half. Once more, there's applause for the conductor; the music begins and the curtain rises to reveal the Land of Sweets. Again, the painted backdrop is superb and depicts a magnificent castle with many turrets and lighted windows, mountains made of ladyfingers with a topping of whipped cream as white as snow, and candied flowers. Clara and the Nutcracker Prince are greeted by the Sugar Plum Fairy and shown to a curtain-draped platform on which two large plush chairs have been placed. The Prince tells his story in gestures of how Clara saved his life and in gratitude the Sugar Plum Fairy places a crown on Clara's head. She and the Prince climb to their seats and the festivities begin much to Clara's delight.

Thea's feet tap to the rhythm as the Spanish dancers dance their fandango to the lively music of trumpets and castanets: the dark haired senorita; the flash of a red petticoat; the senor with his tri-cornered hat, stomping and raising his black coated arms in the air, fingers snapping. The Arabian women take over, dancing in veils and moving their sultry bodies—the silver threads in their exotic tunics catching the light, the bells on their ankles jingling. The Chinese Dance is tight and confined compared with the Russian dancers who leap and crouch pushing their red boots out in front of them, arms crossed over their chests. Dancing flowers enter to the tune of a harp and move around the stage in intricate patterns to the most beautiful waltz.

A handsome cavalier enters the scene and he and the Sugar Plum Fairy dance to the most recognizable tune in the entire work—a role to which all ballerinas aspire and Thea is sure Izzie is no exception. They perform flawlessly with grace and athleticism. She is sure they are both breathing hard, but ballet isn't for the faint-hearted and the only way to succeed is to be superbly fit. She has nothing but admiration for anyone who takes up ballet as a profession and even if you love it above all else, it is still hard work.

The festival concludes when all the dancers come together and bid Clara and the Nutcracker Prince farewell. The stage dims and silently the backdrop is changed and the stage comes alight to the final scene of Clara waking up the next morning under the Christmas tree with her Nutcracker still in her arms.

The applause is thunderous—a standing ovation. Thea's water bottle falls to the floor with a thud as Clara and the Nutcracker Prince come to the front of the stage. She wants to whistle and shout, but she restrains herself. Her arms are aching, but still she claps for Herr Drosselmeier, the Sugar Plum Fairy and all the other members of the cast who surge forward in a great wave. They move back and the curtain falls, only to rise again.

The Nutcracker Prince comes forward and gestures to the conductor in the orchestra pit below and opens his arms to the crowd and the clapping continues. How splendid to have a full theater and an enthusiastic audience for their first night. The curtain comes down and the lights in the auditorium come on and it's over.

Thea looks down at her feet searching for the water bottle, but it has rolled out of sight on the sloping floor. She gathers her coat, her pocketbook and the crumpled program and follows Margaret and Bill out of the row. "I have flowers for Izzie in the car," Margaret says. "Do you think we'll be able to go backstage?"

"I'm sure we will. I'll wait just inside the door for you."

People nod to Thea as they walk out. Some of them know who she is and there are murmurs of congratulations. "Your daughter did beautifully." "You must be so proud," they say. She acknowledges their compliments, her cheeks flushed with pure delight, oblivious to the cold night air seeping into the lobby through the open doors. Margaret and Bill are having a hard time making their way back in, fighting against the throng, Bill holding the bunch of flowers aloft to protect them from being crushed. "This wasn't the smartest thing we ever did," he says, beaming from ear to ear.

"Oh, but Izzie will be thrilled," Thea says.

And indeed she was, greeting the three of them, her face still covered in makeup. Margaret holds out the flowers and says, "Well done, my dear," totally ignoring the surrounding chaos with children and parents connecting up with each other, saying, "Goodnight. See you tomorrow," as they drift away.

Bill, caught up in the excitement of it all, stands by the wall just observing. Looking at all the children's faces, somehow made older by the makeup, he understands the lure of the greasepaint. He has never had any desire whatsoever to make a spectacle of himself either on or off stage, but being here in the thick of the theatrical world makes him realize how addicting it is. But it is a fickle world full of drama and high stakes and he is glad Nan didn't have similar aspirations. Izzie walks over to him. "Thank you for coming, Uncle Bill."

"Aye, lass, we wouldn't have missed it for the world. You did us proud."

Thea comes up behind her daughter and gently puts her arm around her shoulders. "It's time to go. Go get your things. I'll hold your flowers."

Simone Beauchamps appears as they are waiting. It is odd to see her in regular clothes. Thea has seen her in nothing but a leotard and tights with her hair pulled tightly into a bun. Tonight she is elegantly dressed in a deep burgundy coat, her dark sleek hair falling into soft waves around her shoulders. "Good evening, Mrs. Chamberlin. How did you like the performance? I thought it went well. Oh, there were a couple of small hiccups, but only I and the dancers would have noticed."

"It was dazzling. I am always blown away by how professional the production is seeing as you have limited resources and a smaller stage to work with."

"Ah, but that's what makes it so special. We are forced to be creative and pull in all the talent we have. That way no one takes anything for granted. We've worked in collaboration with the Down East Ballet Company for many years; it is a good partnership. And then when we find an exceptional talent like your Isabel, it makes the show come alive."

"Thank you. Watching my daughter tonight I could see why you chose her. And the best thing of all, I get to see the next two performances, although I find it exhausting."

"I'm sure you do. Goodnight, then. See you tomorrow."

Izzie, having made a half-hearted attempt at removing her makeup, looks pale and tired. "Time to get you home and into bed."

"I do feel kinda droopy."

"I'm sure you do."

The four of them leave the theater together and part ways in the parking lot. There are "thank-yous" and "goodbyes" and "see you soons" and kisses on cheeks in the frosty air before settling in their seats, turning on their engines and driving away. Izzie dozes on the way home and Thea guides her gently into the house, putting a finger to her lips to MaryAnn and helps Izzie into her pajamas. Sleep is more important than clean teeth so she tucks her into bed, kisses her on her greasy cheek, pulls Jess's covers up and goes off to find MaryAnn.

"Do you know how wonderful it is to come home and find you here?" She collapses into a heap on the sofa.

"How come?"

"Because you're a rock. Nothing seems to faze you and you've no idea how nice that is."

MaryAnn raises her eyebrows. "You make me sound rather dull."

"Now you know that's not true. I'm sorry I'm not explaining myself very well, but I've never met anyone quite like you. You are so good with the kids."

"I guess there are advantages to being the oldest of seven. Bringing up kids is second nature to me because I always helped out with my siblings."

"But it's more than that . . ."

"I was never afraid of anything until I lost Sam, but because of his death, I have a greater appreciation for life. Does that make sense?"

"It does."

"I'm finally at peace and the fear is gone. I love my life the way it is now: for Jim and what he has done for my boys and for my friendship with you. My life is so full."

"I wish I could say the same. My problem is I live with too many regrets. I've made a lot of stupid mistakes."

"But you've come through them. I was consumed with guilt over the way the boys and I had to live after Sam's death and Will put me straight by saying it hadn't done them any harm, that Johnny's weak chest wasn't caused by living in that dreadful rental, but by losing his daddy. And I believed him because I had to. So, yes, your kids have had a rough time of it too, but look how great they are and how much strength of character they have. You're a great mom and it shows. They know you love them."

Thea looks at MaryAnn with tears in her eyes. "Thank you."

"You haven't told me anything about Chris, or should I just mind my own business?"

"We had such a good time together. I was drawn to him, just as I was drawn to you because he's calm and yet he was able to make decisions. There was none of that awkward standing around trying to make up our minds where to go; he just told me he knew just what I needed and took me to this delightful restaurant. He didn't ask me personal questions and I was able to forget about being a mother just for a little while. He gave me a hug at the end of the evening and that's all it was, just a hug between two friends and I can't believe he'll be here tomorrow. Have I done the right thing?"

"Judging by the expression on your face, I would say so."

"My mom and dad really like Chris, and I even sensed a little bit of matchmaking going on there. They couldn't say enough good things about him."

"You'll know what to do without being influenced by anyone else."

"I'll know as soon as he meets the kids that's for sure and I'm just going to tell them he's a friend, just as you are, and let it run its course. I'm certainly throwing him in at the deep end, aren't I?"

MaryAnn laughs. "You sure are. That would test anyone's character, and on that note I need to go home."

"Home or Jim's?"

"Home, if you can call it that; too much temptation at Jim's."

They both stand up. "Thanks for babysitting."

"I wouldn't call it exactly that. We just enjoy being together."

CHAPTER THIRTY-FIVE

VISITORS

"Ah, smell that air," Theodore said, breathing in deeply, standing in the parking lot of the Harbor Inn. "Salty and invigorating—just what the doctor ordered." The sky above, cloudless, blue and empty except for the occasional gull wheeling lazily, a faint mist forming on the rust-colored salt flats. "Shush, stop your chattering, don't you hear the sea?"

Dorothy, Enid and Henry put down their bags and moved close to Theodore. "Isn't it wonderful?" he said. Enid and Henry nodded in agreement, happy in the knowledge this landscape would soon be their home.

The Harbor Inn, weather-beaten but welcoming, lured them to its front step where they peered at the notice pinned to the red front door. "Ring both bells for the innkeeper," and Henry did just that. They waited, their bags at their feet, eager now to get into the warmth, the afternoon drawing in, the air damp. Dorothy could feel the tendrils of hair that had escaped her bun curling uncontrollably; Enid, fearing for her perm, dabbed at the dewdrop on the end of her nose. Sally Connolly opened the door, face wreathed in smiles. Short blonde hair, bright blue eyes, softness and kindness emanating from her slender apron-wrapped figure, she beckoned them inside. "Welcome," she said. "Let me help you with your bags."

"Thank you," Henry said, stepping through the front door, the others following close behind, into a quaint and old-fashioned room, redolent with the lingering smell of baking. Floor to ceiling bookshelves lined one wall, the titles tempting a cozy seat in a corner, an escape on a rainy day.

"Would you please fill these out for me," Sally said, handing them each a large card where they would write their names and addresses, the registration and make of the vehicle, how they would pay, and the length of their stay. "What's the date today?" Theodore asked, sinking, knees cracking, onto the sofa. "I can never remember anymore."

"It's the twenty-second," Dorothy said, smoothing back her dark hair and smiling kindly at Theodore. Brown eyes set wide apart, outer corners wrinkled with laugh lines, belied an expression of innocence. Her sixty-five years had been kind to her, swimming keeping her fit; her legs her finest feature, never ashamed to be seen in a swimsuit. Life was an adventure, to be lived to the fullest, and she was the perfect companion for Theodore— someone to gently prod him out of his lethargy.

Henry was meticulously filling out his card, his neat handwriting following the lines. Enid stood in her usual stance, her pocketbook held in front of her clutched in nervous anticipation of what was going to happen next. A fish out of water gasping for air in unfamiliar surroundings, she made every attempt to not let Henry down. "Help yourself to brownies," she heard Sally say. "They're freshly baked," but she was frozen to the spot and telepathically willed Henry to hurry up, her brow furrowed. The ticking of an unseen clock only served to increase her agitation and she jumped when the doorbell rang.

"My, this is quite a party," Sally said, opening the door to reveal Chris, duffel bag slung over one shoulder. There were greetings all around. "Good to see you, son," Henry said, shaking his hand. Enid took a big breath and smiled a greeting. "How are you Mrs. Marchant?" "Good, good," she said, letting go of her pocketbook long enough to shake Chris's hand.

Sally, wisely giving the older folks the two rooms on the ground floor, handed them each two keys. "This one's for the front door," she said, dangling one of the keys from her fingers. "Breakfast is at eight o'clock. Is there anything you need?"

"We're all set, but thank you. We'll be off to my daughter's soon. We might be a little late because we're going to see *The Nutcracker* tonight. My granddaughter is playing Clara," Henry said, his stance important with pride.

"How wonderful. What a treat that will be."

There was a parting of the ways, with an agreement to regroup at five o'clock. Chris and Dorothy made their way up the steep flight of stairs, stepping sideways on the narrow treads. Chris's room was small but adequate with a full-size bed, shutters over the windows, a dresser with a mirror, braided rugs on the bare wooden floor, and a tiny en suite bathroom with a shower. The baseboard heating registers clicked and dinged when he turned up the thermostat—the Spartan temperature a little too cold even for him. He stood and looked out of the side window over the top of the salt marsh, the spindly grasses stretching up through the mist like the skinny fingers of a drowning man, to the ocean beyond. There would be time to walk on the beach tomorrow, to run and stretch his legs, something he longed to do after being cooped up in Jasmine for hours. He pulled his cell phone out of his pocket, looked at the bars, reception better than he had expected, and rang Thea's number; a little shiver of excitement coursed through his veins. "Hello," he heard her say.

"I just wanted to let you know we're all here at the Harbor Inn safe and sound."

He could sense her relief, heard music playing in the background, children chattering. "That's good. What time will you be here?"

There was no "I can't wait to see you" on either of their parts, but he could hear the eagerness and the lightness in her voice and she could probably sense the same in his. He just said, "About five fifteenish. Does that work?"

"Perfect."

"Do you need me to pick up anything for you on the way?"

"I'm all set, but thank you. See you in a little while. Bye."

And she was gone. His heart dimmed with the connection lost, and the room seemed empty and sparse. He had loved Meggy but never like this.

⁂

Thea talked to the children about the visitors who would soon be arriving for supper and she casually mentioned Chris. Told them he was coming to help out with the older folks, unsure they were buying it. Peter gave her a funny look, an "Oh, yeah, and who are you kidding?" expression coloring his bright blue eyes. He was going to keep a close eye on this one because there was no way he was going to allow his mother to get herself into a mess with another man. He'd threaten to run away from home if he had to, taking Honey with him. That should stop her in her tracks.

Izzie sat in the kitchen eating a light supper, picking absent-mindedly at the food, far too absorbed in thought about the evening's performance to pay much attention to the impending visitors. In any case, she would only be with them for a short time because MaryAnn had saved the day for her mother by offering to come and pick her up. She liked MaryAnn and had absolutely no problem in going with her. In all honesty, it would be a relief to escape her mother's nervousness.

Tires crunched on the gravel driveway. Thea, temporarily blinded by the headlights, turned away from the kitchen window, walked through the hallway and opened the front door. "Please come in," she said. Enid, Henry, Dorothy and Theodore stepped into the warmth, the smell of the outdoors clinging to their clothes. Chris, the last one in, handed her a big box of chocolates, the gold wrapping opulent, glinting in the light. "Oh, my, these are the best. Thank you."

Chris recognized the dark-haired boy who had manned the cash register at Aladdin's Cave and they nodded to each other, shook hands. "Hello, Peter. Please call me Chris." Honey held out her paw to be gladly shaken, Peter's hand resting on her head in proprietary ownership. No words were necessary. Chris remembered what it was like to be that age, had been the victim of many a grownup patronizing remark, so he just smiled and gently held Honey's paw. Thea asked everyone if they would like something to drink and then collared Peter to go help her. When he returned, tray of drinks carried carefully, the liquid barely moving, a little girl followed close behind, dark curls awry, freckles dusting her snub nose. She eyed the people in the room and he stepped forward. "We haven't met."

Shoulders back, chin high, she said "I'm Jessica."

"It's very nice to meet you."

"You must be my mommy's friend, Chris. She told us about you."

He acknowledged her with a smile, amused by her bad grammar, but it wasn't his place to correct. He could tell she was summing him up, glancing up at him with her big blue eyes, ignoring him, wandering over to greet her grandparents and to say hi to Dorothy and Theodore.

Dinner was a simple, but lively meal. Chris met Izzie briefly as she was heading out the door with MaryAnn, her reddish-brown hair shining under the hall lamp. A shy smile and she was gone. "See you later," he said. He sat in Thea's dining room and observed; his offer of help declined.

Enid had followed Thea into the kitchen and they fell into an easy pattern of familiarity; the kitchen a place to ease out any awkwardness between them. She didn't voice her thoughts. Now was not the time to deal with her regrets. She set to work helping her daughter carry plates and dishes and they worked quickly and efficiently; Enid, even in her shyness, undaunted by feeding a crowd, shady images of the orphanage flashing through her mind. Of course there was no comparison: her daughter's house colorful and bright and the people at the table nothing like the children with their haunted faces, of which she had been one. Thea's children didn't know how lucky they were. Even if they didn't have a dad, they had a home. Peter came forward and said, "Here, Grandma, let me help you," and she gave him the stack of plates, returned to the kitchen, nearly bumping into Thea as she turned the corner, both of them bursting out with laughter.

Henry was having the time of his life. He was puffed up with pride because he and Enid, finally brave enough to toss their inhibitions aside, were actually in Thea's home—a just reward for leaving their comfort zone. "Having a good time, son?" he asked, turning his head to look at Chris, sitting on his left ladling his fork with a generous helping of lasagna. He'd tried not to sound too eager when Thea had told him Chris would be part of the group, but he genuinely liked the young man, and if for once in his life he had yenta-like tendencies, so be it. Henry was thawing, a little late perhaps, but being in the midst instead of on the outside looking in, made his old heart thump vigorously.

Thea sat at the end of the table in a kind of daydream waiting for her guests to finish. The fact her parents were actually sitting in her dining room was something she thought she'd never see. She was afraid to blink in case none of this was real. Chris's presence added to the fantasy and he fit right in with his easy nonchalance, drawing in the kids, talking to Peter about skiing and snowboarding; to Jessica about books; fielding Henry's questions with a gentle easiness; asking Dorothy about her family; bringing Theodore into the conversation, coaxing the old man out of his fatigue. He glanced at Thea at one point, smiled his lazy smile, and caught unawares her body lit up like a Christmas tree. "Please pass the plates down if you're finished," she said, in an attempt to hide the flush warming her cheeks, a sun from beneath the clouds—the hopes of just a friendship dashed like a shattered glass on a ceramic floor.

Nan, looking smugly plump, and Stanley, his wiry hair a little longer than the last time Thea had seen him, arrived to save the day. Again, there was a wave of introductions and instructions to leave the dishes, to have Jessica in bed by eight—at which Jessica pulled a face and said it wasn't fair—to help themselves to anything they wanted. In the end Nan said, "Shoo, otherwise you'll all be late."

Once outside, she told Dorothy just to follow them. "We will, but don't worry if you lose us because I have directions. I printed them out before we left." Thea, reassured, walked with Chris to Jasmine and he opened the door for her, making sure she was settled before shutting her in. She sank down into the warmth of her down coat thankful it came all the way past her knees. The darkness filled the car once they were away from the house, the dimly lit dashboard a feeble glow.

"Do you know, it's so nice to have someone else do the driving for a change."

"Even in Jasmine? I'm afraid she's a bit of a bone shaker."

"Yes, even in Jasmine."

"Thanks for dinner."

"I'm glad you came."

"Do you mean that?"

"Yes, I do. I enjoy your easy company."

"I'll take that as a compliment," he said, taking his eyes off the road for a split second so he could turn and smile at her.

"You should. It was meant as one. You need to make a left-hand turn at the next traffic light. Are the others still behind us?"

Chris glanced in the rearview mirror. "Yes, they are."

They sat at the light, the turn signal clicking like a metronome, breaking into the silence. Thea felt the electricity between her and Chris, thankful they had kept the conversation light. Surprised by the depth of her attraction, she needed time to reflect, to stay at arms' length, to remember she had children to consider. Done with regrets, moving forward she must be wise.

"The school's just down here on the right, where all those cars are going."

"Gotcha."

If anything, the performance of *The Nutcracker* was even better than the night before. This time they had front row seats in the balcony right in the center, and although they were a little further from the stage, Thea preferred them. Mr. Blunt produced opera glasses from his jacket pocket. "I like to look at the dancers' faces," he said. Enid's expression was one of delight and she settled down into her seat, quiet as a mouse as soon as the music started. Finding the picture of Izzie in the program, she folded back the page and looked no further. Thea was conscious of Chris sitting to her right. The warmth of his leg so close to her own distracted her, but she maintained her composure, forgot all about him once the curtain rose.

Chris, equally aware of Thea's closeness, longed to reach over and take her hand, but his wiser self held him back. Making a wrong move now would jeopardize his hopes for the future so he concentrated on the ballet, watching Izzie. She enchanted him, and he wasn't the only one. The rustling and the coughing stopped as soon as she took to the stage and danced with the Nutcracker—you could have heard a pin drop. Thea's tension, obvious by the way she leaned forward, hands clenched in her lap, visibly relaxed once Izzie's solo was over.

Intermission came, the clapping thunderous as the curtain sank slowly, its luxurious dark blue velvet folds resting gently on the stage. Theodore, Chris and Thea stayed in their seats and the others went off to get a drink. "Oh, Thea, I am so glad we came. Izzie is marvelous. The whole production is so well done. Thank you for inviting us. We're having such an adventure, Dorothy and I."

"It means a lot having you here," and she squeezed Mr. Blunt's hand. "Are you sure this isn't too much for you?"

"Not at all, not at all," he said, removing his spectacles and polishing them madly with his handkerchief. "Getting away from all the old sad memories and making some new happy ones is just what I needed. I'm tired, but it's the right kind of tired, so don't you worry about me, my dear."

The lights flickered and people returned to their seats, shuffling down the rows, getting settled. Dorothy passed a couple of bottles of water down; Thea handed one to Chris and she hoped she wouldn't drop hers this time. Applause broke out for the conductor, young and a little disheveled in his ill-fitting suit, blonde hair falling over his forehead, but while his appearance might lack finesse, his expertise at making the orchestra come alive was passionate and accomplished. The curtain rose and Thea sat back in her seat and relaxed. As always, the music tugged at her emotions and she never tired of watching the dancers. She wondered whether Chris felt the same way. Ballet wasn't a guy thing as a general rule, many a disparaging remark being cast about men in tights. It wasn't something they'd discussed.

Again, there was a standing ovation. Even Mr. Blunt managed to struggle to his feet. "Oh, well done, well done," Thea heard him say. His enthusiastic clapping, especially when Izzie stepped forward to take her bow, caused perspiration on his brow and eventually when the curtain finally went down, he mopped his face with his handkerchief. There were too many of them to go backstage, so they stood to one side out of the way waiting for the crowd to subside and Dorothy slipped out to their car to retrieve a bouquet of flowers just as Bill had done the night before. "If you wait here, I'll just go find out how much longer she is going to be," Thea said and Chris watched her retreating figure, the scent of roses lingering in the stale air. They chatted amongst themselves, trying to decide what they should do tomorrow, and with Christmas on their minds, concluded a little last minute shopping would be a great idea. "It's about sixty miles to Portsmouth. That's a great place to shop and then there are the outlets at Kittery. Or we could go to Portland, that's closer. Don't look so horrified, Theodore, we can always find a dusty old book shop for you to sit in!" Dorothy said.

"That's settled, then," Henry said. "What an adventure this is turning out to be, right, Enid?"

"It all seems like a dream."

"What about you, Chris? You probably don't want to spend the day with us old fuddy-duddies."

"Speak for yourself, Henry," Dorothy said, winking at the group.

"Now that's certainly put me in my place."

Chris, highly amused by their assumptions, was saved by the appearance of Thea with Izzie in tow, her face greasy from the makeup, shadows beneath her eyes, but she perked up when she saw them. "Thank you all so much for coming."

Dorothy held out the flowers. "These are from all of us."

"This is so kind of you," she said, looking into their faces one by one.

"You deserve more than this for your splendid performance," Theodore said. "You took us all by surprise."

"I surprise myself sometimes. It's like I'm two different people because I just seem to be able to become another person."

"As long as you come back to us and stay as Izzie," Enid said, her soft voice no more than a whisper.

Izzie stepped forward and gave her grandma a hug. "I'm so happy you're coming to live close to us, and you too, Grandpa."

Henry, his eyes moist, patted her on the shoulder. "I'm glad too."

"I hate to break this up," Thea said, "but I need to get this young lady home."

Coats were buttoned and zipped, gloves removed from pockets and they headed out into the cold where they said their goodbyes. "We'll call you in the morning," Dorothy called over her shoulder as she walked away, her breath frosty in the frigid air.

Once back at the house, Chris politely asked Thea whether she would just like him to head back to the inn. "I'm sure you're tired," he said.

"Not too tired for a little conversation and I'd like you to meet Nan and Stanley properly."

They both got out of the Jeep and he opened the rear door to reveal a sleeping Izzie. "Would it be all right if I carried her? It seems such a shame to wake her up." After a fraction of hesitation, Thea said that would be great, but he was puzzled by her reaction and wondered whether he had overstepped his mark. Izzie, light in his arms, smelled of stage make-up and apples; her long dark lashes rested on her freckle-dusted cheeks and she was definitely gone, deep in that worry-less sleep of childhood. She didn't even stir when he gently laid her down on the bed. Nan and Stanley hovered in the doorway, luring Chris away to the kitchen with the promise of a hot drink.

Stanley folded his long, lean body onto one of the chairs and put his arm around Nan's now expanding waist. "How was the show?" she asked. "We're going tomorrow."

"You are in for a real treat," Chris said. "Izzie's performance was magical. My mom used to drag me and my sister off to *The Nutcracker* at the Boston Opera House every Christmas, and even though this production was much simpler, I still enjoyed it just as much. My dad wouldn't come. Told my mother she'd turn me into a nancy boy. I'm sorry; I'm talking too much. It's been a rather long day."

"That's okay. You've outdone Stanley for once. He could talk the hind leg off a donkey," Nan said, punching her husband to-be playfully on the shoulder. "What would you like to drink?"

Chris pulled out a chair, sat down opposite Stanley and said coffee would be great. He and Stanley immediately started up a conversation, filling each other in on their respective occupations. "Your job sounds a lot more interesting than mine, Stanley. I'm really ready for a change."

"Uh-oh," Nan said. "Don't let my mother hear you say that. She and Dad are always looking for someone to manage the Country Store. You've no idea how many people they've tried to recruit over the years. I'm an only child, you see, and too restless to stay in small-town Maine, much to their disappointment. Stanley and I are worried they will start grooming our grandchild as soon as he or she pops out of the womb!"

Stanley wanted to know how Chris and Thea had met, and looked at him in surprise when he just said it was a brief encounter at Aladdin's Cave. "You're not from around here, then?" Stanley asked.

"No, I work and live in Great Barrington and my parents live in Lennox."

Nan poured three mugs of coffee, placed a jug of cream on the table and magically produced a wooden board of cheese and crackers and a brownie-filled plate. "Please help yourself."

Thea found all three of them sitting around the table, deep in conversation. She poured herself a cup of coffee, went and joined them. "I see you've made yourselves at home," she said, sparking fresh laughter. Four compatible people enjoying each other's company was more intoxicating to Thea than a glass of champagne. The bantering and the teasing went back and forth. Chris's story-telling matched Stanley's, their take on life a never-ending rich adventure; Thea and Nan bobbed along in the tide of their words, quite content to listen. Nan thought Chris was a keeper, but wondered whether Thea was ready.

The clock in the hall struck twelve, reminding the four of them it was time for sleep. Nan and Stanley shook Chris's hand and told him how much they had enjoyed meeting him. "Likewise," he said. Thea thanked them for staying with the kids. "See you tomorrow," she said and Nan winked at her before she and Stanley stepped out onto the porch. Thea said, "Goodnight," and closed the front door on the slice of cold air threatening to turn the hallway into a block of ice. Chris had come up behind her and said, "I should be going too." She summoned her willpower and resisted the urge to touch him.

"Stay just a minute. I'm so sleep deprived at this point, a little while longer won't make any difference."

"Only a minute and I'm not going to sit down again because we'll end up talking all night. I think we've gone a little bit beyond asking each other what makes us happy," and thrusting his hands into his pockets, he looked down at his feet before glancing up and staring her full in the face. "I think I'd better leave now."

"It would be best, but I don't really want you to go."

"Come here." She moved towards him and he wrapped her in his arms. She rested her head against his chest and curled her arms around his waist, eventually stepping back out of his embrace and looking up at him.

"Can we just do hugs until we're really sure? I'm afraid of passion; it's too intense, and it doesn't last. It confuses and burns me. Love, on the other hand, is sustaining—it gently reaches into all the dark corners of our souls and heals. Am I making sense?"

"Thea, I've been burned too. I'm not looking for a wham, bam, thank you ma'am kind of relationship. In fact, I wasn't looking for a relationship at all until I met you, but you intrigued me so I had to try and find you. I'd be perfectly content with hugs, just as long as I can hold you when we're on our own, give you a hug before we go our separate ways, that's all I ask. I need to feel connected to you."

"It's uncanny you should say that because that's how relationships work for me. There has to be a connection and that's how I sum people up. I never had that with my parents, but I'm building bridges now and it's working."

"I never had it with my dad and I never will, but I am completely in tune with my mom and my sister. We don't always see eye to eye, but our respect for each other and the connection is always there."

"I have that connection with my kids, although it's getting harder and harder with Peter. Hopefully, you can give me some insight into what it was like to be an eleven-year-old boy. I'm fumbling in the dark despite all the books I've read. Now, I really am going to send you off to the inn. You will come for supper tomorrow?"

"I'd love to, but only if you let me bring something."

"A couple of Margaret's loaves from the Country Store would be great. I have beef stew in the freezer. Now, I really must send you on your way. Let's say five thirty. We should be back from the matinee by then."

Chris shrugged into his jacket, gave Thea one final hug. "This one will have to last until tomorrow," he said. "Then I'll be back for another fix."

"Thanks for the chocolates," she said. He touched her cheek with the tips of his fingers and then he was gone.

Thea hummed while she got ready for bed. Neither she nor Chris had discussed the practicalities of their budding friendship, but it would take care of itself. In the meantime, she would enjoy him while he was here, not worry about the future. His mom was obviously important to him, and even though she was unable to observe their interaction, instinctively she knew he treated her well. She had read somewhere to always choose a man who was good to his mother—advice she planned to pass on to her daughters when the time was right. She definitely owed Mrs. Morrison a debt of gratitude and she looked forward to meeting her someday, Mr. Morrison not so much. And with that final thought, she snuggled beneath the covers and fell asleep.

CHAPTER THIRTY-SIX

CHRIS

Chris's internal alarm always went off at seven o'clock, regardless of how much sleep he'd had the night before and Friday morning was no exception. He lay on his back watching the early morning light sneaking its way into the room where the shutters didn't quite meet the window. When he closed his eyes, he could easily visualize Thea's lovely face, her expression from the night before—one minute joyful, the next perplexed and fearful—her pretty brow furrowed in concentration, trying to find the right words. But daydreaming wouldn't make her magically appear.

The shower turned out to be somewhat of a challenge; he had to fight off the plastic curtain which billowed inwards, but at least the water was hot, the towels fluffy. Relieved not to have to wear a shirt and tie, he went down to breakfast in his favorite navy sweater and jeans, his feet snug in his well-worn winter hiking boots. His deep auburn hair had a curly mind of its own, neatly shaping itself to his head as long as he kept it short. Clean-shaven now, he often thought about growing a beard, but had never managed to get past two days of stubble; he wondered what Thea's take would be. Unable to get her out of his mind, his thoughts went in circles, endlessly curious as to what her opinions might be about books, politics, religion, music; he was impatient to find out.

Breakfast turned out to be a lively meal. Sitting at a large pine table in the rear of the dining room, Sally plied them with coffee, or tea in quaint earthenware pots, cranberry or orange juice, slices of sweet honeydew melon, light and fluffy sourdough blueberry pancakes, crisply grilled sausages and real maple syrup. They discussed their plans for the day and both Enid and Henry agreed it would be a good idea to stay out of Thea's hair. Chris declined to accompany them on their shopping trip to Portsmouth, said he was going to do some exploring locally. They all talked about *The Nutcracker*, how they were now in the Christmas spirit, couldn't wait to part with their well-earned dollars and come back to the inn laden with gifts. Chris didn't say much, just sat back and listened to the older folk. From where he was sitting, he could see partially into the adjoining kitchen. The charming dining room, obviously an addition, boasted huge windows overlooking a wintery garden—the lawn white frosted, the bushes and trees bare of leaves silhouetted against the harsh blue sky. Plants hung from the ceiling in front of the windows, brilliantly green in contrast, the asparagus fern trailing its delicate foliage, brushing Chris's head as he made his way out of the room.

Sally showed them maps of the local area and Chris grabbed one to take up to his room, but not before telling her how much he had enjoyed his breakfast. Her smiling face was his just reward and Enid and Henry, Theodore and Dorothy were as equally enthusiastic in praise of her delicious food, especially the pancakes. "Never tasted anything like them," Henry said, patting his stomach. "We'll be all set for hours." After agreeing to rendezvous at Thea's at five thirty, they went their separate ways.

Chris, anxious to find his way down to the beach, followed Sally's directions, making a right out of the inn's driveway and walking along the road. There was little in the way of traffic, but he was still pleased to see the sidewalk once he came to the end of the salt marsh, where it turned into sand and then pebbles. He always pictured Maine as wild and rocky with pine trees close to the water, but this beach was devoid of rocks until you got closer to the ocean. He made his way over the pebbles to the grainy sand below, firm beneath his feet, much easier to walk on, his boots making shallow water-filled dents. The air was spray-laden and cold where the rhythm of the waves alternately rushed in to hit the rocks, only to be sucked back into the shallows. A cormorant stretched high, its sleek dark body poised to dive, waited at the end of a rocky promontory; a few black-headed gulls sat silently, their backs to the wind, and herring gulls with their bright yellow beaks flew lazily above Chris's head. He knew better than to feed them, predatory and bold by nature, you were asking for trouble. He decided to avoid the rocks, slick and covered with seaweed, and walked briskly along the beach until he was forced to turn back by the incoming tide and a water-filled estuary too deep to cross. But he had expanded his lungs with sea air, ironed out the kinks from yesterday's inactivity and now he was anxious to satisfy his curiosity about the Country Store. Even if things didn't work out with Thea, he still longed for a fresh start. The thought of assisting in the running of a country store, not exactly on his career path, had its appeal. He had no doubt he'd be able to pick up a computer programming job somewhere in the area to augment his income, besides which he could turn his hand to almost anything. Being practical by nature, unable to completely ignore the ever present and niggling problem of medical insurance, he reluctantly admitted there were advantages to having a steady job.

Melford Point intrigued Chris, and after parking Jasmine, he decided to walk the length and the breadth of Main Street to see what the town had to offer. Observant and curious, he decided the only thing missing was a supermarket. Other than that, one could exist quite nicely on Italian food, fresh fish, and all that the Country Store had to offer. The bookshop would feed one's brain with literature and sharpen it with caffeine; then there was a dance studio for those so inclined and a real estate agent to help in the search of a place to live. He chuckled at some of the names: "It's a Fishy Business" for one, and "Harry's Hardware" another. He had no doubt that the proprietors, hidden behind their shiny windows full of tantalizing merchandise, were a bunch of interesting characters and he couldn't wait to meet them. He walked as far as the park, the pond set up for skating with a sign saying the ice was thick and safe. A makeshift wooden shelter with benches on either side offered a place to lace skates and get out of the wind. Chris wondered whether Thea's kids skated and realized how much fun it would be to go skating with them all. He would have brought his skates, hockey stick and puck if he'd known, but he wasn't in the least bit discouraged because he sensed in his heart of hearts he would be back.

Retracing his steps past Mario's Italian Restaurant, One Woman's Treasure and The Scrapbook Nest, he suddenly noticed an "apartment for rent" sign down in the right hand corner of the window of the only empty store on Main Street. Pulling his phone out of his jacket pocket, he made a note of the number. Was this meant to be? With a considerably lighter step, he walked across the street and into the Country Store.

Bill looked up at the jangling of the bell, immediately recognizing Chris from Nan and Stanley's apt description. They had discussed the young man at length while eating breakfast and Bill wondered whether his ears had been burning. He would have been pleased to know they painted him with glowing colors and if he ever needed a character reference, Chris wouldn't have to look any further than Bill's daughter and his future son-in-law.

Chris took his time, lingering over the items which interested him most, taking note of the way the merchandise was tastefully displayed: the loose candies in huge glass jars; the tiny rubber toys to tempt little hands; a glass case with Swiss Army knives safely locked away; whimsical porcelain animals in another, on top of which sat an old-fashioned scale, the brass weights shining in the light. A notice invited customers to help themselves, a shiny metal scoop and paper bags sitting on the counter just for that purpose. He wandered to the back of the store checking out the dish towels; a wall of kitchen gadgets; a central display with wooden chopping boards, amongst which nestled jars of jams and jellies; relishes and mustards; local honey; boxes of gourmet crackers, and packages of fancy pancake mix. A rack of children's books sat in the back corner, together with soft afghans in muted shades of beige, pale green and blue slung over wooden rods. Greeting cards occupied one small section. Lured by the beautiful artwork on one of the cards—a bright pot of gerbera daisies in vivid reds and yellows—he picked it up just out of curiosity. He nearly dropped it when he saw Thea's signature. He ran his finger along the rack and found a few more bearing her name, from soft misty Maine landscapes to whimsical creatures with big soft eyes. He dragged himself away, even more intrigued by a woman he still knew so little about.

Eventually, Chris turned towards the deli counter, leaving behind the smell of the soaps and candles, the fresh scent of the dishtowels. Lured by the tantalizing aroma of fresh baking and pungent coffee, he realized he was hungry. There was one vacant stool at the counter and he squeezed himself in between a smartly dressed woman and an old weathered man, his chin sprinkled with sparse gray stubble, his hair tied back in a ponytail with a green rubber band. He turned to look at Chris with faded cataract-clouded blue eyes and said, "Ayeh," before returning all his attention back to his soup. Bill looked over the top of the counter. "Don't mind Harry. He doesn't get out much, being stuck in that hardware store all day makes him testy." Harry just grunted.

"I believe you must be Chris Morrison. Am I right?"

Chris looked at Bill in surprise. "How did you know?"

"Well, for one thing you stick out like a sore thumb. We don't see many outsiders at this time of the year and Nan and Stanley described you to a tee."

"Of course."

Margaret waited behind the counter observing Chris and liking what she saw. As far as she could tell, he seemed relaxed and friendly, not at all put out by Harry's cold shoulder. Marjorie Franks, sitting to the right of him, had introduced herself and he soon became involved in a discussion about the real estate business. As soon as there was a break in the conversation, Margaret asked Chris what he would like to eat, and unable to resist the clam chowder, he ordered a bowl and half a turkey sandwich on multi-grain bread.

Marjorie excused herself and Harry also got up to leave after mopping up the remainder of his soup with a large piece of bread that he masticated to death with his few remaining teeth. The three men sitting at the end of the row talked amongst themselves in sparse sentences about the weather and their next poker game. "You're not winning this time, Andy," and how their businesses were going. They nodded to Chris, but made no attempt to introduce themselves; unperturbed, he was perfectly content to sit and listen, taking it all in. He didn't expect to be welcomed with open arms—the reputation of Maine folk preceded them with their reluctance to welcome strangers. If he stayed, it would be up to him to eventually find a way to get to know them.

Chris finished his lunch, asked Margaret if she would please be kind enough to save a couple of loaves of bread for him, telling her he would be back a little later after he had been to the bookstore. They all said how much they had enjoyed meeting each other and Chris told Margaret the lunch was delicious. "There's too much good food in Maine. I shall get fat," he said.

"Aye, I'm sure you will if you eat Sally's breakfasts and Margaret's lunches. Best grub around," Bill said, rubbing his ample belly. "See what it's done to me?"

"You look well on it, sir," Chris said, trying to be polite, shrugging into his jacket and turning to leave. "See you in a little while."

"We'll be here," Margaret said.

He didn't understand why, but leaving was difficult. It seemed with each remark Margaret and Bill wanted him to stay, even though the conversation had been stilted and desultory. It made no sense unless they had an ulterior motive, summing him up as a future employee just as Nan had suggested. He had no idea what Nan and Stanley had said about him and he sensed Bill and Margaret were at a loss as to what to say, fearing they may put their foot in it.

Once outside, he walked across Maine Street dodging the traffic. A Good Read was all he thought it would be, absolutely stuffed with books, both old and new—the spines with their intriguing titles leading him from shelf to shelf. A lady about his mother's age, her softly curling gray hair pulled up into a bun, half glasses perched on her tiny nose, sat behind a large mahogany desk, the surface covered with piles of books. She looked up and smiled a welcome, saying to please ask if there was anything he was specifically looking for. He said, "I will."

Chris was in heaven. He found an old leather-bound book of *A Christmas Carol* for Theodore, and even though the print was small, he thought it would appeal from a collector's point of view. Able to visualize the stack of antique books he remembered seeing in the old man's living room, he was pleased with his choice. For Enid, he picked the first of the *Mitford* series by Jan Karon, hoping she would enjoy reading about Father Timothy. For Henry a beautiful book about Maine, and for Dorothy, *Open House* by Elizabeth Berg—a favorite author of his mother's. Thea was posing a problem until he spied *A Feast of Flowers* by Jacquelin Heriteau, a beautiful hardcover book with exquisite illustrations, tucked into the gardening/household section. He was stumped when it came to the kids so played it safe by buying gift cards for each of them.

The smell of coffee was irresistible, and with time to kill while his books were gift wrapped, he ordered a small hazelnut, laced it with cream, sank into a cozy chair, and sat daydreaming. Even though he had spent time with Thea, albeit brief, he still didn't know much about her; they both seemed to be extremely adept at keeping conversation away from the personal. He was awoken from his reverie by Beverly Forest telling him his packages were all wrapped. "I've stacked them in the same order as the list on the receipt so you will know which is which, and I've put the gift cards in little boxes. Would you like some gift tags? I have some pretty Christmas ones here," she said, pushing a box full of tiny cards towards him. "Take your time." At twenty-five cents apiece, Chris couldn't resist, and placing his coffee cup on the desk, he chose several and Beverly added them to the bag.

"Thank you," he said, pulling out his wallet and giving her his credit card. "You've certainly made my shopping experience nice and easy."

"We aim to please, and I hope you'll come and see us again. You're not from around here, are you?"

"No, I'm just visiting."

"Enjoy your stay and Merry Christmas."

"And Merry Christmas to you too."

Chris was a contented man, exceedingly pleased with his purchases—the personal warmth of the bookstore so much more pleasurable than tramping around a mall. A nurturer and a giver, he liked nothing better than to buy gifts or do things for other people. He was having a good time, life finally giving him direction and meaning after his period of loneliness following the breakup with Meggie.

The bell on the door jangled as he entered the Country Store; the simple old-fashioned sound pleased him, his mouth twitched at the corners and he suppressed a Cheshire-cat grin. Margaret and Bill welcomed him and didn't seem to notice anything out of the ordinary. Margaret handed over the loaves of bread safely tucked inside their brown paper bags, fragrant and still slightly warm. "These smell heavenly," he said, juggling the bread and the bag of books as he attempted to retrieve his wallet.

Margaret watched in amusement. "Why don't you put the bread down on the counter."

"Good idea. Melford Point has cast a spell over me. I'm not sure which way's up anymore."

Margaret was of the opinion Thea had been the one to cast the spell, but she kept her thoughts to herself. She liked this young man and Thea deserved some good luck. She just hoped he was man enough to be able to handle her because he certainly had no idea what he was letting himself in for.

CHAPTER THIRTY-SEVEN

CHRISTMAS EVE

MaryAnn, standing at the kitchen sink absent-mindedly washing the breakfast dishes, stared out of the window at the potholed driveway and the bare arms of the stark winter trees swaying in the wind. In only two more days her view would change forever and the excitement bemused her, made staying on task virtually impossible. Washing and rinsing the last dish, she set it in the drainer and wiped her hands. Without realizing it at first, she had allowed her life to be taken over, given in to the friendly hands who wanted to pull her along, not necessarily to make decisions for her, just suggestions and offers of help in planning the wedding. She loved it.

The boys were running around the house, possessed by the devil of their own excitement. She put her head out of the kitchen door when she heard them thundering down the stairs. "Whoa," she said. They stopped mid-way, panting, their cheeks flushed from exertion, Johnny's hair flying, shaking their heads when she suggested the yard might be a better place to get rid of their excess energy. "We'll be good," Ian said, turning around, going off to his room, Johnny following close behind.

She stood, watched their retreating figures and called out to them, "We'll be going out soon so why don't you go get dressed."

"We will," Johnny said, looking back over his shoulder, blowing her a kiss, before disappearing from sight.

She did a mental checklist: Jennifer was in charge of the food, flowers and the cake; the wedding bands, purchased from Gems Fine Jewelry in Melford Point, were now with Ben for safekeeping as best man; the Reverend Matthews was on board with the wedding service; her dress was hanging in a closet at Jim's house, and Thea had agreed to help her put up her hair with the pretty rhinestone clips she had found at One Woman's Treasure. This morning was a trip to the beauty salon for a manicure and a pedicure, something that had not even occurred to her. Both Jennifer and Thea were horrified. "It's tradition," they both said. She had given in without too much of a fight and now she was looking forward to a little pampering.

Jim, home for lunch, walked with Carrie in the yard, hunched over deep in thought about MaryAnn and how much he loved her, his coat pulled up around his neck, his gloved hands clasped behind him. He longed for her to be with him every day and hated the separation when she and the boys went home. He did have to admit she had been right about not moving in, but he didn't have to like it, did he? And he still didn't, but his relationship with Ian would never have made it this far without the distance between them, without a bolt-hole for the boy back to the familiar. Thank goodness he had heeded MaryAnn's warning to let Ian come to him, and slowly, brick by brick, they were building a relationship. He turned, Carrie close behind, and retraced his steps alongside the edge of his property, a tall hedge of hemlock trees trimmed flat as a mortarboard marking the border. He straightened up and stood looking at the house—candles at the windows, festively decorated for the first time since his mother died—it seemed alive to him, the empty rooms begging to be filled. Overcome with excitement over Christmas and the upcoming wedding, he danced a jig down the path. He was a little crazy, but so what? Right now he was going to make the most of every minute and he went back to work with a song in his heart and a silly grin on his face.

The Chamberlin household was in chaos. Thea had no idea what to do with her parents, Dorothy and Mr. Blunt. It was awkward with the four of them being together and only having one car. She wondered how her mother was doing; unused to going out in the world, even a trip to Maine must seem huge to her. And then there was Chris. Peter, Honey and Jessica were getting under her feet and she shooed them all out of the kitchen. Izzie, still tired from her three outstanding *Nutcracker* performances, was upstairs wrapping her gifts, the only person off Thea's radar screen. This was the most disorganized Christmas ever, and up until this point, she hadn't given it much thought because she had been totally immersed in getting Izzie to and from her performances and staying to watch them. The simple meal last night had gone well and her mother had seemed all right then so she decided to stop worrying and let the day take care of itself. She took three meat pies out of the freezer and asked Jessica whether she would like to make gingerbread men from the dough they had made yesterday. Chris showed up out of the blue and he and Peter went off to the park with Honey to check out the ice skating, saying they would bring lunch from the Country Store. Dorothy and Mr. Blunt dropped off Enid and Henry, refused Thea's offer to stay and drove away. Enid was delighted with the whole gingerbread men creation and Henry went off to the living room for some quiet time with the newspaper and the crossword. Izzie appeared from her wrapping and joined in with Jessica and Enid, freeing Thea to make an apple pie for tomorrow's meal. She went over to her mom and put her arm around her shoulder. "It's so good to have you and dad here."

The Country Store was buzzing with activity. Margaret had last-minute gift baskets to put together and when Peter and Chris arrived, she didn't hesitate to put them to work. "What about Honey?" Peter asked.

"I promised to take lunch to your mom so if it's all right with you, Peter, I could run Honey home and then come back."

Peter hesitated, not sure he wanted to let Honey out of his sight; after all she was his responsibility. He took a deep breath, decided Chris could be trusted and said, "Sure."

Chris, picking up on Peter's reluctance, said, "I'll take good care of her, I promise."

Peter nodded.

Margaret, biding her time, watching the interaction, waiting for the right time to speak, said, "Why don't I give you a couple of large containers of soup and some bread rolls? How does that sound?"

"Absolutely perfect."

After Chris and Honey had left, Margaret told Peter how good it was to see him. "I'm sorry we haven't been around much," he said. "I've missed coming to the store."

"We've missed you too, but we realize how little time you have once school starts."

"Yeah, I know. Then there was soccer and now basketball. And of course we weren't here for turkey day and now I have Honey and she takes up a lot of time."

"Don't worry. Things change and we do understand, we really do. And whatever happens, we will always love you."

"I love you too. Where are Nan and Stanley?"

"Off shopping and the high school kids couldn't work today, so you and Chris are sent from heaven, but chatting won't get these baskets made up. Here's the list of what needs to go into each one. Okay?" Margaret, in her wisdom, didn't say anything about Chris. She decided he must have made a favorable impression because there was no way Peter would have let anyone he didn't trust take Honey. There were times to comment and times to stay silent and this was one of those situations where it was best just to observe. Thea's instinct to trust was shaky, made worse by Jessica's abduction, so she too must be comfortable with Chris in order to allow him to spend time with one of her children alone. Margaret's prime concern was for Peter, but she suspected he had the ability to remain detached until it was safe to let his guard down. Once Chris returned, she briefly observed the teamwork between the young man and the boy before returning to her baking. Chris was quite happily taking instruction from Peter and made no attempt to take over. This pleased Margaret no end so she gave a discreet thumbs up to Bill and went back to her tasks with a song in her heart.

Nan was tired and she and Stanley lingered in A Good Read. She sank down into one of Beverly Forest's comfortable chairs with a fragrant cup of pomegranate-flavored tea thoughtfully provided by Stanley. He was happily talking to Beverly whom Nan had known all her life, telling her about the upcoming wedding and how they were going to be parents. "I'm afraid we kinda shut the door after the horse had gone," he said, scratching his head and turning and winking at Nan. He was incorrigible and she never knew what he was going to say next, but she loved him for his honesty and his lack of airs and graces. He enjoyed life to the fullest, always seeing the funny side, drawing people in, always wanting more. He had the uncanny knack of being able to diffuse awkward situations, and even though he did sometimes talk that little bit too much, conversely he did have the ability to listen.

Nan sat and sipped her tea, resting her other hand on her growing bump, her happiness indescribable when she felt the baby flutter. Her job, for once in her life, was taking a backseat and she would take as much time as she needed after the baby was born. Of course, she wished her mom and dad were closer and she had no illusions it was going to be easy, but they had so little time with the running of the store—a grandchild would just be an added burden. Not that they would think that way and "burden" was a poor choice of word.

Nan was worried because Stanley, unable to take any more time off work, had to leave the day after Christmas and she dreaded a winter storm that would prevent him getting back for the wedding on New Year's Eve. "Aha. You're afraid I'm going to run away and not make an honest woman of you."

"Oh, Stanley, that's not it, but you know how unpredictable the weather can be."

"I'll make it back, my lovely, I promise. Mother Nature wouldn't dare mess up the most important day in 2005."

"I only hope you're right," she had said, full of misgivings.

Margaret had persuaded friends and family to attend the six o'clock carol service. Peter and Chris had finished the gift baskets in the nick of time and folk dropped by to pick them up. She sent them off home at four o'clock, locking the door behind them and turning the sign around to say *Closed*. Switching off lights as she walked through the store on aching feet, she removed her apron and wearily climbed the stairs to the apartment above. "Shopping successful?" she asked Nan and Stanley, who were sitting together on the couch.

"It was, but I'm tired," Nan said.

"Well, that makes two of us," Margaret said, sinking down into one of the armchairs and resting her feet on a tapestry-covered stool. The room was an odd shape, long and narrow, but she had made the best of it with a large pale-yellow sofa along one wall and two chairs placed kitty corner at either end—one in deep red and one in navy. Matching lamps with pale-yellow shades, bases striped to match the furniture, rested on dark honey mission-style tables either end of the sofa. A television sat in the corner by the window and the cream painted walls were covered with watercolors of Maine, collected over the years. The built-in shelves housed a library of books old and new, together with all the family photo albums. A pretty rug in a bright floral pattern complementing the colors of the furniture rested on the dark wood floor; the windows were shuttered, the shutters painted the same color as the walls—open during the day, but closed snugly at night. The whole effect was airy and light—a refuge for Margaret and Bill after a long and busy day in the store.

The church was only a brief walk through town, but both Bill and Stanley, worried about Nan, asked her if she needed a ride. "Oh, stop fussing, you two. I'm fine. The fresh air will do me good."

"We'd better get going, then. You know how quickly the pews fill up and I want to make sure you and your mom get a seat," Bill said, helping Nan up from the couch.

Main Street came alive on Christmas Eve. The retail stores stayed open later in the hope of making some last minute sales. The street lamps, fairy lights wrapped around their pillars, created a magical world, transforming the dowdy daylight faces of the buildings into places of invitation. The beauty of the church always took Margaret's breath away. She liked it best when she came alone for sanctuary when the pews were empty and she could kneel in silent prayer. Now, jostled on the steps by her fellow townsfolk all making their way inside, some regular churchgoers and some Margaret named "the ones with a guilty conscience," she smiled her greeting. Never forgetting a face, she recognized some from their trips to the store, but she didn't know all their names. But it didn't matter. It was Christmas and they had all come to praise the Lord; this made her happy. She paused to look at the nativity scene in the church entranceway, but Bill moved her along.

Margaret's eyes wandered taking it all in, deriving comfort from the familiar: the green-wreathed candlelit decorations at the end of the pews lighting up the high ceiling and casting shadows in the gothic spines; the stained glass windows, the color less intense in their evening glow, depicting angels and saints; the altar resplendent in its wrapping of gold laced cloth; the poinsettias placed up and down the steps on either side magnificent in their festive foliage; Jesus on the cross high on the distant wall; the carved wooden pulpit, its dark wood reflected in the candlelight, and on the right-hand side, the board for the hymn numbers empty because there would only be carols tonight. The choir, bright in their scarlet robes, stood on the left; the organ behind them, the deep gold pipes reaching up in majesty towards the ceiling. Margaret removed her gloves, placed them on the pew beside her, opened her program and read the *Notes to our Guests and Congregation*. Seeing MaryAnn, Jim, Ian and Johnny as she walked down the aisle was no surprise, but she had been surprised to see Thea. Never in a million years had she believed Thea would set foot inside the church. Margaret had tried, but after much persuading, eventually gave up. Once the service started, all her attention focused on the age-old readings, the beautiful music and the raising of the voices of the congregation in celebration of the birth. But there was one voice that rang out clear as a bell above all others and she wondered who it was. Even the singers in the choir could not match the sweetness, and Margaret's breath caught in her throat.

The Reverend Tim Matthews, towering over the congregation in his pulpit, welcomed them all, his robe-clad arms spread wide. His bald head, with its thin streak of dark hair combed over the top, shone in the light; his brown eyes twinkled behind his round-framed spectacles, his smile broadly welcoming. "This is my favorite time of the year," he said, placing his hands flat on the open Bible resting in front of him. "This isn't going to be a long sermon so you young whippersnappers can stop groaning because I know you would all rather be someplace else." The congregation tittered. "I just wanted to remind us all to say a special prayer for those less fortunate than ourselves and some of you may be in this very place tonight. If you are, please remember the church is always open and I am always available for counsel no matter the problem. Christmas is a joyous time for some and for others a miserable reminder of what they lack. At the risk of sounding like a broken record, the commercialism of the holiday has created pressures and hardship where there should be none. I believe the world has gone completely mad when I read stories of Black Friday shopping trips where physical fighting occurs over a bargain. Life isn't about things. Life is about love. Without love we wouldn't survive, so my Christmas message to you all is to love one another as Jesus truly loves you and remember to give because to give is to receive. Let us pray. *Our Father which art in heaven . . .*"

Thea couldn't believe how well Jessica had behaved herself. An hour and a half was a long time, even for an adult, but the child had been mesmerized. Even though she didn't know all the words of the carols, the melodies were familiar and she tunefully hummed along. Izzie ran her finger along the words and Jessica concentrated on trying to read. Izzie carried a tune well, her voice sweet and soft. Chris surprised her with his deep baritone. She and Peter, even though they both loved music, found it hard to stay on key; Dorothy, a contralto, helped their row along. Mr. Blunt, a little shaky, but obviously enjoying himself sang as well, as did her dad; her mom just mouthed the words. She silently thanked Margaret for giving her one more push, but she doubted she would have come if it hadn't been for her visitors. Chris had mentioned he always went to church with his mom and had asked whether there was a local service, so she could hardly let him go on his own. She always felt uneasy in a church and she just didn't know why. She envied those with a deep faith; thought it must be so comforting to believe in all the age-old rituals; to have a sense of community. She sat in awkward silence while one by one people left their pews to go take communion—Chris, Dorothy and Mr. Blunt included. Jessica wanted to know what all the people were doing, but Thea didn't know how to explain. "Why don't you ask Chris or Mr. Blunt when they come back to the house. They will be able to help you understand." Thea's only concession to Christianity was the baptism of her children, and Michael and his family had taken charge of that. The church the Chamberlin family attended was high Episcopalian with a great deal of incense waving. Thea, acutely uncomfortable, had no choice but to go along with it. The church was as cold as Michael's family except for Mimi, his grandmother, and Thea wanted no part of it. The fancy christening robe passed down from generation to generation sat nestled in its box, forgotten until now. She dragged her mind back to the final carol and stood up, program in hand, and sang *O Come All Ye Faithful* to the best of her ability.

Jim sidled back into the pew and squeezed MaryAnn's hand. They too stood to sing along with Johnny and Ian. Ian's voice was as flat as a pancake, but Johnny took after his mom, and even though like Jessica, he didn't know the words, he only had to hear the stanza once and he could hum it perfectly. Jim, bowled over by MaryAnn's voice, barely managed to croak out the words. He knew she could sing, but he wasn't prepared for the emotion. At the end of the service when everyone turned to wish each other a Merry Christmas, surrounded by neighbors, friends and strangers, each one of them complimented MaryAnn, including Ben, Jennifer, Poppy and Daisy. "You should join the church choir." "Where did you learn to sing like that?" "I could listen to you all night." "Well done." "You have such a gift." MaryAnn just said, "Merry Christmas and thank you."

They shook the Reverend's hand at the door. "I hear you can sing," he said to MaryAnn. "We'd love to have you in the choir."

"Thank you and I'll think about it."

He grabbed hold of Jim's hand, pumped it up and down. "See you both on the twenty-sixth."

Once outside, they all split up—all going their separate ways to take up their various Christmas Eve rituals.

⊙⧉⧉⊙

For Thea and all her visitors, it was home to cookies and eggnog, one gift each for the children, and an evening of questions from Jessica about Jesus, and communion, and why they had put money in a big silver plate. Packed into the living room like sardines with the children sitting on the floor with Honey, Jessica said, "Mr. Chris, will you answer my questions now, please?"

"I'll try. My mother always took my sister, Maddy, and me to church. She wanted us to experience lots of things so that when we were older we would be able to make up our own minds. Besides taking us to church, we went to ballets, theaters, museums, art galleries, and libraries. She took us to New York to the top of the Empire State Building; inside the Statue of Liberty; we rode the ferry to Staten Island; took a bus to Cony Island and ate their famous hotdogs. We rode the subway into Boston to baseball games at Fenway Park and hockey games at Boston Garden. We went to zoos and aquariums, helped out at soup kitchens, visited the elderly and the sick. She knew her history and what she didn't know we would find out together by poring over books. She told us we were lucky and never to take that luck for granted. She is a remarkable person and I hope you'll meet her someday. But, I'm sorry, Jessica, I didn't answer your question."

"It's okay. I like listening. Will you tell me now."

"Let's see. I'll try and make it as simple as possible. When we went to church this evening, we were celebrating the birth of Jesus. Do you know the story of how there was no room at the inn and how he was born in a stable?"

"Kinda, but tell it again."

"Well . . . this might take a while, so let me know if you want me to stop." And Chris began, "Long ago, about 2000 years when King Herod ruled Judea, which is now part of Israel . . ." and the only interruption came from Jessica when she heard Chris say, "Joseph was worried when

289

he heard Mary was expecting a baby before their marriage had taken place . . ."

"Just like Nan," she said.

"Let's hope she has her baby somewhere comfortable unlike poor Mary who had Jesus in a stable and had to lay him in a manger."

Thea, surprised by Jessica's comment, sat and listened while Chris, Theodore, and occasionally Dorothy, answered her children's questions. It made her realize the narrowness and inadequacy of her own life. Was it too late to give her children a thirst for knowledge? Looking at their eager faces, she didn't think so, their questions tumbling over themselves in an earnest quest to be heard. Chris told the age-old story well. "There's a lot of mystery in religion and many things that can't really be explained, but the rituals—and each and every religion has its own—are comforting and give people a sense of community. This is one of the reasons for communion, but it is also an opportunity for people to have a lifelong friendship with Jesus."

"But how can people do that? He's dead isn't he? And what's a ritual?" Jessica asked.

"A ritual is something that gets repeated at set times of the year. I'm sure your family has rituals or traditions on special holidays. Can you think of one?"

Jessica, cross-legged, resting her elbows on her knees, her chin in her hands, said, "I know. Mommy always lets us open one present on Christmas Eve, but how can you make friends with a dead person? It wouldn't be any fun because they wouldn't be able to play with you."

Dorothy rescued Chris. "Have you ever had an imaginary friend?"

"Uh-huh."

"Well, that's how it is with Jesus. He's somebody in your mind who you can talk to and ask for help and if you listen really hard, he will give you an answer. There are all sorts of stories in the Bible, which will make him seem real to you."

"Mommy, can we get the Bible?"

Thea, hiding her discomfort, said, "I'm sure we can find a children's bible in the library." Appeased, Jessica lapsed into silence.

Jessica had sidetracked the group away from the subject of communion, so Chris decided to let sleeping dogs lie. It was a complicated process for children to understand, especially these three with their scant knowledge of Christianity, and he was relieved he didn't have to try and explain the mystical transformation of the bread and the wine into Christ's body and blood.

"What happens to all that money we put in the silver plate?" Jessica asked.

"A church is like a business and there are many expenses and the money the congregation gives either each week, or by tithing—which means committing to a fixed amount of money on a regular basis—goes to things like costumes for choir members, candles, outreach programs, decorations at different times of the year for different ceremonies and so on . . ."

"What happens if there isn't enough money for the church to do all it wants to do?" Izzie asked.

"Then there are fundraisers like special breakfasts, spaghetti suppers, corned beef and cabbage on St. Patrick's day and rummage sales."

"What's that?" Jessica asked.

"It's where people donate household items and clothing they no longer need. A sale is then held, usually for two days in a row, where people can come and buy," Dorothy said.

"What happens to the leftover stuff?" Peter asked.

"Some of it goes to the Salvation Army and they sell it in their Thrift Shops and, unfortunately, some of it just gets thrown away."

"Oh, Miss Dorothy, I guess church is a really busy place," Jessica said.

"It is. Do you think you'd like to go to Sunday school? You could learn all about Jesus then and all the stories from the Bible."

This was too much for Thea. Going to church on Christmas Eve was one thing, but to actually get involved with the church on a regular basis filled her with fear. Her mom and dad didn't add anything to the conversation, hardly surprising since neither of them was religious and when Jessica said, "What do you think, Mommy?" Her reply was, "We'll see."

Theodore leaned forward in his chair. "I think it is time for us to leave. We've had a lovely time haven't we, Dorothy, but, Thea, you must feel as though you've been invaded and we don't want to get in the way of your Christmas rituals."

Thea smiled, hoping her relief didn't show, thankful for Mr. Blunt's sensitivity. "It's lovely having you here. Usually, it's just the four of us so it makes a nice change for us to be social and I'm looking forward to us all being together for our Christmas feast tomorrow. Shall we say three o'clock?"

Thea noticed Chris lingering in the hallway listening to the goodbyes and thank-yous. She felt bad pushing her mom and dad out into the cold, but judging by their nods and smiles, they appeared unperturbed. Once they had gone, Thea poured oil on Chris's anxiety. "I'd like you to stay," she said.

"Are you sure?"

"I am."

The kids, excited to have their one gift, were waiting in the living room. Thea lit the row of candles nestled in amongst their festive greenery on the mantle, and put on some Christmas music and relaxed. The lights from the tree, the soft flickering of the vanilla-scented candles and the glow from the gas logs softened the room; Thea loved it this way. Peter, Izzie and Jessica sat on the sofa holding the gifts Thea had produced by magic. Chris sat in the chair by the fire and said not a word. Peter ripped the paper impatiently; Izzie methodically and gently unwrapped hers, sliding her slender fingers beneath the tape, and Jessica pushed her package towards Honey. "Come on girl, give it a rip." The dog didn't need any encouragement, and grabbing the paper between her teeth, she tugged hard. Thea had to tell her not to eat it and she obediently spit pieces of paper onto the floor. Inside Jessica's box there was a soft golden teddy bear, for Izzie, a scrapbook with decorative papers and stickers, and for Peter, a CD, *Funeral* by Arcade Fire. "I don't think the lyrics are too horrible," she said. Thea also produced a gift-wrapped toy for Honey and they all laughed as she tore off the paper, getting pieces stuck to her nose. She immediately went to work chewing on the rubber bone, holding it with her paws, notoriously trying to remove the squeaker. "Hopefully, this one will last a bit longer," Peter said. "Thanks, Mom."

"You are quite welcome. I think it's time to put out carrots for the reindeer and cookies for Santa and then off to your rooms with you. I don't expect you to sleep, but at least get yourselves ready for bed. Peter, don't forget Honey needs to go out."

"You'd better be quick. You don't want Santa to see you," Jessica said. Peter hurried off to placate his sister.

"Well, Chris, it's been quite a night."

"Would you like me to leave?"

"I'm happy to have you stay, but haven't you had enough of us?"

"I'm not going to answer that. Let me help you take these dishes out into the kitchen."

"Your mother certainly put your hat on right."

"I'm sorry if I made her out to be some kind of saint, but she isn't. She threw shoes at my bedroom door one day because she was tired of asking me to put them away. When it comes to standing up for whatever she believes in, she would have cast the likes of Emily Pankhurst into the shade. She is passionate about her beliefs and I think Maddy and I became her crusade. Because she started our education when we were so young, it never occurred to us it wasn't normal to spend our weekends at museums rather than going to a Saturday matinee, or running riot with our friends through the woods. She gave us her time and not many parents actually do that. I know my dad didn't, but we won't go there.

"Obviously, things changed as we got older, but she grounded us, made us feel we could accomplish anything, instilled us with good values and especially a concern for others. Intellectually, we were miles ahead of the other kids—a problem sometimes because we were easily bored. Eventually it evened itself out, but as kindergarteners, we were definitely way ahead of everyone else. But most important of all, she made our activities fun. I could never understand why my friends complained about homework. For me, it was just one more problem to be solved, one more piece of research. She brainwashed us with her favorite mantra—*I can't believe how easy this is*—and that's how I tackle every task with those words running through my head. Don't look so skeptical. It really works, and I'm sorry, I'm talking too much. Your turn."

"I can't match your idyllic childhood, but my parents did the best they knew how. You've met them so you can see how they are. Mom grew up in an orphanage and she only told me recently. I wished I'd known earlier because it would have explained so much—her nervousness, lack of ambition and social skills—but my parents were always there for me. I never came home to an empty house. They gave me stability, and like you, a good sense of values. Unfortunately, I haven't always lived up to them and just kinda let life happen to me, but I've learned my lesson. No more ignoring that nagging inner voice. If only I'd listened."

"We all make mistakes. I've ignored my inner warning signs too and that blindness led to heartache. But don't you see, you have to get it wrong in order to get it right. Without those mistakes . . ."

"I know, but my mistakes have made life difficult not only for me, but all those associated with me, including my children and I can't forgive myself for that. I put my children in harm's way because of my stupidity and it gives me nightmares." Chris wisely remained silent and let her continue. "Are you sure you want to hear my tale of woe?"

"Of course I do."

Thea sat down on one of the kitchen chairs and Chris pulled out a chair and sat down opposite her. "What I am about to tell you isn't going to put me in a good light and if you want to walk away, I will quite understand, but I'd like you to know and then we won't have to talk about it ever again. I met Michael Chamberlin, the children's father, when I was twenty years old. He was thirty-three, sophisticated and worldly; I was naive and swept off my feet. That's why I told you I'm afraid of passion because it doesn't last. We came down to earth with a bump when I became pregnant with Peter, and despite the fact Michael was a terrible father, we still went on to have Izzie and Jessica. I have absolutely no regrets. I loved being a mom and still do, but parenting brought out the worst in Michael. Peter is the one who suffered most and I worry about his inability to control his anger sometimes. He looked out for me and grew up too fast." She got up to get a glass of water, standing at the sink for a moment to compose herself. "This is hard to talk about," and she sat down again.

"Michael and I divorced in 2002 when Peter was eight. I was on my own for a while and should have remained that way, but I made the foolish mistake of taking up with a man called Kenny Evinson. I met him at Hudson's Hardware shortly after Michael and I first moved here. I never gave him another thought—he was just an employee who rang up my purchases and occasionally made deliveries to the house. Anyway, to cut a long story short, I allowed him to move in here with us. I had no idea he was an alcoholic and when he wasn't drinking he was sweet and kind, but once he had a couple of drinks under his belt he became belligerent and downright nasty. Eventually, things came to a head in September of this year. I asked him to move out and that's when tragedy struck. He went on a drunken driving spree and knocked down and killed a young woman; he didn't see her in the dark. Needless to say, there was a court case and I agreed I would be there." She paused, took a deep breath, rubbed the back of her neck with her left hand, took another sip of water and continued.

"I had instructed Jessica to get off the bus at the Country Store, but she had forgotten; the note for the bus driver lost. Peter still blames himself for not taking better care of his sister. Kenny had befriended a man named Bart Robinson, an unsavory character who lodged at his mother's house, little realizing Bart was obsessed with Kenny and out to get me because I had hurt Kenny. He abducted Jessica." Thea looked at Chris with tears in her eyes and swallowed. "I can't go into all the details of that now; the memories are too painful. The only reason I am telling you all this is because Kenny is still a threat. He tried to break in a few weeks ago. Fortunately, I was able to hold him off until Jim Hudson and Kenny's brother got here, but it shook us up, I can tell you. This was one of the reasons why we went to Massachusetts, to make a fresh start, but that didn't work out because of Ellie dying. So you see, I seem to bring bad luck. Now I'm back here with my tail between my legs trying to get back into the good books of the townsfolk."

They sat in silence, Chris assimilating what Thea had told him. Finally, he said, "Don't hit me, but another of my mother's favorite sayings is, *Life isn't about waiting for the storm to pass, it's about learning to dance in the rain.* I think you've learned to dance in the rain rather well."

Thea gave Chris a watery smile. "Thank you." He reached across the table and covered Thea's cold hands with his own. "Cold hands, warm heart," he said.

"My, you're full of sayings. Now I have one of my own. I decided the other day that life is like a flower garden—Michael and Kenny are weeds. I successfully pulled out Michael, but Kenny keeps growing back. Now I have to decide what you are," she said, giving Chris a wide-eyed look. "I refuse to have any more weeds in my garden."

"Only you can choose. I know what I want to be and I hope I'm not acting like a weed," he said, winking at her.

"So far so good," she said, grinning mischievously, pulling her hands away. "Now I have to play Santa."

"I guess that's a signal for me to leave," and he stood up and moved the chair out of the way.

"I'm afraid so. It's getting late. Thank you for listening to me."

"Despite what you may think, I enjoy being with you, warts and all. Oh, and by the way, I found the display of cards you made when I was at the Country Store today. I was blown away when I noticed your signature. You are extremely talented and your children are a credit to you, so don't sell yourself short. All kids have issues to deal with even in the most Pollyannaish of households, me included. That's just part of life."

"You are a wise old owl, Christopher Morrison. I think you should just oversee the garden and make sure the weeds don't grow."

"Now that's an idea."

This time as they stood in the hallway, Chris put his fingers beneath Thea's chin and tilted her face for a kiss and she didn't object. "You make me feel safe," she whispered.

❧❧

Once in the house, Jim wandered off to the library to light the fire he had laid earlier. MaryAnn and the boys followed along behind. Surprised to find he was nervous, eager to resurrect his family traditions of Christmases past, but not wanting to override any wishes the Wilkinsons might have, standing with his back to the fire, he said, "This is our first Christmas Eve together. Do you guys have anything special you would like to do?"

"Can you tell us what your family used to do?" Ian asked.

"We always went to the carol service, and we've already done that so that's a Hudson tradition. And then when we came home, we always had mince pies, eggnog and cookies."

"And after that?" Johnny asked.

"We would all gather around the fire here in the library and listen to the story of *The Littlest Angel.* Would you like to tell me what you used to do?"

"I don't 'member much. Mommy, what did we do?"

MaryAnn swallowed, sat down on the sofa, wishing she and Jim had discussed this without the boys. Ian sat down beside her, his face serious. Johnny came and rested against her knees, facing Jim. "Johnny, after making you a special supper we would put you to bed—only because you were so little, not because we didn't want you with us. Daddy would read you a special Christmas story and while you were sleeping Santa would come. We used to do the same for Ian when he was little too, but because he was older we allowed him to stay up with us for our grown-up meal, followed by a Christmas movie." She didn't need to ask Ian whether he remembered, she could tell by the look of longing on his face. "For the last three years, we've had little enthusiasm for traditions. We just hung on to the memories."

Jim, catching MaryAnn's eye, noticing Ian's unhappiness, regretting the can of worms he seemed to have inadvertently opened, said, "I'll be back in a little while."

MaryAnn turned to Ian, head bowed, elbows resting on his knees, and made no attempt to pull him into her arms, knowing he would resist. Johnny sat on the floor, looked up into Ian's face and said, "What's up?"

"It's easy for you. You don't remember the good Christmases. And I wish I didn't, but I do and it's so hard."

"What can I do to make things better? Would you rather the three of us were on our own?" MaryAnn asked.

"No," Johnny said, jumping to his feet, folding his arms across his chest. "I want to be *here* with Mr. Hudson and Carrie. I'm *not* going back to our house."

"I'd really like to watch a movie," Ian said. "Do you think Mr. Hudson has any Christmas ones?"

"Why don't you stay here, read a book for a little while. I'll go talk to him. I'm sure we can figure something out."

Johnny turned on Ian as soon as MaryAnn had gone. "Why did you have to spoil our Christmas Eve?" he said. "You must be mad if you think I'm going to go back to that awful house."

Ian hanging onto his bad mood like a dog with a rag said, "You don't understand."

"I sure don't. I was the luckiest kid in the world 'til . . ."

"Johnny, just leave me alone."

MaryAnn found Jim sitting in the kitchen half-heartedly putting cookies on a plate, warming mince pies, pouring eggnog and milk. "Jim, I'm so sorry."

"It was bound to happen. I'm sorry if I handled things badly. I didn't mean to upset anyone. I just wanted you to have a say in what you would like to do."

"I know."

"What do we do now?"

"Ian would really like to watch a Christmas movie. I know that's not your tradition, but that's what we used to do with Sam."

"That's fine with me. To tell the truth, I was getting a little bored with *The Littlest Angel* anyway."

"Sorry, I don't believe you. You're just saying that to make me feel better and I'd love it if you would read it to me after the boys have gone to bed."

"You've got yourself a deal, lady."

"And there will be times when we need to discuss things before we talk to the boys."

"And this was one of those times."

"I'm afraid so."

"Just be patient with me. I'm still learning."

"Oh, Jim, we all are. Ian will come around, and sometimes it's best not to try too hard. For the last three years, I've wished I could forget Christmas altogether. To tell the truth, I'm a little overwhelmed."

"I don't know what to say. Saying we'll get through all this together doesn't quite cut it, does it?"

"No, but it helps. Let me go get the boys."

This wasn't how Jim had envisioned his Christmas Eve, and he was a fool for thinking he could recreate his childhood through the eyes of Johnny and Ian. They weren't he and Ben. Watching a movie with the three people he loved best would dispel the awkwardness and put them back on track.

Ian wandered into the kitchen. "I'm sorry," he said.

"I'm sorry too. Grownups can be really stupid sometimes. And Christmas has the habit of undoing a lot of folks. So let's go watch a movie and forget all about it."

"Thanks," Ian said—Dad on the tip of his tongue, but he just wasn't quite ready to say it.

MaryAnn and Jim created their own tradition after the boys had gone to bed. They sat together in the library by the dying fire, bayberry candles flickering on the mantel, and she listened to Jim read *The Littlest Angel*. Emotions already rubbed raw, the story made her cry. She thought of Sam, wondered whether he was in the company of angels, and found the idea strangely comforting.

Jim, distressed by her tears, walking down his own memory lane, remained silent. Sometimes, it was best to be quiet. He gently kissed MaryAnn. "I love you so much."

"I love you too," she said, putting her hand up underneath his sweater to get as close to him as possible. There was nothing sexual in their embrace, just a mutual longing to be held.

Together, they climbed the stairs, took the stockings they had filled earlier and placed them at the foot of the kids' beds. They kissed each other good night, said Merry Christmas, and went off to their separate rooms.

CHAPTER THIRTY-EIGHT

DECEMBER TWENTY-SIXTH

Monday saw a mass exodus from Melford Point. Mr. Blunt, Dorothy, Enid and Henry said their goodbyes to Sally, standing in the hallway of the inn, bags packed at their feet, dust motes dancing in the wintry sunbeams filtering through the dining room windows. They thanked her for staying open over the holidays especially for them. "It was a pleasure," she said. "You picked a good year. My daughter and grandkids are with her in-laws so I would have been on my own. Having you here filled the empty spaces. I hope you will come back for another visit."

"We'd like that," Theodore said, speaking for the others. "I'm not much of a traveler but in all the years I don't ever remember being quite as comfortable away from home."

"That's a fine compliment and one I'd like for my Visitors' Book, if you wouldn't mind."

Theodore, happy to oblige, made himself comfy in the chair by the bookshelf, and in a surprisingly firm hand, wrote his accolade. Sally, in the meantime, took care of business by settling their bills with a deft swipe of their credit cards. "Have a safe journey back," she said, handing Dorothy and Henry their cards and receipts. Enid miraculously produced a large, beautifully gold-wrapped, beribboned box of chocolates from behind her back and held it out to Sally. "These are for you," she said, awkward in her shyness, immediately stepping backwards. Henry rescued her. "They are handmade by the owners of a shop in Portsmouth. We picked each chocolate individually and it was hard to decide on the flavors. We hope you like them."

"This is so kind of you," Sally said, holding the box up to her nose. "Even through the paper, I can smell just how delicious they are." She in turn handed them a bag of muffins. "Something for the road."

Chris, who had been asked by Thea if he would like to stay another day to attend MaryAnn's wedding, and didn't take much persuading, went out into the parking lot to see the old folks off. He helped them stow their bags, and Henry shook his hand before climbing into the driver's seat. "I hope you've had a good time, son."

"I have, sir," and Henry winked before snugly fastening himself into his seat belt. Chris stood and watched while they drove away, Enid's pale face peering out of the back window, she, Dorothy and Theodore waving goodbye. He raised his hand and waved until they were out of sight.

Chris had no desire to leave Melford Point, but he was expected back at work, his sense of decency preventing him from letting his co-workers down. As it was, he would be returning a day later than planned and he hoped they would understand. Because he and Thea avoided talking about the future, he didn't quite know how to broach the subject. He had no doubts in his mind; he wanted to find out about the empty apartment, give in his notice and move to Melford Point. But Thea had to want it too.

Stanley, bag packed, felt bad for making Nan miserable. "I should just come back with you," she said. "At least we'd be together."

"But your mom and dad would be so disappointed. I'm sure they are looking forward to spending time with you without my being around as a distraction."

Nan pursed her lips. "You're right," she reluctantly agreed. "It's just I feel as though part of me is missing when you're not with me."

"Oh, Nan. You're not making this any easier."

"I'm sorry. It must be being pregnant that's making me so emotional."

"I have no frame of reference for that. I'm an animal doctor, not a human one."

"Oh Stanley, are you comparing me with a horse? I'm sure I shall be the size of one pretty soon."

"You could be compared with something worse. Just be glad you're not an elephant—their gestation period is thirty-six months."

Nan smiled. "You certainly know how to cheer a gal up, so I suppose I'd better let you go."

"I'll call you as soon as I get home, I promise. I love you."

"I love you too." Stanley kissed her firmly on the lips and placed his hand gently on the slight roundness of her belly beneath her nightgown. "I love you too, Little Bump."

Nan stood at the door of the apartment and watched him go down the stairs and leave via the door at the side entrance to retrieve his car from the parking lot out back. "Well, Bump," she said. "It's just you and me because your daddy's gone, so we'll just have to make the most of it," and resting her hands where Stanley's had been, she didn't feel so alone anymore. And in any case, the day promised to be a busy one. Happy to oblige when both Thea and MaryAnn had requested her help, she decided perhaps it was just as well Stanley wouldn't be underfoot.

Thea was standing looking out of the kitchen window wondering where the best place would be to put the bird feeder Mr. Blunt and Dorothy had given her. Delightedly surprised by the thoughtful and unusual gift, her mind took her back to yesterday. What a day it had been—one to treasure for the rest of her life. Christmas Day had always been a time for the Chamberlins alone, unlike Thanksgiving, which up until this year they had always spent with the Gilsons. Thea, content with their relatively quiet family time, suddenly catapulted into catering for an extra five people, initially overwhelmed, surprised herself by taking it all in stride. She decided it was the pleased expression on all her guests' faces, their gratitude to be sitting around her table, eating her food, talking to her children, that made all the hard work worthwhile. It was pure joy teaming up with her mom and Dorothy to prepare the meal and tackle the dishes while Theodore, her dad, and Chris entertained her children with a rousing game of cards followed by story telling to calm them down. It was a Norman Rockwell day, right down to Honey sleeping in front of the fire and Smokey always underfoot. Peter, Izzie and Jessica had not pouted about expected gifts not received; they had reveled in all the attention, and best of all, they all just enjoyed being together. Chris had slotted himself into their family life, unintentionally, but seamlessly, and while she found this a little disquieting, she refused to let any negative thoughts worm their way into her mind.

Jennifer arrived on Jim's doorstep bright and early; her car filled with fresh flowers. Nestled in a box, together with boutonnières for Jim and Ben, was a small bouquet for MaryAnn of tiny ivory roses, tied with trailing cream ribbons. She had tried not to go overboard, to get carried away in her excitement about gaining MaryAnn as a sister-in-law. She knew MaryAnn and Jim wanted to keep it simple and they were right, especially with all the existing Christmas decorations, but she just couldn't resist making arrangements for the tables as well as two to go either side of the stairs and she planned to weave more of the ivory roses in between the fairy lights already twisted around the banisters.

MaryAnn helped Jennifer unload the car, including the cake, nervously transported even though the box was sturdy. MaryAnn set it down in the center of the dining room table and Jennifer couldn't resist a "Careful now." MaryAnn peaked over the top of the protective cardboard and gasped, "Oh, it's beautiful. Just as I imagined." The cake, simple but elegant, boasted two tiers, silver dragées around the edges of the white frosting dotted like pearls, a diamond pattern on the top, repeated on the sides, but with tiny ivory fondant roses in the center of each diamond.

Quite content to have Jennifer take over, there was little for MaryAnn to do except maintain a tidy house. The boys were up in the attic playing imaginary games, their bags all packed for their sleepover at the Chamberlins' house. Jim and MaryAnn would at least have one night to themselves and she shivered with the prospect. She watched Jennifer's deft fingers magically transform the banisters; MaryAnn helped by handing her the roses one at a time and holding the trailing end of the ribbon. "I really would have liked to add some red, but I didn't want to clash with your dress."

"I like the ivory. It's calming and fits in well with the existing Christmas decorations."

"You're right, but I love bright colors. You should have seen the flowers at my wedding, but this is your day and I want to make it special the way you want it."

"Jennifer, believe me, you are. I just love the informality of it all, but what you have done with the roses balances out the tree and the poinsettias, adds a little elegance and makes the space feel appropriate for a wedding."

"Thank you." She stood back and admired her handiwork. "Let me place these just right," she said, taking hold of one of the large, square silver vases they had brought in earlier, bending over and pushing it to the left of the stairs. She had continued the theme of the ivory roses, but this time they were larger and interspersed with baby's breath and honesty pods, their silvery translucence giving an ethereal quality to the whole design.

"These are amazing," MaryAnn said. "I would never have thought of using honesty pods. How clever of you. You really listened to me when I said I like simple things."

"That's my job," she said, smiling up at MaryAnn, putting her hands on her waist and standing up. "I think we should put them either side of the last stair, but not until later. We don't want anyone falling over them."

"I agree."

"Well, I think I'm done for now, and unless you can think of anything, I'll get out of your hair. Talking of hair, I'm pleased you didn't ask for my help. I'm useless, as you can see. It doesn't matter what I do with it, my curls have a mind of their own." She laughed, brushing back a stray blonde strand with the back of her hand. "See what I mean?"

"But it suits you. You might find it frustrating, but you wouldn't be Jennifer without your unruly mop."

"The day will come when the twins will curse me for their wild-hair inheritance."

"Believe me, Jennifer, there are worse things."

"I know, you're right, and now I must go. You know me; I'll just stand here talking all day. Call me if you think of anything. I'll be back at three to help with the caterers and set up the chairs."

"I will, and thank you."

The grandfather clock, resplendent in its finery, occupying a place of importance in the corner of the hallway, struck twelve times just as Jennifer was about to leave. "You'd better ask Jim to put a stop to the chimes. You don't want it doing its chiming thing right in the middle of your wedding vows!"

"You're right. I've become so used to it I don't notice it anymore."

Jennifer looked around the hallway at the dark wood paneling, the wide-planked floor, the high ceiling, and the decorative molding. She glanced at the tree: the ornaments haphazard; the angel slightly tilted; yesterday's gifts replaced by six strategically placed creamy poinsettias. "You were right to have the wedding here. I love this house with its spacious rooms. It is meant for parties."

"It was the first place I thought of when Jim asked me to marry him. I truly cannot believe how lucky I am."

"Jim's lucky too. We never thought he would get married and we were always worried about that whole Thea thing."

MaryAnn, having no wish to gossip, ignored Jennifer's remark. "I think I'd better go see what the boys are up to and heaven only knows where's Jim's got to."

"You're right. I'm keeping you." She reached up and kissed MaryAnn on the cheek. "See you later. I can find my own way out."

"Thanks for everything."

"You're welcome," Jennifer said, looking back over her shoulder as she stepped out of the front door.

Sitting in the chair by the window at the inn, Chris called his mom to let her know he would be back a day later than planned. She was eager to hear how things were going, but he said he would fill her in when he got home. He could tell by her voice she was disappointed. "Sorry, Mom, I would much rather talk to you face to face."

"Okay, I'll just have to settle for that."

"Afraid so."

"As long as you're all right. That's all that matters."

"I am. I'm fine."

"Please give me a call when you get home, or better yet, if you're not too tired, swing by."

"I will."

Chris's feelings for Thea were deepening. He wasn't the least perturbed by the kids. He was a little puzzled by his reaction, but came to the conclusion that because he had always looked out for Maddy, looking out for Thea's kids was second nature. He didn't feel like a father though. He couldn't imagine ever having to discipline them—teaching them, advising them, loving them and spending time with them, yes, but telling them what to do, he didn't think so. Boy, was he jumping ahead of himself, but he and Thea had such a rapport as well as common interests, and he wasn't about to let that go. She had given him directions to Jim's and said she would see him there just before four thirty. He had the day to himself and decided to drive to Portland. The possibility of a job there crossed his mind and exploring would serve two purposes—exercise by walking around the town and getting the lay of the land with a view to the future.

⁂

MaryAnn, after taking a quick trip to the attic to make sure the boys weren't into any mischief, finding them happily playing with the trains, and knowing hunger would eventually bring them downstairs, went in search of Jim. Neither he nor Carrie was anywhere in the house, so deciding he had probably escaped to his workshop, she threw on her coat, crossed the yard, and knocked before opening the door of the little wooden building. "Can I come in?"

"Of course." She went over to where he was sitting, rested her arms on his shoulders, leaned over to kiss him on the cheek, breathed in the scent of him: the soap he used; the fresh, clean, aromatic smell of wood. She picked a shaving from his hair. He turned, put his arms around her waist, and lay his head on her chest. "I thought I'd stay out of the way," he said, looking up at her.

"Oh, so you think all this wedding paraphernalia is woman stuff, do you?"

"When it comes to flowers and Jennifer's chit-chat, yes."

"Am I marrying a grumpy old man?"

"A grumpy old man and a disorganized woman, now that's a great combination! And could you please move, I'm getting a terrible crick in my neck."

She laughed and stepped away from him so he could stand up and he grabbed her hand before she could walk away. "I'm only teasing, you know," and he leaned over and kissed her.

Flushed and breathless, she pushed him away. "Carrie is giving us a strange look and I don't really want to find out what it's like to make love in a wooden shed, even though I love it in here. It's so raw and masculine."

"I think you'd better leave. My imagination is running away with me. Give me a minute to compose myself and I'll come in for some lunch."

She stood at the door, eyes wide, cheeks flushed. "It's a good thing we're getting married soon," she said. Halfway across the yard, sensing Jim was watching her, she turned to see him standing at the window.

Ian and Johnny were standing side-by-side staring at themselves in the full-length antique mirror in what they now called "their bathroom." Jim had come to help them tie their ties and now they were on their own in their shiny black shoes, neatly pressed gray pants, dazzling freshly ironed white shirts, and navy blazers. Hair neatly combed, faces squeaky clean, teeth freshly brushed, they looked at each other in wonder. Johnny reached out and touched his reflection. "Can you believe this is us?" Ian shook his head.

"What time is it?" Johnny asked.

"Four o'clock. Dad told us to be downstairs at four twenty-five so what are we going to do for twenty-five minutes?"

"I'm afraid to sit down and make baggy knees."

"If we sit on our beds with our legs straight, that should be all right."

"Good idea."

Pausing outside their mother's bedroom, they wondered what was going on. Not stopping to linger, the sound of laughter, muffled by the closed door, carried them along to their own room where they arranged themselves carefully like a couple of old ladies, plumping pillows and leaning back. Too excited to read, they talked. "Ian, is this a dream do you think?"

"If it is, it's a pretty good one."

"Do you like our life now?"

"I do. I've got used to it. I can call Mr. Hudson Dad now, but it doesn't mean that I will ever forget our real dad, but thinking about him doesn't make me sad anymore. For a while, I felt bad because I thought I should always feel sad otherwise I would be letting him down. Then I realized he wouldn't want me to be unhappy and what's made it easier is that our new dad is so easy to talk to."

"I'm happy because Mom's happy."

"That too, and I know it's been hard for her to stop being sad, but our real dad would want us to have this second chance so I've stopped worrying about things quite so much."

"And I'm getting fat," Johnny giggled, patting his non-existent belly beneath the brand new leather belt with the shiny buckle. "What time is it now?"

"Ten more minutes, that's all."

Nan and Thea had worked wonders with MaryAnn's flyaway hair. Now piled on the top of her head, held in place with the glittering rhinestone clips, tendrils framing her face, she looked stunning. A little subtle makeup brought out the amazing color of her pale blue eyes, darkened her lashes, put roses in her cheeks and a touch of pink to her full lips. Standing in front of the mirror on the closet door, she asked, "Is that really me?"

Nan and Thea stood behind her. The mirror reflected their beauty; their individual coloring in stark contrast—MaryAnn with her silver blonde, Thea with her sandy redness and Nan with her shiny black bob. Thea's soft sage green dress fell to just below her knees, the sleeves to her wrists, the skirt full, the bodice snug, accentuating her slender figure. Nan's pale blue disguised her expanding waistline with a loosely draped top over a two-tiered skirt. "We're going to leave you now," Thea said. "Will you be all right?" MaryAnn nodded.

"I can't believe how calm you are," Nan said.

MaryAnn just smiled. "I'll see you downstairs and thank you so much for helping me." She walked over to the window. She could see Jim's workshop— the outline softened by the gathering dusk—and the yard below, the path flanked by the untidy winter foliage of the sprawling flowerbeds. "Give me your blessing, Sam," she whispered, drawing a heart with her finger where her breath had misted the windowpane. "I will always love you."

Thea and Nan walked down the staircase, arms linked, into the throng of guests gathering below dressed in their wedding finery—hair coiffed, lipstick perfect, mingling perfumes, suits pressed, ties knotted. Folding chairs, strategically placed in the limited space, including the doorways leading into the den, living room, dining room, kitchen and library, cleverly disguised with ivory covers, prettily decorated with creamy satin ribbons, offered the grownups a place to sit. Thea went over to help Jennifer take people's coats. "The kids can sit on the stairs once MaryAnn is here."

"Jennifer, that's a great idea. I'll go round them up."

Margaret and Bill, taking Chris under their wing, made sure he was introduced to everyone. He nodded and smiled, shook hands, said, "I'm a friend of Thea's." Watched their eyebrows rise. "No, I'm not from around here. I live in Massachusetts."

"That's quite a drive." "How long are you staying?" "What do you think of Melford Point?" He answered their questions, enjoyed being gathered into the fold.

Thea, on the other side of the room, formed the children into a tidy group with the shortest in front. She pulled out her camera. "Say cheese," she said. Poppy and Daisy, in matching dresses—one pink, one purple—their curly blonde hair piled on top of their heads, feet shining in Mary Jane's, grinned happily. It was harder to make Peter and Ian smile, but Jessica in her red velvet Christmas dress, Izzie slender in her soft blue and Johnny smart in his blazer gave it their all. "Thank you," she said. "Now if you just wait here, I'm sure it won't be long."

Thea caught Jim's eye and he smiled. He looked handsome in his dark suit, ivory rose in his buttonhole, and she pondered the puzzlement of attraction of one human being to another. The Reverend Tim Matthews, his robes substituted for a suit, his clerical collar still clearly visible, was talking to Ben—shorter and more slender than Jim, his hair darker, the family resemblance unmistakable. Thea wondered if Jim was nervous. He didn't appear to be. She sat down on the only remaining empty chair, and decided she would like a wedding such as this if the occasion ever arose.

A hush came over the room as soon as the sound of the music started. Thea recognized the haunting melody immediately—Enya's *Shepherd Moons*. A speaker had been strategically placed in the corner by the grandfather clock—thoughtfully silenced—and the tone was pure and magical. She watched MaryAnn pause on the landing. In a way, she reminded Thea of Izzie—they both possessed the same fluidity of movement, a natural grace and poise, effortless in its simplicity and beauty. She seemed to float down the remaining stairs, her silver sandals catching the light, the richness of her deep red silk dress falling softly around her. She turned her gaze to look at Jim and his look of naked longing took Thea's breath away. MaryAnn glanced at the children and smiled, walked towards Jim and stood beside him, arms touching. He took her hand. The kids tiptoed, arranged themselves on the stairs, the girls sitting primly, their colorful skirts spread around them; Peter, elbows on knees, looked resigned. She wondered what was going through Ian and Johnny's minds; Ian seemed calm, Johnny more nervous. Jessica took his hand and leaned over to whisper in his ear. He visibly relaxed.

Jim and MaryAnn turned to face the minister. Jennifer held out her hand for the bouquet, and the Reverend cleared his throat and said, "We are gathered here today to join MaryAnn and Jim in holy matrimony. I've known Jim for many years and there is nothing more satisfying than performing a wedding ceremony for a trusted friend. I only met MaryAnn recently, but I knew immediately Jim had chosen wisely. We sat and talked and I was impressed by her calmness and her capacity for love, not only for Jim but also for her sons. Jim and MaryAnn's love for each other is deep and strong, but it is no way exclusive and that is how it should be. Your wedding is . . ." Thea's mind wandered. She thought about MaryAnn and how quickly they had formed a friendship. Initially, MaryAnn, reticent about her circumstances, chose not to confide, but she wasn't the only one in need. Thea had also longed for a friend. The young woman standing with Jim, her silvery blonde hair shining in the light from the Christmas tree and saying, "I will," was nothing like the pale shadowy creature Thea had first met. Rings exchanged, the ceremony over, she heard, "I now pronounce you husband and wife. You may kiss the bride." Jim held MaryAnn's hands and kissed her gently; respectful and sensitive he kept the kiss chaste, fully aware Ian and Johnny were in the room. No wonder MaryAnn loved him so. Reverend Tim, a patient soul, said, "Ladies and gentlemen, I proudly present Mr. and Mrs. Hudson."

Jim and MaryAnn turned to face their guests to the sound of clapping, cameras flashing, Thea's included. Jim held MaryAnn's hand and kept looking at her as if he couldn't quite believe his eyes. "I've quite forgotten my manners, but I just can't get over my good fortune, so please forgive me. Before we all go get something to eat, I would like to dance with my wife, and of course, you are all welcome to join in. Unfortunately, we are going to need a little manpower to move the chairs out of the way." There was no shortage of willing helpers.

Jim and MaryAnn's choice of song sent a shiver up Thea's spine. How uncanny they should play *Lady*, a song Kenny had dedicated to her in his attempt to make her fall in love with him. Instead of invoking pleasant memories, Kenny Rogers' husky voice sent her into a tailspin of memories best forgotten. She wished she could vanish into thin air. Jim and MaryAnn had the floor to themselves; no one wanted to break the spell. Oblivious to their surroundings, they moved together flawlessly, fluid in their harmony—MaryAnn's skirt swirling as Jim swung her gently, their footwork nimble. Thea didn't hear Chris coming up behind her. "They could win a contest," he said. "I'm afraid I'm not much of a dancer." Startled out of her inner turmoil, she didn't reply.

Flushed and slightly out of breath, MaryAnn fanned her face with her hand and smiled at Thea. Jim said, "Can I have your attention, please. We are going to set up a folding table outside the dining room. That way we can sit and eat and be as close together as possible. If you kids would like to help out, please go talk to Poppy and Daisy's mom, the other Mrs. Hudson! This party is for you too, not just for us grownups, and I want you all to have a good time."

Chris wandered over to help; the children gathered around Jennifer, and Nan came to stand next to Thea. "This isn't any fun without Stanley, but I'm putting on a smiley face, and making the most of it. However, you look like a wet weekend."

"Sorry, it was that song. Reminded me of Kenny and that's never a good thing."

"Whoops, but you have to snap out of it. You don't want to worry MaryAnn and ruin her day."

"I honestly don't think she'd notice."

"Thea, that's not the point. And then there's Chris to consider. You can't sink into one of your weird moods now. Let's go see what we can do to help."

"Thanks, Nan, for giving me a kick in the pants. I deserved it."

Nan scowled, and unwittingly echoing Thea's words to Michael, she said, "You always have been your own worst enemy."

The wine flowed; the conversation hummed. The little kids, boosted up on cushions, felt important. Johnny remembered his mom's pep talk about being polite to his cousins and not to ignore Poppy and Daisy just because he would rather be with Jessica. But the precocious twins weren't about to let him forget. "Come sit with us," they said, each grabbing a hand. Jessica wasn't about to be left out and she hoisted herself up next to one of the twins—deciding it was impossible to tell them apart—so she could make sure she kept a motherly eye on Johnny. He gave her a grateful smile.

Ian and Peter, their help no longer required, went off together. Elizabeth, noticing Izzie looked a little lost, asked her whether she would like to sit with her. Pat made a beeline for MaryAnn, unable to contain her excitement. "Welcome to the family, my dear. I have never seen two people so happy. Congratulations."

Thea and Chris were in a fog of their own making. The ceremony had tugged at their emotions, moved them both in different ways, and now they were a little tongue-tied. Margaret and Bill walked among the guests, introducing themselves to Pat and Bruce, the only people they didn't know. Will went off to sit with Peter and Ian. That left Marjorie and Tom, Lily the pianist and Reverend Tim and his wife, Cecilia. Somehow, it all worked. Plates full with food from the cold buffet: succulent slices of roast beef, oven-baked honey-glazed ham, moist turkey breast; potato, pasta and green salads; crispy bread, still warm; glasses brimming with wine, they all found places to sit. Chatting amongst themselves, they said, "Doesn't MaryAnn look wonderful?" "I just love this house." "What a great way to celebrate, informally like this." "No awful loud music." "This is great, nice and light after all the Christmas food." "Didn't think I'd ever see old Jim get married." "He's a lucky man."

Jennifer, in her element playing hostess, retrieved the wedding cake from the pantry and carefully wheeled it out into the hall on Jim's mother's antique cart, still surprisingly sturdy. People gathered around, champagne glasses in their hands; corks popped and flew and bubbles tickled noses; the kids, not to be left out, sipped ginger ale. Jim placed his hand over MaryAnn's and together they carefully cut through the frosting into the succulent carrot cake inside, removing a slice and placing it on a plate. "Please don't smush it in my face," MaryAnn whispered. Glasses were raised. "A toast to the bride and groom." "Where's the best man?" "Speech, speech, speech," they chanted, and Lily walked briskly into the library to turn off the music.

Bruce pulled index cards from his jacket pocket, handed Jennifer his glass. "First of all, I didn't think this day would ever happen. I expected my brother to remain a crusty old bachelor until the day he died, but we were all taken by surprise by MaryAnn. And I must say, bro, you didn't waste any time and I can't say I blame you. Letting MaryAnn slip through your fingers would have been a huge mistake, and we mustn't forget Ian and Johnny. Welcome to the family and what a wonderful addition you all are.

"I can't say enough good things about my brother. He wears many hats—all of them well—from volunteer fireman, to managing the family business, to being a great uncle and now a great dad. He is loyal and trust-worthy and he's never let me down, even taking the blame for some of the evil things I did as a kid. Anyway, I'm not going to embarrass him any further. So let's all raise our glasses to the happy couple and wish them a long and satisfying life together. I know, firsthand, what it is to be happily married, thanks to Jennifer, and there's nothing better. Congratulations, you two."

"I know it's not customary, but would it be all right if I said something?" MaryAnn asked, first looking at Ben, then Jim.

"Of course," Ben said. "This is your day."

Thea envied MaryAnn's poise, taking her time and glancing around the room, she smiled and said, "You have no idea how happy it makes me to see you all here. I have to tell you this wedding would not have happened without one special person, besides Jim of course." She turned to look at him and they all laughed. "We could not have pulled this off without Jennifer, my sister-in-law. Jennifer, where are you?"

"I'm right here." People turned their heads.

MaryAnn continued, "She worked miracles, right down to the tiniest details, so please raise your glasses. To Jennifer . . ."

Thea watched as Ben placed his arm around his wife's shoulders and gave her a squeeze. Caught off guard, Jennifer looked around the room with her big brown eyes, scanning the faces of friends and family, her hands crossed in front of her. "I wasn't expecting this, and for once I don't know what to say, except I can't remember when I've enjoyed myself so much. MaryAnn is so easy to get along with and didn't seem to mind me organizing her." She looked at MaryAnn and smiled.

"It's no secret that I couldn't organize myself out of a paper bag."

"Too right," Jim said. "How many times have I had to find your keys?"

"Uh-oh, ladies and gentlemen, I think my husband is already finding fault with his bride." Laughter filled the room.

"Not so," Jim said, kissing her on the cheek. "Now let's go enjoy the cake. And I believe there's coffee, and hot water for tea, set up in the kitchen if you'd like to help yourselves."

Thea summoned up her remaining energy and joined Chris and the kids to dance *YMCA*, raising their arms high, forming the letters, and even Peter and Ian joined in. They jigged around the floor to *Mashed Potato*, bumping into each other in the confined space. They formed a line to do *The Loco-Motion*, clinging onto the waist of the person in front, weaving in and out of the various rooms, giggling as they went. Thea and Chris took to the floor to Elton John's *Your Song*, slightly out of breath from the conga line. Their dancing, more of a shuffle, paled in comparison to Jim and MaryAnn, Margaret and Bill, but it didn't matter. Will had pulled Nan to her feet and even the two of them were in sync. The kids sat on the stairs, drinking cups of water, eyes shining, brows damp, hair in disarray. The boys had long discarded their ties and jackets, thrown abandoned on the library sofa. They all got up to dance again to Lionel Ritchie's *Cinderella*, moving to a faster beat, stomping their feet on the floor, laughing into each other's faces. For the final song, Abba's *Happy New Year*, they all gathered in a circle and clasped hands. "I know it's not quite the New Year, but it's such a happy song for us all to sing together," Jim said. And sing they did, MaryAnn's beautiful voice keeping them all in tune.

The circle broke; people wandered away. Thea walked over to MaryAnn. "I'm going to take the children home with me now. It's getting late for the little ones."

"Oh, won't you please stay for the sing-a-long—at least for a couple of songs. It's going to be hard to let the boys go. I just want to have them with me for just a little bit longer. I hope you understand."

Thea's heart sank, but how could she refuse. With every relationship comes obligation and in this instance, her obligation was not to burst MaryAnn's bubble or damage their friendship. "Of course I understand."

"Thank you. Let me go get Lily and gather everyone. The song sheets are on top of the piano."

Lily, the proverbial wallflower, choosing to stay on the sidelines, came alive as soon as her fingers touched the piano keys. They all sang a hearty rendition of *Rudolph the Red-Nosed Reindeer*, just to set the mood, the grown-ups lapsing into silence to allow the kids to sing the funny parts—next on the list, one of Jim's grandfather's favorites, *Daisy Bell*. The melody was easy to follow and they quickly caught onto the chorus:

Daisy, Daisy, Give me your answer, do!
I'm half crazy, all for the love of you!
It won't be a stylish marriage,
I can't afford a carriage,
But you'll look sweet on the seat of a bicycle built for two!

They followed that with *Frosty the Snowman* and then Johnny said, "Mommy, would you sing for us?"

"I will, if you will sing with me. Come here, you can sit on the piano. Do you remember the words to *Away in a Manger*?"

"Uh-huh."

MaryAnn lifted him up and she stood in front of him, her hand on his knee. "Ready."

Lily started to play and their voices filled the room—Johnny's sweet and high, MaryAnn's deeper, but clear as a bell. They looked at each other as they sang, and they didn't miss a beat. There wasn't a dry eye in the room. Johnny on eye level with all the grownups for once, chest puffed up with pride, enjoying the applause, kissed his mom on the cheek before being lifted from the piano. He walked over to where Jessica was standing. "Wow, you are really good," she said

"Why don't we finish with the *Twelve Days of Christmas*," MaryAnn said. "It will be a good test of all our memories."

The rendition wasn't perfect by any means and there was a great deal of giggling from the kids when not only they got messed up, but the grownups did too. They all agreed it was a good way to round out the evening.

Thea's feet were killing her and she couldn't wait to get home and get into her pajamas. She watched MaryAnn climb the stairs with Ian and Johnny and she wondered what she would say to her sons. One thing she did know, they were lucky to have her as a mother; she had never known her to be anything but kind, forgiving, generous of spirit, patient and loving. She had seen them through the worst of times and now their life with Jim would open up a whole new world for them all. She gathered her own children around her and waited at the bottom of the stairs. Chris stood with them. She turned to him and smiled. It was going to be all right, and thanks to Nan's stern words, she'd been able to banish her earlier mood.

Ian and Johnny were all smiles and MaryAnn helped them into their coats. They had changed out of their best clothes and looked much more comfortable in their jeans, sweatshirts and sneakers. They gave their mom one last hug, and went off to find Jim. MaryAnn walked over to where the Chamberlins were standing. "I'd like to thank all of you for making my day so special." She hugged Thea, Jessica and Izzie, looked tentatively at Peter, who, surprisingly, walked into her embrace. "I love you all and I'll see you tomorrow."

Jim came towards them with Johnny in his arms, Ian by his side. "I'll take Johnny to the car," he said.

It took a while for people to find their coats, to say their goodnights and their thank-yous. "We had such a lovely time." "Thank you for inviting us." "It was one of the best weddings I've ever been to." "The food was delicious." "We'll send you the pictures once they're developed." And they meant what they said. Jim and MaryAnn stood in the doorway, oblivious to the cold, watched all their guests maneuver their cars out of the driveway, the vapor from the exhaust pipes white in the frosty air. They did one final wave and closed the front door.

"I know I'm supposed to carry you over the threshold, but there's no way I can carry you up two flights of stairs," Jim said.

"Shush," MaryAnn said. "Just kiss me."

MaryAnn removed her shoes and she and Jim went up the stairs hand in hand. When they got to the bedroom, he said, "We've waited a long time for this."

"Too long," she said, turning so he could unzip her dress. He slid it down her arms; she pulled the sleeves over her hands and let the silky fabric fall to the floor. He removed his jacket, dropping it behind him and she leaned into him. The rhinestone clips in her hair ended up on the floor together with the remainder of their clothes, tantalizingly piece by piece. They took their time, their touches intimate, no need for words until ultimately they ended up beneath the sheets. Their cries of release disturbed the silence of the room and MaryAnn lay nestled against Jim, tears streaming down her face. He was fighting emotions of his own. "I love you so much," he said. "Finally, I have someone to hold, to treat tenderly, to entrust with my dreams—someone who will forgive my inadequacies. Now I can be a whole man."

MaryAnn leaned up on one elbow so she could look into Jim's face, dimly lit by the light from the hallway. He reached over and wiped a tear from her cheek. "I hope those are happy tears," he said.

"Very happy tears."

"I've imagined this moment so many times in the last few weeks. I've longed for the intimacy of having you close, but more than that I've wanted someone to talk to. I know we talk all the time, but it's different somehow lying here in the dark. There are things I have never shared with anyone and now I have you. Sometimes I have nightmares and when I do we will talk about it, but for now it's just enough to have you here. I just didn't want you to be scared if I cry out."

"Oh, Jim, you could never frighten me. We're in this marriage together and you're getting much too serious for a honeymoon night," and she rolled over and sat on top of him, putting her finger to his lips. "No more talking, I'm not done with you yet." Eventually, they slept; Jim spooned around MaryAnn, wrapped in comfort, her hair tickling his nose. Satiated by the mutual rhythm of their lovemaking, they were warm and at peace.

And best of all was waking up together, lying side by side, listening to the noises of the house: the metallic click-click of the radiator under the window, the wind whistling its icy fingers into any crack it could find, and Carrie whining softly at the bottom of the stairs. Pale wintry sunbeams filtered into the room through undraped windows, casting shadows over the furniture and a pool of light on the old wooden floor. The boards creaked beneath Jim's feet and MaryAnn watched his retreating figure. "I'll be back in a minute," he said. "Don't get up."

MaryAnn stretched, pulled the soft cotton sheets up to her chin, and inhaled the lingering scent of lavender. Inevitably, her thoughts went to Sam, to that other honeymoon, so different from this. Their relationship, uncomplicated by age difference and children, dark secrets and emotional pasts, had been happy and carefree. She and Sam had not needed each other and this is where the difference lay. She didn't like the word "need." It implied dependence. Jim's relationship to her was unique for him—the first taste of a marriage bed. With last night's lovemaking their relationship had changed, moved to the next level and she was comfortable with that. Amazingly so in fact and she smiled, wiggled her toes and cleared her mind of the past; never one to dwell for long on anything, always content to live in the moment, she fingered her wedding band and waited for Jim to come back.

⁂

Thea arrived home with her band of exhausted children. Johnny had fallen asleep in the car and Jessica was over-stimulated and cranky. Peter and Ian had ridden with Chris and they all arrived in the driveway at the same time. She had to admit she was glad of the help of another adult. Chris carried Johnny, Izzie walked sedately, Jessica stomped—her scowl clearly visible by the porch light—Peter and Ian followed along behind. Peter, worried about Honey, had wanted to leave earlier, had visions of her being desperate to go out and he planned never to leave her for as long again without making arrangements for her comfort. Problem was, all the people they usually relied on were at the wedding. As it turned out, his fears were unfounded. Needless to say, she was overjoyed to see her family, but didn't seem particularly anxious to go out.

Chris dressed a sleeping Johnny in his pajamas. It was difficult, his limbs rubbery, a dead weight. Eventually, he was snugly encased in his sleeping bag on the airbed on the floor in the girls' room, oblivious to the world. Chris made himself scarce.

Jessica was being obstreperous, sitting on her bed with her arms folded, swinging her legs and narrowly missing Johnny's head. Thea, exhausted and losing patience, said, "Stop it." In the end, she decided she was making things worse and left the room.

Izzie came back from the bathroom, took one look at Jessica, shrugged her shoulders, decided her sister was impossible, and just got into bed. Jessica, still pouting, pulled off her shoes, but she was stuck in her dress. She would have slept in it, but it was uncomfortable, the skirt stiff and prickly, but she was reluctant to back down. Eventually, she came to her senses, practicality kicking in, and she slid off the bed and padded over to Izzie and touched her on the shoulder. "Would you please undo my dress?"

"Of course I will, you silly goose. Turn around," and she patiently undid all the buttons, pulled the dress over Jessica's head. "There," she said. "Get yourself into bed and you'll feel much better."

"Thanks, Izzie."

Chris had taken matters into his own hands and turned on the electric teakettle. If he hadn't been leaving in the morning, he would have just said his goodbyes. He was beginning to wish he hadn't gone to the wedding. Thea had seemed to retreat into some lonely world of her own and barely knew he existed. Should he cut his losses and run? He just didn't understand women, except his mom and that was a problem—anyone he met seemed to pale in comparison. What was it that had made him pursue Thea? The slight connection he had felt meeting her that day in Aladdin's Cave—he knew that was the reason. He looked at her when she walked into the kitchen. "I boiled the kettle. Would you like something to drink, or would you rather I just leave?"

"No, don't leave. We do need to talk, but first I need to get out of these uncomfortable clothes. And I'd love a cup of chamomile tea; the bags and mugs are in the cupboard just behind your head."

"Okay," he said, turning away from her. He made the tea and sat at the kitchen table waiting for her to return, believing the situation hopeless. Cradling his tea, he noticed the chip in the old blue mug, the bright daisies in the center of the table in a room he had begun to unwisely think of as home. He had intruded into Thea's life, and up until this point, thought it was something she wanted, but now he wasn't so sure. He heard her soft footsteps on the stairs and realized she made him nervous, an alien emotion for him.

Her face devoid of makeup, made her seem younger somehow, but small bruises of shadows under her eyes showed her exhaustion. She sat down opposite him, pulled her tea towards her and took a sip. She smelled of roses and toothpaste. The silence hung heavy between them like a wet sheet on a washing line. Chris sensed her fear and it matched his own. Finally, she said, "I'm afraid of saying the wrong thing." He didn't say anything.

"I have a tendency to make things complicated. I also spend too much time inside my own head. I don't think I would be fair to you if I allowed you to move here because I would feel under some kind of obligation to make the relationship work."

"That's a risk I'm prepared to take."

"But, I'm not sure I am. I know that sounds selfish, but it's far better we air things now."

"I agree with you, but I don't want us to say a lot of things we might regret."

Thea sat silently, her brow creased. "One of my favorite books is *Gift from the Sea*, by Anne Morrow Lindbergh. It is a wise and beautiful book about the balance of personal needs with obligations, something that is difficult for me. I am not sure what love between a man and a woman truly is, aside from romantic love upon which I have, in the past, placed too much importance." She paused, sipped her tea. "I don't know whether I am capable of sustaining a relationship because I quickly become smothered and feel like a fly caught in a web, helpless and trapped. I love my children fiercely, become a tiger when they're threatened, but I just don't have the energy or the passion to love a man that way and I don't think I ever will. Chris, I'm so sorry . . ." Voice choked with emotion, she rubbed her upper arms.

Chris resisted the temptation to get up and go to her; unnerved by her tears, he chose his words carefully. "Thea, you are being much too hard on yourself. Self-criticism is a dead-end street. It's our responsibility to treat ourselves well. I know that sounds like self-indulgence, but it's not. Treat yourself kindly and that is how you will view the world. It isn't only you and me who are connected; we are all interconnected, not just with other human beings but everything in our environment—the tree in your back-yard, the food we ate earlier."

"You really are a wise old owl," she said, sniffing, reaching for a tissue from the box on the table and wiping her nose. "I get so buried inside my own misery sometimes, I forget."

"I believe you. I have my own demons too, and sometimes it's not healthy living alone. I'm not some lovesick teenager, but my coming to Maine was a gamble, a whim. For me it paid off, stopped me sitting at home thinking about you. I may decide to come anyway, but it won't be because of you, I promise. I like Melford Point and the surrounding area. I drove into Portland today and it looks like a good place for a job prospect. I may also be the answer to Bill and Margaret's prayers. Helping out at a country store appeals to me for some reason."

It was hard not to get caught up in Chris's enthusiasm. Thea took a deep breath, leaned back in her chair, and looked at him. "It sounds as though you've got it all worked out. And, if you do come, you could certainly help me with Aladdin's Cave if that whole thing takes off."

"Talking of Aladdin's Cave, do you know anything about the apartment that's for rent above the vacant store?"

"You won't believe this, but you'd be subletting from MaryAnn. She signed a six-month lease back in November before Jim asked her to marry him so you'd definitely be helping her out. It's a beautiful apartment."

"Are you opening a door for me?"

"Perhaps."

"Thea, you have nothing to fear from me. Your friendship is more important than anything and if it develops into something else, so be it. I would never smother you and I would always respect your need for solitude. I believe we can enrich each other's lives without treading on each other's toes. I would also like to spend time with Peter if you'll let me."

"He trusted you enough to let you walk Honey home from the Country Store and that's huge, so that has to be a yes."

"Are we good?"

"Very good. You have this uncanny knack of being able to draw me out, stop me from going any further down my dark road. If I sent you away, it would only make me miserable and that's not being kind to myself, so I do see what you mean."

Chris stood up, pushed the chair away with the back of his legs, and took his mug over to the sink. "I am what I am," he said, turning to look at Thea. "I have no hidden agendas; I have no tolerance for intrigue. The only person I ever get mad with is my dad, but that's a story for another day. I read poetry and cry at sad movies; I also quite like shopping. I'm a terrible cook, but willing to learn and I'm insanely obsessed with Jasmine, which . . ."

"I already know and you'll be pleased to hear the apartment comes with a garage. That's, of course, if you choose to come." She walked over to him and he put his arms around her.

"You're nothing but trouble," he said, "all wrapped up in a tiny five foot package."

Thea rested her head against his chest, listened to the rhythmic beating of his heart, breathed in the scent of him. He leaned down and kissed her. "There's no way I could have just walked away from you and if we ever do end up living together, it would be so I could give you the opportunity to do with your life what you want. We also need empty space. Our lives become so crowded, we forget that sometimes and your life is more crowded than mine. I don't want to add to that crowd if it is more than you can safely handle."

She moved away from him, stood holding onto the back of a chair. "I will be all right as long as we recognize we won't feel exactly the same about each other every day. We have to accept the relationship for what it is at any given time. I believe relationships fail because we expect too much, but there are going to be days when we are out of sorts, will go our separate ways. The only way it will fail is if we lose respect for and trust in each other. We will be dancing partners in the same pattern, but we will be free. I know this sounds like pie in the sky stuff, but my friendships with women have always been successful. We help each other out, make no demands, cry on each other's shoulders, tell our most intimate secrets without the fear of it coming back to slap us in the face. It's a tall order to think we can accomplish the same thing as a man and a woman, but I would like to try."

"You won't get any arguments from me," he said.

"Anyway, I suggest you go home and think this through carefully. I find writing a list of pros and cons always helps."

"Yes, ma'am."

"It was only a suggestion, but I really think you should go back to the inn now. You have a long drive tomorrow."

Thea stood at the kitchen window and watched Chris drive away. For once in her life, she had done something right; opened her heart for all the right reasons, gone with her instincts. She went off to bed with a spring in her step and peace in her heart, happy to add Chris to her flower garden of life.

EPILOGUE

⸾⸾⸾

Chris did indeed come back to Melford Point and wove himself into the intricacies of the small town with Bill and Margaret's help. Unassuming and always willing to lend a helping hand, he won the hearts of the locals. His mother, Audrey, became a frequent visitor and charmed Thea and her children, especially Jessica. She came and helped out at the Country Store where Chris was now part-time manager, taking over the baking while Margaret was in Massachusetts for the birth of Nan's son—Frederick William—born on the fifteenth of June, 2006. Chris augmented his income working Monday, Tuesdays and Wednesdays as a computer programmer at a small company in Portland.

Aladdin's Cave had a shaky start, but once the summer folk started to arrive, filling the cottages and bed and breakfasts to bursting, business boomed. Michael, as promised, financed Thea by paying for the inventory once Theodore Blunt came up with a reasonable sum. He and Dorothy arrived one day with a huge U-Haul and with the help of MaryAnn, Jim, Ben, Jennifer and Chris they made light work of the unpacking. The local shop owners came out of their doors, hands on hips, tongues wagging, too curious to stay inside, to see what was going on and Thea began to feel she had, finally, become one of them. There was still the odd cold shoulder, but their memories seemed to have dimmed over the disaster with Kenny Evinson. She called Chris "her redeemer" because his likability rubbed off on her by association. Their friendship blossomed. True to his word he didn't crowd her in any way, but their relationship was no longer chaste. However, they were the souls of discretion. They went out on date nights and even though she went back to his apartment, she never stayed over. They cracked up when she said she was being kind to herself! Chris restored her faith in her sexuality because he never tried to dominate her. She would have run a mile had he tried, but it wasn't in his nature. He was gentle and caring and their lovemaking was mutually satisfying.

The Chamberlin kids went back to helping out at the Country Store during summer vacation. As Ian and Peter became older, Thea and MaryAnn gave them more freedom. They could be seen all over town on their bicycles or walking down Maine Street with Honey. Chris took them skiing and snowboarding in the winter and all of them would skate on the pond in the park. The Chamberlins, Chris, and the Hudsons, always in and out of each other's houses, had a great time together. The reciprocal babysitting they provided for one another gave Thea a sense of freedom. Little did she know she would be looking after Jim and MaryAnn's daughter, Josie Victoria, born in May 2007. Ian and Johnny, well established in their new life, took the baby's arrival in stride and loved her to bits. Jim, of course, over the moon, didn't play favorites—his stepsons were never made to feel second best. A hands-on dad, he was out of bed like a shot as soon as he heard Josie's cry through the baby monitor. Gathering her in his arms, he would bring her to MaryAnn. Sitting up in bed, pillows plumped behind her, she would nurse Josie and as soon as his daughter was done, he would take her back to the nursery, change her and sit in the rocking chair holding her gently, rocking back and forth, breathing in her soft baby smell, reluctant to lay her in her crib. The *Winnie the Pooh* nightlight kept the scary dark away—more Jim's fear than Josie's—and dimly illuminated the cheerful nursery rhyme wallpaper. With Jennifer's help, a room had been created fit for his daughter, to his and MaryAnn's taste instead of the pink frills Jennifer loved. Never a day went by when he didn't count his blessings.

MaryAnn gradually reduced the hours she spent at the diner until finally she cut the umbilical cord and handed in her notice, but she and Will remained friends. She didn't want him to think she had used him in her hour of need and then forgotten him. She would take the boys with her after school at least once a week for a bowl of ice cream with hot fudge sauce and Will would join them at the table smiling and nodding, listening to her sons answering his many questions. She also invited him over for dinner on several occasions, but he always declined. She didn't need to ask him why.

MaryAnn chose not to pick up the threads of her photography, pigeonholing the too painful memories of the business she had built with Sam. Instead she put her college education to good use by helping Thea with Aladdin's Cave and Jennifer with her home decorating business by handling their accounts and filing their taxes. Jennifer, creative but hopelessly disorganized, welcomed MaryAnn, told her she was her salvation. MaryAnn loved the challenge, undaunted by the large brown carrier bag of receipts Jennifer dumped in her lap. Starting from scratch with Thea was easier. Firstly, she was methodical and tidy, and secondly, with Chris's help, they were able to set up a computer program for keeping track of inventory. She also joined the church choir and fulfilled her dream and learned how to play the piano. The Hudson house was always full of music.

Enid and Henry finally sold their house at the end of March 2006. The closing date was April thirtieth and they arrived that same day to take up possession of their ground floor rental in a converted Victorian just past the park on the left-hand side. There were four apartments in all with the stipulation from the landlord of "no pets" and "no children." This suited Enid and Henry just fine, not relishing the possibility of children running about over their heads. Thea's kids would go visit and the landlord was okay with that. In fact, Peter and Ian would quite often stop by and take his grandparents off for a walk to the park. Enid and Henry loved Melford Point, especially Henry, who would walk every morning to get his newspaper and stop in at the Country Store for coffee. Handy with a hammer and a screwdriver, Bill quite often put him to work. He had never been happier. For Enid, Aladdin's Cave was the lure, and she made a huge effort to overcome her shyness so she could help her daughter. Their lives were busy and full of purpose, something Henry had lacked after his retirement. The novelty of being able to walk everywhere never wore off and occasionally he would treat Enid to a meal at Mario's. Manny's fake Italian accent didn't fool them, but they were charmed and it made for a fun night out.

Kenny Evinson never caused any more trouble because he was now six feet under—the victim of an unfortunate motorcycle accident in August 2006. They all decided it couldn't have happened to a nicer person!

Thea put all her troubles behind her and became a successful businesswoman, eventually able to support herself and her family without Michael's help, giving her a sense of relief and a huge leap in confidence. She socked away his child support to help with the kids' college education. As far as Michael himself was concerned, he continued to distance himself from their lives and perhaps it was just as well . . .

ABOUT THE AUTHOR

Pamela Frances Basch is the author of EACH TIME WE SAY GOODBYE and A SCARY KIND OF HONESTY, the first two books in the trilogy about the Chamberlin family. She firmly believes stories connect humanity and this inspires her to create her novels. Although a piece of her heart will always be in England, Pamela lives with her husband on the East Coast of the United States. She can be reached at storiesconnecthumanity@comcast.net and would love to hear from her readers.

Made in the USA
Middletown, DE
16 February 2015